Sue Fortin is a *USA Today* and #1 Kindle bestselling author. Sue was born in Hertfordshire but had a nomadic childhood, moving often with her family, before eventually settling in West Sussex. She is married with four children, all of whom patiently give her the time to write but, when not behind the keyboard, she likes to spend time with them, enjoying both the coast and the South Downs between which the family is nestled.

Sue is a member of the Crime Writers' Association.

🐦@suefortin1
📘www.facebook.com/suefortinauthor
www.suefortin.com

Also by Sue Fortin

SUE FORTIN

THE BIRTHDAY GIRL

A division of HarperCollins*Publishers*
www.harpercollins.co.uk

HarperImpulse an imprint of
HarperCollinsPublishers
The News Building
1 London Bridge Street
London SE1 9GF

www.harpercollins.co.uk

This paperback edition 2017

First published in Great Britain in ebook format by HarperCollinsPublishers 2017

A catalogue record for this book is
available from the British Library

ISBN: 9780008275501

Set in Birka by Palimpsest Book Production Limited,
Falkirk, Stirlingshire

Printed and bound in the United States of America by
LSC Communications

For more information visit: www.harpercollins.co.uk/green

To my lovely friends, Laura, Catherine and Lucie who, without hesitation, accepted my invitation of a weekend away all in the name of research

friend

1. countable noun
A friend is someone who you know well and like, but who is not related to you.
2. plural noun
If you are friends with someone, you are their friend and they are yours.

Chapter 1

Friendships are made up of all the little things that matter, the common ground of lives, shared interests, loves, dislikes, the highs and the lows. They matter and they are matter. Like stars in the night sky, friends can light up the darkness. Sometimes we might forget they are there and yet know they will always be there. Others can come in a burst, dazzling us with the excitement of newness, seducing us with promises of adventure. Some will deliver on this promise, others will fizzle away while some will shoot across the night sky in one last hurrah before they disappear from our lives.

I think of my best friends, I can count them on one hand with digits to spare. Joanne, Andrea and Zoe are the stars in my night sky. Together, we make a good constellation. We stick by each other. We look out for each other. We forgive each other.

I remind myself of the last fact as I hold the invitation in my hand, knowing that I should accept, with grace and maturity, the olive branch it represents.

Dear Carys, Zoe and Andrea
My Fortieth Birthday Celebrations
Come and join me for an adventure weekend, full of
mysteries and surprises, the like of which you can't
imagine.
With the grand reveal on Sunday evening.
Friday 8 September – Monday 11 September
Meet at Chichester Cathedral 09.00 Friday morning
Love Joanne
P.S. As it's also Carys's birthday on the Monday,
I thought we could celebrate that as well.

Two months ago, Joanne had told us to save the date, or rather the weekend, and said she'd let us know nearer the time what was happening. I could have quite happily ignored my thirty-ninth birthday, but Joanne had been insistent the weekend was to be a double celebration. She also insisted that, despite it being her birthday, the whole weekend was to be a surprise for me too. I had hoped we'd find out the details sooner and, I have to admit, leaving it until the night before is cutting it fine but she has steadfastly refused to give us any more details until now.

I flip the card over and see there is a handwritten message, the tall spiky writing unmistakably Joanne's.

PPS. I know things have been difficult lately but amends need to be made. Do come, it's important you're there.

I sit down at the kitchen table and read the invitation again. I'm not sure what it is about the PPS on the reverse, but it sounds . . . odd. I think that's the best way I can describe it. I mull over the significance but before I can settle on anything meaningful, my mobile rings.

Andrea Jarvis's name flashes across the screen.

'Hiya,' I say, kicking off my running shoes. Flakes of dried mud from my afternoon cross-country run scatter across the tiled floor like dirty snowflakes. I sigh inwardly at the mess. Sometimes I'm no better than my teenage son. Stepping over the debris, I go to the fridge, hook out a bottle of wine and pour myself a glass, something I would normally reserve for a Friday night, but seeing as we're off on our jolly tomorrow, I feel a drop of alcohol is justified. 'Don't tell me, you've seen the invitation.'

'Too bloody right,' says Andrea. 'Did you get the PPS on yours?'

'Where it says about making amends?'

'What is that all about?'

I shrug even though Andrea can't see this action. 'No idea. Maybe, she just really wants us to go. Maybe she thought we'd change our minds now that it looks like it's going to be an outdoor adventure type of weekend.'

'I'm not bothered about that,' says Andrea. 'It's not like we haven't done this sort of thing before. Last year we all did that charity walk up Snowdon. Before that, the mountain bike trail. You'll be in your element anyway.'

It's true, I am an adventure junkie and working at the local outward-bound centre tends to satisfy my addiction for kayaking, rock climbing and the like these days. I also help with the outdoor activities for the Duke of Edinburgh Award, so I'm not particularly fazed by the prospect of what Joanne has in store for us. 'It's going to be like a busman's holiday for me,' I say. 'And you'll be OK yourself.'

'Yeah, that's as maybe, but I'm stuck behind the desk most days since I took over the gym. I headed up a high-impact aerobics class the other day and thought my legs were going to seize up afterwards.'

'You'll be fine. Have you spoken to Zoe about the invite?' I ask, taking my seat at the table again. I glance at the official-looking letter which was also waiting on the doormat when I got in this evening and push it to one side to read later.

'She hasn't a clue what it means either. But she's gone into full-on cute Labrador puppy mode. All excited – can't wait for the weekend and thinks Joanne is utterly wonderful.'

I give a small laugh into my glass as Andrea does a perfect imitation of Zoe, whose voice gets squeakier the more excited and enthusiastic she gets about anything. 'It's too late to change your mind,' I say.

'It would be awful if I was struck down with a stomach bug, though,' says Andrea.

'Don't even think about it. We made a deal, remember?'

'I might have been under the influence of alcohol when I did that one-for-all-and-all-for-one shit.'

'You promised and you can't break a promise. Not to one of your best friends. Besides, it's my birthday too.'

'I think that's called blackmail.'

I laugh as I imagine the scowling look on Andrea's face. 'No, seriously, Andrea. You can't back out now. Joanne will kill you.'

'Hmm. When she said it was a surprise, I was hoping it would be more of a spa weekend. You know, fluffy white dressing gowns, manicures. Lots of pampering and relaxation.'

'Look, like I said before, I think this is her way of making up for being so distant lately.' In saying this, I silently acknowledge that I'm referring more to the way my own relationship with Joanne has been in recent times. We had once been so close, but things happened and the balance of our friendship shifted, leaving a hiatus in our alliance.

There's a small silence while we both contemplate the sentiment of the weekend. Andrea speaks first. 'I suppose I owe it to her. You know, give her a chance to make up for the way she's been since I took on the gym.'

'Is all that still going on between you two? I thought the dust had settled.'

'Sort of. I've certainly drawn a line under it all, but not Joanne. I have this sense that she's still angry at me. I can't put my finger on it or explain it, but when I speak to her, it's like an undercurrent of tension. Do you know what I mean?'

'Mmm . . . I do.' Andrea could be describing my own relationship with Joanne.

'Anyway, as I say, I'll give her a chance to *make amends*, but if she starts again, about having to work for me now instead of being a partner, I'm sorry, I won't be keeping my mouth shut. Fortieth birthday or not.'

'And when do you ever keep your mouth shut, my darling?' I say.

'I think I did once, in 1986 – I might be wrong though,' says Andrea with a laugh. 'Anyway, so now you're not letting me skive off, we'd better sort out what's happening tomorrow. Is Alfie still coming to mine for the weekend?'

'He's not in from college yet – five-a-side football, I think he said. But yes, he's all good to come to you. He's going to go home with Bradley. Are you sure Colin is up to this?'

'Oh, he'll be in his element. Takeaways and gaming. It's totally a boy's weekend.'

'That's kind of him. I appreciate it.'

'Anytime. You know that. Although, I'm surprised Alfie's not staying at Joanne's, with Ruby and Oliver.'

I ignore the little drop my stomach gives at the mention of Joanne's daughter. It's the sort of weightless feeling you experience when the rollercoaster tips over the edge of the first big dip and it takes a few seconds for your internal organs to catch up with the fall. I'm used to that sensation. As sure as night follows day, I get that every time Ruby comes up in conversation. As always, I make a faultless recovery. 'Fortunately, Tris is away this weekend too, so Ruby is going to stay with Joanne's mother.' I try to keep my tone neutral as my thoughts are thrown off course and on to a different trajectory. If my friends are the constellation by which I navigate life, then Ruby is the black hole whose gravitational pull is so great that nothing, not even light, can escape from being drawn in and swallowed up. I know. I've witnessed stars in my night sky pass the point of no return, the absolute horizon of the black hole, and disappear forever, while other stars are teetering around the edges, unwittingly being drawn closer and closer until it will be impossible to turn back.

I force myself to focus on the conversation. Andrea is talking about a film showing at the cinema that Colin might take the boys to see. I let her chatter on for a while, before the conversation comes to a natural halt and Andrea closes with, 'Right, well, I'd better get on. I'll see you tomorrow morning.'

'Yep. See you then. Don't let me down.'

'When have I ever let you down?'

For some time after the call, I remain sitting at the kitchen table, looking at the invitation with Andrea's words on repeat in my mind.

She's never let me down. In my darkest hour, when Darren had committed suicide, she was there for me. 'That's what friends do,' she had said once. 'They look after each other.'

A sigh leaves my lips and I blink away thoughts of Darren to focus on the next four days. Despite my assurances to Andrea that it's going to be a great weekend, my own doubts are beginning to surface. Perhaps I'm expecting too much by way of reconciliation. Can we honestly put everything behind us? Even if we want to, can we truly repair our fractured friendship or is it another black hole on the not-too-distant horizon?

How many times have you lied to yourself? I suspect you've lost count. You must lie to yourself every single day of your life. So much so that it trips off your tongue with ease; you probably even believe it yourself now. You may be able to fool everyone else, but you can't fool me.

I hear the pity in people's voices, I see the compassion in their eyes as they exchange knowing looks when they talk about you. I can't tell you how much I loathe that. You are not deserving of their sympathy and yet, I can forgive them. You've been very careful in cultivating a false history, hiding behind the status of a grieving widow if friends come too close to the truth or show too much of an interest in your past and ask questions that could unpeel the layers of deceit you've created.

As Shakespeare said, 'The truth will out.' I have been extremely patient, waiting for the right moment to make you pay for what you've done. And now the time has come, I can hardly believe it's here. My body trembles in anticipation and excitement at the prospect of the next few days. I have the power and I will get my revenge.

FRIDAY

Chapter 2

'OK, Alfie, I'm heading off now,' I say, popping my head round the door to my son's room. I'm dismayed to see him still in bed. 'Hadn't you better be getting up?'

'Don't nag,' comes a reply muffled by the duvet he pulls over his head.

I check my watch, I can't afford to hang about any longer and without giving it too much consideration, I yank the end of Alfie's cover, exposing his head and shoulders. 'Come on, you need to get up now.'

'Oi!' Alfie sits up and snatches at his cover. 'What did you do that for?'

'To make you get up. You'll be late for school. I need to go.'

'I'm not stopping you. Go.'

'Alfie! Get up. Now.' I go to pull the cover again, but this time he's prepared and holds it tightly around his shoulders.

'Pack it in. Just piss off.'

I ignore his bad language. Some battles are not worth the fight. 'Get out of bed,' I insist.

I don't expect him to move so fast but in a split second, Alfie has jumped out of bed and is standing directly in front of me. 'I'm up now. All right?' he snarls at me, his face inches from mine as I get the full force of his stale breath.

'OK,' I say, taking a step back, instantly wishing I had thought twice before going into battle. My heel hits the bottom of the bedroom door, which vibrates violently as the edge digs between my shoulder blades. I let out a small cry of pain.

'I think that's called karma,' says Alfie. He pushes past me, knocking his shoulder against mine as he does so. 'Hadn't you better go? You'll be late if you don't get a move on.' He slams the bathroom door shut behind him.

My attempts at garnering a response from Alfie by calling bye to him through the bathroom door are met with the sound of the shower on full-blast.

Normally, I'd make an effort to smooth things over before leaving, but today I haven't got time and I think Alfie is deliberately spending longer in the shower than usual to avoid appeasing my guilt by parting on amicable terms.

As I walk down the road, I reflect that today's battle was tame. Sometimes the arguments and confrontations can be much worse and I find myself thinking about the future when we don't live together and wonder if our relationship will be any better then. I'm tired of the emotionally draining status quo we're at, and I long for quieter days ahead when I'm on my own. Before I reach the end of the road, I already feel guilty for wishing the days away as I remind myself it's not Alfie's fault he's the way he is. It's mine.

My spine aches from carrying my rucksack the mere half a mile from my home and I'm sure the knock to my back earlier isn't helping matters as, even to the touch, it feels tender.

I turn the corner into South Street where the dark shop windows and closed doors, yet to be roused from their slumber by the arrival of early morning shop assistants, serve only to reflect the prospect of rain later today. I adjust the straps of my rucksack and hitch it further on to my shoulders as I head towards the end of the road where the four main shopping streets meet and the city cathedral occupies one corner. I scan the benches which line the pavement and overlook the cathedral grounds.

Andrea is sitting on the middle bench, a Styrofoam coffee cup in one hand and her mobile in the other. She spots me and waves, phone still in hand.

I lumber over to her. 'Yay! You came. And you're the first one. You must be keen.' I wriggle my arms free of the straps and dump the rucksack on the ground, then take a seat beside Andrea on the bench.

'Keen as mustard, me,' says Andrea. 'To be fair, Colin dropped me off this morning so I didn't have to get the bus. Don't mistake my dislike of the bus service for enthusiasm to be here.' She reaches down and retrieves a cup from under the bench, presenting it to me. 'Here, I got you a latte.'

'Thanks.' I take the cup and tentatively lift it to my lips, taking a minuscule sip to gauge the temperature. 'No sign of Zoe yet?'

'She texted me. Said she'll be five minutes.'

'And no word from Joanne as to what happens now?' I take a more confident sip of the latte, having deemed it to be of an acceptable drinking temperature.

'Nope. Nothing. So we sit here and wait,' says Andrea. She

leans against the wooden slats of the bench and purses her lips in the way she does when she has something on her mind. I wait for her to speak. 'I know you said it was a chance to put our friendships back on track, but I'm not sure things will ever be the same between me and Joanne. The dynamics have changed and I don't think she can deal with it.'

'Try to be positive about it. This could be her way of saying sorry.' I don't wish to reignite the flames of doubt that I had successfully extinguished before I went to sleep last night. 'Look, it's Joanne's fortieth. Maybe she's realised the importance of having good friends. Yes, we may have our little disagreements or falling outs, but at the end of the day, friendship is worth more.'

Andrea gives me a sideways look. 'You need to try harder than that to convince me.'

'I'll be honest. Last night, after I spoke to you, I did think maybe it wasn't such a great idea. Maybe it's best to leave the past alone.'

'Isn't that what I've been saying all along?'

'I know, but another part of me thinks if this is Joanne's way of saying sorry, it could be a good opportunity for us to clear the air with her. That way, maybe things *can* get back on track.'

'True, but it will be awkward for Zoe. I don't think her and Joanne have fallen out about anything.'

'I thought about that too. My theory is that Zoe's the goodwill ambassador for this trip.'

'But why all this big secrecy? Why not a meal out? Isn't that what normal people do?'

'Remember, this is Joanne we're talking about. She loves all this cloak-and-dagger stuff.' I give Andrea a playful tap on her thigh. 'I'm sure we're going to have a great time.'

As we both sip our drinks, I spot Zoe's unmistakable five-feet-ten frame cutting across the lawn of the cathedral. She has a sports holdall hanging off her shoulder, her blonde hair tied in a ponytail and is wearing leggings with trainers. She looks more like she's off to the gym than an adventure weekend. I wave to her.

'Hi, guys,' says Zoe. 'I made it. Ooh, coffee, is that for me?' She takes the cup that Andrea holds out to her. 'Lovely. We all set for this mysterious adventure weekend?' She smiles broadly, reminding me of an excited child on Christmas Eve.

'Yeah, Andrea can't wait,' I say, winking at the new arrival.

Zoe pulls a card from her pocket. I recognise the white lettering on the black invitation immediately and the PPS written by Joanne. Zoe reads it out loud. 'An adventure weekend, full of mysteries and surprises, the like of which you can't imagine.' She looks at both of us. 'What's not to like?'

'It's the surprise bit I don't care for,' says Andrea. 'Not to mention the bit about making amends.'

Zoe gives a shrug. 'I love surprises. I wonder what she has planned for us?'

'Oh God, I don't know if I can cope with your enthusiasm this early in the morning,' says Andrea, shaking her head. 'Thank goodness I packed some vodka. Where is it?' Andrea makes to rummage around in her rucksack.

Both Zoe and I laugh. 'If only your clients knew the truth

about you,' says Zoe. 'Right, what happens now? Anyone know?'

'We wait for Joanne, I suppose,' I say, looking around to see if there is any sign of our infamous host.

As if on cue, a black MPV pulls up alongside the pavement. The rear door automatically slides open and the driver gives a toot of the horn.

'This must be for us,' says Zoe. 'How exciting.'

'Either that or we're about to be abducted,' says Andrea, picking up her rucksack.

I hoist mine up on to my shoulder and follow Zoe to the car, dropping my half-drunk latte into the waste bin as I go.

Zoe hops into the vehicle without a moment's hesitation. 'Ooh, it's very swish in here,' she calls to us.

I exchange looks with Andrea as we reach the edge of the path. Andrea surveys the vehicle. 'I suppose it's not a van. I'm slightly reassured that it looks like a swanky MPV, exactly the sort of thing Joanne would hire.'

'Come on, there's loads of room,' says Zoe. 'And there's an envelope, addressed to us all.'

'No sign of Joanne, then?' I push my rucksack in first and climb into the vehicle, taking the rear-facing seat. I look over my shoulder at the driver. He's a middle-aged man and, as far as I can see, is dressed in a shirt and tie. 'Morning,' I say with a smile.

'Morning,' he replies, not turning but looking in the rear-view mirror at me.

'Where are we off to?'

'I'm afraid I can't tell you that. Need-to-know basis,' he says, giving a tap to the side of his nose with his finger. He shifts in his seat and reaches over to the passenger seat, retrieving a small blue cloth bag. 'Mrs Aldridge has requested that you all put your mobile phones in this bag.'

'What?' Andrea plonks herself down in her seat. 'I don't think so.'

'I'm sorry, but Mrs Aldridge has said it's all part of the surprise. It's all there in the envelope apparently.'

'Give me that,' says Andrea, taking the envelope from Zoe's hand. She rips it open and reads out loud the letter inside.

Dear lovely ladies,

So now you're all aboard and on Phase One of the journey. I hope you approve of your mode of transport. Only the best for my best friends!

I expect Zoe, you're all excited and can't wait to find out where you're going. You love secrets and surprises, probably even more than I do, but I think I'm going to have the last laugh this time.

Andrea, I imagine you're frowning right now and cursing me for keeping it all hush-hush. Sorry, I know this goes against your natural instinct to be the one in charge!

Carys, you, I imagine are sitting there, taking it all in and trying to second-guess my next move, wondering how to play this one and if you can out-smart me. Am I right? I bet I am. Hahahaha!

Well, my lovely friends, don't waste time trying to

quiz the driver, I've paid handsomely for his silence.
You've got about an hour's drive, so sit back and relax.
  Please be very sweet and hand your phones over. I
don't want anyone cheating and turning on their maps
app.
  Oh, yeah, bubbly under the seat. Chink, chink!

Love Joanne xxx

The driver shakes the bag and passes it to me. Reluctantly, I place my mobile inside. 'Better play along,' I say, even though I'm not happy about it myself. What if Alfie needs to speak to me? Or Seb? I console myself with the idea that Joanne will no doubt let us have them back once we arrive and this is only her way of keeping the location a surprise.

'It is Joanne's birthday treat,' says Zoe. She too places her phone in the bag.

We both look at Andrea expectantly. A small expression of defiance settles on her face for a moment and then with a big huff and drop of her shoulders, she produces her phone from her jacket pocket. 'Don't want to upset the birthday girl, do we?' she says with little grace. She hands the phone to me, which I pop in the bag and then hand to the driver.

'Right, that's that,' I say.

'Hmm,' says Andrea, dumping the letter in Zoe's lap, before rummaging under the seat. 'Where's this bubbly?' She pulls out a cool bag and we hear the distinct sound of glasses clinking. 'Aha. Here we go. Right, what's in here? Prosecco and three glasses. Typically, Joanne-style, they're glasses and not plastic ones.' Formalities pushed aside, Andrea dishes out the glasses and pops open the bottle as the car pulls away from the kerb. Despite jolting over some potholes, Andrea successfully fills each of the glasses. 'Cheers!'

I'm not entirely sure I can stomach too much alcohol this early in the morning, but not wanting to be a killjoy, I decide to join in with the celebrations and take a small sip.

'So, who's looking after Alfie?' asks Zoe.

'He's over at Andrea's for the weekend. I expect him and Bradley will be glued to their games, only emerging for food.'

'Colin will be in his element too,' says Andrea. 'He'll be able to watch the sporting channels with zero interruptions.'

'Who's looking after your boys?' I ask Zoe.

'I've enlisted the help of my mum. The kids tried to tell me that at fifteen and seventeen they were OK to be left for the weekend.' Zoe gives a roll of her eyes. 'I'm not that daft! If their dad didn't live so far away, they could have gone there, but trying to get them up to Liverpool for just a weekend is nigh-on impossible. Plus, I didn't want to ask any favours from him.'

Zoe emphasises the word *him*. I don't think I've ever heard her refer to her ex-husband by his name. Zoe is the new girl out of the four of us, having moved to the area about a year ago after her marriage broke up. It was a fresh start, she'd told us that first morning we all had coffee together. I can't re-member who made friends with her first. She appeared one day at our regular keep-fit class and the next thing, she'd struck up a conversation and she was sitting with us having coffee afterwards. She had just slotted in. It was like she'd always known us and we'd always known her. A new star to extend our constellation.

As the MPV smoothly exits Chichester, I look out of the window for clues as to where we are going. We are heading north and in my mind I picture a rough map of the area and where we could get to in an hour. Certainly out of Sussex. Although, there is the possibility that it's part of the surprise and we end up back where we started from. I wouldn't put it past Joanne.

About half an hour later the car takes a turn off the main road and down a narrow lane. Trees line the road on either side, blocking out much of the daylight. The car turns off but I don't manage to catch a glimpse of the signpost. Neither of my travelling companions seem to be worrying about where we are heading. The Prosecco bottle now empty, Zoe is busy opening another as Andrea tells us about the spinning class she had taken yesterday for the local rugby team.

'I love my job, but some days, I love it more than others,' she says. 'Those rugby players, Christ, they have stamina. All those muscular legs. I didn't know where to look. Well, I did, if you know what I mean!' She fans herself with her hand and sighs.

'Ah, don't give us that, you've eyes for Colin only,' I say. Much as Andrea likes to make out she drools over all the toned men who come into the gym, her and Colin are a solid couple.

The car begins to slow down and gradually the trees on either side of the road thin out, before disappearing completely on our left. A small airfield comes into view.

'Farnstead Airport,' I read the sign out loud as the driver turns through the gates and pulls up in a parking bay. 'This is definitely where you were supposed to take us?'

'Definitely,' says the driver. He opens the glove box and takes out another envelope. 'These are your next set of instructions. While you read them, I'll take this over to the departure terminal.' He holds up the blue cloth bag and leaves us with the envelope.

Zoe reads it out this time. 'So, you've all arrived at Farnstead Airport, Phase One of the journey is complete. Now for Phase Two. Please proceed to the departure terminal where at reception you will find a flight booked for you under my name. Don't worry, you don't need passports, just the photo ID I told you to bring. Enjoy the view and see you soon!' Zoe looks up at us, her eyes shining with excitement. 'She's only bloody chartered us a flight!'

Twenty minutes later, we are sitting in a small light aircraft, still none the wiser as to where we are heading.

'Obviously the UK,' says Andrea. 'Although I can't say I'm particularly enjoying being stuck in this thing. It's hardly a Boeing 747.'

'I think it's exciting,' says Zoe.

Andrea looks up to the ceiling in despair.

'Oh, come on, Andrea. Don't be a party-pooper,' I say, nudging her foot with my own. 'Joanne's gone to a lot of trouble. Relax and enjoy it.'

Andrea gives another look of exasperation but I can tell it's half-hearted. 'I'll relax when we've reached wherever the hell we're going and my feet are firmly on the ground again.' Andrea peers under the seat. 'No Prosecco this time.'

I exchange a grin with Zoe. Andrea loves playing up to her role of harbinger of doom and gloom.

The pilot is very pleasant but he too has been paid into silence by Joanne, so the three of us have no choice but to peer out of the window and make rough approximations of whereabouts in the UK we are flying over and speculate as to where we could be heading. The uneasy realisation that this is totally out of my control dawns on me. Joanne's idea of a surprise has reached new heights, literally. And I don't like feeling I'm at her mercy now.

Chapter 3

The further north we head, the more convinced I am of our destination. 'I think we must be going to Scotland,' I say.

'Scotland? That's where Joanne went on holiday last year,' says Zoe. 'Her, Tris and the kids went pot-holing, canoeing, all that sort of stuff.'

'Some holiday that was,' says Andrea.

Both Zoe and I look at Andrea blankly. 'I thought they had a great time,' I say.

'Yeah, I'm sure they did.' The sarcasm in Andrea's voice is apparent.

'What's that supposed to mean?' I say.

'Ignore me. I meant all that outward-bound stuff Joanne does, not my idea of a holiday.' Andrea gives me a sideways glance. 'What?'

'You know as well as I do that's not what you meant.'

'You don't like Tris at all, do you?' says Zoe.

Andrea looks as if she's about to protest, but the defiant part of her nature surfaces, fuelled by the earlier alcohol no doubt. 'It's a personality clash, nothing more.'

'Bullshit.' I give a fake cough from behind my hand, to

which Andrea gives her best and totally unconvincing innocent look.

'Ditto to that,' says Zoe. She shifts position in her seat. 'Why is it you don't like him?'

'If you must know, he fancies himself a bit too much,' says Andrea. 'Thinks he's God's gift to women.'

I laugh. 'He's always been like that. I swear he takes longer getting ready than Joanne does. You should see all his beauty products. Anti-wrinkle this, healthy-glow that. He must spend a fortune.'

'I rest my case,' says Andrea.

'Just because a guy looks after himself, it can't be grounds for not liking him. That's a bit shallow, even for you.' There's a prickly tone in Zoe's voice and I sense Andrea's mood shift.

'It's nothing to do with me being shallow, thanks very much. I do actually have other reasons.'

'Such as?' Zoe clearly has no intention of letting the matter drop.

'Such as . . .' Andrea pauses. 'OK, if you must know, he made a pass at me once.'

'What?' both Zoe and I say in unison.

'A couple of Christmases ago. You know, at that Boxing Day party we went to.'

I nod and remember that was the last Christmas Darren had been alive. There had been a funny atmosphere that night and it wasn't solely down to the argument Darren and I had had before we'd arrived. Joanne had been on edge and Tris was quite drunk early in the evening. I have looked back at that night many times since then and realised that Joanne's daughter, Ruby, had already dropped her bombshell and the fallout was happening right before me, but in such slow motion, I hadn't noticed.

'Tris made a pass at you? Really? Are you sure?' Zoe's voice brings me back from my thoughts.

'Of course I'm bloody sure,' says Andrea. 'Waiting for someone to come out of the loo and then bundling them up against the coat rack while you simultaneously try to stick your tongue down their throat and your hand between their legs, is actually more than just a pass.'

Zoe's face is a mix of anger and disbelief. 'He did that? Tris groped you?'

'I think the legal term is he sexually assaulted me,' says Andrea.

'Jesus,' I mutter, letting out a long breath. 'What happened? Did you tell Colin or Joanne?' I wonder if this was the turning point between Andrea and Joanne. If this was where their friendship began to fray at the edges.

'No. I didn't,' replies Andrea. 'We were all pretty drunk. I pushed Tris away and told him to fuck off. He apologised and we laughed it off.'

'Except you don't sound like you've really laughed it off,' I say.

'Not exactly. So, you can see why I'm not Tris's biggest fan.' Andrea looks at Zoe.

'I can't believe it. Not Tris,' says Zoe, and then adds rapidly, 'I mean, I do believe you, but I never thought Tris would do something like that. Why would he? No offence.'

'None taken,' says Andrea. 'I know I'm hard to resist . . .'

She gives a smile and the tension in the air eases. 'I'd like to say it was the alcohol, but Tris is all about strutting his stuff, he's such a poser. I think he tries to make up for his lack of prowess in the bedroom.'

I shake my head. Honestly, Andrea is terrible sometimes.

'And what do you mean by that?' demands Zoe. She must catch the surprised look my face involuntarily offers at the defensive tone in her voice because she quickly clarifies her question. 'I mean, how do you know? Joanne's never said anything to me about . . . bedroom stuff.'

'It's not for me to say.' Andrea looks at us and I can tell that, despite that caveat, she is going to say. 'But, you know how Joanne loves to oversee everything?' We both nod and let Andrea continue. 'Well, that extends to the bedroom. She once told me that she had no intention of letting Tris have the upper hand, that he may be the qualified psychologist, but she was far superior at the mind games.'

'To be honest, that doesn't surprise me,' I say, contemplating our friend. 'Joanne's not very good at taking instruction from anyone.'

'And I should know,' says Andrea. 'If she wasn't my friend, I'm sure I would have sacked her by now, or at least put her on a disciplinary for the way she talks to me, especially in front of the other staff. Honestly, you'd think she was the bloody owner, not me!'

Before the conversation can continue, the plane banks to the right and the pilot's voice comes over the intercom, informing us that we should fasten our seatbelts to prepare for landing.

As I tighten the belt across my lap, I look over at Andrea. Her latest revelations and insight into Joanne's marriage only serve to confirm my own private thoughts; we may all be friends but there's so much we don't know about each other. We all have our secrets and I, for one, intend to keep it that way.

'I think we're landing in a bloody field,' says Andrea, as she looks out of the window. Both Zoe and I do our best to see the ground below us. There's no sign of a runway anywhere.

A minute later the wheels of the aircraft touch down on to grass and we are bumped and jolted as we make our landing. Zoe gives a little screech at one point, but the pilot is obviously experienced and once all three wheels have made contact with the ground, the speed slows rapidly and the engine purrs in a gentle contented way as we taxi along.

'We have literally landed in a field,' says Andrea. 'I can't even see a control tower or anything.'

The plane bumps its way to a halt but the engine remains ticking over. The pilot walks back to us in the plane. In his hand, he holds what is becoming a familiar sight. A white envelope.

'I believe this is for you,' he says, handing me the envelope. 'This is where I say goodbye. I hope you enjoyed your trip.'

'And our phones?' I ask.

'I'll hang onto those for now,' he replies. 'Don't worry, they are going with you though.'

There's distinct chill in the air as we climb out of the plane. I place my rucksack on the ground so I can zip up my fleece. We are indeed in the middle of a field. I look around, wondering if there is a farmhouse or something nearby, but there is no sign of life. The landscape is one of fields merging into a backdrop of hills and in the very distance silhouettes of mountains.

'Are you going to open that letter, then?' says Andrea, dropping her bag on the ground beside mine.

I oblige and read out Joanne's message.

'Welcome to Bonnie Scotland! I hope the plane journey was OK. Now, if you make your way over to the far end of the field, there's a gate and Phase 3 of your journey awaits you. God, I'm loving this. I hope you are too!'

'Are you loving it?' I ask Andrea in amusement.

'Yeah, can't you tell?' comes the grim reply.

I laugh at Andrea's glum expression and grin at Zoe, who is still as enthusiastic as ever as she performs a three-sixty turn to take in the surroundings. I must admit, my own enthusiasm is waning slightly. My stomach is protesting at the lack of food and I could murder a cup of tea. I look down towards the gate.

'Come on, let's go down there,' I say. But when we get to the gate, there is no sign of Phase 3. 'I suppose we just wait.'

'I guess so,' agrees Andrea. 'Doesn't look like Top Gun is going anywhere at the moment, so we won't be stranded. Besides, he still has our phones. I presume he's waiting to hand them over to whoever comes for us.'

'I feel lost without my phone,' I confess, eyeing the blue bag in the pilot's hand. 'I said I'd text Seb to let him know we'd arrived safely.'

'And how is the lovely Seb?' asks Zoe. 'Still lovely, I take it?'

I smile. 'Yes. Still lovely.'

'Ooh, will we be needing to buy hats soon?' says Andrea, giving me a nudge with her elbow.

'I don't think so. Marriage is certainly not on the agenda. Not for me anyway.' I turn around and rest my arms on the gate, hoping we won't be stuck here too long. 'It's very beautiful here,' I say, trying to head the conversation off in a different direction.

'Yes, it is,' agrees Andrea. She leans back. 'Now, tell us, why is marriage not on the agenda for you?'

'Yes, why not?' chimes in Zoe. 'From what I've seen of Seb, he's totally in love with you.'

I give a sigh, resigning myself to the fact that the conversation topic isn't going away. 'It's not only me I have to think about when it comes to marriage. Whether it's Seb or someone else, I've Alfie to think of.'

'True, but he'll be off to university this time next year. You won't have to worry about him then,' says Zoe.

'Sounds to me like you're using Alfie as an excuse.' Andrea fires from the hip as usual. 'What's at the root of it? Darren?'

I can't answer immediately. Andrea is far too perceptive. Zoe stretches her hand over and squeezes my arm. 'You can't put your life on hold forever. Darren is dead. What happened, you can't change. You need to accept that.'

'He can't hold you to ransom from the grave,' adds Andrea. 'You deserve better than that. Fucking hell, what he put you through, I don't know why you're still so loyal. Your marriage was bad enough, the separation ugly, but to do what he did – and not just to you, but to do that to Alfie too. That was evil.'

Having Andrea as a best friend can be wonderful most of the time, but other times, she can be brutal in her honesty. I close my eyes tightly at the two-year-old memory of coming home from work to find Alfie on the doorstep. Darren had forced himself into the house and locked Alfie out. I will never forget the sight that greeted me as I stepped over the threshold. Darren had hanged himself from the banisters. I had tried to shield Alfie and to push him out of the house, but it had been too late. He had seen it. How did a sixteen-year-old lad ever get over that?

'Andrea, don't.' Zoe's voice is soft and full of concern. I feel her fingers rub my hand.

'I'm sorry,' says Andrea. 'I didn't mean to upset you, but sometimes I get so frustrated that you constantly punish yourself about Darren.'

'Andrea!' Zoe cuts in again. 'Enough.'

I give Andrea a half-smile. 'It's OK. I know you're right but I still have this tremendous amount of guilt and, no matter what, I can't shrug it off.' The truth is, I don't deserve to shrug it off, not after what happened that day.

'We understand,' says Zoe. She nudges Andrea. 'Don't we?'

'Yeah, of course we do.'

'Can we not mention it again? Not this weekend anyway.' I look at each of my friends in turn. 'This is supposed to be a fun few days to celebrate Joanne's birthday.' I remain silent about the real reason why I don't want to talk about my late husband. I ponder at the expression *late husband* and think how ludicrous it sounds. Late? What's he late for? He's been dead two years. Shit-husband, self-absorbed-husband, insecure-husband or even bastard-husband would be a better description. As always, I keep these thoughts locked away, allowing my loyalty to Darren to be misconstrued.

The sound of a car engine breaks the silence that has fallen between us. We all look towards the road. The engine grows louder and a black Transit-type van appears from around the corner, drawing to a halt on the other side of the gate.

A man dressed in blue overalls, who I estimate to be in his thirties, jumps out of the vehicle.

'Good morning, ladies,' he says, in a broad Scottish accent. 'Good to see you made it safely.' He slides open the side door and then walks over to the gate, unhooking it and opening it wide. He indicates to the van. 'Climb aboard, your hostess is waiting for you.'

I look towards the pilot and am relieved to see him making his way over with the phones. Only once I witness the hand-over of the bag and I'm convinced the phones are coming with us, do I venture into the vehicle.

The back of the van is boarded out in plywood and fitted with bench-like seats along each side. The rear windows have all been blacked out so there is no danger of us being able to see where we are going. There is a plywood partition between the rear of the van and the driver's seat, with a small rectangle cut out.

'This is ridiculous,' says Andrea, taking a seat next to me. 'What's happened to the plush MPV and private plane? Now we're in a boarded-up Transit van.'

'Oh, stop,' says Zoe. 'It's a bit of fun.'

Andrea makes a grunting noise but doesn't comment

further. The driver appears at the door. 'All belted up? Good. That's what I like to see. We don't want any accidents along the way. I'm sure Mrs Aldridge wants you all to arrive in one piece.'

'Please tell me this is the final leg of the journey,' says Andrea, folding her arms and blowing out a disgruntled breath.

'Aye, in under thirty minutes, you will have reached your final destination,' says the driver, before sliding the door shut, leaving us in semi-darkness. A small shaft of light streams through the gap in the plywood.

I'm not sure why, but I involuntarily shudder at the driver's turn of phrase.

Chapter 4

We sit in an uneasy silence as the van trundles along the road, our bodies swaying from side and side as the driver navigates what I can only presume to be small winding roads. I'm not convinced the lap belts will actually do much to save us if there is an accident and as the van hits a pothole and we jerk forward, I tighten the belt for good measure.

Although it is chilly outside, here in the van there is no air and I begin to feel a little stifled. I rest my head against the plywood which lines the van. Although my mind is clear and I know this is all a bit of fun on Joanne's part and I know we are going to get out of here soon, my body is offering a different interpretation.

I'm conscious that my heart rate has picked up and I can feel sweat gathering under my arms. I concentrate on breathing in slowly through my nose and control the out-breath from my mouth. Techniques I have had to learn since Darren's death.

I stopped seeing the counsellor about six months ago and this is probably the first time I have felt under duress since then. It's the small space of the van that is getting to me. I don't know what it was about finding Darren that caused this claustrophobia, but it's certainly a symptom. My counsellor suggested it could be something as simple as the closing of the front door behind me that day, the sense of being shut in a house and then dealing with the devastation before me. My mind has somehow connected the two things.

I eye my rucksack on the floor of the van. In the side pocket is my little box of pills. I have recently found another way to deal with the panic attacks. Neither Andrea nor Zoe know about the pills. In fact, no one does. Not even my GP.

'You OK, Carys?' Andrea's concerned voice filters into my thoughts.

I sit myself upright and take another deep breath as I open my eyes. I turn and smile at her. 'Yeah. Just finding it not quite so fun now.'

Andrea nods. 'Typical of Joanne to take it one step too far.' She leans forward and bangs on the partition.

'What's up?' comes the voice through the small cut-out hole.

'How much longer?' shouts Andrea over the noise of the engine. 'This is taking the piss now.'

'Patience, ladies, patience,' comes the reply. 'We're nearly there.'

The speed drops and the van takes an unexpected turn to the left. The ground noise changes. It sounds like we are on an unmade track. I can hear stones pinging up against the wheel arches every now and then, and the van rolls and lollops more as if navigating potholes and dips in the surface.

I close my eyes again, resigning myself to the fact that shouting and getting stressed isn't going to get us there any quicker. I make a conscious effort to take my thoughts to a more positive place. It's easier said than done. I think of Seb and my heart lifts as I bring his face to mind. His fair skin and almost translucent blue eyes. I smile as I remember him telling me why he has his hair cut so short.

'It's to stop any of the bad guys being able to get a grip on me, should I get into a tussle,' he had said, referring to his job as a detective with the Met. Once I had made a suitably impressed response, he'd broken into a broad grin before continuing: 'I can't lie. It's really because, if I let my hair grow, it turns into a mass of curls; looks like pubes.' We'd both laughed for a long time at this imagery. I think that was the moment I realised how much I enjoyed being with Seb and relished spending my free time with him. I miss him when he isn't there and want him in my life more. However, my next thought is of Alfie, which should be a positive one. But it's not.

Before I can visit this further, the van slows down. There's a change of gear and the engine noise lowers. We grind to a halt; a small jolt indicates the handbrake has been applied and then the engine is cut.

The driver's voice comes through the gap. 'Could all passengers disembark. This service will now be terminated.'

'Finally,' says Andrea.

The side door opens and we emerge from the bowels of the van, blinking as daylight floods our pupils. The driver jogs over to the croft and opens the front door, places the blue bag containing our phones inside. He closes the door and jogs back to the van.

'Enjoy your weekend, ladies,' he calls, jumping into the van. We watch as the vehicle makes a U-turn and then disappears down the track.

I look at Andrea and Zoe, who return the look with equal bewilderment. 'Well, that was the strangest holiday transfer I've ever experienced,' says Andrea. The fun has worn off and we take a moment to study the building in front of us.

It is a stone cottage made up of a ground floor and a first floor. A solid oak door is centred in the stonework, flanked by windows each side. In the roof, there are two dormer windows and on the side of the building is a single-storey extension which, judging by the lighter colour of mortar between the stonework, was probably added at a later date.

'So, here we are,' I say needlessly. 'I suppose we'd better go in. I assume Joanne is already here.'

'I wouldn't bank on anything right now,' says Andrea. 'Maybe that's her surprise.'

'What?' says Zoe, frowning.

'The surprise is, she's not here,' says Andrea.

I pick up my rucksack. 'There's only one way to find out.' I give my friend a nudge with my elbow. 'Come on.'

Before we take a step, the front door swings open and Joanne appears in the doorway. Her brunette bobbed hair, immaculate as ever, frames her petite features. She opens her arms wide. 'You're here!' She trots over and hugs each of us in turn, the blue phone bag in one hand. 'And all in one piece. I hope you enjoyed your journey. What did you think?' Joanne looks expectantly at each of us.

'Loved it!' says Zoe, injecting possibly rather too much enthusiasm into her voice.

'Yeah, loved it,' says Andrea, her lack of enthusiasm balancing out Zoe's excess.

'Put it this way,' I say. 'I'm glad we're here now. I hope the return journey is rather more orthodox.'

'Oh, don't be worrying about the return journey.' Joanne flaps her hand in the air. 'You'll love that too.'

'That's what I was afraid of,' says Andrea. 'Jesus, let's get inside. I'm freezing my tits off here.'

'What do you expect in that flimsy fleece? I hope you've brought a warmer jacket with you.'

'This has to be your best surprise ever,' says Zoe, hooking her holdall on one shoulder and slipping her free arm through Joanne's.

'Maybe not ever. Just to date,' replies Joanne. 'You have no idea what other surprises I have in store for you three.' Joanne leans into Zoe and squeezes her arm. She then looks around at myself and Andrea, and I don't miss the little glint in her eye. 'Let me show you to your rooms. I have some lunch ready for you and then we can crack open our first bottle of wine.'

'Sounds like a plan,' I say, following on behind. I look over my shoulder at Andrea. 'Come on, misery. This isn't an audition for the seven dwarfs, you know.'

'If it is, then Andrea gets the part, hands down,' calls Joanne. Her laughter echoes around the porch roof.

Andrea pulls a face, which only makes me laugh too.

Inside the croft, the small entrance hall with an oak staircase and a red quarry-tiled floor greets us. Years of feet travelling the surface have worn the shine from the centre of the tiles but the edges have managed to retain some of their former gloss. I look through the doorway on my left. It's the living room, with two big comfortable sofas either side of a large brick fireplace. A wooden chest sits between the two pieces of furniture, acting as a coffee table. The floorboards in this room have been sanded and varnished, giving a more modern feel to the room, and a black-and-white hide is spread out in front of the hearth.

'Cow hide,' supplies Joanne. 'All the rage, apparently. Not so keen myself. Not at two or three hundred pounds each, anyway.'

'I quite like it,' says Andrea, peering over my shoulder.

'Now you're a successful business owner, I expect you can afford these luxuries,' says Joanne.

I shoot Joanne a look. Was there a hint of tightness in her voice? A topic of conversation that is always sidestepped with a sense of awkwardness. I watch now as Andrea gives Joanne a long look, one that Joanne matches without flinching.

'What's beyond the trees there?' Zoe pipes up, as she gazes out of the window.

I don't know if the change in conversation was deliberate on Zoe's part, but it breaks the deadlock.

'More trees,' says Joanne, turning towards the rear window where Zoe is standing. 'That's the edge of a bloody great forest. It stretches around from behind the croft in a big arch and then all the way along the edge of the track.'

Zoe gives a shiver. 'Even in daylight, it looks spooky.'

'After lunch, we're going exploring,' says Joanne. She nods towards the trees. 'There's a walk through there which

40

eventually leads to a clearing. Legend has it that it was once a site for pagan rituals and human sacrifices.'

'Sounds delightful,' mutters Andrea.

Zoe turns away from the window and drops into one of the sofas. 'I'm glad I'm not here on my own. When did you get here, Joanne?'

'Last night, actually.'

'You were here on your own all night?' Zoe leans back and looks up at Joanne.

'No big deal. Anyway, you're on your own at night times, aren't you? Or are you? No secret lover you haven't told us about?' She flicks Zoe's ponytail with her fingers and winks.

'No!' protests Zoe. Her cheeks flush red. She sits upright and looks round at us.

'Ah, you're blushing,' teases Joanne. 'Look how red Zoe's gone.'

Zoe has turned a deep crimson colour and I can't help feeling sorry for her, yet at the same time I wonder if Joanne's teasing has some substance. For all Zoe's bouncy childlike enthusiasm and seemingly innocent charm, I've always felt this has been to cover up the after-effects of a bad relationship. Although she's never gone into details about her ex-husband, there clearly are unresolved issues in that department. To ease her embarrassment, I take it upon myself to divert the topic of conversation this time. 'Joanne, are you going to show us round the rest of the place?'

'Sure. Follow me.'

Across the tiled hallway is another room, identical in size to the living room. It too has a fireplace on the rear wall and to the right of that, in what was once an alcove, is a doorway. A dining table and six chairs occupy the centre of the room and a wing-backed armchair is on the other side of the fire-place with a view over the garden.

'Through here is the kitchen,' says Joanne.

The kitchen looks to have been refurbished recently but it is sympathetic to the age of the property. The units are free-standing and of a farmhouse style with wooden worktops. A Belfast sink is below the window, which overlooks the front of the property. There is an exterior door with glass panels at the top, draped with a net curtain.

I move the curtain to look through. There is a rear porch and beyond that is an outbuilding about the size of a garden shed. 'What's in there?'

Joanne joins me at the door. 'Nothing very exciting, I should imagine. It's locked, but from what I've seen through the window it's full of old garden tools and a lawn mower. Not that they seem to worry about keeping the grass manicured: it's more pasture than lawn.'

True, the rear of the property has no fencing to identify the boundaries and blends in with the surrounding open scrubland scenery. A small area immediately outside the back door has been laid with paving stones to create a patio, and a flowerbed has been dug around the edge which is full of shrubs, but that is the extent of the garden.

'To be fair, we do appear to be in the middle of nowhere. It must be hard to get a gardener up here,' I say. 'I don't suppose they want to pay someone to come up here every week.'

'Exactly,' says Joanne.

'How far are we from civilisation?' asks Zoe, as we walk back through to the entrance hall.

'Bloody miles,' says Andrea.

Joanne gives a laugh but ignores the question. 'Oh, before I forget. I need to take a picture of us all. A selfie. Wait there a moment while I get my camera.'

She disappears into the living room, leaving us waiting in the hall. As with the rest of the house, it's a mix of old and new. Some pieces of furniture and decoration look like they've been here for years, whereas other pieces wouldn't look out of place in an Ikea catalogue. There's a dark wood telephone seat with a faded green velvet cushion, which seems odd as there doesn't appear to be a telephone here. It reminds me of something from the seventies. Above it is a picture of a crying boy, another leftover from a past era. And on the opposite wall is a row of modern pictures in white frames. They have almost a seaside feel to them, depicting stick-men in sailor suits with flags in different positions, each spelling out a word in semaphore. I take a closer look to see if the words are printed underneath, but can't see anything. On the floor, propped against the wall, is a print, about a metre long, of spring flowers, which I personally think would look nicer on the wall.

Joanne reappears almost straight away. 'I treated myself to a Polaroid camera. Instant photos,' she says, holding the retro-looking camera in her hand.

'How very old-school,' says Andrea.

'Exactly. Just like us,' replies Joanne. 'Now, I need you all to stand here in the hall. Zoe, you here. That's it. Andrea here.'

She leaves a space between them and then takes my arm. 'Carys, you stand in the middle. I'll set the timer up and then I'll hop on the end.'

Joanne moves a pot plant from the shelf inside the door and prepares the camera. 'I tested it earlier. It's the perfect height,' she says. 'OK, you ready? I'm pressing the timer button now.'

'Quick, before it goes off,' says Zoe, as Joanne darts back and joins the end of the line. 'Smile!'

We all stand rigidly, while at the same time trying to pose naturally with big smiles plastered across our faces. Just as I think the timer isn't going to work, the camera flashes.

'Now to see the result,' says Joanne, returning to the camera. 'I love this, it's so eighties.' After a few seconds, a photograph emerges slowly from the bottom of the camera. Joanne waves the photograph in the air to dry the ink. 'Do any of you miss the old days? When life was simple, before we had to deal with all the grown-up stuff?'

'I don't know,' says Andrea. 'I actually like my life now, as an adult.'

'Mmm . . . I expect you do,' says Joanne. 'What about you, Carys? Do you prefer life now?'

I catch Andrea and Joanne exchanging a look, the latter appearing confused for a moment and then in a display of realisation, throws her hand to her mouth, the photograph still grasped between her finger and thumb. 'Oh, I'm so sorry, Carys. That was insensitive of me.'

I force my mouth to curve north in a bid to smile. I'm not sure how effective the action is, but the intent is there. 'It's

OK,' I say. 'No one has to tiptoe around me. Honestly.'

An awkward silence straggles behind my words until Andrea sweeps everything up with her none-too-subtle attempt at changing the subject: 'Right, let's see this photograph then.'

We crowd round the image and overly enthuse about it.

'It's lovely,' says Joanne. 'I love the way the real us shines through.'

I'm not sure any of us quite know what she means, but to restore the light-hearted atmosphere, we all agree and allow Joanne to lean the picture against the clock on the mantelpiece of the living room.

'What shall we do with our bags?' asks Andrea, as Joanne takes a moment to admire the photograph from the middle of the room.

Joanne spins round. 'Oh, yes. I'll show you to your rooms.' She leads the way back into the hallway and we climb the narrow oak staircase. 'Two of you will need to share.' She looks at myself and Andrea. 'Are you two OK in the twin room?'

'Yeah, sure,' I say and Andrea agrees.

'Excellent, that's that sorted.' Joanne pushes open one of the doors and stands back to allow us in first.

It's a pleasantly spacious room with dual views from the front and rear of the property. Everything in the room is white, from the walls to the furniture and bedding. The little dormer window at the front looks out on to the track and for the first time I notice a river over the other side of a small brow that must have shielded it from sight when we were dropped off outside. I push my face closer to the glass and away to the left, where the river bends out of sight, I can see a little stone bridge, just wide enough for one vehicle to pass over. It looks picture-postcard.

'It's a gorgeous view,' I say, turning and going over to the window at the back. The view this time isn't so inviting. The trees behind appear even taller from the first floor. They bunch together, swallowing up the daylight, and become one big mass of darkness as I try to look further into the forest.

'Which bed do you want?' asks Andrea.

'I'll have the one near the front window.'

'OK, I'll be near the door.' Andrea dumps her rucksack on to the bed.

'The bathroom is right next to your room,' says Joanne from the doorway. 'It's not exactly en-suite, but it's as good as.' She turns to Zoe. 'Our rooms are across the landing. I'm at the front and you're at the back. Now I'll let you all get settled and freshened up. Come down in ten minutes and lunch will be ready.'

'Any chance we can have our phones?' I ask. 'I want to check in with Alfie.'

A shadow darts across Joanne's face, but it's so fast I almost question whether I saw it. However, the sympathetic look she gives me seems so false, I know I didn't imagine it. 'Sorry. No can do,' she says, hugging the blue bag to her body. 'All part of the game. No communication with the outside world this weekend. Besides, you can't get a signal up here, it's a not-spot.'

'How do people get on in an emergency?' asks Andrea.

'There's a wireless radio in the kitchen, but it looks as old as the hills,' says Joanne. 'It was probably last used in the Second World War.'

'I can't believe there's no phone coverage at all,' says Andrea. 'We really are in the middle of nowhere.'

'You'd think there would be a landline,' I agree.

'What's up?' asks Joanne. 'Is there a problem? Do you need to get in touch with Alfie?'

'Nothing's up. Alfie is staying at Andrea's with Colin and Bradley.'

'Then he'll be fine. Nothing to worry about,' says Joanne. 'Although you know Tris would have been happy to look after him had he not been on his golfing break. Not that Alfie needs looking after, he is eighteen later this month.'

'Yeah, I know, but Bradley and Alfie are having a gaming weekend. Thanks anyway, I'll bear that in mind for the future,' I say, feeling slightly uncomfortable at my little lie. The truth is, I was relieved when I found out Tris would be away this weekend. Alfie had already said he'd like to stay with Tris and Ruby, but I didn't like the way he was attaching himself to Tris. It was almost as if Tris was becoming a replacement for Darren. The amount of time he spends over there concerns me. Next thing, he'll be seeing Joanne as a replacement for me. As usual, this thought provokes a wave of insecurity and jealousy. I turn away from Joanne and start undoing my rucksack to hide the irrational fear that somehow she will be able to read my thoughts.

'He's always welcome, you know that,' says Joanne, clearly not letting me off the hook that easily. 'We like having him over. He and Ruby get on great. You should be encouraging him, not deterring him.'

'Who said anything about deterring him?' I snap, my guilt flaring up in the disguise of anger.

'Don't get all defensive,' says Joanne, folding her arms. 'I've known him so long and he's at our place so much, we're like an extended family.'

'Hey, come on you two,' says Zoe, from the landing. 'Let's not fight. This is supposed to be a fun birthday weekend, remember?'

Joanne and I study each other for a few seconds. I don't want to spoil the weekend. I plaster on a smile. 'We're not fighting.'

'No. We're not,' Joanne says, before turning and ushering Zoe across the hallway to her room.

I begin to unpack my clothes, quietly seething inside. I can sense Andrea looking at me and I meet her gaze. She raises her eyebrows and gives me a look that says she's not fooled for one minute. 'What?' I say defensively. 'We weren't fighting.'

'No. Of course you weren't,' she says, taking a T-shirt from her bag and lying it flat on the bed. 'No tension between you two at all.'

I lob a jumper I've just taken from my bag at her. 'None whatsoever. Don't know what you're talking about.'

We both laugh as she tosses the jumper back at me, but we also both know that Andrea is one hundred per cent right.

Chapter 5

I hang the last of my clothes in the wardrobe, leaving space on one side for Andrea to use. 'It's a nice room,' I say, as I quickly put on a fresh T-shirt. 'A bit on the basic side, but functional.'

'Better than I was expecting,' says Andrea. 'How is everything with Alfie?' She fiddles with her makeup bag in an attempt to seem casual but I suspect my earlier words with Joanne have prompted the enquiry.

'About the same. Actually, that's a lie. I don't know how it's going. He never talks about Darren.' I stop myself from continuing. I feel disloyal talking about Alfie even though Andrea is one of my best friends.

'Do you ever ask him?'

'Not any more. It's a prickly subject,' I admit. I walk over and sit down on my bed, letting out a sigh as I wrestle with my need to talk to someone about Alfie and my desire to project a much rosier picture of my home life. The need wins out. 'He seems more distant than ever lately. And he still has his moments, you know, when his temper gets the better of him.'

'Have there been any other . . . incidents?' asks Andrea. Her tone is gentle.

I shake my head. 'No. Not recently.' I realise I'm rubbing my arm subconsciously. Since Darren's death, Alfie has found it difficult to express his emotions and has taken to lashing out in his temper. Once or twice, I've found myself in the way.

'What's that mark on your back, then?' asks Andrea.

'On my back?'

'Yeah, I noticed it just now when you changed your T-shirt. You've got a red mark, right between your shoulder blades.'

'Oh, that. I did that this morning. Banged into the door by accident.' It's the truth. Maybe not the whole truth, but it is what happened. I feel embarrassed and ashamed to talk about Alfie's behaviour sometimes.

'Can't you speak to his counsellor?' asks Andrea. She squeezes my hand in a gesture of support.

'God, no. I suggested that once but Alfie was adamant I wasn't to get involved. Besides, I'm not sure what the counsellor would say. They're not supposed to divulge anything from the counselling sessions. Patient confidentiality.'

'You could speak to him, though. The counsellor, I mean. You could tell him how Alfie has been at home. He might not be aware of that. Alfie might not tell him the truth.'

'But then I feel I'm going behind Alfie's back, and if he finds out . . .' I leave the sentence unfinished as I gulp down an unexpected lump in my throat.

'Have you thought about getting advice on how to deal with it all yourself? I don't mean going to your counsellor, I mean strategies. A bit like they do parenting help for when you have a new baby. There must be some sort of support group for parents of bereaved children.'

'It's not my thing,' I admit. 'I did mention it once to my GP and she said to follow Alfie's lead for now.'

'Which is?'

'Not to talk about Darren's death unless Alfie wants to, and try to defuse the situation when he gets angry.'

'But doesn't that mean avoiding it so it becomes a taboo topic?'

'It's not just that,' I say, surprising myself at how all my worries are tumbling out. I'm usually very controlled when it comes to Alfie and Darren. 'Alfie spends so much time over at Joanne's house, it's starting to get to me. Like, really annoy me. I don't know why he doesn't want to spend time with me. It's like he's a visitor at home these days.'

'Maybe it's something to do with what happened with Darren.' Andrea moves over to my bed and sits beside me. 'Tell me about it! I can't walk through the hallway without the image of him . . . you know . . . hanging there. It makes me feel sick. God knows what it's doing to Alfie.'

'No luck with the house sale then?'

'No. I had someone view it the day before yesterday and they seemed keen. They were at the point of putting in an offer, but when they found out what happened, they changed their minds. It's the third time that's happened. No one wants to live in a house where the previous owner killed themselves.'

'What about reducing the price?'

'I think I'm going to have to, but that will mean I can't afford somewhere quite so nice to move to. Look, please don't say anything to the others. I don't like talking about it, especially to Joanne.'

'I won't. But have you thought about asking Joanne to encourage Alfie and Ruby to spend time at your house for a change?'

'That's the thing. Ruby doesn't want to come over because of Darren killing himself and Joanne is quite happy for Alfie to be there.' I can feel the little blaze of irritation flare inside me. 'I did actually speak to Joanne once about it and she told me that Alfie needed a safe place.'

'A safe place? What the hell does that mean?'

'According to Joanne, he needs somewhere he can go where he can relax and subconsciously know that nothing bad is going to happen. She said I should be grateful that he was there and not roaming the streets, getting into trouble.'

Andrea gives an indignant huff on my behalf. 'She's got bloody cheek at times.'

The sound of Joanne calling from the bottom of th punctuates the conversation. 'Lunch is ready her sing-song voice.

'Maybe things will be better after the weekend,' says A 'Like you said, this might be Joanne's way of saying so

'Yeah, I might be totally wrong about that,' I say wi wry smile.

We spend a few minutes unpacking our things. 'I'm done,' declares Andrea, pushing her rucksack under the be 'You ready for lunch?'

'You go ahead. I'll be down soon,' I say. 'I want to freshen up first.'

After Andrea has gone downstairs, I sit on the bed and let out a long slow breath, as a sense of claustrophobia settles lightly around me. It's not the house. It's not the company. It's the atmosphere. Joanne definitely seems spiky. Was I naïve to think this was a weekend of reconciliation? If I had my phone, I'd call Seb. To hear his reassuring voice and comforting words, in the way he can be both pragmatic and sympathetic at the same time, is what I really want right now.

I'm annoyed with myself for giving my phone over in the first place. It was a stupid idea and one I had gone along with too readily, hoping to appease Joanne. I decide to tackle her about it after lunch. It's unreasonable of her to expect everyone to be out of contact.

Before I head down for lunch though, I take the little box of tablets from my rucksack and pop a white pill from the foil wrapper. I swallow it down, not needing any water. I feel better even before it has absorbed into my bloodstream. Just knowing I've taken it helps.

In the kitchen, I find Zoe stirring a big pot of soup and the sweet earthy smell of carrots and coriander wafts in the air.

'I'll set the table,' I say, opening several cupboard doors before I find the bowls.

'I was about to do that,' says Andrea, entering the kitchen. 'Joanne's lighting a fire. Apparently, we're in for some colder weather. Joy.' She pulls a glum face.

'Typical,' I say, handing the bowls to Andrea and rummaging around in the cutlery drawer for spoons.

'You OK?' asks Andrea quietly, as Zoe nips through the dining room with a box of matches for Joanne.

'Yeah. I could do with my phone though. I wouldn't mind checking in with Alfie.'

'Only Alfie?' Andrea raises one eyebrow.

'Maybe Seb as well,' I confess.

Andrea gives a laugh as she goes into the kitchen. 'Maybe?' she questions. 'Oh, I think, definitely.'

I look out of the dining-room window and gaze across the driveway to the riverbank beyond. The yellow gorse bushes sway hypnotically from side to side as they are caught and then released by the breeze. It's a beautiful spot and I imagine on a summer's day when the sun is shining it would be a heavenly place to come and escape from the world. However, by contrast, the grumpy skies and agitated weather are only adding to the undercurrent of disquiet.

Andrea comes in with some glasses, which she places at each setting. 'Don't be worrying about Alfie. He'll be fine with Bradley and Colin.'

'I know. Ignore me. I'm fine,' I say, turning from the window and smiling.

'That's the fire lit,' says Joanne, coming into the room. 'Right, I'll bring the soup in. Sit down, everyone.'

'It smells delicious,' says Zoe, sitting at the table. 'I managed to resist the urge to have a little taster earlier when no one was looking.'

'I know what you mean,' says Andrea. 'My stomach has been rumbling like mad.'

'Well, the wait is over.' Joanne brings in the pot and places it on the table, before carefully ladling soup into each of our bowls. 'I'm so glad you all came,' she says as we tuck in. 'I was worried that one of you would drop out if I told you beforehand what I had planned.'

I resist looking up at Andrea, it would be a telltale sign of our guilt.

'Wouldn't miss this for the world,' says Zoe. 'Would we?'

We offer our reassurances that we are as pleased to be here. I take a spoonful of soup to hide my true feelings.

The conversation moves on to the children and I feel myself tense in anticipation of Alfie and Ruby being mentioned. Since Darren's death, the two of them have grown incredibly close. Too close for my liking. As if I haven't been tormented enough by that girl. I say girl, she is nearly twenty, but I've known her since she was six years old and it's hard for me to see her as a grown woman.

As if anticipating my desire to change the topic of conversation, Joanne addresses me. 'Ruby wasn't happy about going to my mum's. She would much rather have stayed at home with Alfie, but she said you had already arranged for him to go to Andrea's.'

My throat feels incredibly tight and the words catch in my mouth. Even though I was expecting this, my physical reaction far outweighs my mental reaction. My body has gone into overdrive.

It's then I feel the burning sensation on my lips and my throat tightens some more. I recognise the symptoms. This isn't a reaction to the conversation, this is a reaction to something I've eaten. I'm going into anaphylactic shock. A symptom of my nut allergy.

I drop the spoon on the table and simultaneously push

the chair back as I get to my feet. My EpiPen is upstairs in my bag. I had completely forgotten to bring it down with me, something I do as a matter of course when I eat where someone other than myself has prepared the food.

'You OK, Carys?' asks Joanne.

'Shit,' comes Andrea's voice and I assume she's realised what is happening.

The rest of the conversation is lost as I race upstairs as fast as I can. My legs feel wobbly and my breathing is becoming harder as my airways tighten in response to my allergy. From my handbag, I grab my EpiPen and flip off the blue cap, before plunging the pen into my thigh. As I wheeze I count to ten before removing the pen from my leg. I flop down on to the bed and, closing my eyes, I make a conscious effort to keep calm, to focus on my breathing as almost immediately the epinephrine takes effect. I massage my thigh at the same time to encourage the muscle to absorb the medication.

'Carys, are you OK?' It's Andrea's voice and I feel the mattress dip beside me as she sits down. She pushes a strand of hair from my face and holds my hand.

I squeeze her hand in response to reassure her as I gradually feel the reaction subside. The numbing sensation in my lips fades first; it's not dissimilar to the feeling of numbness wearing off after a trip to the dentist. My breathing becomes easier as my airways dilate and I take longer, fuller breaths.

'Do you want some water?' This time it's Joanne's voice. She's at the other side of the bed.

I open my eyes and Zoe is standing at the foot of the bed

looking concerned, with Joanne and Andrea either side of me. I sit myself up and look at Joanne.

'There must have been some sort of nut in that soup,' I say, taking the water from her. My hand is a little shaky as I lift the glass to my lips.

'There wasn't. I promise,' she says. 'I'm not that stupid. We all know about your allergy.'

'Did you check the ingredients?' asks Andrea.

'Of course I bloody did,' snaps Joanne. 'You can look at the box if you don't believe me. No nuts. Not even a trace of nuts.'

'It's a bit late for that now,' says Andrea. 'Damage has been done.'

'There's no damage now,' I say, not wanting this to turn into an argument. 'I'll be OK. I just need to rest here for a little while.'

'But there must have been something in that soup,' insists Andrea. 'It's hardly likely to have been cross-contaminated. Maybe you added something?' She looks at Joanne, who scowls back at her.

'I'm telling you, I never put anything in that soup. Why would I?' Joanne stands with her hands on her hips, glaring across the bed at Andrea. 'If there was something else added, who's to say I did it?'

'This is ridiculous,' says Zoe. 'Are you saying one of us put something in the soup?'

'Someone did and it wasn't me,' says Joanne. 'I left you in the kitchen on your own, stirring the soup.'

'Seriously?' says Zoe, shaking her head.

Joanne ignores her. 'What about you, Andrea? Were you in the kitchen on your own?'

Andrea looks slightly taken aback. She looks at me before speaking. 'Well, I was, but I only went in to get the glasses. Look, this is a stupid conversation.'

'It's OK,' I say. 'Obviously, no one did anything on purpose. It was probably some sort of cross-contamination at source.' I realise that my anaphylactic shock has probably shaken everyone up. 'Let's all forget about it. I'll come down. I could do with a cup of tea.'

'Good idea,' says Zoe. 'This has got us all a bit flustered.'

'Too right,' says Joanne. 'Goodness, you gave us all a fright there. Come on, I'll make the tea. We can have a slice of cake I made. And I promise, no nuts whatsoever.'

Andrea insists that I sit in the living room with a cup of tea while they clear away the lunch dishes. I feel a lot better now and am grateful that my allergy is on the milder end of the spectrum. Although it has shaken me up, the reaction wasn't severe enough to warrant any further medical intervention. Which is just as well, considering where we are. I have no idea how far away we are from a hospital.

Andrea, Joanne and Zoe are all very aware of my allergy and, despite my assurances to them that it could easily have been contaminated at source, I know it's unlikely, especially these days with health and safety so stringent. This leads me to poke around in the dark corners of my mind where other thoughts are crouching: what exactly was put in the soup and how did it get there . . . which leads me to question who and why.

I feel restless at the thought and try to distract myself by inspecting the bookcase, idly skimming the spines of the books. There's a wide range of fiction, although most of the novels look several years old and well-thumbed, as if they have been rescued from a charity shop. There are some larger coffee-table books on the lower shelves. Most of them appear to feature the Scottish landscape and traditions. There's one about Victorian London, which seems out of place but, again, probably a rescue book. At the end of the shelf is a small stack of DVDs.

A Disney film, *Lion King*; an old John Wayne western, and a thriller called *Rogue Trader*. None of them appeal to me. It's then I realise that I haven't seen a television in the croft, never mind a DVD player.

'Aha! Caught you,' says Joanne, coming into the room.

I jump unnecessarily and spin round. Joanne is carrying a mug of tea. 'You're supposed to be resting,' she says, placing the mug on the coffee table.

'I was having a look at the books.'

'Found anything interesting?'

'Not really. Although there are three DVDs here and yet no TV. Seems odd.' I hold the boxes up.

Joanne gives them a cursory glance. 'Maybe there used to be a TV here or perhaps the last visitors left them.'

I return the cases and sit down next to Joanne. 'This is a lovely croft,' I say. 'You've gone to a lot of trouble for this weekend.'

'I'd been toying with the idea for a while,' says Joanne. 'It was actually Zoe who made up my mind to go ahead with it.'

'Really?' I give Joanne a quizzical look. 'I didn't think any of us knew anything about it.'

'Oh, she didn't know. It was something that was brought up in conversation one day and it spurred me into action.'

'It's very generous of you.'

'The pleasure is all mine. You know I love organising parties. Who better to organise my own than myself? That's what I told Tris. This way, I get to totally please myself.'

'You have a point.'

'Not to mention your birthday too.' She stands up and calls from the doorway. 'Come on, you two. We've got a game to play!'

Chapter 6

'Is everyone ready for their next surprise?' asks Joanne, once Andrea and Zoe have settled themselves in the living room.

'Ready as we'll ever be,' says Andrea, leaning back in her chair.

'Excellent.' From the pocket of her jeans, Joanne produces three white envelopes. 'Here we go. One for you, Carys. One for Zoe and, Andrea, one for you. Now, don't open them yet. I have to explain the rules.'

'The rules?' says Andrea, inspecting her sealed envelope.

'Listen up. I've called this game "What's My Secret?" Inside each of the envelopes you'll find a card with a name of a famous person who could be living or dead. That's your secret identity for the weekend. Underneath is their well-known secret.' She dabs the air with imaginary quotation marks. 'You can't tell each other who you are. It's up to them to guess and then to try to work out what your secret is. You with me so far?'

'Is there a prize for guessing right?' asks Zoe.

'Oh, yes, there's a prize, but . . .'

'Let me guess,' I interject. 'It's a surprise.'

'A surprise prize,' mutters Andrea, seemingly unimpressed with the game.

'Absolutely,' says Joanne, beaming at us. 'There are clues as to the identity and what the secrets are all around the house. Bonus points for each clue you find.'

'How long have we got to find out the identity and secret?' I ask. I must admit, it is rather intriguing. If I can say anything about Joanne, it is that she has a fantastic imagination and is excellent at these sorts of things. It reminds me of a murder mystery dinner Joanne held some years ago. It had been a great success and she had gone on to make it a murder mystery weekend the following year for Darren's thirtieth birthday. We'd had a lot of fun. As with every time I think of Darren, a stab of guilt strikes me. I push it to one side, not wishing to dwell on it. Blocking it out is probably not the best coping method, but right now, it is the only way I can cope.

'The game finishes Sunday evening,' says Joanne, passing each of us a pencil. 'Once you've decided who you think the others are, you write it down in these notebooks.' She passes A6-size books to each of us. 'You will get one mark for each part you get right. The person with the most points is the winner. If no one guesses you, then you're also a winner. Two winners, two surprises.'

'And if you lose?' asks Andrea.

'The loser also gets a surprise,' says Joanne.

'This is going to be such fun,' says Zoe. 'Just one thing, how do we find out who each other are?'

'You can ask three questions each day, but the person being asked is only allowed to answer yes or no. You must pick your questions carefully. And if you're being asked, you must answer honestly. No cheating! Everyone clear?'

The three of us nod. 'I think I can follow that,' I say. 'When can we open our envelopes?'

'Open them now, but take care not to let the others see them.'

'And what are you going to be doing the whole time?' asks Andrea. 'It's not like you can play, you know the answers already.'

'Exactly. I'm the Oracle. I am the holder of all knowledge. Once you've asked your three questions, if you're still stuck you can come to me for a clue, but if you do, I will deduct half a point off your final score.'

'Let's open the cards,' I say, not even attempting to follow Joanne's convoluted marking system. I lean back in my chair and slip my thumb under the edge of the flap, tearing the paper open. Inside is a black card with the same pattern as the original invitation and with the same white font. I read mine.

DIANA, PRINCESS OF WALES
1 July 1961 – 31 August 1997
First Wife of HRH Prince Charles
Had an affair

'Keep your card with you at all times so no one sees it,' instructs Joanne.

I look up and watch Andrea open her card and then give a small frown before replacing it in the envelope. Zoe is flicking the corner of her card between her finger and thumb.

'Are these real people?' she asks.

'Is that a question for the Oracle?' replies Joanne.

'No, I—'

'Shhh. Don't say anything. Remember the rules. You can ask three questions only and then you can ask the Oracle for one clue only.'

'OK. I get it,' says Zoe. 'Can I go first?'

'Fill your boots,' says Andrea, holding her envelope to her chest.

'I'll ask Carys first.' Zoe turns to me. 'Are you alive or dead?'

Joanne interrupts before I can answer. 'Carys can only answer yes or no.'

Zoe pokes her tongue out at Joanne and looks at me. 'Are you dead?'

I laugh. 'I don't think so. No, sorry, that wasn't the answer. Am I dead? Yes.'

'My second question,' says Zoe. 'Are you female?'

'Yes.'

'Last question for today. Were you born in the nineteen-hundreds?'

'Yes.'

'Hmm, that doesn't help much.'

'Right, let me ask my questions now,' says Andrea, entering the spirit of the game. 'Are you a criminal?'

'No.'

'Did you die before your sixtieth birthday?'

'Yes.'

Andrea drums her fingers on the table. 'This is hard.' She

looks around the room. 'And you say there are clues in the house?'

'That's right. And don't forget you can ask the Oracle for one clue each day. Of course, you may want to ask that in secret, or you can share the information with each other.'

Andrea narrows her eyes. 'I'll ask the Oracle later. Right, Carys, my last question. Do you have children?'

'Yes.'

'That still hasn't helped much,' says Zoe. 'I'm going to have a look for some clues. Unless anyone wants to ask me some questions.'

'I do,' I say.

'And me,' says Andrea. 'Then you can ask me some.'

As we ask our questions and get the yes or no replies, we all scribble in our notebooks. 'So far, I've got this about you, Andrea,' I say at the end of the questions. 'You are female. You are dead. You lived in the 1800s. You were married more than once. You had children. You were a criminal.'

'I have no idea who she can be,' says Zoe.

'Neither do I,' I admit. I look at the next page in my book. 'Zoe, you are male. You are alive. You are British. You are famous for a crime but it's not a violent crime. You are not a celebrity.'

'You're all doing really well,' says Joanne, giving us a round of applause.

'That's easy for you to say – you know the answers,' says Andrea.

'I do. And by the end of the weekend, you all will know too. I can't wait to see the look on your faces,' says Joanne. 'Anyway, if you're clever enough, you'll realise the answer is staring right at you.' For a moment, her smile drops but she quickly recovers her usual cheery expression. Joanne stands up. 'Time for a stroll out to the woods before it rains. The weather is so changeable up here.'

She purposefully avoids looking at me as she busies herself with pushing the chair in and hurrying us along. I don't know why, but that little look I caught on her face has left me feeling unsettled. There was no warmth to it, rather the opposite: cold and hard. I can't help wondering what she was thinking at that moment.

I hang back while Zoe and Andrea make their way upstairs to get their jackets and walking boots. I look out of the window, surprised to see light mist swirling around in the sunless sky and the grey clouds overhead are giving a gloomy appearance to the landscape.

Hearing the footfall on the floorboards upstairs, I seize my opportunity. 'You've gone to a lot of trouble with this secrets game,' I say, as Joanne stands in the doorway, fastening her jacket.

'I like these sorts of things, they're fun.'

'Fun for all of us, right?'

'Probably more fun for me, if I'm honest.' She looks up from her zip.

'And this is only a game?'

'Of course it is,' she says. 'Unless you're worried I might know your secrets.' She gives a fake laugh, as Andrea and Zoe clomp down the stairs. At which point Zoe chides me for not being ready. As I squeeze by Joanne in the doorway, she gives a smile. 'Only a game,' she says, as if butter wouldn't melt in her mouth.

Chapter 7

Pulling down my woolly hat and yanking on my gloves, I feel quite well protected against the elements and ready to explore the Scottish countryside. I fall into place alongside Andrea and we follow Joanne and Zoe round the back of the croft and up the hillside towards the trees.

The forest consists of a variety of trees, mostly tall firs but some deciduous varieties, too, whose foliage is a mix of yellows, reds and browns as the autumn is beginning to take over. Underfoot the ground is uneven; small rocks and stones hamper our stride and we take care where we place our feet. Already leaves have begun to fall, and they lie scattered across the ground like woodland confetti.

As we walk deeper into the woods, I can feel the drop in temperature despite my fleece. 'Is it me, or is it cold in here?'

'Nope, not you. It's definitely colder,' says Andrea. 'Hey, Joanne! You do know where you're taking us, don't you?'

All the trees look the same to me. We are following a track that weaves its way around the trees and climbs the hill.

'Yes, don't worry,' calls Joanne. 'Anyway, like a good boy scout, I'm always prepared. I have a compass and a map but, yes, I do know where we're going.'

Twigs crack underfoot and once or twice I think I hear rustling noises in the undergrowth and bushes. 'This place is giving me the creeps,' I say, and as I do, another noise catches my attention. 'Did you hear that? It was a rustling noise. From those bushes.'

We all stop to listen.

'That's the river,' says Joanne. 'It flows down from the hills and eventually joins up with the main river that you saw outside the croft. There's a walk, Archer's Path, that runs alongside the river. We're going there tomorrow.'

'Never mind tomorrow,' says Andrea. 'What about today? How much further? My legs are killing me.'

'You should be the fittest of us all,' says Joanne. 'You're the one with the gym.'

'Yes, but I'm the owner, remember?' says Andrea. 'Unfortunately, you're more likely to find me stuck behind the desk these days, dealing with a mountain of paperwork, than you are to find me heading up an exercise class. Rugby boys excepted.'

Joanne looks blank.

'She took some sort of spinning glass with the local rugby team,' I supply.

Joanne gives an exasperated look to the sky. 'Oh, my heart bleeds for you. Can anyone hear those violins?' She mimes playing the stringed instrument while humming a sad and mournful tune. Joanne turns and walks backwards. 'Don't think you'll get any sympathy from me, you're the one who wanted to be the sole owner.' She spins on her heel and jogs ahead to catch up with Zoe.

'That's me told,' says Andrea.

'She's still prickly about it all, then,' I say. It's more of a statement than a question.

'You noticed, huh?'

'Don't worry about it.'

'I'm not worried,' says Andrea. 'But it pisses me off that we always make allowances for Joanne. She gets to say what she likes and none of us ever stand up to her. Why is that?'

'It's just Joanne being Joanne. You know what she's like. It's amusing at first, especially when it's directed at other people, but at some point she always manages to turn it on you. Then you're like, "How am I now the butt of her barbed comments?" She does it in such a way that no one wants to say anything because, at the end of the day, she does very generous things. Like this weekend.'

'I know. She can be totally endearing one minute and an absolute bitch the next, and yet we still love her,' replies Andrea. 'At the moment, she's definitely in absolute-bitch mode.'

We walk on in silence for a few more minutes. Ahead of us, Joanne is chatting away to Zoe. She calls to Andrea and me from time to time, chivvying us along.

'We're here!' she announces at last, with a flourish of her hand.

'Praise the Lord!' says Andrea.

We step out from the trees into a small clearing which seems almost circular in shape. In the centre is a heavy stone slab on top of four smaller stones, which have been carved to almost identical sizes of roughly three feet in height.

'It's an altar,' says Joanne. 'Apparently, the Vikings used to make human sacrifices here in honour of their gods. When their chief died, the chief's female slaves would volunteer themselves as sacrifices to follow him into the afterworld so they could tend to him there. They were bathed, dressed in white linen, given some sort of drug to relax them, and then they walked to the altar, where they'd lie down and have their throat cut.'

'Lovely,' I say.

'You wouldn't catch me doing that for my boss,' says Zoe. 'I'd be bloody dancing on that altar.'

'Good thing Tris isn't your boss any more,' says Andrea.

I'd forgotten Zoe used to work for Tris, back when he was still with the local NHS Trust. Zoe was a secretary in the psychology department where he was one of the senior psychologists. Although, since then, Tris has moved into private practice where the money is more lucrative.

Zoe clasps her hand to her mouth. 'Oh, sorry, Joanne. I didn't mean Tris. I only meant I wouldn't do that for any man.'

Joanne grins. 'It's OK. I'm with you on that. I wouldn't be offering myself up as a sacrifice for Tris either. Do you honestly think I want to go to Valhalla and spend eternity washing his dirty socks and pants?'

'What are those petals on the altar?' asks Andrea as we approach the stones.

Now we are closer, I can see a dozen or so red petals have been scattered across the stone. They look like rose petals, but there aren't any roses in sight.

'There's another Norse legend,' says Joanne. 'I can't remember all the details, but Mrs Calloway, the owner of the croft, told me about it once. Apparently, the son of a Viking king fell in love with a local Scottish girl but her mother was against it. She pleaded with the king not to allow the wedding. The king said the gods would be offended, so to atone for angering the gods, the mother would have to sacrifice herself. So she did.'

'Did it work?' asks Andrea.

'I can't remember. But after that, young people who wanted to get married would come here and spread petals on the altar to receive the gods' blessing. Something like that, anyway. The petals are supposed to represent the mother's blood and the sacrifice she made for her child.'

'What a load of mumbo-jumbo,' says Andrea.

Joanne shrugs and looks at the petals. 'I didn't realise people still did it. I thought it was one of those folk stories. I suppose we should be grateful it's only rose petals and not a human sacrifice.'

'Ooh, stop. The thought of people having been killed on this slab is giving me goosebumps,' says Zoe, rubbing her hands up and down her arms.

Andrea gives a sharp intake of breath and grabs hold of my arm. 'Did you see that?'

'What?' I look in the same direction as Andrea.

'I thought I saw something behind those trees.' She moves a step to her left, still holding on to my arm. 'Through there. I definitely saw something.'

'You're getting jumpy,' says Joanne. 'There's nothing out there.'

I watch as Joanne begins to walk towards the outer edge of the clearing. She doesn't seem in the slightest bit bothered.

'I can't see anything out there,' I say, in a bid to reassure Andrea, not to mention myself.

'You're winding us up,' says Zoe. 'Trying to spook us.'

'I'm not. I swear there was something or someone out there,' says Andrea. 'Joanne! Don't go. Stay here.'

'Honestly, there's nothing out there,' says Joanne, continuing to make her way further into the trees. 'I'll prove it. Hello!' she calls out. 'Hello, Mr Fox or Mr Bogeyman. Are you there?' Her voice echoes around the trees and bounces back from all sides.

'What's that there?' says Andrea, pointing to the ground.

As I look, I'm met by the sight of a rabbit carcass, which has obviously been picked at and eaten by other forest animals.

'That's disgusting,' says Zoe.

'Yuk,' says Andrea, turning away and looking in the direction Joanne went. 'Where the hell has she gone?'

I scan the clearing and the trees beyond but I can't see her. 'Joanne? Joanne! Where are you?'

I let go of Andrea's arm and head over to where I last saw her.

'Don't go off on your own,' calls Andrea. She comes running over to me, Zoe hot on her heels.

'She can't have disappeared,' says Zoe. 'You don't think—'

'Shut up,' snaps Andrea. 'Joanne!'

'But you said you saw something or someone out there,' says Zoe.

I call for Joanne again, but there is still no answer. The others follow me.

'All stay in sight,' says Andrea. 'I'll look over here. Zoe, you go over there. Carys, you go straight ahead.'

Remaining in line and within sight of each other, the three

of us move forward into the forest. I can feel my pulse rate increase and tension burrowing into the nape of my neck. Where could Joanne have gone? One minute she was here, the next vanished.

A noise to my left of rustling leaves makes me swing round. Suddenly, a figure jumps out in front of me.

'Boo!'

I scream, which has the knock-on effect of making Andrea and Zoe scream too.

Joanne is standing in front of me, bent double with laughter.

'You stupid fucking idiot!' snaps Andrea. 'What did you do that for?'

'Oh my God, that was so funny,' says Joanne, pausing to laugh again. 'You should have seen your faces. Especially you, Carys. It was priceless.'

'Bloody hilarious,' I reply.

'Ooh, were you worried about me?' says Joanne, her laughter now subsided but her face still beaming with amusement. 'Did you think the Bogeyman had got me? I'm touched by your concern.'

'Not funny,' says Zoe.

'Where's your sense of humour?' says Joanne. 'This is supposed to be a fun weekend.'

'But at the moment you seem to be the only one having fun,' says Andrea.

'Don't be a sourpuss. You're annoyed because you're not in charge.' Joanne turns on her heel and marches off, leaving us to follow.

Chapter 8

'Who fancies a glass of wine?' asks Joanne, as we gather in the living room, jackets and boots discarded in the hallway.

'This fire is lovely,' I say, warming my hands in front of the fireplace. 'I've always fancied an open fire at home.'

'It's nice but it is a lot of work,' says Joanne. 'I'm assuming that's yes to the wine for you all?' We all agree that wine is a good idea and she heads off to the kitchen.

'Have you seen this?' says Andrea. She is on the other side of the room looking at the various photographs that are arranged in different frames on an old whatnot in the corner. 'The owners must be proper royalists, they've put a picture of Diana and Charles on their wedding day in a frame and lined it up with their own photographs. How funny.'

My ears prick up at the mention of Diana and I wonder if it's anything to do with my character card. I casually wander over to the photographs.

'I didn't think the Scottish were fond of the royal family,' says Zoe, from her position on the sofa. 'And if they are, why wouldn't they have a picture of Charles and Camilla?'

'Princess Diana fans?' I suggest. I pick up the photo frame and make to casually inspect it.

'Maybe.' Andrea continues to prowl the room, looking at the books on the shelf along the wall.

'I'm going to nip upstairs to change my trousers,' says Zoe, getting up from the sofa. 'Think I'll put my tracky-bottoms on. Much more comfortable.'

'I did suggest that when we came in,' says Andrea. 'Where's Joanne got to with that wine?'

'I'm doing it now,' comes Joanne's voice from the hallway. 'Just had to nip to the loo.' She comes back into the room with the wine. 'Here we go,' she says, placing the tray she's carrying on the chest in the middle of the room and opening the bottle.

Zoe comes bounding down the stairs. 'Hey, guys! Look what I've found.' She opens the palm of her hand and a gold wedding band glistens in the firelight.

'A wedding ring?' I move closer to get a better look and pick it up from Zoe's hand. 'Where did you find that?'

'It was on my bedside table,' says Zoe. 'Which is weird as I definitely don't remember seeing it there before. I'm sure I would have noticed when I unpacked earlier.'

'It must be the people who rented the croft before,' says Andrea, taking the ring from me. She slides it on to her finger. 'It looks like a woman's ring. It's too small and thin for a man's wedding ring.'

'You'd think they would have noticed by now that they had lost it,' I say. 'It's not like a piece of jewellery you would wear only occasionally.'

Automatically I feel the ring finger on my left hand and thumb the bare skin. Joanne is watching me; feeling like a naughty child who has been caught out, I drop my hands from sight of her prying eyes.

'A wedding ring should never be taken off,' says Joanne. 'I wear mine all the time. Don't you agree, Andrea?'

'I keep mine on twenty-four-seven,' she replies.

Joanne looks at me again. 'It's not yours is it, Carys? You're not wearing one?'

'No, not mine.'

Fortunately, Zoe speaks before Joanne can say any more. 'And it's definitely not mine as I wouldn't dream of wearing it. Not after what that cheating bastard did to me. I wouldn't be stupid enough to make that mistake for a third time.'

'A third time?' says Andrea, raising her eyebrows in Zoe's direction.

'I mean, second,' she says, and then to appease our looks of surprise goes on to clarify: 'The first guy I was serious about, it was a long time ago. We weren't married, only engaged, but that's as good as in my book. He was another waste of space. I sure know how to pick them. So, back to what I meant to say: I wouldn't make the mistake of getting married a second time.'

'How old were you at the time?' asks Andrea.

'Oh, really young. Only twenty,' replies Zoe. She takes a large gulp of wine. 'We were just kids and had some romantic notion about love and marriage. I think my parents were more disappointed than I was when we broke up.'

'Did you finish with him?' Andrea continues with her questioning.

Zoe swirls the contents of her glass in small circular motions. 'He finished with me, if you must know.' Her brow creases into a frown and she drops her gaze, but not before I see the hurt and anger in her eyes.

I feel sorry for Zoe; from what I can tell, she hasn't had much luck where men are concerned. No wonder she doesn't like to talk about it, especially if she's had a failed marriage and a broken engagement.

Andrea gives a sympathetic smile. 'Don't worry, you'll meet someone one day who will love you as much as you love them.'

'I know,' says Zoe. I notice a small blush creep on her face which doesn't go unmissed by Joanne.

'My, my, Zoe, I do believe you're blushing, again. Come on, what's his name?'

'There isn't anyone,' says Zoe. 'No. Seriously. There is no one. Anyway, about this ring. We should let the owners know that we've found it in case the previous guests have reported it missing. It's still a mystery how I didn't see it before, though.'

'Put it on the mantelpiece for now,' says Joanne. 'I'll email them when we get home and let them know.' She takes the ring from Andrea and pops it next to the photograph taken earlier. Then she turns to me. 'How long have you not been wearing your wedding ring?'

I feel myself bristle but realise I will sound childish if I tell Joanne it isn't any of her business. 'About a year,' I reply.

'Don't you feel strange without it?' says Joanne. She passes me a glass of wine she has just poured.

'Not now. At first I did, but it didn't seem right to go on wearing it,' I say.

'You don't feel a tiny bit disloyal to Darren?' She passes the other glasses round and takes a sip from her own.

I feel obliged to answer. 'No. I don't, actually. We had separated and were going through a divorce.'

'What about Alfie? How does he feel about you not wearing it?'

'Really, Joanne, it's nothing for you to concern yourself with. And Alfie's thoughts are definitely none of your business.'

'Don't take offence. I was only asking.'

'I'm not taking offence. Let's just forget about it. It really isn't important.'

'Sure.' Joanne gives a tight smile. 'How is Alfie anyway? He said he was thinking of quitting counselling.'

I have no idea what Joanne is talking about. To say it irks me that she seems to know more about my own son than I do is an understatement. However, it is nothing compared to the hurt I feel knowing my son has confided in Joanne rather than me, his own mother. I compose myself, not wanting to give Joanne the satisfaction of having one over on me. 'I don't think now is the right time to talk about Alfie's counselling.' I look round at the others. Zoe looks down, suddenly finding her shoes very interesting and Andrea pulls a sympathetic, *this is awkward* face.

'No, you're quite right,' says Joanne. 'I'm sorry. Let's have a toast to both our birthdays.'

We all join in with a degree of over-enthusiasm to disguise yet another awkward conversation. Zoe begins to chatter away about the latest diet she's on, which will clearly go to pot now, but who cares, we're here to party!

I force a smile and join in, although the celebratory mood has left me. I was foolish to think this weekend would be some sort of reconciliation. Right now, far from forgiving Joanne, I want to throttle her.

Chapter 9

'Hey, what do you make of Zoe being engaged before?' asks Andrea as we get ready for bed. 'Did you know that?'

'No, but then she's quite private about her marriage.'

'Yeah, she doesn't like to talk about it. All I know is that he was a rotten bastard and he lives up in Liverpool now.'

'I don't think they're even on speaking terms. When they need to make arrangements for the boys, they do it via text messages.'

'She's pretty bitter about her ex.'

'Bitter. Yes, you could say that. Probably just as well they live so far apart. She absolutely loathes him.' I let out a sigh as I think back to Darren and wonder if we would have gone down that path and ended up hating each other. I'd like to think not.

'You all right?' asks Andrea.

'Me? Yeah, I'm fine,' I say, although I'm aware I don't sound particularly convincing. Thinking of Darren, together with Joanne's comments about Alfie, has left me feeling emotionally exhausted.

'Joanne was out of order earlier,' continues Andrea. 'She should keep her nose out of your business.'

'Try telling her that,' I say, as I pull off my T-shirt and fish out my pyjamas from the drawer. 'She sees Alfie as her business.' Pulling my pyjama top on, I slide my hands round my back and unfasten my bra and slip the straps from my shoulders, before yanking it out from under my top. 'As I said to you before, Alfie spends so much time there, he tells her more than he tells me.' I fling the bra on to my bed. 'And that really hurts.'

'Perhaps he finds it easier to talk to her. He's at that age where sometimes it's hard to speak to your parents. I'm sure Bradley doesn't tell me half of what he's thinking or doing.'

'I appreciate that, but it still hurts. All I've ever done is try to support him, to look after and look out for him. He hates me. I'm sure about that.'

'He doesn't hate you,' says Andrea. She sits down on her bed. 'You're his mum and he loves you. He's obviously still having a hard time coming to terms with what happened.'

'It's bloody damaged him psychologically,' I say. The effect of the wine from earlier is loosening my tongue. 'It's my fault. I shouldn't have had that huge argument with Darren. If I hadn't, then he wouldn't have been so desperate . . .' I conquer the urge to say more.

'None of that was your fault,' says Andrea. She knows I feel guilty, but the depth of her appreciation of that guilt only reflects what she knows. She doesn't know everything.

I fling myself back on the bed and put an arm over my face. If I hide my face, she can't see there's something else that weighs heavy on my conscience. 'I wish I could have shielded

Alfie from seeing Darren like that. I can cope with it; I'm strong enough. He's not.'

'You can't change what happened.'

'You know what the worst bit is?' I sit up, guilt making way for anger. 'Darren knew Alfie was outside, waiting for me. He knew we'd come in the house together, but he didn't give a damn. In his warped mind, he was punishing me. He was going to make sure I lived with this for the rest of my life. He hated me for wanting a divorce and he wanted to get some sort of revenge. Not once did he consider what he would be putting his son through.' I scrunch the bedspread in my fists as the anger storms through me. 'That's the bit I cannot forgive. He bloody well knew Alfie would see him, and that was his way of punishing me forever.'

'At best, he was mentally ill and at worst a selfish bastard,' says Andrea. She moves to sit next to me and puts a comforting arm around my shoulders.

'Joanne's not helping either. She shouldn't be bringing Alfie into it. She's out of order.'

'I can speak to her, if you like?'

'No. Don't do that.' I shake my head vigorously. 'I can deal with her. But thanks anyway.'

Andrea gives my shoulder a squeeze and kisses the side of my head. 'Right, no more talk of Darren. Not for tonight anyway.' We exchange a smile before she continues, 'This game of Joanne's. What do you think to it?' Andrea gets up and takes her washbag from her rucksack and extracts her face-wipes. 'She's gone to a lot of trouble.'

'That's Joanne for you.' I resume my horizontal position on the bed and stretch out my legs, thankful that my hobby of cross-country running has stood me in good stead for the ramble up the hillside and through the forest earlier.

'Do you want to team up?' says Andrea with a grin.

'I'll show you mine if you show me yours, type of thing?'

'You got it.' Andrea rubs her face with the wipe.

'Appealing as the idea may be, I think we should at least try to work out who each other is,' I say. 'It's a bit unfair on Zoe if we team up.'

'Spoilsport,' says Andrea with good humour. 'Maybe tomorrow we should try to find the clues Joanne mentioned.'

I think back to the photograph of Charles and Diana. I'm pretty sure that's a clue about my character, left for one of the others to find. I take out my notebook and go back over the information I've found out about the other characters. 'We get to ask each other three more questions tomorrow.'

'I'm going to need more help,' says Andrea. 'I haven't the patience for all this. I'm never going to be able to work it out. We'll have to ask Joanne for a clue.'

'Good idea. We'll consult the Oracle.'

'That's if we make it back from the all-day hike she has planned for us.' Andrea drops the used face-wipe into the bin and picks up her washbag. 'Where did she say we were going?'

'Archer's Path,' I reply. 'She said it's a fabulous walk and takes a couple of hours. I hope the weather holds out, it wasn't looking so good this afternoon.'

'I'm going to brush my teeth,' says Andrea. 'Won't be a moment.'

I pull back the duvet and climb into bed. I need to think of something other than Alfie. I don't want to spend the night replaying my confrontation with Joanne and worrying about what Alfie may or may not have said to her.

Andrea comes back into the room. The look on her face instantly alerts me, something is not right. I sit up. 'You OK?'

'No. I'm not. Look what I just found in my washbag – and I sure as hell didn't put it in there.'

How are you feeling now? Enjoying the weekend? Probably not, and that's such a shame. You don't think anyone has noticed, do you? That no one has seen your body language, the way the pallor of your face changes when you're upset. The way it goes from a pinky glow to a deathly white, almost translucent. And the way your pupils dilate and your breathing quickens when the 'D' word is mentioned. They are only small modifications to your behaviour, small enough to go undetected by those who are not looking for them, but not small enough for someone like me to miss.

I don't mind admitting this is giving me much more of a thrill than I thought it would. I love how I have the power over you. I have the control. I am the puppet master. I am Geppetto and you are Pinocchio.

Are you unnerved? You probably don't know why, but you can sense something is wrong. I like the thought of the fear and panic this makes you feel. I wonder if that's how you reacted before? When you had to confront your worst nightmare? Did you panic then? You never speak about it. Why is that? Don't answer. I know why that is. If you speak about it, people will feel entitled to ask you questions, awkward questions. Ones you'd sooner not face. You've never told anyone your secret.

And the reason for that? Because you feel guilty – and rightly so. You are guilty. You have ruined my life and I am about to ruin yours. I'm coming for you, so you'd better watch out.

SATURDAY

Chapter 10

Any idea that I might be able to sleep in the following morning is dashed by Joanne banging on the bedroom doors at eight o'clock and then poking her head into the room to announce breakfast will be ready in half an hour.

'Is she serious?' groans Andrea, snuggling further into her bed. 'I was hoping I'd have a nice gentle wake-up call, breakfast in bed, even.'

I laugh. 'Oh, she's serious all right. I think she wants to head off on this hike at about ten.'

Andrea pulls the duvet back down. 'I suppose I'd better show willing.'

I swing my feet out of bed and perch on the edge of the mattress. 'Are you going to show the others what you found last night?'

'I guess so. It must be part of the game. Although, I don't know what the significance is.'

I reach over and pick up the dollar bill that Andrea found in her washbag. 'It's definitely meant for you, no mistake. I was wondering last night if that wedding ring Zoe found was put there by Joanne as part of the game. It could be a clue.'

'Yeah, I thought that too. But again, I've no idea what the significance is. And if both Zoe and I have had something left for us, that means you've got something coming to you.'

'I'm a bit nervous now,' I say with a laugh. 'I'm going to be on edge the whole day, waiting for something to turn up.'

I get up and make my way to the bathroom. As I stand under the shower, I let my mind drift to the game and the clues so far. Something is nagging at the back of my mind and I can't quite put my finger on it. Something to do with the wedding ring.

It isn't until I have finished showering and am brushing my teeth that it suddenly comes to me.

My character card, Diana, Princess of Wales, the wedding ring and the out-of-place photograph of Diana and Charles must all be connected. My card said I was an adulteress. The wedding ring signifies the marriage, the photograph is the out-of-place thing in the house.

I spit the toothpaste down the sink and rinse my mouth while musing over the US dollar bill Andrea has been left. Obviously something to do with money. I think back to yesterday where we discovered that Andrea's character had committed a crime but not a violent one. Was bank robbing a non-violent crime? Was she a famous bank robber? Bonnie and Clyde come to mind straight away. I'll have to look at my notebook to check. Then I will look around the house for another clue.

I can't help grinning to myself. I quite like this game now. Of course, I won't be able to tell Andrea. No. I'll have to keep this to myself.

Ten minutes later, I'm downstairs with the others, tucking into a cooked breakfast Joanne has been kind enough to prepare. 'This is really good of you,' I say, trying to get the new day off to a fresh start. 'I wouldn't normally eat this at home, but somehow it's different when I'm away. I can always manage a full English.'

'I'm exactly the same,' says Zoe.

'We need to have our energy levels high for today's hike,' says Joanne.

'Notice she didn't say walk,' says Andrea, raising an eyebrow. 'The word hike is slightly unsettling me.'

'You'll love it,' says Joanne. 'It really is a beautiful walk, and the waterfall and vantage point at the end is well worth the effort. I've prepared a packed lunch for each of us. If you can all carry your own, that will save one of us carrying too much.'

'Before we head off, I have something to tell you,' says Andrea. She puts her knife and fork together, pushing the plate away. She leans back so she can get her hand in the front pocket of her trousers and produces the money she'd found the night before. She puts it on the table.

'What's that?' says Zoe, picking up the note.

'That was in my washbag last night.' Andrea looks over at Joanne.

'Don't look at me,' says our hostess.

'Too late,' I say with a laugh. 'You most definitely got the look.'

'Anyway, as I say, it was in my washbag. I definitely didn't bring it with me, so I can only assume it's part of the game,' says Andrea.

'What does it mean?' asks Zoe, inspecting both sides of the note.

'We haven't worked that bit out yet,' says Andrea. 'Feel free to share any ideas.'

Zoe frowns. 'Sorry, I don't have any. I don't think I'm going to win this game. I have no idea what's going on.'

'All will become clear,' says Joanne. 'Keep playing.'

'Can we ask our next three questions?' I ask. 'That will give me something to think about today.'

Ten minutes and nine questions later, we can add some more details to our notebooks.

'To summarise,' I say. 'Zoe, we now know these things about your criminal activities. You acted alone. You went to prison but you are now out. You were in the newspapers. It was to do with a bank and it was in the last twenty years.'

'Aha, I think I know who you might be,' says Andrea, a satisfied look on her face. 'All I need now is to find a clue around this place.'

'Remember, don't say anything until tomorrow evening,' says Joanne.

Andrea mimes zipping her mouth closed and sits back with folded arms.

'OK, Miss Clever-Clogs,' says Zoe. 'Let's ask Carys her questions. I'll go first.'

'Fire away,' I say.

Five minutes later, Zoe is studying her notebook. 'This is hard. I can't think who you might be. You were in the public eye. You were very popular. You were not a TV celebrity. You were not a singer. You married someone famous. Wait a minute

. . . I think I know who you are. Damn it, I want to ask another question but I can't.'

'What about you Andrea? You any the wiser?' I ask.

'Possibly.' Andrea taps her notebook with her pencil.

'We need to get off on our walk soon. Are you going to ask Andrea any questions?' says Joanne.

'I'll ask first,' says Zoe. 'Andrea, we know from yesterday you are a criminal, so my first question today is, are you a murderer?'

Andrea nods. 'Yes.'

'Question two. Were you caught for your crime?'

'She must have been,' I say. 'We wouldn't know about it otherwise.'

'But you've asked the question and can't change your mind now,' says Andrea. 'And the answer is yes.'

'Knickers,' huffs Zoe. 'I didn't think of that. OK, last question from me. Did you hang for your crime?'

A stilled silence swamps the room. Joanne throws me a sideways look and then exchanges one with Andrea. Of all the questions Zoe could have asked, she had to mention hanging. It seems like minutes but in fact it is only a couple of seconds. I realise everyone is waiting for my reaction. I swallow, fake a smile and urge Andrea to answer the question.

'Oh, God, sorry,' says Zoe, her hand flying to her throat. 'I didn't mean . . .'

I wave her apologies away and give her a reassuring smile. 'Don't be silly. It's fine. Honestly. So, Andrea, yes or no?' I'm not sure who I'm trying to convince the most that I'm fine, them or me. I will Andrea to answer the question so we can move on.

'Yes. I did,' says Andrea.

'My questions,' I say. I want to get this over with as soon as possible. The air in the room is thick and oppressive. Indoors is where the demons lurk. I need fresh air. I need space. Open space. I concentrate on asking my questions. 'Did you live in the UK?'

'Yes.'

'Was it in the north?'

'Yes.'

'Manchester?' I've no idea why it would be Manchester, I just want to get my questions over with.

'No.'

'That's that all done,' I say. The claustrophobia won't go away. The walls of the dining room have moved in several metres. The windows are smaller and the doorway is disappearing like something from *Alice in Wonderland*. I get up abruptly. The scraping of the chair legs on the floor is amplified by the small surroundings, the noise claws at my eardrums. I need to get out before the door gets any smaller and the walls squash the air from me.

I fumble with the door handle on my first attempt, but manage to stagger out into the hallway. Not bothering to grab my coat, I make for the front door. The fresh cold air of the Scottish countryside hits me full in the face, knocking the breath back down my throat. I gulp. Stand tall. Gulp again. I take a deep controlled breath in, hold for the count of three and then release slowly. I repeat this several times.

'Carys! You OK?' It's Andrea.

Before I can turn, I can feel the weight of my jacket being

rested on my shoulders. 'Put your coat on, it's cold out here this morning and you're shivering.'

I hadn't noticed, but now that I'm more in control I can feel the difference in my body temperature. I glance over my shoulder and Joanne and Zoe are standing in the doorway, concern etching their faces.

'I'm OK,' I call. I give a smile and then turn to Andrea. 'Sorry about that. Had a funny turn.'

'I didn't think you had those any more.'

'From time to time. Certain things can trigger them off.' I zip up the jacket.

'I'm guessing it was the . . .' Andrea's voice trails off.

I nod. 'Yeah, it was that bit. Took me by surprise, that's all. Forget about it. I feel a bit of an idiot.'

'Don't be daft. No one thinks that. It was insensitive of Joanne to include a character who'd . . . well, you know.'

'I'm sure it wasn't intentional,' I say, noting my voice lacks conviction.

Chapter 11

'Why do they call this Arrow's Path?' I ask, as we make our way along the track.

'I'm not sure, something to do with it being a perfectly straight path, scored out through the countryside by a Scottish hunter,' says Joanne. 'The path leads to the edge of a gorge and a rock the shape of an arrowhead juts out over it. Apparently, the arrow hit the cliff and made the gorge, which then allowed the water to flow down into the river, hence the waterfall called Archer's Fall.'

'Is it a popular tourist spot?' asks Andrea. 'I thought we might see some other hikers.'

I look at the empty path ahead of us. The forest is on our left over the other side of the hill. Here the landscape is bleak. Hills roll in from either side as the path leads through the centre of a valley. Long grass, brambles and heather add the only texture.

'It's not hugely popular,' says Joanne. 'When we were here last year, we only saw one other family all week. There's not much else around to bring the tourists in.'

'How far from civilisation are we?' asks Andrea.

'About fifteen miles. There's a small town to the south called Gormston. Other than that, I wouldn't like to say, but you'd certainly need a vehicle to get anywhere. Aberdeen is about a hundred miles to the east.'

I call up my rough mental map of Scotland which, I confess, is very sketchy. I have a general idea of where Aberdeen is, but that's about it.

'We really are in the middle of nowhere,' says Andrea. 'What if there's an emergency? You've got no landline, no mobile phone coverage and I haven't seen a car parked at the croft.'

'I told you, there's a radio in the kitchen.'

'But what about now? What if we have an accident out here?' Andrea gives me an incredulous look.

'Relax,' says Joanne. 'You've all got the survival packs I gave you, but I also have a small hand-held radio with me and a flare. Stop worrying.'

I must admit, encountering a problem out here isn't exactly appealing but we do have a basic emergency pack and first-aid kit. It's what I would take with me normally if I was out on a hike. On a run, I only have my mobile phone with me, having the luxury of phone coverage, unlike here. At least Joanne has a backup device, even if it is at the croft. I make a mental note to check it out when we return.

After about another hour walking, we stop for a refreshment break.

'I've got flasks of hot tea when we get to Arrow's Head,' says Joanne, 'but for now we can have water.'

I open my flask and look around. The path cuts its way between two hills, inclining slightly as it does so and then disappearing over the brow. With another hour to go, I guess our final destination is some way off yet.

Final destination.

The words resound in my head and remind me of the comment the guy in the van made yesterday. Why did it make me feel the same now as it did then? Uncomfortable. Nervous. I shake my head to be rid of the negative thoughts that are threatening to get out of control. I am overreacting and have no idea why. To distract myself, I take my camera from my pocket.

'Group photo,' I announce to the others. 'Let's get a selfie.'

The others huddle together while I balance the camera on a rock, checking they are in the frame. I set the timer and then run to join the group, where we all strike a pose and wait for what seems like far longer than ten seconds for the flash to go off. After examining the photo and all agreeing it was quite a good one, I take some snaps of the landscape.

'Let's get going now,' says Joanne, popping her water bottle in her rucksack. 'Tell me, has anyone got any more ideas about who the mystery characters are?'

'Oh don't,' groans Zoe. 'I'm useless at this game. I'm going to have to ask the Oracle tomorrow, that's for sure.'

'How did you choose our characters?' asks Andrea, as we begin our ascent along the path. 'Was it a random choice or was there a method to it?'

'There was definitely a method,' says Joanne. 'I hand-picked each character with great care for their qualities and relevance.'

I try to work out why I have been given my character. Someone who married a Prince and who Joanne has branded as an adulteress. How was that connected to me? Darren and

I may have been getting a divorce, but I certainly hadn't had an affair. 'Did you definitely give us the right characters?' I ask.

'Yes, but that doesn't necessarily mean I've given you a character that relates to you.'

'And the secret associated with that character, what's the relevance of that? Or was that random?' asks Andrea.

'You should know the answer to that,' I say. 'Nothing is ever random where Joanne is concerned.'

'I thank you,' says Joanne, turning around and giving a small bow to the rest of us. 'Spoken by someone who knows me only too well.'

We trudge along the path and I think of the clues once again. So, the character I have could be Andrea or Zoe and the secret is that of an adulteress, which Joanne has specifically chosen to fit one of us. I know it's not me, so that must mean Joanne believes either Andrea or Zoe have had, or are having, an affair.

I run the idea through my mind with each of them. I can't imagine Andrea having an affair. She and Colin have a rock-solid marriage. I dismiss the notion almost immediately. Could Zoe be having an affair? She's single, so that must mean she's having an affair with a married man. Again, I want to dismiss the notion straight away. I can't see Zoe doing that, not after her own husband did it to her. It's simply not her style. Joanne must be wrong about this. At least, I hope she is.

At least the weather is on our side; the grey clouds of this morning have been blown south by the gentle breeze which has brought whiter and thinner clouds our way. After another fifty-five minutes, I can see the path ahead level out and widen.

'We're here,' announces Joanne.

As we reach the wider part of the path, we are met by the beautiful sight of Archer's Falls. The waterfall is on the other side of the gorge, which is about fifty metres across. The narrow breadth of water sloshes lazily over the rocks and down the side of the gorge, tumbling into a pool below.

'This is breathtaking,' I say, as we stand at the edge of the path. A large rock juts out over the pool. 'Is this Arrow Head? Is it safe enough to walk out on to?'

'Perfectly safe,' replies Joanne. 'We definitely should take another picture of us all standing out there.'

I walk a few steps closer to Arrow Head.

'I'm not going out there,' says Zoe. 'Not in a million years. It's bloody dangerous.'

'No, it's not,' counters Joanne. She marches out to the edge of the rock and turns to face us, her arms wide open. 'Look!' Joanne jumps up and down a few times, before sitting on her bottom and hanging her feet over the edge.

'Don't be so stupid!' shouts Zoe. 'Come back this minute!'

'I'm not one of your kids!' Joanne's response is terse.

I make my way towards the edge but stop short of sitting on the end of the rock. I've rock-climbed and abseiled regularly with the outward-bound centre I work for, but always with sufficient safety ropes and precautions. 'This is the most beautiful view ever,' I say, taking more pictures of the vista before me. 'No towns or buildings, just valleys and mountains.'

'Now you see why I brought you all here,' says Joanne. She looks below her. 'That pool down there leads out into a small river which eventually winds its way past the croft and on into Gormston.'

I shuffle a little closer to the edge for a look. 'Wow. Is there any way we can get to the pool?'

'Yes. This is one of my surprises,' says Joanne, swinging her legs up on to the edge of the rock and standing up. She brushes non-existent dust from her trousers. 'This is where you come in handy.'

'I do?'

'We're going to abseil down there.'

'We are?' I raise my eyebrows and look at Zoe and Andrea. 'I take it they don't know that.'

'Of course not. They wouldn't have come. Don't worry, they won't have any choice. It's a fait acompli.'

Chapter 12

'No. Fucking. Way,' Andrea says, folding her arms and looking at Joanne as if she is completely off her head. I have every sympathy for Andrea. Abseiling may be something that doesn't faze me, but I appreciate it's not everyone's preferred method of descent.

'Don't be such a baby,' says Joanne, as she kneels and begins to unfasten her rucksack. 'It's my birthday, think of it as the ultimate gift to me.' She looks up at Zoe. 'You're up for it, aren't you?'

Zoe glances uncomfortably at both myself and Andrea, before looking back at Joanne. 'I can't say I'm keen on the idea. Where exactly are we abseiling from? Please don't say over the edge there.' She points to where Joanne has been dangling her legs.

'There's a place further round the gorge – it's lower, about fifteen feet.' Joanne pulls out two large coils of rope, a harness, a safety helmet and an assortment of hooks, clips and wedges. She looks up at Andrea. 'It's no different to rock climbing, except we're going in the opposite direction. You did fine at the Bradleys' rock-climbing birthday last year.'

'That was different,' says Andrea. 'It was in a sports hall with instructors. A safe environment. Crash mats. Safety ropes.'

'And this is no different. We'll all be wearing the proper safety equipment. Why do you think I lugged this bloody great rucksack with me? I have everything here. It's perfectly safe. I'll be at the top and Carys will be at the bottom.'

'Would have been nice to know that beforehand,' I say.

'But then that would have ruined my surprise.'

'Point taken.' I look at the kit Joanne is setting out on the ground. It is amazing how she managed to fit everything in. 'How's this going to work?' I ask, noting there is only one set of equipment.

'You go down first and then we hoist the equipment up for the next person. Once they're down, we send it up again,' explains Joanne. 'I couldn't carry four helmets, harnesses, gloves and everything else, could I?'

'Where exactly is this lower edge?' asks Andrea, looking around.

'We have to make our way down this path here and it takes us round to a lower level.' Joanne stands and turns towards the gorge. 'See over there, where it juts out? That's where I abseiled last year with Tris, Oliver and Ruby.'

'And what happens when we get to the bottom? Don't tell me we have to climb back up.' Andrea still doesn't look convinced, but the fact she is asking questions tells me her opposition is waning. 'And if you tell me there's a path or steps, then I sure as hell am NOT abseiling down. I'll be taking those steps.'

'That's my next surprise, but if I tell you, it will spoil it,' says Joanne, grinning. 'Trust me, there are no steps down and we are not climbing back up.'

Zoe gives Andrea a little nudge with her elbow. 'It will be—'

Andrea cuts across her. 'If you say fun, I swear I'll scream. I can think of many words for this, none of them being fun.'

For a few seconds, I wonder if Andrea is going to refuse after all. She turns and looks over her shoulder at the way we have come and then takes a few steps closer to the edge, eyeing up the abseiling point. She purses her lips. 'And you're sure there are no steps?'

'Positive,' says Joanne.

Andrea blows out a long breath. 'Seeing as I don't even know my way and it's a two-hour walk, it looks like I don't have any choice.'

'Excellent,' says Joanne, a broad smile stretching across her face. She gives Andrea a hug. 'This is why I love you so much. You always work out the odds and play the right hand.'

Andrea gives me a confused look from over Joanne's shoulder. I shrug. I have no idea what Joanne means either, but am grateful Andrea has agreed.

Before we take up the abseiling challenge, we decide to have something to eat. Joanne has been kind enough to provide us all with a packed lunch.

'It reminds me of being at school,' says Zoe. 'Sitting down with our lunch boxes.'

'Funny, I had that feeling when I was making them up,' says Joanne. 'And this is the school trip.'

'As long as we don't have to call you Miss and ask if we can go to the toilet,' says Andrea.

'I wouldn't dream of it,' says Joanne. 'Anyway, I'd end up excluding you. You would be the naughty disruptive child, who'd never do what the teacher told them to.'

'Sounds about right,' I say.

'I call that being strong and independent,' says Andrea, biting into her sandwich.

'I call it being a pain in the arse,' I respond good-naturedly.

'Amen to that,' says Joanne. 'Oh, and if you do want to go to the loo, I suggest you do that now. You won't have the chance again until we get back to the croft.'

'Al fresco?' says Zoe, with a groan. 'I remember when we did that Snowdon walk and had to find somewhere to have a pee.'

'No need to be shy,' says Andrea. 'All girls together and all that.'

'Oh, I don't think Zoe's shy at all,' says Joanne. She gives Zoe a playful nudge. 'And I don't think she'd be worried if it wasn't just us girls. Go on, off you go.'

Zoe gives a little laugh as she gets up, clearly wondering if she should be reading between the lines. Something I'm also wondering.

About forty minutes later, having eaten our lunch and chatted without any further ambiguous comments, we make our way down the track to the lower level. From where we are standing, I look over the edge to get an idea of height. As Joanne said, we are about fifteen feet from the bottom of the gorge. We will be landing on a bed of shingle which extends along this side of the pool.

I look at the rock face behind us for three good places to secure the anchors for our abseil. There are plenty of jagged rocks and boulders to anchor from. I must admit to being a little nervous at abseiling an unknown rock face. Whenever I've done this sort of thing before, it's always been on well-established descents that are safe and easy for the youngsters under my charge.

'What's the rock face like going down?' I ask Joanne.

'From what I remember, it's a straight drop, nice and easy, even for beginners,' Joanne responds with a much more confident tone than I feel.

She hands me a small net bag and I remove the safety harness. Placing a foot through each of the leg loops, I pull the harness up, rather like pulling on a pair of trousers, then fasten the belt tightly around my waist. Once that's secure, I fasten the strap at the back.

'I've got chocks over here,' says Joanne, pulling out three pieces of rope, each with a metal wedge on the end, designed for sliding into gaps to act as anchors. 'There's a place here and another over there.'

'What about a third?' I ask. 'I always like to work with three anchors.' I inspect the rock face and after agreeing on the two places for the chocks, decide that the third anchor could be a large rock half-buried in the side of the gorge which I can loop the rope around.

It only takes a few minutes to secure the three anchor points. I attach the rope to the gate rings and check and double-check before I'm happy with everything.

'Are you sure about this?' says Andrea as I begin to take the slack of the rope against the weight of my body and manoeuvre myself backwards over the edge of the ledge.

'Absolutely,' I reply. I can feel the adrenalin pump through me. It has been a while since I've abseiled, but suddenly that rush of excitement, laced with a dash of trepidation, washes over me. I used to do this all the time before I had Alfie. Darren and I had spent many holidays hiking, abseiling, kayaking and generally enjoying the wilder side of the outdoors. For a moment, the memory of us on honeymoon, yomping over Exmoor, gatecrashes my thoughts. Most of our friends who married went on beach holidays and fancy destinations, but Darren and I opted for much less conventional locations. We didn't care. We loved it. Darren loved lots of things then. Darren loved life. I force the memory from my mind. I can't afford to go down that route; it's too painful.

I take a deep breath, nod and smile at the others. 'It's like riding a bike,' I say. 'Now, remember: this is the worst bit, but you must trust us. I wouldn't do this if I thought it was unsafe and I certainly wouldn't let either of you do it. OK?'

'If you say so,' replies Andrea.

'Let the rope take your weight. Lean back so your legs are straight out from the wall and bend your body so you're an L-shape.' I continue to give clear and concise instructions how they are to hold the rope with one hand and let it glide through the other. 'All the time this rope is behind you, you're not going anywhere. Gently release and you can walk down the cliff face.' I lean back and for the benefit of Andrea and Zoe, I very slowly show them how to walk down the cliff. When I'm about halfway down I call up. 'I'm going to jump out now, but you two, you keep walking your way down. OK?'

When I reach the bottom, I feel another rush of adrenalin.

I thoroughly enjoyed that little abseil and the excitement that came with it. I take off the harness, safety helmet and gloves, hook them to the rope and call to Joanne to pull it all up. While I wait for the others to get organised, I check out the surroundings.

There is a muddy embankment closer to the rock face, the grass petering out into the mix of shingle and pebbles which lines this side of the pool. The waterfall on the other side of the gorge gracefully tumbles down the rock face, slipping into the pool with a degree of elegance and dignity. There's a calm and tranquil feel about the water as it ripples out. Looking to my left, I can see it wend its way through the narrowing embankments and around the corner, joining the river I saw from up above. The one that Joanne said eventually runs past the croft.

As I turn round, I notice for the first time, tucked away in the far corner, two kayaks. So, this is what Joanne has planned for us. We are going to paddle downstream. To me, it sounds like a great idea, but I'm unsure whether Andrea or Zoe will be quite so pleased. Although, to be fair, neither of them made too much fuss about the abseil. A gentle paddle home could be quite relaxing after that.

A shout from above tells me they are ready. Andrea slowly comes into view as she takes teetering steps backwards over the ledge.

'You'd better bloody catch me if I fall,' she shouts.

Amazingly, after a little hesitation, she begins a relatively smooth descent for a beginner. The first few steps are always the worst, but once you've taken them and allowed yourself to trust the ropes, then it really is very easy.

Anxious to be on terra firma, Andrea rushes the last few feet of the descent and lands rather unceremoniously in a heap at my feet.

'You did it! It wasn't that bad after all,' I say, heaping on the praise. I hoist Andrea to her feet and help unfasten the safety belt while she takes off her helmet.

'Hmm. I can't say I would do it again,' she says. 'Not in a hurry, anyway.'

It's not long before Zoe is at the foot of the cliff with us. Her descent was a rather more noisy and squealy affair.

'Oh. My. God. That was amazing,' she says. 'I can't believe I did that. I feel like a proper adventurer now. Woohoo!'

I can't help laughing at my friend's enthusiasm. That's what I love about Zoe, she is so eager about everything she does.

Joanne is cheering from above. 'Way to go, Zoe!' She leans over to look down at us and my stomach lurches. Jesus, she is close to the edge. I hurry to get the harness off Zoe and, hooking everything up, I call to Joanne to hoist it all up for the third time.

Joanne disappears and the rope begins its rather jerky journey to the top of the ledge. We wait around, looking upwards every now and then, expecting her to appear over the edge.

'What happens to all the equipment?' asks Zoe.

'The chocks? I expect Joanne will come back for them another day,' I say. 'It's not unusual to leave them behind for the next climber who comes along.' I look up, expecting to see Joanne hopping down the cliff face, but there's still no sign of her. 'Joanne! Are you OK?' Silence. 'Joanne!' I try again, only this time, properly shouting. 'Joanne!'

Then from out of the grey sky, a white piece of paper flutters down over the ledge. It swirls and turns numerous times before landing at our feet. I pick it up and unfold the paper.

'See you at the croft,' I read out loud.

'What?' says Andrea, taking the paper from my fingers. 'What the fuck is she on about? Joanne? Joooooaaannne!' She looks at me and Zoe. 'Is this some kind of fucking joke?'

'It's not very funny if it is,' I reply. My gaze climbs the rock face and scans the ledge above, half-expecting Joanne to appear and announce that this is another of her pranks, like in the forest yesterday. I try calling up to her again. In fact, we all do, but there is no response whatsoever. 'She really has gone and left us,' I say, surprise now replaced with anger at her irresponsible behaviour. Not only has she left us to fend for ourselves, but she is also now on her own. What if she has some sort of accident on the way back to the croft? And then I remember, Joanne said she had a radio with her in case of emergencies. Well, good for her, but what about us? I mutter an expletive under my breath at Joanne's recklessness.

'I'll bloody kill her when I see her,' says Andrea. 'What are we supposed to do now?'

Chapter 13

I must admit, even by Joanne's standards, this is taking things too far. I know she would think it hilarious and, to be honest, the prospect of kayaking down the river doesn't bother me, but it's the way this has been thrust on us which annoys me. I'm sure Andrea can manage the kayaking, but for Zoe, despite her athletic frame, it may be a tad outside her comfort zone. Zoe is more yoga, tennis and swimming than intrepid adventurer.

Without Joanne, I am the only experienced kayaker. It's unfair of her to put me in this position. However, there's not a lot I can do about it now. Once again, Joanne has manipulated us into a situation; what was it she called it earlier? That's right, a fait accompli.

I look at the kayaks. They are two-seaters, which means one of us will have to paddle alone.

'How are your paddling skills?' I ask the others with an enthusiasm I don't particularly feel. I nod in the direction of our transport.

'You have got to be joking,' says Andrea. She looks up at the ledge we have descended from. 'Joanne! If you're up there,

115

you'd better get your arse down here quick.' She turns to me. 'Can't you climb up and see what's happening?'

'Climb up? Even if I thought that was a good idea, which it's not, I've just sent the harness and ropes back up.' I look at the rock face. There are a few hand and footholds but only a fool would attempt it without any equipment.

'The last thing we want is for Carys to fall and hurt herself,' says Andrea, a slight impatience creeping into her voice. 'We'll be well and truly in the shit then.'

'Sorry. Stupid idea,' says Zoe.

'We haven't even got any way of calling for help,' I say. 'Joanne has the radio in her rucksack. Well, I assume she does. I should have checked.' While my anger simmers beneath the surface, I'm aware of a different sensation now taking prime position. One of unease. I can't help but question Joanne's motivation for pulling this stunt. It's not the physical danger she is putting us in that worries me most but the psychology behind her actions. She's an intelligent woman, married to a psychologist, she must know this will cause stress and anxiety to us as individuals and to us as a group. I don't want to voice my concerns out loud, not yet. This isn't the time or place. Right now we need to adopt a pragmatic approach. However, in my head, misgivings about this entire weekend have gone from a distorted hum to a coherent whisper.

'This it totally irresponsible of her,' says Andrea, her hands on her hips. I nod my agreement.

'Let's not waste any more time moaning about it,' says Zoe. 'We don't have a choice. It's canoeing or nothing.'

'Kayaking,' I say needlessly.

Zoe shrugs. 'Whatever.'

'Hey, what's that?' Andrea says, pointing up to the ledge again.

As we all look up, another small white piece of paper floats down towards us. Andrea makes a couple of grabs for it, but the paper flutters away from her grasp and lands on the stones at our feet. As Andrea stoops to pick it up, something makes me look up again. I barely have time to register it, but I see something falling towards us.

'Look out!' I shout, covering my head with my hands and diving out of the way. I feel a whack on my shoulder and I cry out in pain as whatever it is lands on the ground by my side.

'It's the rope,' says Andrea. 'Oi! Joanne! Talk about bloody stupid!' I can hear the anger in Andrea's voice.

Unsurprisingly there is no response. 'That kind of puts an end to any notion of climbing back up,' I say, rubbing my shoulder, which feels a little tender. I will probably have a bruise or a burn mark as a result. 'Anyway, what does the note say?'

Andrea has picked the note up from the floor by now and unfolds it.

SEE YOU LATER. HAVE FUN!

'Have fun!' repeats Andrea. 'I'll give her fun when I see her.'

'OK, let's get this over with now,' I say, sensing Andrea is on the verge of having one of her unstoppable rants. They don't happen often, but when they do, anybody in her way had better look out. All sorts of scenarios race through my mind, involving Andrea telling Joanne exactly what she thinks of this latest stunt. I wince at the thought of the two of them locking horns again. If this weekend was Joanne's attempt to patch things up, then she has seriously misjudged how to go about it.

'Are either of you any good in a kayak?' I ask, distracting Andrea from her murderous thoughts about Joanne.

'I've only kayaked a few times,' says Zoe.

'I've canoed,' says Andrea. 'When I was the activities co-ordinator for the sea cadets. You know, when Bradley went through a phase of thinking he wanted to join the navy?'

I smile, remembering it well. Bradley had roped Alfie into going along with him for a couple of meetings, but then Darren died and Alfie had stopped going. I never nagged him to go again; maybe with hindsight I should have. If Alfie'd had something to occupy himself with, to take his mind off things at home, rather than shutting himself away in his bedroom, maybe he'd be a different lad to the one he is now. Once again, the guilt rises in me.

'You can take one kayak,' says Andrea before I have a chance to speak. 'And I'll go in the other one with Zoe.'

'I can take the lead, all you two have to do is to follow me.' I step nearer to the edge of the water and look down towards the river. The embankment becomes steeper further along and changes from grass and stones to rocks and boulders. On the other side of the river, the cliff face is about sixty or seventy metres high, towering over us. The river bears off to the right downstream and I can't see any further, but the water itself is calm. The gentle waterfall on the other side is having little or no impact on the pool.

'How far do we have to paddle for?' asks Zoe, coming to join me at the water's edge.

'I'm not sure. Joanne said the river runs right past the croft. There's probably some sort of landing point around there.'

The kayaks are quite stable in the water and Joanne at least had the foresight to provide life jackets and safety helmets. I gather up the rope that was thrown down from the cliff and wind it into a neat coil around my hand and elbow before dropping it into the front of the boat.

'What do you make to this?' asks Andrea, her hands on her hips again, one foot resting on the edge of the other kayak.

'What's that?' I say, looking into the boat. 'Safety helmets, life jackets. What's the problem?'

'Count them.'

'Four of each,' I reply, not understanding what Andrea is getting at. Zoe looks equally blank.

'Four helmets and four life jackets,' says Andrea. 'And how many of us are there? Three. Why would she put four in if she wasn't planning on coming?'

'Does seem odd,' I agree, trying to make sense of Joanne's actions. I find myself questioning everything she has done this weekend. Joanne doesn't appear to have left anything to chance but I'm struggling to rationalise her actions. 'I suppose she may have put four there in case she changed her mind and decided to come with us. You know what Joanne's like.' As I say the words out loud, I'm aware they don't sound particularly convincing.

'It's possible,' says Andrea, and I can detect the scepticism in her voice. 'Wonder what made her change her mind?'

'Who knows.' I try to concentrate on getting back to the croft; we can analyse Joanne's actions later. One by one, I pick up the helmets and hand them out, repeating the process with the lifejackets. We spend a few minutes getting organised and I issue some tips to Zoe and Andrea about getting into the kayak. 'We'll have to wade out into some deeper water,' I say.

'It's bloody freezing,' squeals Andrea. We've all rolled our trousers up to our knees and the water is now overlapping the tops of our socks.

Zoe is on tiptoe. 'Quick, get me in that boat.'

The water is extremely cold. There has been no sun today to take the chill off even the shallow water. I hold the kayak still as Zoe clambers in first. Fortunately, it is the type of kayak that you sit inside. Zoe wriggles around and gets herself comfortable.

Andrea sits behind Zoe and the kayak rocks from side to side as they take up their paddles. I give the boat a little push out into the middle of the pool. 'Tandem paddle,' I call over to them as I go back to the shore to retrieve my kayak and bring it into deeper water.

Despite my intention to forget about Joanne and her games, I can't stop my mind returning to the undercurrent of tension I have sensed all along from Joanne. I'm beginning to think my interpretation of the rationale behind the invite was totally wrong.

A shriek from the other kayak makes me look up. Andrea and Zoe are heading for the bank. Andrea is barking instructions at Zoe, who seems to be having trouble working out her left from her right.

'Right hand down!' Andrea shouts. 'Right. In. Pull. Out. Left. In. Pull. No! Not like that. You've got to do it faster.'

'Zoe! Stop paddling for a second!' I yell. 'Now, left. Left. And again. Keep going! Left!' I watch through half-closed eyes as the kayak heads straight for the bank. Somehow Andrea manages to avert a complete disaster and the kayak bears away from the bank, but not before going under an over-hanging branch. Zoe dodges out of the way, sending the kayak to one side and then the other.

The splashes and screams echo around the gorge as they both end up in the water. The kayak, now without the weight of the passengers, pings upright.

'You fucking idiot!' Andrea shouts, rather uncharitably, at Zoe, who shouts back that it wasn't her fault, that she thought Andrea was steering and didn't she see that bloody branch?

As they somehow manage to haul themselves into the kayak, much to my relief, laughter erupts from both of them. I paddle over and, pulling alongside, steady their kayak with my hand.

'Are you two all right?' I ask once I've managed to stop laughing myself. 'Honestly, I wish I had a video camera, that was hilarious.'

'Good job the water isn't very deep here,' says Andrea. 'My bottom half is soaked. Are you OK, Zoe? Sorry about shouting at you.'

Zoe waves away Andrea's apology. 'It's fine, don't worry. I

am freezing, though. When I see Joanne, I'm going to make her pay for this.'

'She's not watching us from up there somewhere, laughing at us, is she?' I ask, scanning the top of the rock face and then the tree-lined embankment. Not that I can see much through the dense woodland. I take my jacket off and hold it out to Zoe. 'Take this. I've got my thermal vest on underneath my jumper, I'll be fine. Sorry, Andrea, I don't have anything else you could borrow.'

'It's OK. I'll survive. Let's get going or it will be dark at this rate.'

We paddle down the river, Andrea and Zoe eventually settling into something of a rhythm. Despite there being two of them in one kayak, I make better headway. Twice I slow down to wait for them to catch up as they tack their way along the river.

The skies are darkening by the time we round a bend in the river and see the bridge near the croft in the distance. I glance up to the left and can see the two chimneys of the croft poking above the brow of the embankment.

'Thank goodness for that. Well done, you did it!' My arms are burning from the effort of paddling a double kayak single-handedly and I'm glad we're finally here. We paddle over to the embankment where there is a small pontoon, just big enough for two people to stand on.

After faffing around, we manage to successfully exit the kayaks and tie them up to the small scaffold post on the side of the pontoon.

The grey skies look a menacing charcoal colour now and

with dusk creeping up on us and mist settling on the water, the croft is a welcome sight.

'I can't see any lights on,' says Andrea.

'No smoke from the chimney either,' I comment. I had hoped Joanne would be waiting for us with a healthy fire roaring away in the hearth. Sadly, it doesn't look to be the case.

'Don't tell me this is still part of her joke,' huffs Andrea.

As we near the croft, with Zoe leading the way, she stops and turns to us. 'That's odd. The door is open.'

'I was the last one out this morning and I definitely closed it,' says Andrea. 'I remember checking with Joanne that she had the key.'

I venture ahead, pushing the door gingerly. 'Joanne? Are you there?'

'Where the bloody hell is she?' says Andrea.

'What if she got lost? Or had an accident?' says Zoe, verbalising my own fears.

'If she's not here, we'll have to go back and look for her,' I say. I glance outside, not wanting the others to read my expression. I'm not relishing the prospect of going on a manhunt in the dark when we're all cold and wet. Joanne's behaviour is pissing me off now.

'This is a stupid game. ' Andrea huffs loudly, having finally lost her patience. 'I want to say it's her own bloody fault for going off alone.'

I raise my eyebrows at my friend, who glares at me defiantly. 'I'm only saying what you two are thinking.' She bundles her way past me and switches on the light. 'I'm going up for a shower.' Andrea stops at the foot of the stairs, lets out a sigh and turns to face us. 'Look, I'm sure she's here somewhere but I'm not in the mood right now to play hide and seek. I'm cold, I'm wet and I'm tired. I'm going to have a shower and if she hasn't turned up by then, we'll go and look for her. I'm not pandering to her and her stupid games any more.'

Zoe gives me a questioning look, which I answer with a shrug. Then after a second or two of internal debate, she unzips her jacket. 'OK, I must admit, I can't wait to get out of these wet clothes either. But if she's not turned up by the time we've showered and changed into dry clothes, we have to look for her. Agreed?'

'Agreed,' I reply.

Zoe hands me my jacket. 'Thanks for the borrow. See you in five.'

I take the jacket and hang it on the peg. 'Let me grab some dry clothes first and then I'll put the kettle on and light the fire.'

Dressed in a dry pair of jogging-bottoms and T-shirt, I go into the living room, half-expecting Joanne to be sitting in the armchair, smiling smugly at me, but the room is empty. I have a quick look in the dining room and kitchen, in case she's in there, but again, there is no sign of her.

I shiver and goosebumps run down my spine. I can't shake off that undercurrent of something not being right. The sight of my reflection in the window makes me jump and I scold myself for letting the strange atmosphere in the house get the better of me.

As I go about setting the fire and lighting it, I can hear the shower running upstairs and then Andrea calling out to Zoe that she has finished. Doors open and close, footsteps patter across the landing and the shower runs again, this time accompanied by the muted sounds of Zoe singing.

The fire takes ages to light, but eventually the little pieces of kindling and white firelighter blocks catch. The smell of paraffin from the blocks seeps into the room as the fire takes hold. I stand up and from the corner of my eye, I catch a movement through the window. I spin round to face the glass, but only my reflection looks back at me.

I wonder if it's Joanne outside, attempting to creep into the house without being noticed. The anger that has been simmering quietly below the surface all afternoon flares up and I stride down the hall to the front door, intending to turn the tables and catch her by surprise this time.

I grab the torch from the shelf and yank open the door but am greeted only by the advancing dusk, the daylight long since swallowed up by the grey tones of the evening and deteriorating weather. I flick the light switch by the front door and the driveway is illuminated in a soft amber glow which fades and fizzles out as it stretches away from the croft.

I peer into the monochrome landscape, wafting the torch from side to side, the beam sweeping the driveway. 'Joanne? Is that you?' As I step out from the shelter of the porch, the wind catches a loose strand of my hair, whipping it across my face. I hook it with my finger and hold it against the side of my head. 'Joanne, are you there?'

The bushes rustle as a stronger gust of wind chases its way across the driveway. The branches of the trees yield to the wind, bowing in deference to the elements. The wind buffets against my ears, distorting the sound and for a moment I am thrown off balance as I lose my orientation and stumble to one side. The front door slams behind me and while my brain registers the sound as unthreatening, my body is a nanosecond ahead and sends adrenalin rushing through my nerve endings as I jump and let out a small shriek.

Every instinct is telling me to go inside, but another sound, a stifled high-pitched noise, one that is out of place with the surroundings and weather conditions, breaks through the momentary pause in the wind. I shine the light to the left, where the sound came from. 'Joanne? Is that you?'

My feet involuntarily lead me towards the rear of the croft.

Nothing is giving me greater pleasure than knowing that the whole weekend is not going at all like you planned. That you are nervy and uneasy. That things are not within your control and other people are calling the shots, forcing you to do things you don't want to do. All the time people are challenging you, questioning you. And you won't like that one little bit.

You must know that things aren't going to get any better. I bet the alarm bells are ringing in your head but you don't want to say anything for fear everyone will accuse you of being paranoid or overreacting. You probably think they'll mention your nerves and ask you if you're still taking your medication or whether you should perhaps go back to the doctor. And by the same token, if no one voices their fears, you'll certainly be wondering if that's what everyone is thinking.

It's not nice when that happens. Trust me, I know. And that's your fault. They say revenge is a dish best served cold. Soon my patience will be rewarded. You'd better watch your back.

Chapter 14

'Boo!'

I scream and drop the torch while simultaneously realising it is Joanne. 'You stupid idiot!' I hear myself yell. 'You frightened the bloody life out of me.'

Joanne is laughing as she picks up the torch and hands it to me. 'I should say sorry, but it's just too funny.'

I ignore the offer of the torch and spin on my heel, marching indoors, with Joanne following me, laughing as she does. Andrea appears at the top of the landing.

'Oh, look who it fucking is,' she says, on spying Joanne. She folds her arms. 'Our illustrious leader.'

'Ooh, do I detect a hint of unrest in the troops?' says Joanne, clearly enjoying herself. 'Don't be spoilsports.'

Zoe makes an appearance alongside Andrea. Wrapped in a towel, her hair drips down her shoulders. 'I thought I heard your voice,' she says. 'There was me thinking something had happened to you. I should have saved my worry for someone more deserving.'

'My, my, we are all touchy, aren't we?' says Joanne, and for a change she looks slightly miffed by our reaction. 'I knew

Carys would take care of you both and lead you to safety.' She pats my shoulder. 'We can rely on Carys to do the right thing, can't we?'

'Leave it,' I say, going into the kitchen. 'Sometimes you take things too far.'

'Don't be such a bore,' retorts Joanne, following behind me. 'You never used to be. I know it was pretty miserable of Darren to do what he did, but you can't let it carry on affecting you this way.'

I can feel the words balling in my throat as I almost choke on them, but before I can speak, Andrea launches in.

'You're so insensitive sometimes, Joanne,' she says.

'I'm being honest, that's all,' comes the reply. 'I don't mean to upset you, Carys, I promise. But what sort of friend would I be if I didn't tell you the truth?'

I flick the kettle on. 'You're assuming that I want your opinion.'

'Look, regardless of whatever relationship you're in now, I know you've never got over Darren's death – and for good reason.' I go to interrupt but she holds up her hand to silence me and carries on. 'But you have to think of the effect your disposition is having on your son.'

I slam the cup I'm holding down on to the worktop. 'You know that expression about treading on dangerous ground, or that one about skating on thin ice? Well, that's exactly what you're doing right now.' I step closer to Joanne, who doesn't flinch. 'Keep your opinions and theories about what I'm doing and how that relates to Alfie, to yourself. You know nothing.'

I storm past her, allowing my shoulder to brush her own

as I go and I'm instantly reminded of how Alfie did this to me on Friday and for a moment I have a small glimpse into his mindset. I'm not sure I like it. I hear Andrea tell Joanne that she's an idiot and should keep her mouth shut. I pause on the stairs and march back through the dining room to the kitchen doorway. 'You know what, I thought this weekend would be fun, a chance for us all to get back to the sort of friendship we used to have, but I was wrong. This weekend isn't for that at all, it's for you, Joanne, to bitch and make catty remarks at every possible opportunity. OK, I get it, you're pissed off with me and probably Andrea and Zoe too, but this is the wrong arena for it. If I'd known what this weekend was really about, I'd never have come. And if there was any way I could leave now, right this minute, I would.'

This time I make it all the way up to my room without going back for another rant. I slam the door to underline my fury at Joanne.

Taking deep breaths, I stand at the window and look out across the rear garden at the cordon of trees which hems the croft. I turn and go over to the opposite window, hoping the open landscape will give a sense of space and light. The mist that is now rolling off the river obscures my view and only adds to the suffocation.

I pace the room and finally force myself to sit on my bed. My anger, as always, is short-lived. I'm not one for sudden outbursts and I put my display of fury down to a physically tough day and an emotionally challenging thirty-six hours. As my equilibrium returns, I can feel the guilt begin to form and take shape. Did I overreact? Possibly. My reactions remind me of Alfie when his temper erupts. Maybe he is more like me than I realise, although I certainly don't take it to the extremes he does. Fortunately, I can exercise control and I come down much quicker. I should have spoken to Joanne in a calm manner and explained to her quite clearly how her comments were upsetting me.

After a few more minutes of contemplation, I decide that I should speak to her to clear the air, but before I can do anything, the door opens and Andrea comes in.

'Hiya, is it safe to come in or do I need a flak jacket and hard hat?'

I wave her in. 'None needed. All is calm once more.'

'I'm glad to hear it.' She sits on the bed opposite me. 'Feel better for it?'

'Kind of. But I also feel embarrassed about flaring up like that. I was thinking I should go and speak to her.'

'She's downstairs.'

'Is she OK? I didn't upset her, did I?'

'Upset Joanne? You've got to be kidding! I have the distinct impression she enjoyed winding you up.'

I let out an agitated sigh. 'I'm still going to speak to her, though.'

'Well, I'm going dry my hair out and then go downstairs and open the wine,' says Andrea. 'Zoe's sorting herself out too. Now would be a good time to speak to Joanne.'

When I venture downstairs, Joanne is nowhere to be found. The fire is burning nicely and the flickering flames jitter around the log, illuminating the room in a soft yellow hue.

I go upstairs and pause outside Joanne's bedroom door. I

can't hear any movement inside but I knock gently and press my mouth to the doorframe. 'Joanne? You in there?' There's no response. I remember the notebook in my room and quickly scrawl Joanne a note.

Sorry for getting so cross earlier. Can we chat later?

I poke the paper under the door so she will see it before she leaves the room and hope she interprets it in the spirit it's been written in.

When I go back in the bedroom, Andrea is asleep on the bed. I take the blanket from the wardrobe and drape it over her. Today's exertions seem to be getting the better of everyone and as Zoe hasn't emerged from her room either, I guess she's taking a catnap too.

Not wanting to disturb Andrea, I make my way downstairs again, pausing in the hallway to inspect the semaphore pictures on the wall. They must be spelling out something but without a copy of the semaphore alphabet, I have no idea.

As I browse the bookshelf in the hope of finding a book which will reveal the code, I get the sense of being watched. I turn around and Joanne is standing in the doorway.

'Didn't want to make you jump again,' she says, with a small raise of the eyebrows.

'Thanks,' I say, aware there is an awkwardness between us.

She holds the note that I'd slid under her bedroom door in the air. 'Shall we go outside? It's more private.' Joanne doesn't wait for me to answer but heads off towards the door.

Through the mist and gentle glow from the kitchen light,

everything outside appears a little distorted, sharp edges and definitions lost. It's like looking through a grimy net curtain where the light is diffused and detail is missing. The shed is a grey shadow hovering above the lawn in a swirl of fog and the trees up on the hill resemble a smudged charcoal sketch, as they loom over the croft.

Joanne is standing on the patio with a cigarette in her hand. She lights it and blows the smoke out in front of her.

'I thought you'd given up?' I say.

'I have. Let's call this a relapse.'

I wonder if I've upset her more than I realise. 'I'm sorry for getting so angry earlier. I didn't mean what I said.'

'Yes, you did. We both know that.' She continues looking straight ahead, her cheeks hollowing as she draws on the cigarette and holds the smoke in her lungs before expelling it through her nose. 'You really do wish you'd never come.'

I push my hands into my pocket. 'Only because of all the tension.'

'I was merely being honest. No need to get so uptight.'

'You don't get it, do you?' I give a small shake of my head. It is exhausting even trying to apologise to Joanne. I feel my temper rise again. 'If we're being honest here, then I'll tell you a few things that have been bothering me. I don't like the way you feel you have an automatic right to say what is good for Alfie and what isn't. I appreciate that he spends a lot of time at your place with Ruby, but that doesn't give you the right to lecture me about my son.'

'I wasn't lecturing you. I was letting you know that you've changed. You're more serious, more cautious, more guarded.'

'And your point in listing my character flaws is . . . ?'

'Because I can see what's happening to you, even if you can't. You're heading for a fall, big time.'

'Joanne, I have no idea what you're on about.'

'OK, I'll be blunt.' She turns to face me. 'You know as well as I do that Ruby's affection for Darren wasn't one-sided. I've found something out since then. Something that backs up what I've always suspected.'

Fear and panic ravage my brain, I feel light-headed from the verbal blow and air evacuates my lungs as I struggle to breathe.

I wheeze out a reply. 'What are you talking about?'

Joanne's eyes narrow and her jaw tenses. 'You might have forgotten or chosen to forget how charismatic Darren was. He could be very charming, very flirtatious and very persuasive.'

I want to dispute this, but the truth is, Joanne is right. Darren was all those things. 'Where's this going?' I manage to say and I can hear the surrender in my own voice. While I don't want to have this conversation because of the end destination, I need to know what Joanne has found out. I need to know what I'm up against and how much harder I must fight to keep Alfie safe.

'You need to open your eyes, Carys, and see Darren for what he really was.'

'Which was?'

'A manipulative, lying bastard.'

I can't refute this. That's exactly what he was. 'No one's perfect,' I say.

'But where is that line of what's acceptable and what isn't?

135

I know Ruby was eighteen at the time, an adult in the eyes of the law, but she was his student. He was in a position of power. She looked up to him. Yes, she had a crush on him, but he took advantage of her. He abused his position.'

I can't control the fear that is building up inside me. How can I, as a mother, ever admit that maybe Darren did have an affair with a student? How will that make me look now? More importantly, what sort of effect will that have on Alfie? How will he deal with the possibility that his father had no morals? I can't let Joanne continue with this, even if it is true; I've gone too far down the denial path, I can't turn back now.

'What is the point of all this, Joanne? What do you want from me?'

'I want you to admit that you covered up for your pervert of a husband.' Her voice hardens and she jabs her finger in my direction. 'Not once but at least twice. For all I know, there might have been other times.'

'You talk about this new information, this new proof. What is it?'

'You don't need to know that yet. You'll find out soon enough.'

'This is a load of rubbish,' I snap. 'You don't have proof. I don't believe you have any proof, you're making it up because you can't let go. You can't bear the thought that your precious daughter might have been lying about the depth of their relationship in the first place and the fact that she was a silly infatuated teenager.' I say it with such conviction that I almost believe it. 'I'm not having this conversation,' I say, but before I can turn to go indoors, I feel Joanne's hand on my arm.

'You're not walking away from this. Not now. You're going to listen to me.'

Something about the look in her eyes makes me freeze. This is a different Joanne from the one who confronted me about this two years ago. That Joanne didn't have the conviction in her voice. That Joanne was upset but in a disbelieving way. 'Spit it out,' I say, with a confidence that's at odds with the vulnerability I'm feeling.

'It's not the first time Darren has had more than a professional relationship with one of his students.' She pauses and studies my face before continuing. 'I can see the fear and guilt in your eyes. Your reaction tells me everything I need to know.'

'Which is?'

'That this isn't news to you. You're not shocked. In fact, you're angry and scared.'

'You're clutching at straws.' My heart is pounding and my stomach rolling.

'Leah Hewitt. Hammerton College.' She punches the words out, the impacts hitting me in the stomach each time.

I gasp for breath in my winded state and my legs want to buckle but I somehow remain on my feet. 'Shut up. Shut the fuck up.' I hear the words and recognise my own voice, surprising myself as I have no knowledge of even thinking it, let alone saying it.

'Hit a nerve, have I?' Her grip on my arm tightens. I try to shrug her off but her grip tightens even more. 'That's why Darren moved colleges, isn't it? He was asked to leave and the college didn't want a fuss made, it was all hushed up, wasn't it? Wasn't it?' She shakes my arm.

I find the inner strength from somewhere and yank my arm away, but Joanne doesn't let go, even though she is thrown off balance and almost falls into me. We struggle, sway back and forth as we wrestle with each other. I feel her hand loosen on my arm and with both hands I push her away. She stumbles backwards and trips over her own feet. Joanne hits the ground and her head makes contact with the porch wall.

I stand there, shocked. Looking at her. Her eyes are closed. She doesn't move. Somewhere in my mind, I know I should be kneeling beside her, checking she is OK, helping her. But I do none of those things.

And then she groans and her eyes squeeze tight before she opens them. Her hand lifts to touch the side of her head. When she takes her fingers away there is blood. She looks up at me. 'You stupid bitch. Look what you've done.'

I look at her and try to summon up some sort of concern or sympathy. But I can't. And in a moment of brutal honesty, I acknowledge my feelings, first of disappointment and then of fear. I can't let Joanne tell anyone the truth.

Chapter 15

The warmth of the living room comforts me in the same way a hug from Seb does. I wish I was with him. I've had enough of Scotland and everything I am beginning to associate with it.

I swirl the vodka and Coke I have mixed myself around in the glass. The ratio of alcohol to soft drink well in favour of the former. Movements upstairs, gently squeaking floorboards and muted thuds of feet tell me that the others are awake now.

I hear footsteps on the stairs but the door is closed and I don't bother to call out. I want to put off having to face anyone as long as I can. My enthusiasm for false jollities and friend-ships has been lost in the fog. I finish my drink and push further into the sofa, allowing my mind to wander into that place between conscious thought and sleep.

I am not sure how long I've been dozing when a scream of utter terror penetrates the thick walls of the croft. I'm cat-apulted from my slumber immediately. I jump up, the empty glass falling from my hand, but fortunately landing on the sofa. I ignore it and rush out into the hall where I almost collide with Andrea as she reaches the bottom of the stairs.

'Where did that come from?' she asks, a nervous inflection in her voice.

'Outside.' I slip my feet into my walking boots without bothering to tie the laces. Another scream punctuates the night air as I open the front door and we both rush out.

Andrea has a torch in her hand. 'It's Zoe,' she says. 'Sounds like she's round the back.' Without thinking what might await us, we bundle round the side of the croft.

Zoe is sitting on the edge of the grass, her knees drawn up and cradled by her arms. She's staring straight ahead. She's wearing her pyjamas and a towel is wrapped around her head. She reminds me of a frightened child.

I rush over to her. 'Zoe. What's the matter? What's happened?' I crouch beside her and put my arms around her. 'Are you hurt?' She clings to me and buries her head in my arm. Her body heaves and another sob escapes.

Andrea is standing in front of the porch. 'Oh my God—' The words are barely audible.

I follow the shaft of light from the torch and recoil at the sight illuminated on the ground.

'Fuck,' I hear myself say. My head swims and I feel faint but I force myself to my feet and drag one foot in front of the other until I am standing next to Andrea.

Joanne is lying across the threshold of the porch on her back. Her eyes stare blankly up to the night sky and a pillow of blood circles her head on the ground.

Zoe scrambles to her feet and throws herself on the ground beside Joanne, grabbing her hand and patting it, as between sobs she calls Joanne's name. She cuffs her nose with her sleeve and looks up at us. 'We need to call an ambulance. Do something!'

'How can we? We haven't got a bloody phone,' says Andrea desperately.

'We can't just leave her. She needs help,' insists Zoe. She jumps to her feet and looks around in a panic. 'Carys! Andrea! Do something.' She grabs my arms with her hands and shakes me.

The act triggers my brain into action. My first-responder training kicks in and I kneel beside Joanne. I slide my fingers around her limp wrist to locate a pulse, while calling her name.

'Is she breathing?' asks Zoe.

'Is there a pulse?' asks Andrea.

'I can't find one.'

Zoe lets out another wail. 'Oh my God, she's dead.'

'Check her neck. See if you can find a pulse in her neck.' Andrea's voice is controlled but the panic and fear are evident. She turns to Zoe. 'Shut up, Zoe, just for a minute. Let Carys check her. We don't need you losing it right now.'

I feel a brief moment of sympathy for Zoe, who whimpers and claps her hands together in front of her mouth, as if in prayer. I turn my attention back to Joanne, my fingers now pressing underneath her jaw against her soft, but cold, neck.

I cannot feel even the faintest of pulses. I lean forward and try to feel her breath against the side of my face or hear the tiniest whispers of breath.

Nothing.

'Check again,' Andrea insists. 'Check. Again.'

I hear the intensity and desperation in Andrea's voice. It takes a moment for me to think straight. Have I made a mistake? Have I missed the pulse because it's weak? Can people keep their eyes open, unblinking, if they are knocked out?

My fingers shake as, once again, I try to locate a pulse, both in her neck and on her wrist. I listen intently for the slightest sound of a breath.

'I can't find anything,' I say.

'CPR. Try CPR,' instructs Andrea.

I once again take in Joanne's unblinking eyes and the crimson crown of blood and the coldness of her skin. I squeeze my eyes tight to stop the rapidly gathering tears from falling.

'Carys, do what Andrea says.' Zoe is close to hysteria.

I find myself beginning chest compressions even though I know that Joanne can't be helped. The actions are as much to appease Zoe and to pave the way for ease of conscience on my part when I will need it in the days and weeks to come. I've seen death before. I know what it looks like. And I know the guilt that follows.

I try for five minutes, but all attempts to resuscitate Joanne are futile. Eventually, I lean back on my heels and, looking up at the others, I shake my head.

Zoe buries her face in her hands and emits gentle sobs which are carried away into the night by the wind before she rushes to the edge of the grass and throws up.

'What the hell happened?' asks Andrea.

I shake my head as I feel the enormity of events begin to push away the detached and focused element of my first-responder training. I fight back, not wanting to break down.

'I don't know,' I reply steadily, wiping the sweat from the palms of my hands down the sides of my trousers. 'Looks like she's had a fall and hit her head on the side of the porch.'

I try to remain divorced from the notion that this is Joanne, my friend, lying dead on the ground. I've dealt with serious injuries and even a death during my time as a first responder. I have to convince my mind that this is someone I have no connection with. If I start to think of it in any other context, I know I will go to pieces.

Tears swamp my eyes and trickle down the side of my nose. I wipe them away with my hand but they keep coming. 'Oh, Joanne,' I say, so quietly I can barely hear my own words. 'Oh God. What happened to you?'

'Is she definitely . . . you know . . . ?' Andrea leaves the word hanging silently in the air.

Before I can say anything else, there's a roar behind me and Zoe grabs my shoulders, spinning me round as I crouch and throwing me off balance. 'What did you do?' she screams at me. 'What did you do to her?'

Andrea is pulling Zoe back. 'For fuck's sake, Zoe. Pack it in!'

I manage to scramble to my feet, shocked by this unprovoked attack. Zoe pushes Andrea away, takes several steps backwards, holding her hands up towards her; a signal that Zoe has it under control and Andrea is to back off.

'Take it easy, everyone,' says Andrea. She looks from me to Zoe as she maintains her position between us. 'You all right, Zoe?'

'Yeah, I'm fine,' she replies, before looking over at me. 'You were out here talking to Joanne. I heard you from my room upstairs. What happened?'

I don't miss the challenge in her tone.

'Nothing happened,' I reply evenly. I'm not sure if Zoe believes me or not, but at this moment, I don't particularly care. 'It's not important right now,' I say, as more tears breach the rims of my eyes.

It's Andrea who takes control of the situation. 'We need to get inside. It's freezing out here,' she says. 'We'll all freeze to . . .' I'm unsure if it's the tears or the thought that prevents her from finishing the sentence.

'What about Joanne?' says Zoe, her tone now one of uncertainty.

'We'll work that out in a minute,' I say. 'We'll have to do something with her. We can't leave her out here.'

'What about the police? We should call someone,' says Zoe between sniffs.

'And how are we going to do that?' says Andrea. 'We haven't got our phones, and even if we did, we're apparently in a not-spot.'

'The radio,' I say, suddenly remembering Joanne said she had one with her when we were setting off this morning. 'Joanne took one with her.'

We all look at Joanne. 'Someone needs to search her pockets,' says Zoe. 'I'd sooner not.'

I take a deep breath. 'I'll do it.'

Kneeling once again beside Joanne, I avoid looking at her face as I begin to pat the pockets of her padded coat, hoping to identify the radio. Both pockets are empty.

'You'll have to undo her jacket,' says Andrea.

I feel so intrusive as I pull the zip down and check the inside pockets and the waistband of Joanne's trousers in case she has it strapped on to her belt.

'I can't find it,' I say. 'Maybe she already took it indoors. We'll have to look for it when we go in. We can try to find our phones while we're at it. We might be able to get a signal from higher ground.'

'You're not seriously planning on going out tonight in the dark on the off-chance you'll get a signal?' says Andrea. 'That's a stupid idea. What if you get lost, or something happens to you?'

I stand up. 'Have you got any better ideas?'

'As it happens, I do. And it doesn't involve standing around here freezing our tits off while I convince you that going out in the dark is not simply stupid, it's bloody stupid.'

'Andrea does have a point,' agrees Zoe.

'And even if you did somehow manage to find a signal,' carries on Andrea, 'how are you going to tell them where we are?'

'They could tell from my phone. Or, if I've got a signal, I can put the location setting on and check with the map app.' I feel a small ray of hope as I let this idea grow in my head.

'Still not going out tonight. The weather is closing in and it's dark now,' says Andrea.

'But we can't do nothing,' I protest.

'We'll go inside and try to find the radio and phones,' says Andrea. 'I don't know about any of you, but I need a drink. A strong one.'

Reluctantly, we follow Andrea inside the croft where, for want of something to do rather than out of necessity, I fill the kettle and switch it on to boil. Andrea disappears into the living room and returns with a bottle of vodka tucked under one arm and carrying a bottle of cola and three wine glasses in her hands.

'It's the best I can do. There's no whisky.' She puts the glasses on the table, takes the bottle and twists the red screwcap until the seal cracks. Then she pours three large measures. She pushes a glass to each of us.

'There's some Coke here, if you want to dilute it,' I say, offering Zoe the bottle. I know from nights out, neither of us are ones for drinking neat spirits. Andrea knocks her shot back in one go and is already topping up with another.

'Thanks,' says Zoe, taking the bottle and adding plenty of Coke to her vodka. I drink mine down in one go and nod to Andrea when she holds the bottle over the empty glass.

'I'll have some more vodka,' says Zoe.

I decline the offer of another. Two is enough. What I long for, now that the alcohol has taken some of the sharp edges off the shock, is a nice cup of sweet tea.

'What are we going to do?' asks Andrea.

'I thought Joanne said there was a radio out here, in case of emergencies. You haven't seen it, have you?'

'Nope. It must be here though. What are you supposed to do in emergencies otherwise?' Andrea begins searching the kitchen, opening cupboard doors, inspecting the contents and closing them again. 'Do we even know what it looks like?'

'No idea,' I reply. After a good search of the downstairs, we give up. 'What about our phones? Do either of you know what Joanne did with them?'

Their blank faces say it all. 'God knows why we agreed to her confiscating them,' says Andrea. 'What was the point of that?' She has one final look in the wall cupboard next to the door. As she closes the door, she peeks through the glass. She gives a shiver. 'We can't leave her out there. Or at the very least we should cover her up.' Her voice cracks and she turns swiftly away from the door, closing her eyes and taking slow deep breaths.

'We shouldn't move her,' I say.

'What? You want to leave her out there all night?' snaps Zoe. 'We can't do that. What if some fox or wild animal comes along?' She pushes her face into her hands, then flaps her hands in the air as she fights off more tears. 'I can't bear the thought. It's too awful to even think about.'

'I still don't think it's a good idea to move her,' I say.

'You've been watching too many police programmes,' says Andrea. 'This isn't foul play, it's an accident. A terrible accident. We've already contaminated the scene anyway, so I don't care what you say, I'm not leaving her out there all night.'

'I don't want to leave her there either,' says Zoe.

I sit down in the chair and push my hands through my hair. 'I don't know what to do. I'm trying to keep it together and do the right thing, but I agree with what you're saying,' I concede. 'Leaving her out there doesn't seem right. It's . . . disrespectful. But at the same time, I don't think moving her is right. Can't we keep a vigil by her for the night? Take it in turns?'

'In this weather? We'd get hypothermia or something,' says Zoe.

'I'm making the executive decision, in that case,' says Andrea. 'Both Zoe and I want to move her, so I say we should.'

I can feel the will to fight seep from me. 'OK, we'll move her'. I massage my temples with my fingertips and close my eyes, only to be confronted with a new wave of helpless anxiety as the enormity and knock-on effect of what's happened swamps me. 'This is all so bloody surreal. What are we going to tell Tris? And the kids?'

'God knows,' says Andrea. She goes to pick up the vodka bottle but changes her mind and sets it on the table. 'I need to keep a clear head, tempting as it might be to get totally wasted.' She sits at the table and takes a sip of the tea I made. Her hand shakes as she picks up the cup and lifts it to her lips. Andrea is far more affected than she is letting on but, for now, I'm grateful for her pragmatic and stoic front. I'm sure if one of us starts to crack, the other two will follow. We need to stay strong, at least until help arrives.

'How long do you think Joanne's been dead?' asks Zoe, staring into her mug as she swirls the spoon around in slow circles.

'I don't know. She was stone cold, so maybe a little while ago. I'm sure a person doesn't go cold that quickly.'

'It's not exactly the tropics out there,' says Andrea. 'It wouldn't take long for the body temperature to drop. You think it happened earlier?'

'I don't know,' I say honestly. I give a sigh. It's hard to think logically about it.

'Were you outside with Joanne?'

I nod. 'I was apologising for earlier. That's all.'

'Why go outside though?' Andrea folds her arms.

'Joanne suggested it. Said it would be more private.'

'I could hear you talking,' says Zoe. 'I couldn't make out what you were saying, but I could hear your voices.'

I wonder if Zoe's telling the truth. Could she have heard what we were saying? Joanne and I weren't exactly keeping our voices down, especially towards the end. Zoe's room is right above where we were standing, I'm pretty sure she'd have heard us. 'We talked, then I came back in and dozed off on the sofa.' I can hear the defensive tone creep into my voice. I don't like the assessing look Andrea gives me. 'Maybe she slipped or something. I don't know.' I rest my head in my hands again as I try to process the chain of events. 'Earlier, I thought I'd seen someone at the window, but it was my reflection.'

'You sure about that?' asks Andrea.

'Yes. That's what made me go out and look,' I reply. 'I went out to the front with a torch. It was very spooky. I felt like I was being watched. That was when Joanne jumped out on me.'

'You don't think it was anyone else?'

'What are you getting at?'

'That maybe there was someone else out there?'

Chapter 16

'What are you saying? There's someone else out there and they killed Joanne?' says Zoe, looking shocked. 'What's to stop them coming in here for us?'

'Wait a minute,' I say, holding up my hand. 'This is getting ridiculous. For all we know, Joanne could have fallen and we didn't hear her. All this talk of someone being out there is making us jumpy.'

'But you're the one who said you saw something,' says Zoe.

'I might have been wrong. I can't think straight.' I blow out a breath. It's true, I am having a hard time keeping a handle on everything and what it all means.

'I'll go and see if I can find our phones,' says Zoe. 'They're probably in Joanne's room somewhere.'

We sit in silence for a while, the only sound being Zoe's footsteps as she moves around Joanne's room right above us.

My body feels weary and I rest my head against the sofa. 'I can't quite believe this is all happening,' I say.

'It's been a bizarre weekend from the start,' says Andrea. 'All the secrecy leading up to it, and the business of actually getting here. And then that stupid bloody guessing game.'

'I know. What was that all about?'

'No idea.' We lapse into a silence once more before Andrea speaks again. 'What I can't stop thinking about is, when I asked Joanne about the game, she said that the answer was staring us straight in the face. I've no idea what she meant.'

'I haven't thought much about it.' I open my eyes and my gaze falls on the photograph of the four of us that Joanne took when we first arrived. A subliminal message nudges an unconscious observation to the fore of my mind. 'The photo. It's got to be the photograph.' I jump up and take the picture from the mantelpiece.

'I'm not with you,' says Andrea.

'The answer is staring straight at us. This photograph has been up there all along. I might be barking up the wrong tree, but at the time I thought Joanne was being rather fussy about where we stood for the photograph. And in an odd place too. Why the hallway? Why not in here or out the front?'

'What are you getting at?'

'Look at the background. Those stickmen with flags – that's semaphore. Each of those pictures must be spelling out a word.'

'How the hell are we going to work that out?' asks Andrea.

I go out to the hall and take the four pictures from the small nails that are tapped into the wall. It's then I notice there is a fifth nail. A larger one. I look down at the picture propped up against the wall. 'My guess is this big picture of the flowers was here originally and Joanne put these smaller ones in its place.' On closer inspection, it's more obvious that these have been produced on an office or home printer; they're not the professional-quality prints you see in shops. 'She must have made them herself.'

'I still don't get why, though,' says Andrea, taking a picture from my hand and studying it.

'Her idea of fun. The joke was on us, except we didn't know it.'

I look up as Zoe comes down the stairs. She pauses halfway. 'I heard what you were saying. Look what was pinned to the back of my door.' She unrolls a poster and holds it up for us to see: *Semaphore Alphabet*. Against each letter of the alphabet is a corresponding stick man with flags in various positions.

'Good work,' says Andrea. 'What's that you've got there?' She nods to the red A4 notebook Zoe has tucked under her arm.

'I'll show you that in a minute,' she replies. 'First let's crack the flag code.'

We go into the living room with the four pictures and spread the poster out on the coffee table. We begin with the picture I was standing under. Letter by letter we write the word on to a piece of paper. I gulp as we read the final word.

M U R D E R E R

'What the . . . ?' says Andrea. She looks up at me. 'Any idea why she's put that?'

Despite the fire burning and the warmth of Zoe and Andrea's bodies, a chill rushes over me and my arms begin to prick with cold. I shake my head. 'No idea.'

'Let's do the others,' says Zoe.

It takes a few minutes, but finally we have decoded the other semaphore pictures.

Above Zoe the word S L U T is spelled out. Above Andrea the word F R A U D S T E R and finally, above Joanne is the word J U D G E.

'What the hell was she planning?' asks Andrea of no one in particular.

'It's starting to make more sense to me,' says Zoe. Both Andrea and I look at Zoe, the questioning looks on our faces need no words to back them up. She picks up the notebook from where she left it on the floor and places it on the table. 'I didn't find the phones, but I did find this.'

Andrea takes the notebook and opens it. Her eyes scan the first page and I crane my head to try to read from the other side of the table. Andrea flicks through some more pages. 'It's a dossier. On us.'

'Let me see properly,' I say, taking the notebook before it is even offered. Sure enough, there is a page on each of us. I automatically flick to the page headed up with my name.

'Each of those pictures ties in with what she's written about each of us,' says Zoe, as I scan the pages.

Carys Montgomery
Character: Mary Ann Cotton
Crime: Murdered her children and her HUSBANDS.
Secret: Carys Montgomery murdered her husband.
Covered up what happened between Darren and Ruby.

My hands slam down on the book, as if I can hide the words and un-see them.

'I've already read it,' says Zoe. 'You might as well read what she's said about us.'

I move my hands away and turn the page to Zoe's name.

Zoe Coleman
Character: Diana, Princess of Wales
Crime: Had an affair with a married man.
Secret: Zoe is having an affair with a married man.
The married man is Tris.

I look at Zoe. 'Is this true?'

'Is it true what she said about you?' replies Zoe. 'Or you, Andrea?'

'Give that to me.' Andrea takes the book and opens it at her name. Once again, I peer across the table.

Andrea Jarvis
Character: Nick Leeson
Crime: Defrauded bank.
Secret: Andrea Jarvis has committed fraud.
Conned me out of the gym.

'What a bitch,' says Andrea. She quickly reads through the pages, letting out a low whistle. 'Joanne sure was pissed off with us.'

'But I didn't have the Princess Diana card,' says Zoe. 'She must have got muddled up.'

'No, I think she did that on purpose,' I say. 'We were given each other's cards because Joanne didn't want any of us to get suspicious about what she was up to. She didn't want us to guess the game was about our personal secrets.'

We all fall silent as we take a moment to catch up with the theory. Andrea speaks first. 'So Joanne's game wasn't a game at all. Or at least, not a nice game. She was going to expose each of our secrets. Or should I say, alleged secrets?'

'But why?' says Zoe.

'Humiliation. Satisfaction. Revenge.' I check each one off on my fingers. 'We thought this weekend was a peace offering. We've all crossed swords with her recently for various reasons, that's why she's been distant. But this weekend wasn't about reconciliation, it was so she could have her revenge.'

'You're talking as if it's true, as if these allegations have substance,' says Andrea. 'I swindled her out of the gym, Zoe is having an affair with Tris, and you killed Darren over something that happened with Ruby?'

'In her eyes, yes. Of course, I didn't kill Darren.' The words tumble from my mouth. I ignore the reference to Ruby. I don't want to talk about that. My leg begins to shake involuntarily and I squeeze it tightly with my hand. The thought of those accusations being dredged up again makes me feel physically sick.

Andrea is unusually quiet. I watch my friend look at the notebook again.

'She was going to expose us,' Andrea says at last. 'Zoe, are you having an affair with Tris?'

Zoe stands a little taller, her jaw clenching. It's difficult to take Zoe seriously, standing in her checked pyjamas with a teddy bear on the front and the words *Sweet Dreams* underneath.

'I don't actually think that's any of your business,' she says.

'That's a yes, then,' retorts Andrea. She turns to me, ignoring the goldfish open-and-close motion Zoe's mouth is making. 'And what does Joanne mean when she talks about Darren and Ruby?'

'Nothing. There's nothing to tell,' I reply.

'Carys, this isn't a game any more. There must be something to it, otherwise she would never have mentioned it. This is part of Joanne's game. She wanted to expose our grubby secrets.'

'Oh, God, please don't tell me Darren and Ruby were having some sort of an affair,' says Zoe. 'Is that why you two split up?'

'They weren't,' I snap. 'And, no, that's not why we separated.' I fold my arms and sit in my chair. I have no intention of telling them the truth.

'What did Joanne mean then?' Andrea won't give up.

I consider denying it again but decide against it. I'll have to offer some sort of explanation. I go for the least damaging: 'It's stupid and totally untrue,' I begin, my brain working overtime. 'Ruby asked Darren to help her with her personal statement for her university application. Naturally, Darren agreed, and he ended up helping her several times. Joanne didn't like it. She thought Ruby had developed a crush on Darren and asked Darren not to help her any more.' I look at the others. 'That's it. That's all there is to tell.'

I watch while they dissect this information and consider the plausibility.

Zoe speaks first. 'Fair enough. Although she never mentioned it to me at any point.'

'It was just between us,' I say.

Zoe gives Andrea a nudge. 'What about you? What's Joanne's problem with you?'

'She accused me of buying the gym behind her back. She thought we should have been partners in the deal. The fact is, I asked her to come in with me, but she didn't have the funds.'

'Is that it?' I ask, suspecting, as in the case of my own story, there must be more to it than that.

Andrea huffs loudly. 'All right, Joanne thinks, or rather thought, that I forged her signature on a document and withheld information about the sale of the business and its valuation.'

'And did you?' I press.

'What do you think?' Andrea drops the notebook on the table. The slap of the cover hitting the oak makes both me and Zoe jump. 'Of course I didn't.'

I allow the revelations to roll around in my mind for a while as I try to assess each one and its credibility. Or even plausibility.

'Whether we deny these allegations or not is irrelevant,' I say finally. 'The fact is, Joanne believed them. She was so convinced, she set up this elaborate game to expose how we were supposed to have wronged her. And now, before the grand reveal, when we're all getting close to working out who these mystery characters are and how their "secrets" connect them to us, she ends up dead. If I were a police officer, I'd say that each of us had a motive for killing her.'

Andrea bursts out laughing. 'You seriously believe one of us killed Joanne?'

'It's a possibility.'

'You're letting your imagination run away with you,' says Andrea. She opens the vodka bottle and pours another shot. Zoe pushes her glass forward for a refill and Andrea obliges.

'What's your theory?' I ask.

'Let's run with your crazy notion that one of us did it,' says Andrea. 'We'll come back to mine in a moment.' She takes a big slug of vodka. 'We were all together when we last saw Joanne.'

'Agreed,' Zoe nods.

'Then we went upstairs and you stayed downstairs. Suddenly we hear you scream and run down to find you outside with Joanne,' Andrea continues. 'Now, who would you say the prime suspect is?'

'Wait a minute,' I say, registering the uncertain look on Zoe's face. 'I was in the living room, asleep. It was Zoe's screams that woke me up. How do I know what you two were doing prior to that? You weren't together, were you?'

'You think one of us did it?' Andrea gives a laugh. 'We were both upstairs. Asleep.'

'Carys does have a point,' interrupts Zoe. 'I was in my room with the door closed. I don't know for sure what you were doing. Likewise, you don't know what I was doing. Technically, you could have crept downstairs without Carys hearing or seeing you.'

Andrea looks stumped and I give Zoe a mental pat on the shoulder. It's true, I did close my eyes for a few minutes and the door to the living room was pushed to.

Andrea shakes her head in disbelief. 'And how do we know you didn't do the exact same thing?' she says, glaring at Zoe. 'Either that or Carys could have crept out of the house, or something could have happened when Carys was talking to Joanne.'

I glance away from Andrea, not wanting to meet her eyes, and then rub my hand over my face to conceal my guilt at the accuracy of this last statement. Something did happen when I was talking to Joanne, but she was definitely OK when I left her. I let out a long sigh and try to compose myself. 'Look, this isn't getting us anywhere. All we've established so far is that any one of us could have done it.'

'What about motive?' asks Andrea. 'Zoe, you were shagging Tris by all accounts, so you have a motive.'

'That's not fair,' snaps Zoe. 'You have a motive too. You swindled Joanne out of the business. You know how much that gym meant to her and how she had plans to take it over, but you wouldn't let her. In some underhand, illegal way, you conned her out of it.'

Andrea holds up her hands. 'Even if that was how it happened, it doesn't make me a murderer – that's no reason to kill someone.' She turns to look at me. 'You have the strongest motive, Carys. If there was something between Darren and Ruby, that would look very bad indeed.'

'Why would that bother me now?' I say, hoping my false bravado will deflect suspicion. 'Darren's dead. It can't exactly harm his reputation.'

'No, but it could harm yours. If it was to get out, people would no doubt ask questions about whether you were suspicious, or even knew. If you're married to someone who likes young girls, then you're bound to know things like that.'

'Shut up, Andrea. You don't know what you're talking about,' I snap, and immediately regret it. This will only shore up her belief that I knew something.

'Hit a nerve, did I?' she says, clearly not deterred. 'Then there's Alfie.'

Pinpricks of sweat pierce my top lip in an instant at the mention of Alfie's name. I feel the muscles in my body tense and I fix Andrea with a glare through narrowed eyes. 'Watch it,' I warn.

Andrea drums her fingers slowly on the table before speaking. 'If it was to get out that Darren did have an affair with one of his pupils, who would suffer the most? Probably not you. Whatever comes your way, you can deal with. You're quite a resilient and tough cookie underneath the surface. You'd be OK, but Alfie, he's much more volatile.'

'Best you stop now.' I grind the words out.

'Too late for that,' says Andrea. 'How would Alfie cope with being teased and taunted about his dad shagging a student? Calling his dad a paedo? Some might even decide to take justice into their own hands and make Alfie pay for his dad's actions. It seems to me that gives you the strongest motive of all.'

Chapter 17

'You know what, Andrea?' I say, my jaw tightening with anger. 'You need to know when to shut up.' The urge to jump to my feet and hurl a torrent of denials at her is almost overwhelming. It's taking a Herculean effort to restrain myself.

'I'm only stating facts.'

I conjure up a tone of civility from deep within me. I've done this before. I can ride it out. Taking a deep breath, I tell her, 'Leave my husband, my son and Joanne's daughter out of this. If Joanne was here, she'd say the same thing.'

'Would she?' Andrea fires me a challenging look.

'Hey, come on, you two,' says Zoe. 'Let's not fight. I don't believe any of us killed Joanne. It's a ludicrous suggestion. What happened was an accident, that's all. Joanne was messing around, slipped on the patio and hit her head. Simple as that. A tragic accident. Us falling out like this isn't going to help.'

Andrea weighs up Zoe's words. 'Yeah, you're right. Sorry.' She looks at me and gives a small smile. 'All this is freaking me out.'

'It's OK,' I reply, although I can't say I truly mean it.

'There is the other option mentioned earlier,' says Andrea.

She pauses to make sure she has our attention. 'There could be someone else out there. And it may not have been an accident.'

'Oh, come off it.' Although I'm grateful the spotlight of blame has shifted away from me, I can't help feeling we are all overreacting now. 'Who would be out there? And why? Why would someone randomly kill Joanne?'

'Perhaps they tried to attack her and she fought back?'

'Andrea's got a point,' says Zoe, her eyes widening. 'All that stuff yesterday in the woods. Maybe there is a weirdo out there, watching us. Maybe they followed us here.'

'Stop it,' I say firmly. 'I'm sure that was Joanne's warped sense of humour at work. She was having fun at our expense. I wouldn't mind betting she made up that story about the mother sacrificing herself at the altar, to make us jumpy. I'm not buying that there is some crazed killer out in the woods.'

Zoe dips her head. She reminds me of a scolded child. 'Sorry. You're right. I'm getting carried away too.' Her bottom lip trembles and I go to give her a hug. Zoe waves me away. 'No. Don't. I'll be reduced to a quivering wreck at this rate and be of no use to anyone. I wish we knew what happened out there.'

'Let's keep calm,' I say. 'And think what to do next.'

'We can't bring her in here,' says Andrea. 'I couldn't cope with a dead body in the same house.' She glances over her shoulder in the general direction of the back door. 'Sorry, Joanne. No offence.'

'There's a shed out there,' I say. 'We could wrap her in a blanket and leave her in the shed. Probably the best place. It will be colder out there than in here.' I bat away the images of dead bodies and the smell of rotting flesh. 'We'd better do it soon. It's dark enough as it is.'

'And we need to find our phones or that radio, so we can get help,' says Andrea.

'Agreed.' Zoe moves to the dining-room door. 'I'll get the duvet cover from Joanne's bed. We can wrap her in that.' She pauses in the doorway and looks at us. None of us say anything. I am sure we are all thinking the same. This is a godawful situation and we are making decisions and carrying them out in an almost businesslike way.

'It will be OK,' I say softly. 'We've got to stay strong and get through this. Extreme situations force people to take extreme actions. But it will be OK. I promise.'

Zoe presses her lips together and gives a small nod before leaving the room.

'I hope you're right,' says Andrea.

Outside, the air is damp from the mist and tiny droplets of moisture form on my clothes and hair. As we round the corner of the croft, the scent of pine needles, combined with an earthy smell of damp grass, drifts down.

I brace myself to see Joanne's body again. I look at the others and we exchange silent nods.

Joanne is exactly how we left her. I don't know what I was expecting. Maybe somewhere in the recesses of my mind, I had hoped it was some sort of group hallucination or another of her clever but cruel jokes, but there's no escaping the fact this is real.

'Lay the duvet as close as possible to Joanne,' I instruct. 'One of you take her legs and I'll lift her arms.'

'I don't think I can,' says Zoe. She takes a step back, the bedding still bundled in her arms.

Andrea pulls the cover from her. 'I'll do it.' She spreads the duvet out and I'm relieved that Andrea seems to be over the shock and back to her usual no-nonsense self. I don't think I'd be able to do this if both of them were flaky. I'm not exactly relishing the prospect of moving the body myself, but I know it must be done.

I manoeuvre myself behind Joanne's head and the inside of the porch. All I have to do is to pretend she is sleeping and not to think of her as anything else. I bend down and force myself to put my hands under the arms. Andrea takes the legs. Joanne's body is still supple, rigor mortis hasn't yet set in, so it is easy enough for us to move her.

We lift her swiftly on to the duvet. I place Joanne's arms by her sides and we fold the duvet over her.

'Sorry. Sorry, Joanne.' I can feel the tears building up in my eyes and my nose begins to run. I fumble in my pocket for a tissue to wipe my face.

'We need to get her into the shed,' says Andrea.

'I'll get the door open,' says Zoe. She has the torch and heads off to the end of the patio and nips across the grass. She rattles the door. 'Bugger. It's locked.'

'For fuck's sake!' says Andrea.

'It's actually padlocked,' Zoe calls.

'I saw a key hanging up by the back door,' I say. 'Wait here, I'll get it.'

I sprint round to the front of the croft. The mist is thicker now and the trees and bushes have been reduced to shady outlines. I hurry indoors and grab the key from the hook. On closer inspection, it doesn't look like a padlock key and I'm dubious as to whether it will unlock the shed.

Deciding that I will break the shed door down if it comes to it, I look around for something that I can use as leverage against the lock. I take the wooden broom and, as an afterthought, grab the iron that is sitting in a cradle on the back of the door.

'What the hell have you got an iron for?' asks Andrea as I reappear next to them at the shed.

'Makeshift hammer, in case I have to smash the lock. Don't worry, I'll buy the owners a replacement.'

'That's the least of our worries,' says Andrea.

I'm right in my assumption that the key I've brought won't fit the padlock. It's too big for a start and looks more old-fashioned than the relatively new padlock on the shed. I don't have time to work out which lock it will open, so I shove it into my jacket pocket.

'Shine the torch closer,' I instruct Zoe.

The padlock is holding a metal plate across the door. It hasn't been fitted that well and there is a certain amount of slack between the door and the frame. I succeed in wedging the broom handle behind the metal plate and try to jemmy the door open. There's a cracking sound and something gives. I pull harder on the broom handle. Suddenly there is a splintering noise and I can see the screws on the plate begin to loosen, but the handle of the broom snaps and I'm sent flying backwards.

'The iron it is,' I say, getting to my feet and picking it up. I smash the iron down hard on the edge of the metal plate where the screws have worked loose. It takes several attempts but finally the force and weight of the iron smashes the screws from the wood. 'Bingo!'

We all peer inside the shed from the doorway. Zoe shines the torch around. The shed is about six by four feet and, from what I can see, houses a few old garden tools, a hosepipe and a couple of bits of old furniture: a dining chair and a chest of drawers. On one side is a shelf which is mostly filled with plastic plant pots and old hand tools that look like they should be in a museum.

'What's that?' says Zoe, resting the torch beam on the shelf, illuminating a rectangular black box with dials on the front.

'It's a bloody radio!' says Andrea. 'What the hell is that doing out here?' She steps inside and lifts the set down. A coiled wire with a handset on the end yo-yos up and down.

'Thank God for that,' says Zoe. 'We can contact someone now. Assuming it works, that is.'

'And assuming we know how to work it,' I say, tamping down my relief, not wanting to get carried away with any thoughts of an imminent rescue.

'Oh wait, I saw some sort of instruction sheet in Joanne's room,' says Zoe. 'It was in the drawer with that notebook. I didn't think anything of it. I'll get it when we go in.'

My relief increases. This is our lifeline to the outside world. Imminent rescue suddenly seems a real possibility. 'Let's move Joanne in here,' I say, feeling energised by our good fortune.

It is harder to move Joanne now she is swaddled in the

heavy duvet, but at the same time, it is easier mentally as I can no longer see her face. The definition of her body and limbs is also less obvious. Andrea takes the legs and as I hold the upper part of the body, we shuffle our way over to the shed. Zoe is standing behind us, shining the torch into the dark recesses of the outbuilding.

Carefully, we rest Joanne's body on the shed floor and I take a few moments to arrange the quilt so that she is properly covered and looks to be in a comfortable and respectful position. I acknowledge this is a ludicrous notion, but it's important to me that we are deferential to our friend, even in death.

Confident that we have done everything we can, we close the shed door. Gathering several of the small rocks that are scattered around the edge of the garden, we pile them against the door to keep it shut.

Inside the croft, I notice Andrea double-checking the doors are locked and watch as she goes around closing all the curtains. The fire has died down and she pops another log on the dancing flames. 'We need to see if we can get that radio working,' she says.

Zoe has put the radio on the chest in the middle of the living room and hurries upstairs to fetch the instructions.

'I'm going to nip to the loo,' I say. 'Why don't you put the kettle on.'

'Kettle be buggered,' says Andrea, standing up and walking out of the room. 'I'm having something stronger than tea.'

I head upstairs to the sound of glasses being picked out of the cupboard and guess Andrea is pouring us all a vodka. It doesn't seem like a bad idea. I'm not sure how I'm going to sleep tonight. I can't stop thinking about Joanne's wide-open eyes staring up at me and the weight of her body in the duvet as we hauled her into the shed.

As I open the bathroom door, I glance across the stairwell towards Joanne's room. The door is half-open but I can't see in. Hopefully, Zoe has found the radio instructions and within a few hours the police will be here. Morning at the latest.

When I come out of the bathroom, I take the opportunity to change out of my damp clothes and pull on a fresh T-shirt and jogging-bottoms, along with a zip-up hoody. My bed looks so inviting, I could sink into it right now. My arms and legs feel heavy but I know if I were to lie down now, I wouldn't be able to get up again. All that abseiling, kayaking and lifting Joanne, has taken its toll; my limbs ache and my back protests every time I lean forward.

My mind, however, has other ideas and even if I did rest my weary body, I know my brain will be jumping all over the place and I won't get any sleep. I consider taking one of my pills, but find myself hankering after something stronger. Maybe the vodka will help me sleep later. I need something to keep the awful images of Joanne at bay. I can't allow myself to visit these thoughts, as I know I'll go to pieces.

In the living room, I take the vodka that Andrea offers and sit down on the sofa beside her. The radio-set is in front of us. 'It's a CB radio,' I say. There is a dial on the right-hand side of the face, bigger than the others with a square screen above it. There is an array of dials and switches, many of them labelled: dimmer, MIC gain, volume and talk back. On the left is another, smaller screen with a dial and a needle. On the side is a coiled cable, like the old-fashioned telephone wires, with a square handset attached to the other end.

'I don't suppose you know how one of these works?' asks Andrea.

'Nope. The only thing I know is you say "breaker-breaker".' It's a feeble attempt at humour, one which neither of us finds amusing.

'What's taking Zoe so long?' asks Andrea, giving the hallway a glance before returning her attention to the CB. She reaches around the back and picks up two long black cables. One has a connection at the end not dissimilar to a phone charger for a car and the other has a normal plug. 'I guess this must plug in somewhere.'

'Maybe in the kitchen?' I suggest.

We take the CB radio through to the kitchen and look around for a socket.

'Over there,' says Andrea, pointing to the skirting board near the door where a phone socket and a regular power point are. 'Here, pass me the wire.'

I place the set on the worktop and Andrea stretches the wires across the kitchen to the sockets. I switch the power dial on and a little red light glows as the sound of static fills the room. 'Looks like we have power,' I say, smiling for the first time this afternoon.

'Don't get too excited,' says Zoe, standing in the doorway of the kitchen. She holds out her empty hands. 'I can't find those instructions anywhere. They're gone.'

'What do you mean, gone?' asks Andrea, standing up.

I note the look of tension on Zoe's face. 'Exactly what I say. They're not there. Gone. Vanished.'

'They can't have vanished.' Andrea turns the volume down and the static crackle fades out.

Zoe places her hands on her hips and looks directly at Andrea. 'Well, I'm telling you they have.'

The tension in the room fizzes like a broken electrical cable flipping wildly from side to side. We all stand there looking at each other and, I suspect, wondering the same thing. Which one of us has moved the instructions, and why?

Andrea speaks first. 'Are you absolutely sure that what you saw earlier were the instructions for the CB?'

'Pretty sure. I didn't read them in detail, I only skimmed a few pages. But whatever it was I saw, it's now gone.'

'You definitely didn't move them earlier?' I ask.

'No. I was fascinated with the notebook and its contents. I didn't even take the instructions out of the drawer.'

'Then one of us must have,' I say, although in reality, I acknowledge that it can only be Andrea who has moved them. Zoe wouldn't say they were there and then pretend she couldn't find them if she didn't want us to see them. I certainly haven't moved them, so logically, Andrea has.

'Oh, this is ridiculous,' says Andrea. 'You must have scooped them up by mistake. Not realised. Anyway, we haven't got time to debate this. Our priority is to get this radio working.' She turns her attention to the rig. 'It can't be that difficult.' She switches it on again and, as before, the sound of a million twigs being snapped swamps the room.

'Try turning this dial here,' I suggest. 'It looks like a tuner. There must be different wavelengths to choose from.'

Andrea picks up the microphone and clicks the dial. The number sixteen appears in the red digital LED display. 'Push that button down on the side.' I point at the handset Andrea is grasping. 'Say something.'

'Hello? Anybody there?' says Andrea. She gives a shrug. 'I've no clue what you're supposed to say.' She releases the button but all that comes back across the airwaves is more static.

'Try the next station,' says Zoe.

Andrea clicks the tuner round to the next wavelength and repeats the process. We get the same result as before.

'We must be doing something wrong,' I say, frustrated. 'Perhaps we just have to keep trying different stations.'

'How do we even know this bloody thing is working?' asks Andrea. 'Surely, if we were getting a signal we wouldn't hear all that crackling. It can't be any different to when you're trying to tune in a car radio.'

'Maybe it's the aerial,' I suggest. 'Isn't it out there, fixed to the back of the house?'

'Don't say we've got to go outside again,' says Andrea, making a big huffing noise. 'It's dark now. You won't be able to see a thing.'

'I like the way you automatically assume it's me that's going out,' I retort. 'And don't be so negative anyway. Doing nothing won't get us any help.' I'm aware my frustration has broken free but at the same time, I don't care. What we need right now is positivity. I ignore the raised eyebrows of Andrea and continue: 'If you both stand by the door with the curtains open to throw some light out there, I'll take the torch and trace the wire up the wall. If it's come out of the aerial, I might be able to poke it in.'

Andrea and Zoe don't look particularly convinced. 'You're going to just poke it in?' says Andrea.

'Have you got a better idea?' I snap.

As I step outside, not only is it dark, but the building is surrounded by the mist. Or does it qualify as fog now? I idly wonder what the difference between the two might be.

Andrea and Zoe are standing side by side in the outer porch while I trace the wire from its exit point, up the outside wall, across the porch roof and down the other side, where it then runs along the bottom of the wall to the end of the extension. The aerial is attached by two brackets just below the roof. I follow the wire halfway up the wall to the last clip, where it then hangs limply over.

'It's broken here,' I call through the mist. Or fog. Whatever the correct name for it is. I aim the torch beam at the end of the wire. It is a clean sharp end, there are no frayed or broken pieces of wire where it might have gradually worked its way loose. No, this end has been cut.

I have a flashback to the abseiling rope. That too had a clean neat end. Both the rope and the wire have been cut intentionally.

Chapter 18

'It's broken,' I say, as we all squeeze through the doorway. I lock the door behind us, leaving the key in the lock. Then I change my mind and place the key on the worktop near the kettle.

'Can you fix it?' asks Andrea.

In the few seconds it takes for me to come inside, I debate whether to tell them the truth about the wire. Something inside my head is urging caution but in the end I dismiss the notion, the crazy notion that it could be one of them sabotaging the radio because that would mean one of them didn't want the police coming. And the only reason they wouldn't want the police involved at this stage is because they were responsible for killing Joanne. However, I then find myself arguing that, sooner or later, the police are going to get involved, so what could they have to gain by delaying the inevitable? And it's this thought that bothers me. Is something else about to happen?

I realise I must have hesitated a fraction too long. Andrea is pressing me for an answer.

'Broken? How would that happen?' she asks.

I let out a sigh, dismayed by my own wild imagination. These are my friends. Neither Andrea nor Zoe would do anything like this on purpose. No. I'm letting myself get carried away.

'Come on, spit it out,' says Zoe. 'What's happened to the cable?'

'It's been cut,' I say. 'On purpose.'

They both look incredulously at me as they take in what I've said. 'Cut? You're sure about that?' asks Andrea eventually.

'Certain.'

'What the fuck is going on around here?' Andrea runs her fingers through her hair.

'What are we going to do?' says Zoe. There is a touch of hysteria in her voice, her eyes widen with every word. 'I want to get out of here.'

'And how exactly do you plan to do that?' says Andrea, impatience rising to the surface.

'Can't we walk out of here together? Right now?'

'That's the worst idea,' I say. 'Look, let's all sit down and think this through rationally.' I usher Zoe into the living room, grabbing a bottle of lemonade as I go. Andrea follows but has different ideas about the choice of drink and immediately pours out three vodkas.

We perch on the edge of our seats; I'm sitting next to Zoe, while Andrea positions herself opposite.

'So, what's your masterplan?' she asks, pushing the vodka glasses to each of us.

'I wouldn't call it a masterplan. I think we should stay here the night. It's safer indoors than out,' I say, topping my glass up with lemonade. 'Out there, we have no idea where we're going, what sort of terrain it is. Visibility is poor. We could easily stumble and hurt ourselves, or worse, fall down an embankment or go hideously off course.'

'I don't like it here,' says Zoe.

'Neither do I, but we haven't got a choice. The doors are all locked. No one can get in or out. We only need to get through the night and as soon as it's light, we can set off.'

'You're not actually making me feel better by saying no one can get in.' Zoe pouts and takes a swig of her vodka.

'I was trying to make you feel better,' I say with a smile. 'Sorry it didn't work.'

'Do you think there is someone out there who wants to harm us?' asks Zoe.

'If there is, I can't think why. Besides, they've had plenty of opportunities to bump us all off, and they haven't.'

'Don't be so flippant,' snaps Zoe.

Andrea leans forward, swirling the clear liquid around in her glass. 'I don't buy it. I don't believe there's someone out there.' She looks up from under her eyelashes.

'You think it's one of us?' Zoe flings herself back in the sofa.

'Stop it,' I say. 'We're going round in circles. I'm sure what Andrea means is that Joanne's death was an accident and we're all getting worked up for no reason.' I purposefully look at Andrea, willing her to agree, if only to calm Zoe down.

'Of course that's what I mean,' says Andrea. 'Look, I'm as gutted and upset about Joanne as anyone, but I'm sure it happened exactly the way Carys says.'

'How do you explain the cut wire then?' says Zoe.

'Simple,' replies Andrea. 'It was probably broken or cut before we even got here. The owners knew about it and that's why the radio was in the shed: so no one would think it worked and try to use it.'

It's a logical explanation and I'm inclined to agree with Andrea. Zoe doesn't seem quite so reassured. 'What about our phones?'

'That's Joanne's joke. She must have hidden them. Shame we can't find them,' says Andrea.

'OK, so first thing in the morning, we're out of here,' says Zoe. 'Agreed?'

Both Andrea and I agree.

We sit in silence for a moment, lost in our own thoughts, and as I allow my gaze to rest on the log basket, I realise it's empty.

'I suppose I'd better fetch some more logs,' I say, getting up. Much as I would like to leave it, I remember Joanne saying the hot water was heated by the fire.

'Do you want me to come with you?' Andrea offers, but I can tell from her tone of voice she isn't enthusiastic.

'No, it's OK. The logs are only out by the back door.' I sound rather more casual than I feel but putting on a brave face, I rise and take the empty log basket with me. I head out to the kitchen, stopping in the hallway to slip my feet into a pair of wellington boots by the door.

Armed with the torch, I venture outside. It's pitch-black now, apart from the lonely beam of light coming from the torch. The logs are neatly stacked against the wall of the croft under a little pitched roof about three feet high.

I can just about make out the shape of the shed through the darkness and have a fleeting moment of nausea as I think of Joanne's body lying in the cold damp building.

Suddenly I have a distinct sensation that I'm not alone. Under the thickness of my jumper and fleece, I can feel goose-bumps prick my arms and spread across the back of my neck. I spin around. Something is close to me. I can't see anything.

I can hear my own breathing quicken and recognise the signs: I'm on the verge of a panic attack. One where everything around me starts to close in. Where I feel compressed by empty spaces. Where the air around me is sucked away, leaving a void of nothingness.

Shit. I don't think I can ward it off. I can hear myself humming out loud. I can't identify the tune but think it's an old school hymn. I snatch a couple of logs from under the wooden shelter, constantly glancing over my shoulder.

I'm singing out loud now. It's 'Jerusalem'. We used to sing it every morning in school assembly. Funny how these things stay with you. I don't consider myself particularly religious, despite a Church of England education, but when I feel most afraid I find myself digging into some deeply instilled idea there is a God out there and if I sing loud enough, he will protect me.

I throw the third log without looking. It misses the basket and bounces off the rim, on to my foot. I can't focus on the pain. All I can do is concentrate on keeping the urge to flee at bay long enough to allow me to get inside and lock the bloody door.

I hurtle into the kitchen, dropping the basket on to the

tiled floor. I slam the door shut and lock it, then snatch the key out. Panting for breath, I lean against the worktop.

'You OK?'

Zoe's voice makes me jump. I feel embarrassed at my over-reaction. 'Yeah, sure. Just didn't want to hang around out there. It's cold.' I rub my arms as if to prove my point. Leaving the key by the kettle, I carry the logs into the living room, Zoe following behind with the dossier Joanne complied under her arm.

'I made you a hot chocolate,' says Zoe, sitting down on the sofa. 'I've got one too, but Andrea declined.' She gives a disapproving school-teacher look to Andrea.

'I aim to sleep like the proverbial log tonight,' says Andrea.

'I don't know how you can say that. I won't be able to sleep at all, not after everything that's happened,' says Zoe. She takes a sip of her hot chocolate and then, placing it on the chest, flicks the edge of the incriminating notebook she has brought in with her.

I sit down and pick up my drink. 'Thanks for this. I'll probably go to bed quite soon.' I suddenly feel exhausted. It's been a long and difficult day, not only physically but mentally as well. My head is so full of thoughts and feelings, I'm not sure I have room for much else tonight.

'Do you think Joanne hated us?' asks Andrea. She's resting in the deep folds of the corduroy sofa. 'I mean, to have arranged all this, gone to all this trouble, she couldn't have liked us, could she?'

'I was thinking that myself,' admits Zoe. 'I'd thought this weekend was all about us bonding. I thought Joanne had missed us all being so close and this was her way of saying sorry for being paranoid.'

'But was she paranoid?' says Andrea. She has the look of the devil in her eyes. She swirls the liquid around in her glass before downing the last drop. 'She must genuinely think I swindled her out of the gym. Whether it's true or not doesn't matter. What counts is what Joanne believed.'

'And the point of all this?' I ask, rather impatiently. I don't want to go down this route again.

'I'm still working out who has the most to lose from Joanne revealing our secrets,' says Andrea.

I can feel my impatience turning into annoyance. 'I thought we agreed we'd stop this speculation. You've had too much to drink, it's late, we're all spun out by what's happened and we should all go to bed,' I say. 'Sitting here picking over the details of what Joanne may or may not have against each of us, isn't actually going to help in getting us out of here in the morning. Sleep, however, will.'

I plonk my cup down on the coffee table and a slop of hot chocolate hits the floor. I mutter several unnecessary swear words as I get up and fetch some kitchen roll to clean it up.

'I think we should be honest, that's all,' Andrea calls after me. I ignore her and take my time finding the kitchen roll before coming into the room. As I wipe the hot chocolate from the floor, Andrea leans forwards. 'Just between us, what exactly did happen between Darren and Ruby?'

'Give it a rest, Andrea,' I say.

'And what about you, Zoe? You never confirmed nor denied you're having an affair with Tris.'

'Like Carys said, give it a rest.'

'Ooh, getting touchy, are we? Well, seeing as we're all stuck here for the night, I'm going to tell you the truth about me and Joanne and what went on about buying the gym. Then it will be your turn to confess all.'

'I'm not playing this game,' I say, screwing up the kitchen roll and tossing it into the hearth.

'It's not a fucking game,' says Andrea, her eyes boring into mine. 'Not when one of us has ended up dead. So, I suggest we all stop being so secretive and tell the truth.'

'Go on then,' I say, even though I have no intention whatsoever of telling the truth.

Andrea waits for me to resume my position next to Zoe and then begins. 'When the gym came up for sale, Joanne and I talked about buying it together as a joint venture. Unfortunately, she couldn't raise the funds. She asked Tris about getting a loan against the house, but he was reluctant to do so and he didn't want to take any money from his business. Anyway, while they were trying to work out what to do, aka arguing about it, the owner was putting pressure on us to close the deal. He was threatening to take up someone else's offer. I told Joanne I couldn't wait any longer and I didn't want to miss out. She asked if I would buy it outright and then sell half back to her, which she would pay using a bank loan.'

'But I'm guessing that never happened,' I say.

'No. To be honest, I didn't feel comfortable with it. If Joanne defaulted on the payments, then I would be out of pocket. She and Tris had some awful rows about it. And . . .' she pauses. 'Well, put it this way, I wasn't one hundred per cent sure their marriage was very stable.' She looks at Zoe, who shifts in her seat. 'If their marriage went tits up, then I could get stung for the repayments. Joanne might not have any money, Tris might not continue with the payments. No, it was too big a risk. So I went ahead and did the deal on my own.'

'But surely, if you could afford it on your own, you would have been able to cover any payments Joanne might miss,' says Zoe.

'Yeah, but what if Joanne didn't tell me she'd missed payments, what if the debt collectors came in? As a joint venture, we'd both be equally responsible and, much as I loved Joanne, I wasn't taking on her debts and getting stung for interest. Or she might sell her share of the business without me knowing. No, it was too risky.'

'Wow. You really are the hard-nosed businesswoman,' I say. 'When you and Joanne discussed this, was it amicable?'

'Fuck was it!' scoffs Andrea. 'She came round the house to talk to me about it and it descended into a slanging match.'

'I still don't understand what Joanne thought she had on you,' says Zoe. 'You're telling us all this, but it's no big deal.' Zoe picks up the notebook and flicks to the page about Andrea. 'Joanne thinks you committed fraud.'

'It's bullshit. Joanne wanted to humiliate me. To get some sort of personal satisfaction from making me feel uncomfortable. Perhaps she was going to tell us what she thought of us and then fuck off and leave us here. So maybe what happened to her was karma.'

I shoot Andrea a look. She's knocking back the vodka way too fast now and her sharp tongue is going freelance.

'That's out of order,' says Zoe.

'I don't care,' says Andrea. 'Anyway, when we speak to the police about this, they'll see I have nothing to hide and that I had nothing to gain from seeing her dead.' Andrea gives me a smile of satisfaction. 'Can either of you say that?'

'I've no reason to harm her,' I say. 'As in your case, Joanne was making something out of nothing.'

'You're not being straight,' says Andrea. 'Why would Joanne randomly suggest there was something going on with Darren and Ruby? It has to have come from somewhere. Is it linked with Darren's death?'

The simmering anger inside of me erupts. 'Give it a rest!' I shout, louder than I intend. 'Who the hell knows what was going on in Joanne's mind?' I pause, close my eyes for a moment while I rein in my temper. When I speak, my voice is under control. 'Like you said, she was making something out of nothing.'

'Keep calm, I was only thinking out loud,' says Andrea.

'Well don't.'

Andrea turns her attention to Zoe. 'It would be unfair of me not to ask you,' she says. 'But there's no smoke without fire. Why did Joanne think you were having an affair with Tris? Is it still going on? Or was it only a one-night stand? Perhaps it's you who has most to lose by this coming out.'

Zoe jumps to her feet, her half-drunk hot chocolate suffering a worse fate than mine and spilling all over the floor. 'You, Andrea, need to know when to shut the fuck up,' she hisses. She snatches at the kitchen roll and tears several sheets off to soak up the spillage.

'Another touchy one,' says Andrea.

Zoe finishes mopping and stands up. 'I'm going to bed. When you're sober in the morning, you can apologise for being a drunken, shit-stirring bitch.' With that, she stomps out of the room and up the stairs. Her feet are heavy on the floorboards above. The little croft almost shakes as she slams her bedroom door shut.

I look at Andrea and shake my head.

'What?' she says with mock innocence. 'Just getting to the truth.'

I rise. 'She's right, you are a shit-stirrer at times. I'm going to bed. Sober up and I'll see you in the morning.' I leave the room to the sound of Andrea giggling to herself.

So, Joanne is dead. It's not looking like a great weekend, is it? And you know what? It's not going to get any better. Oh no. I'm going to make sure of that.

I bet you're lying in bed wondering what happened to your friend. Was it an accident? Did she slip? Or did she have a delayed reaction to you pushing her?

I use the word 'friend' with a degree of artistic licence. You were never a good friend to her. You let her down when she needed you most, but that does seem to be a particular habit of yours. Always thinking of yourself and not of others. I'm not the only one to see through your pretence. I can see your true colours.

I can't wait for this all to come out in the open. Once the police start investigating Joanne's death, it won't be long before they come looking for you. I'll see to it that they'll have help, point them in the right direction. I won't have to say much, just enough to give them the heads-up. I'll drop in things like the tablets you secretly take, the ones I've seen in your bag. Those beta-blockers which you clearly haven't got on prescription.

I'll also mention your increasing paranoia and how bad it's

been getting. *The police will only have to look at how you've behaved this weekend to work that one out for themselves. The food tampering allegation was only the start. Now that Joanne's dead, I expect your behaviour is going to become a lot more erratic.*

I bet you wish you hadn't accepted the invitation. I can't say I feel sorry for you. You don't deserve to be happy after what you've done. I, on the other hand, am going to be extremely happy.

SUNDAY

Chapter 19

On the landing, I tap on Zoe's door. 'You all right?' I call gently.

Zoe opens the door and although she's not crying, I notice her eyes are red-rimmed and she's holding a scrunched-up tissue in her hand. I give a sympathetic smile. 'Ignore Andrea. You know what she's like. Gobby. Especially after alcohol.'

'It's OK. I should be used to her by now, but sometimes she pisses me off.'

'Try to get some sleep. It's late. As soon as it's light in the morning, we'll get out of here. I think what happened to Joanne is getting to us all.' I give Zoe a hug and we say our goodnights.

The floorboards creak as I make my way across the landing into my own room. It's hard to take in everything that has happened. I can't wait to get away from this place. I have a sudden overwhelming yearning for Seb. He told me he loved me last week. I'd felt embarrassed for some reason. I had wanted to tell him that I loved him too but hadn't been able to bring myself to say it. For some reason, I'd had a pang of guilt. Not guilt for Darren; no, I'd stopped loving him as a wife a long time ago. The guilt was towards Alfie. I'm in love with a man who isn't his father. A man who my son hasn't exactly welcomed into our lives with open arms. If I tell Seb I love him, then it will mean our relationship has officially taken on a new meaning at a deeper level. I'm scared of the implications. How the dynamics will change and, ultimately, the impact it will have on my already difficult relationship with Alfie.

Tonight, however, I have no such feelings of guilt. At a time when I feel scared and lonely, it's Seb who I want to hold me and to tell me everything will be OK. At this moment, I don't care what Alfie thinks; he'll be an adult soon and, as Andrea says, off to university. I don't want to waste any more time not loving and not being loved. I make up my mind to tell Seb how much I love him the very next time I see or speak to him, whichever is first. Who knows where that might lead? If anything has come out of Joanne's death, it is the realisation that time and life are precious and not to be wasted.

I gaze out of the window into the night, onyx shadows against a dappled background making for some strange and indistinguishable shapes. Nothing looks the same as it does in daylight. The wind has picked up and the shapes morph from one distorted arrangement to another.

Again, I have that feeling of not being alone, of being watched. Something out there is dangerous and hostile. I can sense it. I don't know what it is, but my blood runs cold. I snap the curtains shut and climb into bed. I'm over-tired and my senses are on high alert. I need to relax and go to sleep.

I eye the pocket of my rucksack where the little white pills rest. One won't hurt. I need something to take the edge off my nerves, something to help me relax. Ironically, my heart beats a little faster at the prospect and without giving it any further consideration, I slice the foil with my fingernail and pop the tablet into my mouth, swallowing it down without the aid of water.

I pull the duvet up to my chin. I close my eyes and begin the relaxation methods I have learned. Breathe in. Breathe out. I think about each part of my body, the function it performs, letting each muscle relax, right from my neck to my toes, one by one. I concentrate on the here and now, not letting my mind wander to all the fears and worries around me. I bring my thoughts back when I feel them drifting into dangerous territory.

It's beginning to work. I can feel myself easing into the early stages of sleep. And then Andrea bowls in through the door like a SWAT team. The door hits the stopper and bounces against Andrea's foot.

'Shit! Sorry,' she hisses. Andrea is trying to whisper but making a lousy job of it. I keep my eyes closed in the hope she will think I'm still asleep. Wrong. 'Carys. Carys, are you awake?'

I can hear her footsteps travel between our two beds. I open my eyes. 'No, I'm not asleep. What is it?'

'I want to talk to you.'

'Can't it wait until the morning?'

'No. It can't. Please, Carys.'

'It had better be worth it,' I say, sitting up. The quicker we get this conversation over with, the quicker I can go to sleep.

'Do you believe Zoe?' Andrea rocks slightly on the edge of her bed.

'About what?'

'About not having an affair with a married man and that married man not being Tris.'

'I don't know. I can't think straight this evening,' I confess. 'And you can't either. Whether Zoe's telling the truth or not isn't that important, not in the scheme of things.'

'Of course it is! She's lying and I know it. Her and Tris are definitely having an affair.'

'But you've no proof. I'm sure Tris wouldn't be unfaithful to Joanne anyway. Not with her friend. And Zoe wouldn't do that to Joanne.' I lie back down, wishing I'd never engaged in this conversation. 'Go to sleep.'

'I wouldn't put it past Tris. I told you what a randy bugger he was that Christmas, remember?'

'Maybe he's been flirting with Zoe and Joanne has got the wrong end of the stick,' I say in an attempt to placate Andrea.

'I don't think so.'

I'm about to defend Tris and Zoe, but I stop before I speak. What if there is some truth in it? The last thing I want is to admit to Andrea that she might be right, because if I do, then that means I also have to admit to her that there's some truth in what happened between Darren and Ruby. I choose my next words carefully. 'I honestly think it's Joanne getting everything out of proportion. Like she has with you and the gym, and the way she said I killed Darren. We both know that's ridiculous. Maybe Tris and Zoe flirted a couple of times and Joanne saw them and read more into it.'

'It's possible,' says Andrea. She rubs her forehead with her fingers. 'I'm so tired. I probably shouldn't have had that last vodka.'

'Shouldn't have had the last *three* vodkas, more like.'

She stands and wobbles slightly on her feet. 'You know Tris would never leave Joanne, even if he was having an affair with Zoe.'

'Shh, keep your voice down.' I glance towards the door, which is slightly ajar, and hope Zoe is fast asleep. 'No, I don't think he would either. They've been together a long time.'

'You know as well as I do, that doesn't mean anything.' Andrea gives me a look. 'But you're right, Tris wouldn't leave Joanne. Because, no matter what his feelings are for Zoe, his feelings for money are stronger.'

'What do you mean?'

'It's surprising what you hear at the gym,' says Andrea, whose speech is remarkably coherent, considering her earlier vodka intake. She plonks herself down on the end of my bed and leans over. 'I heard two guys from the bank talking. They were in the coffee bar and I was in my office, but had the little fanlight open above my desk which happens to open right above where these guys were talking. Anyway, one of them was saying how much debt Tris was in with the bank and the other was saying how much money Joanne had. Obviously not enough to buy the gym with me, but a fair sum. They said that Tris would have to persuade Joanne to bail him out.'

'So, why didn't Tris ask her to help him? Surely she would?'

'I wouldn't be at all surprised if Joanne was making him

sweat on it. It's the sort of thing she'd do purely for the sadistic pleasure she'd get from it.'

'I don't know what to think,' I say with a sigh.

'What if Tris was only staying with Joanne because leaving her would be too expensive? What if he and Zoe are having an affair? What if Zoe loves him but he doesn't love her enough to leave the security of his family?'

'Andrea, stop. You're rambling. You've had too much to drink,' I say. 'I've honestly had enough of all this. You need some sleep. We all do.' I pull the duvet up and snuggle down. 'Go to bed.'

Andrea makes a few protests, accusing me of being a misery. While she fumbles around getting ready for bed, I can hear her muttering to herself. I can't understand what she's saying but I can hear Zoe's name being mentioned every now and then and it's clear whatever is being said isn't favourable.

Andrea makes it successfully to bed and after about ten minutes her breathing regulates and deepens as she finally succumbs to sleep. I, on the other hand, am now wide awake. Despite Andrea being worse for wear, her accusations fill my head. Is she right about Tris and Zoe? Has Tris got money worries? Is that why he stayed with Joanne?'

Inevitably, my mind turns to Darren and Ruby. I always thought Joanne believed Darren's version of events, just as I had. Now I wonder if I'd got that wrong. What had happened to make her think differently?

I have no answers. Nothing makes sense.

My mind makes the jump from Darren and Ruby to Alfie. It's a never-ending loop. One always leads to the other. Not always in the same order, but always those three. I think of how much Alfie has gone through.

Did it all start with Ruby? Were our lives destined to play out the way they have right from the start, all those years ago when I first met Joanne, when she and Tris had got married and Darren and I were dating? We'd met through the hiking club Joanne and I were members of. If I hadn't joined, I would never have met Joanne. Would that have meant that none of the trouble with Ruby would have happened? Would Alfie still be the confident, happy-go-lucky teenager I always thought he was?

How far would I have to turn the clock back to stop the chain of events?

And now, after all that, after everything that has happened between our two families, Alfie is finding comfort in the Aldridge household. That hurts. I'm his mother and I want to be the one to comfort him, the one he turns to when things get too hard. Alfie and I have a shared tragedy and yet he doesn't want me. Every day I feel he's moving further and further away from me.

Tears prick my eyes. This is no good. I can't cope with these thoughts at the best of times. Thinking about the disintegration of my relationship with my only child in the middle of the night, stuck in a croft, God knows where, while Joanne lies dead, wrapped in a duvet in the shed, is not a good idea.

I skulk my way round the end of the bed, grabbing my jumper on the way, and slip out of the room. I pause on the landing to pull my jumper over my head and wish I'd grabbed a pair of socks but don't want to go back in and risk waking Andrea.

It's then I realise I can hear a voice coming from downstairs. It's only a low murmur, but definitely someone speaking. Zoe must be downstairs. Who the hell is she talking to? Maybe she's found the phones.

Excited by this prospect, I take the stairs light-footedly and head for the kitchen. When I reach the dining room I see that the door to the kitchen is closed. The handle squeaks as I pull on it.

Zoe jumps and lets out a squeal. 'Oh God, Carys!' she gasps, her hand flying to her throat. 'You scared the life out of me.'

'Sorry, I was coming down for a glass of water. Who were you talking to?' It's then I notice Zoe is holding something in her other hand which she is shielding with her leg.

'I . . . er . . . I found this,' she says, holding out her hand. 'It's a walkie-talkie.'

'Where did you find that?' I move swiftly to her side and take the handset. 'Does it work? Have you been able to speak to anyone?'

'No. I don't even know if it's working.'

The hope that was rising within me dies instantly. 'Where was it?'

'At the back of the pantry. I couldn't sleep after the things Andrea said, so I thought I might as well get up and have another look for the phones.'

'You haven't found them?'

'No. Only this. I had a go at twiddling with the knob there

to tune it in, or whatever you do with a walkie-talkie, but it's stuck.'

I try to move the dial but it won't budge. 'What were you doing then, just holding the button and speaking?'

Zoe nods. 'Yeah, I didn't know what else to do.'

I depress the button on the side and hold it down. I put the handset to my mouth. 'Hello? Hello? Can anybody hear me?'

'Release the button now,' says Zoe.

We wait for a reply but can only hear static. 'What is it with the bloody radios around here?' I say in frustration. 'First the CB won't work and now this.'

'I suppose there has to be someone on the other end to hear us. I don't even know how far this thing works.' Zoe runs her hand through her hair. 'I want to go home. I wish we'd never come.'

'Hey, hey, don't be upsetting yourself,' I say, putting an arm around her shoulder. 'Hang in there for a few more hours. As soon as it's light, we're getting out of here. I promise.'

'You sound like some sort of action hero.'

'Let's give this thing another go,' I say, hoping I sound upbeat. 'Hello? Can anybody hear me? We need help. It's an emergency.' I stop speaking and look at Zoe. She motions for me to try again. 'This is an emergency. Is there anyone there?' I release the button and we both lean closer to the handset. Suddenly, the crackle is disrupted and we hear a voice speaking to us.

'Hello. This is the park ranger station. We can hear you. Can you hear us? Over.'

We both give a squeal of excitement. 'Hello. We can hear you. Over.'

'Is everything all right?' The Scottish accent is distinguishable, despite the transmission breaking up slightly.

'No! We're on holiday. Staying in a holiday home. There's been an accident. We need help. We need the police. Over.' I don't know how much to say over the airwaves. The relief is flooding through me. We are speaking to someone. We are not alone.

'Are your injuries serious? Over.'

I look at Zoe before replying. 'Yes. Someone has . . . has died. Over.'

'Can you repeat that, please? Over.'

'Our friend has had an accident and she's dead.' I can feel a lump in my throat. 'Please can you send someone to help us. We're stuck in this croft and need help. Over.' My voice breaks at this point as the emotion and enormity of what has happened suddenly seem much more real now that I'm saying the words to someone else.

'How many of you are there? Over.'

'Three. Over.'

'And are you safe? Is anyone else injured? Over.'

'We're safe. No other injuries. Over.'

'OK. I'll contact the police as soon as I can. They will send someone out to you. You need to stay where you are until then. Over.'

'What time will that be? Over.' I grasp Zoe's hand and nod. Everything is going to be all right.

'I can't say exactly. But someone will be with you as soon as they can. Over.'

My initial excitement is dulled. I want someone out here now. 'You did hear me, that there's been a death? Over.'

'Aye, I did. I'm sure the police will make this a priority,' he replies. 'Now, I don't want to scare you, but you need to make sure all the doors are locked. There's been a few break-ins of holiday homes recently. Lock the doors and stay inside. Do you understand? Over.'

'Understood. Over.' I don't bother to explain that's exactly what we have done.

'Good. I'll keep you up to date. As soon as I hear anything, I'll be in touch. Keep the radio with you. Understood? Over.'

'Understood. Over.'

'OK. Don't worry, help is on the way. Over and out.'

The crackling sound is back and the ranger has gone.

'Thank God for that,' says Zoe. 'You don't know how happy I am. I could bloody cry.'

'I wonder if this is the walkie-talkie Joanne had on the walk. Maybe she hid it in the pantry for some reason. What luck, you finding this.'

Zoe takes the handset and turns it in her hand. 'It must be set to this channel on purpose. It must be the emergency channel to the park ranger. I reckon it has to be the one Joanne said she had.' She slips the walkie-talkie into her pocket. 'I'll take it up with me in case he calls us.'

'Perhaps now I'll be able to sleep,' I say, taking a glass and filling it from the tap. 'You should try to get some sleep too. Hopefully, we won't have to wait long before help arrives.'

We make our way upstairs and say goodnight to each other on the landing.

Andrea is still fast asleep when I enter the bedroom. She doesn't look like she's moved. I pause to check her breathing and, satisfied she's OK, I climb into my bed.

As I rest my head on the pillow and replay the conversation with the ranger in my mind, I feel I am missing something but can't think what. My mind wanders into an uneasy sleep, one where I wake several times and, without making a conscious effort, recall the conversation again. Still I can't work out what is bothering me.

Chapter 20

The remainder of the night stretches into a pattern of waking, thinking and drifting into a half-sleep as I monitor the digital display on the bedside clock. At six, I give in and decide to get up. Andrea hasn't stirred at all in the night despite my tossing and turning. The weather has taken a turn and in the early hours of the morning I could hear the wind pick up and rain splatter against the window panes.

In the kitchen I flick the kettle on to boil. The rain is steady and I wonder how long we will have to wait before the police turn up. Will they believe what's happened? What will they make of the notebook and its contents? I don't want them digging up the past and asking awkward questions. Maybe for all our sakes it would be best if they didn't know about the notebook.

'Morning.' Andrea shuffles into the room. She comes over and gives me a hug. 'I was hoping yesterday was a bad dream.'

'Me too.' I return the hug and fight to stop myself welling up. 'You're up early,' I say, pulling away from the hug. 'You want a cup of tea or coffee?'

'That would be great, thanks.' Andrea sits down at the table in the dining room. 'I feel like I drank a bottle of vodka last night.'

'Very nearly. You were knocking it back,' I reply, taking two cups from the cupboard. 'While you were playing Sleeping Beauty, Zoe and I managed to make contact with the outside world.'

Andrea frowns and rubs her eyes with the heels of her hands. 'What?'

'Zoe found a walkie-talkie and we managed to speak to the park ranger. He's putting a call in to the police.' The kettle rumbles to a boil and I make the drinks.

'Run that by me again.'

'Zoe found a walkie-talkie in the pantry and we managed to get it working. Help is on its way as we speak.' I pass the coffee cup to Andrea.

'Did you tell them about Joanne?'

'Yes, but I didn't go into detail, just that there had been a fatal accident. I wanted them to know that the call was serious and we need help ASAP.'

'What did they say?'

'He told us to sit tight and wait for the police. I was hoping they'd have turned up by now.'

'Thank goodness for that. I didn't fancy hiking out in this weather. And that's not simply because of the hangover,' says Andrea.

A clatter on the stairs and a cry of pain, followed by a distinct thud, cuts through our conversation. We both race from the kitchen, through the dining room and into the hall.

Zoe is on the floor, her left ankle clasped between her two hands. 'Aghhh, my ankle!' she cries, scrunching her eyes tight shut but unable to prevent a few tears escaping.

'Oh my God, Zoe! Are you OK?' I drop to my knees beside her.

'I fell down the stairs,' she says. 'I've twisted my ankle. It's killing me.'

'Let me have a look,' I say, gently moving her hands away. I carry out a visual inspection of her bare ankle but can't see any obvious signs of injury. 'I need to run my hands down your leg and ankle. Where exactly does it hurt?'

'Here, under the bone,' she says, indicating with her finger.

As gently as I can, I check Zoe's ankle and foot with my hands. She winces when I apply pressure to the area under the ankle bone and when I gently rotate her foot. 'On a scale of one to ten, how painful are we talking?' I ask.

'About seven,' she says. 'You don't think it's broken, do you? That's all we need.'

'No. Although, it's hard to say, I'm no expert. Andrea, grab a damp tea-towel and some ice. Then we need to get you in the living room, with your foot elevated. It will help reduce the swelling. What did you do, miss a step?'

'No. I fell over this.' Zoe reaches behind her. 'Your boot. It was on the third stair up. I didn't see it until the last minute and tried to avoid it.'

'What was it doing on the stair?'

'I guess that's where you left it.'

'I didn't. I mean, I wouldn't have.' I look round at the footwear lined up under the coat pegs. 'Look, there's my other one. Someone must have moved it. Andrea, did you notice my boot when you came down?'

Andrea shrugs. 'Can't say I did, but that doesn't mean it wasn't there. I'm not properly awake yet.' She rubs her head with her fingertips. 'Hanging a bit here this morning.'

'And it was definitely on the stair?' I ask Zoe.

'Let's not have an inquest now,' says Andrea as Zoe insists it was. 'Shall we get Zoe into the living room and I'll fetch the ice.'

I take the boot and put it with the other one, a little peeved that the blame seems to be heading my way for leaving the boot there. I definitely put it with the other one. I'm sure. At least, I think I'm sure.

We settle Zoe in the living room and I apply the makeshift ice-pack Andrea managed to put together. 'It doesn't look like it's swelling,' I say, inspecting it. 'Hopefully, it's only a slight sprain.'

'Good job it was only the last three steps,' says Zoe.

I'm about to protest my innocence about leaving the boot on the stairs when, once again, Andrea speaks first.

'Carys was telling me about the walkie-talkie you found last night and how she managed to speak to the park ranger,' she says. 'That was a stroke of luck.'

'I know. Thank goodness,' says Zoe. 'All I want is to go home. I don't think I can cope with anything else.'

We all make agreeing-type noises as we consider our predicament and the awful events.

'I'm going to light the fire,' I say, not wanting to dwell too heavily on Joanne's death. I need to keep busy. 'It's freezing this morning and it could be a few hours before the police arrive.' As I stand up and look across the hallway to the dining room, I notice Joanne's notebook on the table. 'You know the police are going to ask us lots of questions,' I say as I fetch the notebook.

'Mmm. That's their job,' says Andrea.

'I was thinking . . . it may muddy the waters if we start telling them all about this book and what Joanne thought of us.'

'Go on,' says Andrea.

'I don't particularly want the past raked up and I'm sure you two don't either. They don't need to see this.'

'But that's evidence,' says Zoe.

'No, it's not,' says Andrea. She puts her cup on the coffee table. 'It's only evidence if it is linked to Joanne's death and one of us killed her as a result of the contents of that book.'

'None of us killed her,' I say, looking directly at Zoe. 'Did we?'

She shakes her head. 'No, but . . .'

'If the police read this, they are going to automatically assume that one of us had a strong enough motive to kill Joanne. It will throw a tremendous amount of doubt over the truth, which is that Joanne's death was an accident,' I say.

'Do you want them to go into every little detail about your relationship with Tris?' asks Andrea. 'Yes, I know you said you're not having an affair with him and, quite frankly, right now I couldn't care less, but the police will consider it a strong motive.'

'She's right,' I say.

'What are you suggesting?' asks Zoe.

'That I burn the book,' I reply.

'And those stupid game cards she gave us,' says Andrea. 'And we don't mention the game or the book again.'

'OK,' says Zoe. She sounds hesitant but both Andrea and I reassure her that it's the best thing to do in the circumstances.

'I'll get the fire lit. You get the cards. I've got mine here with me,' I say.

As I set the fire, Andrea helps Zoe up the stairs so they can get dressed and retrieve the game cards.

When I go outside to fetch some logs, the rain has eased and the once gunmetal-grey clouds are now a softer opaque colour. Puddles have formed in the dips and mini rivers in the gullies as the water has found its own path.

I remember how frightened I was out here last night in the dark and note how different it feels in daylight. The threat of what I can't see has gone, but as I look up to the forest and see only the darkness within the trees, once again the unsettled feeling returns.

I turn my attention to the task in hand. As I stand in front of the log store, I notice something that I don't remember seeing before. Hanging on a hook is a climbing rope, like the one we used to abseil down the gorge yesterday. Leaving an expensive climbing rope exposed to the elements seems odd. As I pick a couple of logs from the pile, I look at the rope again. It's then I notice the end.

My heart misses a beat and I draw in a sharp breath that burns its way down to my lungs. My body is immobile. I close my eyes and open them again, hoping I'm imagining things.

I'm not.

The end of the rope has been fastened into a hangman's noose. Immediately, images of Darren flood my mind. I see myself opening the front door, laughing at something Alfie has said – I can't remember what. I push open the door and as I step into the hall, in my line of sight, Darren's feet dangle in mid-air. He's wearing his black lace-up work shoes and his dark-blue suit. My favourite one. My gaze travels over his body and, dear God, his face. His eyes. They are bloodshot and bulging.

I will never forget that sight. I remember screaming and trying to bundle Alfie out of the door, but it is too late. He has seen his father. And then, amongst the scuffling, Alfie is yelling at me to do something.

I don't remember running into the kitchen, but the next thing I'm aware of is that I have the bread knife in my hand. Alfie is grappling with Darren's legs, trying to lift him up to relieve the weight of his father's body on the rope. It is the saddest and most heartbreaking sight I have ever witnessed. He looks up at me, tears, panic and sheer desperation filling his eyes. I race up the stairs and frantically saw at the rope, calling to Alfie to get out of the way as Darren's body drops to the floor with a thud.

Now, here, at the back of the croft, as I look at the noose, my legs go numb and my knees want to buckle. I drop the log basket and reach out to grab the little roof of the log store to steady myself.

Why haven't I noticed this before? It can't be a coincidence. No one randomly ties a noose at the end of a rope, least of all a climbing rope.

I spit out the bile that rises from my stomach. Surely the rope isn't another of Joanne's games. She wouldn't be that cruel. Would she?

Anger replaces the fear and I grab the rope from the hook and dump it in the corner where I won't see it any more.

Fuck Joanne and her stupid games. This is one step too far.

And then I remember Joanne is dead and I can't take my anger out on her. Why do I feel guilt for being mad at her because she's dead?

I pick up the log basket and go inside, locking the door behind me. The whole weekend has become a living nightmare.

I spend the next twenty minutes fiddling around with the fire, getting it started, then sit mesmerised by the flames as they lick and spread their way around the kindling and the larger pieces of wood. There is something comforting about the flickering orange flames, the odd crack as the fire attacks the wood, and the heat that becomes more intense with each minute.

I curl up on the sofa and pull one of the blankets over me. I think about Joanne, her game and the clues we've found so far. There was the dollar bill, the wedding ring and the photograph. Each item linked to the accusation levelled at us by Joanne. So why have I now found another clue, if that's what it is? It certainly fits with Joanne's warped mind. The noose can only be meant for me.

I must have nodded off at some point, my sleep-deprived night catching up on me, because the next thing I'm aware of is Andrea waking me with a mug of hot chocolate.

'Hey, you OK?' she asks, sitting down on the opposite sofa. She drops the notebook and cards onto the middle of the table. 'Nice and warm in here. It's no wonder you fell asleep.'

'Any sign of the police yet?' I ask, sitting up and sliding my legs off the cushions. I glance at my watch. It's now ten fifteen.

'Not yet.'

'Do you think we should try to contact the ranger again, make sure he got through to the police?'

'Let's give it a while longer. I'm sure they'll be here soon.'

'You'd think they'd be here quicker, especially as there's been a death.' I sip my hot chocolate and look up as Zoe hobbles into the room and sits herself on the sofa opposite me. 'How's the ankle?'

'Still sore but not quite so bad,' she replies, sinking deeper into the cushion. On the face of it, she looks relaxed, but on closer inspection, I can see her body language is telling a different story. Her hands are wrapped around her cup, but her fingers are drumming the side in an agitated way. Her shoulders look tense and her eyes are darting from the fireplace to the window behind me.

'Try not to worry,' I say. 'It's been an awful weekend but it will be over soon.'

'I hope so,' she says, and wipes a tear from her eye. I move to comfort her but she shakes her head and gives me a small smile. 'Probably best if you don't offer me any sympathy right now, I'm likely to go to pieces.'

I was going to mention the noose I found outside, but I change my mind. I don't want to upset her or freak her out.

Not when she's obviously feeling the way she does. I pick up the notebook and cards. 'Shall I do the honours?'

'Fill your boots,' says Andrea.

Zoe gives a shrug which I take as no objection, so I drop the incriminating evidence through the open door of the wood burner, before returning to the sofa. We all sit in silence as we watch the paper swiftly engulfed in fresh flames. 'Have you got that walkie-talkie?' I ask once the flurry of activity has died down. 'I might try to speak to that ranger again. Just to check the police are coming.'

'It's up in my room. I don't want to have to tackle the stairs right now.' Zoe leans forwards and rubs her foot.

'Don't worry. I'll get it if you tell me where it is.'

'No. Don't. I mean, I'll get it. Might actually do me some good to exercise my ankle, you know, stop it stiffening up. I was only being lazy.' Zoe rises from the sofa and limps out of the room, returning with the handset a couple of minutes later. 'Probably best not to use it that much, we don't know how long the batteries will last.'

'Good point. I didn't think of that. I'll give it a couple of attempts.' In the hall, I slip my feet in the wellington boots and pull on my jacket. 'I'll try outside, I might get a better signal,' I call over my shoulder.

Zipping up my jacket, I switch the walkie-talkie on. 'Hello. This is Carys Montgomery. I spoke to the park ranger last night. Is anybody there?' As I speak, I realise that I didn't give my name the night before.

I don't know what the etiquette is for these things but right now I don't care. I release the button and wait for a response but all I'm met with is the now familiar buzzy sound of static. I wander down the track and try once more. This time I'm rewarded with a response as a Scottish accent comes across the airwaves.

'Hello, Carys Montgomery. This is the park ranger you spoke to last night. Is everything OK? Over.'

'Hello. Yes, we're OK. Erm, I wondered if you knew what time the police will be here. Over.'

'Ah, it won't be until later in the day, I'm afraid. The stormy weather last night caused a landslide and the road is blocked. They're waiting for it to be cleared and then they'll be up to you. Over.'

Disappointment follows this news. 'How far away are they? The town they're based in, I mean. I wondered if we could walk there. Over.'

'Oh no. Too far to walk. You should not be going walking in this weather. More rain is due this afternoon. You stay where you are. Please confirm. Over.'

I hesitate before replying. Part of me doesn't want to comply with the instruction. Part of me wishes I'd never made this call and I'd taken my chances and tried to get help. The voice of the ranger comes again. 'I repeat. Do not leave the croft. It's too dangerous. Please confirm. Over.'

Reluctantly I reply: 'Yes. I confirm. Over.'

'Good. Stay where you are for now. It's the safest option. Over and out.'

Brooding to myself, I dig the toe of my boot into the mud on the edge of the track which is now soft and mushy from the rainfall. *Stay where you are. Wait for the police.* How long is that going to take?

It's then I notice something odd about the mud. Embedded in the sodden ground is the pattern of a tyre tread. Not big enough for a car but certainly the size of a bicycle wheel. Someone has been here on a pushbike. Right up near the croft.

Chapter 21

'Honestly, Carys, I think you're overreacting,' says Zoe, resting her hand on my shoulder for support, her good leg taking the weight to compensate for her other one, which is resting on the ground. 'Those tyre marks could have been made at any time. They could be dried-up ones that now look fresh because of the rain.'

'I never noticed them before,' I say.

'Are you trying to tell me that you have been around the whole area, making notes of everything you've seen?' Zoe gives me a dismissive look.

'Well, no . . .' I begin.

'My point exactly.'

I'm surprised by Zoe's sharp tone but put it down to frayed nerves.

'To be fair, Zoe has a point,' says Andrea. We are all standing on the track inspecting the tyre marks. 'Even if they are fresh, this isn't a private road, there's nothing to stop anyone cycling up here.'

'It's not a very cycle-friendly place though,' I point out, though it feels foolish to insist.

'True, but that doesn't mean impossible,' says Zoe. 'Let's go indoors, I'm freezing.' She gives a shiver as if to demonstrate her low body temperature and we all trundle into the croft, Zoe at more of a hobble but covering the ground with surprising efficiency.

Zoe and I sit at the dining table while Andrea warms up some soup from the pantry. 'Good old Joanne, she got plenty of food in. At least we won't starve,' says Zoe as Andrea comes into the dining room with three bowls of soup. One in each hand and a third impressively balancing on her wrist. She puts the bowls down in front of us.

I don't like the way Zoe is talking so flippantly about Joanne. It seems disrespectful. Less than an hour ago she was crying about her. I guess everyone has different ways of dealing with traumatic events and perhaps this is Zoe's coping mechanism. I do remember going into some sort of autopilot mode for several days after Darren's death. I had too many things to deal with, and Alfie to worry about, so I couldn't allow myself the luxury of grieving. Maybe that's what I'm doing now. As shocking and upsetting as Joanne's death is, I must remain detached from the raw emotion which is patiently waiting to be set free. The denial stage, someone once defined it. I think of it more in terms of self-preservation. I divert my thoughts elsewhere.

'Tris and the kids are going to be devastated,' I say. 'How will they manage without her?'

'Don't worry about them now,' says Zoe, 'it won't help. You're right, they will be devastated, but you know what?'

I look expectantly at her. 'What?'

'They will be OK. They'll manage. That's what people do. That's what you've done, right?' Zoe tucks into her soup. 'This is delicious.'

I say nothing as I consider Zoe's sudden upbeat and pragmatic view on this. I know she's always been a complete optimist but she is taking it to the nth degree now. How can she find her soup delicious and even be in a frame of mind to comment on such a trivial thing? To me, it tastes bitter. Much like this weekend. As for her *they'll manage* attitude, it sounds so insensitive. I can feel myself getting angry. Zoe has no right to make such assumptions about Tris and the kids. Or me, come to think of it.

I put down my spoon rather more heavily than I intend. 'Honestly, Zoe, sometimes I wonder about you,' I hear myself saying. 'If you think those kids are simply going to dust themselves down after their mother's death and summon up a "we'll get over it" attitude, then you must be living in a complete fantasy world.'

'Easy, tiger,' warns Andrea softly, placing a hand on my arm. I shrug it off.

'I think it's time for some straight talking,' I say, with no intention whatsoever of backing down. 'Unless it's escaped your air-head, I'm still dealing with the aftermath of my son's father dying. Alfie has not just had a cry and then got on with life. He has lots of issues to deal with.'

'But that's different,' says Zoe.

'How?'

'Because Darren killed himself and Alfie saw him . . . hanging. I don't mean to upset you, Carys, but that's the truth of it. Joanne's kids haven't seen their mother dead. She didn't do this to punish them.'

I jump to my feet, sending the chair tipping backwards. 'Darren did not do what he did to punish Alfie. I'll tell you for nothing, he did it because he was ill. He was sick. Mentally ill. If there was anyone he wanted to punish, then it was me.' I can hardly get my words out. I'm gulping for air as if I've competed in an Olympic hundred-metre sprint. 'We don't know for sure what happened to Joanne. What if it turns out she was murdered? How are her children going to cope then? And what about Tris? He'll have to live with the fact that he couldn't protect his wife. And don't give me that look – it's true. Archaic as it might sound, we all feel protective towards our families and Tris is no different. It's not going to be easy for them, having to live with the fact that they may never know exactly how Joanne died.'

I turn on my heel and storm out of the dining room and up to my bedroom where I fling myself on the bed. While my rage bubbles inside, I lie staring up at the ceiling. Of all the things I had Zoe tagged as, a bloody idiot wasn't one of them.

It takes a few minutes, but finally I bring my anger under control by calming my breathing and putting into practice my relaxation strategies. Gradually, I feel my emotions levelling out.

I come to the decision that I am not prepared to sit around waiting for the police to turn up. I can't think why we aren't their top priority; there's been a death here, for goodness' sake.

After thirty minutes' meditating and trying to put myself into a better frame of mind, I return downstairs. I've decided to put Zoe's lack of empathy and tact down to the difficult situation we are in.

'Oh, Carys, I'm sorry,' says Zoe as I walk into the living room. She gets up from where she is sitting and holds out her arms to me. 'I didn't mean to sound as cold and heartless as I did. I was only trying to keep up a positive front.'

'It's OK,' I say, returning the gesture and hugging Zoe. 'I'm sorry too for overreacting. I know you better than that. I didn't mean to upset you either.' As I speak, I'm aware of a certain lack of conviction in my sentiments, but it feels the right thing to say at the right time. We need to stick together and not let our emotions divide us. Not here, anyway.

'That's what I like to see,' says Andrea. 'So let's all relax and wait for the police to come. We don't want to fall out with each other.'

'I was thinking maybe we could walk to the nearest village and get help from there. I can't cope with sitting around doing nothing.'

Andrea sits upright. 'Carys, how does the ranger know where to send the police?'

'What?' I'm not following her train of thought.

'We don't know where we are, right?' Both Zoe and I make agreeing sort of noises. 'So, how does the park ranger know where we are and where to send the police?'

'Maybe he knows this croft?' I say hesitantly.

'But there must be lots of crofts in the area. How does he know which one we're staying in?' She turns to me. 'Think very carefully. In your conversation with the ranger, did he ask you where you were? Did you tell him?'

It dawns on me that this is the thing that was niggling me about the conversation all this time. 'I can't remember. But then again, I don't remember him asking me any specifics. Can he track the radio signal?'

'I don't know. Do radio signals work the same as mobile phone signals?'

I look at Zoe, who hasn't said anything so far. She looks worried. Her emotions are all over the place, another symptom of the high anxiety levels we are all feeling.

'Let's assume the ranger hasn't, for whatever reason, been able to tell the police exactly where we are,' says Andrea. 'What are we going to do? Shall we try to contact him again?'

'To be honest, I've not got much faith in him,' I confess. 'He should at least have taken more details. Some of these rangers are volunteers. I'd sooner be speaking to the police.'

'Let's try to call him one more time,' says Zoe, sliding the locket on her necklace back and forth. I interpret this as another anxiety indicator. She takes the walkie-talkie from her pocket and switches it on. After several unsuccessful attempts at mustering a response from the park ranger, she gives up. 'Maybe he's out of range.'

'I think I should try to make it to the nearest house or village, whichever I come to first.'

'But we're cut off. There's been a landslide,' says Zoe. 'I don't think it's a good idea at all.'

'I'm sure they can get us out of here one way or another. You're not telling me there's no mountain rescue around here.'

'I'm with Zoe,' says Andrea. 'You don't even know where you're going.'

'I've got a rough idea. Joanne pointed a few landmarks out to me when we were up on Arrow Point. If I follow the track down into the valley, I'm bound to pick up a bigger road and sooner or later someone is going to be driving along. I can flag them down and raise the alarm that way.'

'But it's midday. You'll be losing light eventually. You might not even make it to a house before it gets dark,' says Zoe. 'What about the weather? It might rain again or the mist might come in and you could easily get lost or fall down a ravine or something.'

'I'll be OK. I've walked in all sorts of weather before, we do it all the time with the Duke of Edinburgh Award kids,' I say. 'I was thinking about cutting across country but, given the potential for bad weather, I'll stick to the road. Then there's the kayaks. Joanne said the river eventually finds its way to a town. I can't remember what she said it was called. Gormsly, Gormouth? Something like that.'

'Sticking to the road sounds like the safest bet to me,' says Andrea. 'There might be waterfalls or rapids along the river. If you capsize, you could be in serious trouble.'

After a few more minutes debating the pros and cons, we finally agree that taking the road is the safest option.

'I still don't like you going on your own,' says Zoe. 'One of us should go with you.' She looks at Andrea.

'When you say one of us, you mean me. You're not exactly up to it with your ankle the way it is,' says Andrea.

'Well, yes. I suppose that is what I mean,' says Zoe. 'One of us should stay here anyway, in case the police turn up.'

'You're happy staying on your own?' I ask, surprised at Zoe's apparent bravery.

'I'll lock myself in. I won't pretend I'm happy at the thought, but it's the best option.'

I look at Andrea for a response. She shrugs. 'I guess there isn't a perfect solution and I'm kind of inclined to agree with you, Carys. Sitting here doing nothing isn't getting us anywhere. If the police do come and we're on the road, then we'll see them.'

'And when we see a house or a village, we'll be able to raise the alarm. They'll have to make us top priority then, especially now we've also got someone with an injury. You'd think they'd be able to send some sort of mountain rescue team up with a police officer anyway,' I say.

'I know, does seem odd,' agrees Andrea. 'But since that's clearly not happening, we'll have to deal with it the best we can.'

'I must admit to feeling happier now we're doing something proactive,' I say. 'I need to keep busy. Keep my mind busy.'

'Let's get ourselves organised. We can take those emergency hiking packs with us, the ones Joanne gave us yesterday.'

'Good idea. There's a first-aid kit, some emergency rations, a flare and a foil blanket,' I say. 'We'll need to make sure we've plenty of water too.'

'Are you sure you're going to be all right?' asks Andrea, turning to Zoe.

'I'll be fine. Just make sure someone comes back for me!'

She gives a half-hearted laugh. 'I'll keep the walkie-talkie close by in case the ranger makes contact.'

'Good idea,' says Andrea.

I must admit that Zoe seems remarkably at ease with being left on her own, which surprises me. Out of all of us, I would have pegged Zoe as the least, for want of a better word, brave. She's always been the one we've mothered when we've been on our outdoor adventures in the past. I'm beginning to see her in a new light. I ponder this some more as I pack my rucksack and decide the inner strength she's displaying now is probably born out of a shit marriage and having to make a go of it on her own. Pretty much the way I've had to.

Andrea comes up to the bedroom and closes the door behind her.

'You OK?' she asks.

'I think so.'

'You don't sound too sure.'

'I'll admit I'm rather apprehensive.' I clip the rucksack closed.

'Not scared?'

'A little, if I'm honest. Part of me thinks this is a good idea, part of me thinks we should stay put.'

'What would your advice be to your Duke of Edinburgh kids?' Andrea walks over to the window and looks out at the trees behind us.

'To stay put. Don't go off. Wait for help to arrive.'

'So, remind me again, why are we leaving?'

I hold my hands up. 'I know, it goes against everything I've been taught. Everything I teach others. Everything my instincts are telling me,' I confess. 'But I feel we should be doing something more proactive.' I pause, wondering whether to confess my next thought.

'What's up?' says Andrea, picking up on my hesitation.

'That park ranger I spoke to. I'm beginning to doubt he was a park ranger at all.'

'What?'

'He didn't ask me my name, he didn't give his name, he didn't ask our location. It's been bugging me and the only thing I can think of is, he wasn't actually a park ranger, just some random bloke who happened to catch our call.'

'Why would someone do that?'

'I've no idea. Maybe he thought it would be funny. Maybe he's some weirdo. Maybe . . .'

'Wait – please don't say that maybe he's the one who killed Joanne.'

We look at each other in silence.

'It's a lot of maybes,' I say, at last.

'Certainly is. And in light of all those maybes, the last one in particular, do you still think it's a good idea to leave Zoe alone?'

Chapter 22

'Look, I'll be fine,' insists Zoe, when Andrea and I speak to her about our worries. 'As I said, I'm not relishing the thought of being on my own, but someone needs to stay here with Joanne and wait for the police.'

'But we don't know for certain that they're coming,' I say. 'That's the whole point.'

'Yes, but I'll lock myself in and it won't take too long before you get to the town. Besides, I have to stay. I don't have a choice. I can't walk that far, not with my ankle the way it is. You need to go. Both of you.'

'Are you sure you can't manage the walk?' asks Andrea.

'Positive. We've been through all this. Please, just go.'

With a certain amount of reluctance, Andrea and I leave Zoe at the croft and head off down the track.

'I hope it doesn't rain,' says Andrea, as we round the bend in the track and cross the stone bridge. She looks up at the clouds above. 'Looking rather grey up there.'

'The ground is completely saturated. It's quite possible there's been a landslide somewhere.' I lengthen my stride to avoid planting my foot in a muddy puddle which stretches across the track. 'I hope Zoe's going to be all right on her own. I feel guilty leaving her.'

'I know what you mean, but you heard her, she's adamant she'll be fine. Hopefully, this will all be over by tonight.'

'God, I hope so.'

We trudge on in silence for a while, each of us lost in our own thoughts.

It's Andrea who speaks first. 'I know this is going to sound bad, and I couldn't say it to anyone else, but I'm not as upset about Joanne as I think I should be.'

'Really?' I say, surprised at my friend's honesty. Even for someone as straight-talking as Andrea, that's some statement.

'No. I don't think any of us are.'

'Speak for yourself. You don't know what I'm thinking and feeling, or Zoe for that matter.' Andrea's comment irritates me but I'm uncertain if it's because there may be an element of truth in it.

I'm not as cut up as I would have expected an almost-best-friend to be. But then maybe that's because these are exceptional circumstances.

'I'm only being honest,' says Andrea.

'It's probably the adrenalin and the fear that's stopping us from being upset,' I say. 'It will hit us later, when we're safe in our own homes with our families.' I think of Alfie, having to deal with another death, someone he's grown close to, someone who has a connection to both of us. Darren's death has been so very hard for him and now he will have to deal with another loss. And, in turn, I will have to bear the brunt of that new grief, probably in the same way I do for his grief over Darren.

Sometimes I think he almost takes pleasure in my pain, both mental and physical. I had always hoped, and still do, that he'll grow out of his extreme behaviour as he gets older and learns, through counselling, how to deal with his emotions. At the moment, the only outlet for his emotions seems to be anger. Extreme anger. It frightens me. Not that I'd admit this to anyone else. I'm ashamed of the way he lashes out; not ashamed of him, ashamed of his behaviour. But I am ashamed of myself too. I've failed as a mother, in the same way I failed as a wife.

I wish I could speak to Seb. He'd know what to do. In fact, I wish I was with Seb right now. I imagine myself sitting on the sofa with him, snuggled up against his chest, his arm around me, stroking my arm with his thumb like he usually does. We'll be watching the television and there will be a bottle of wine open. We'll have drunk half of it by now. Both of us will be totally relaxed and at ease with each other. I will feel loved and I will be in love. And everything in the world will be all right.

A bubble of emotion rises in my throat. I swallow hard. This is not the time to go to pieces. I need to remain strong, at least until we get help. I concentrate on the road ahead.

'You OK?' asks Andrea.

'Sure. Was thinking of Alfie and Seb, that's all.'

'How are things between those two?'

'About the same.'

'It will come good in the end,' says Andrea, with a confidence I'm not convinced by.

'Alfie can barely bring himself to talk to me, let alone Seb,'

I say. Somehow it doesn't seem so painful talking about it as it does thinking about it. I try to rationalise my thoughts. 'Alfie wants to move in with the Aldridges. Apparently, he and Ruby are a thing,' I blurt out. I hadn't meant to say anything, but ever since Alfie dropped this bombshell last week during a heated debate about spending more time at home, the notion has been patrolling the edges of my thoughts like a frustrated caged animal.

'What? Alfie and Ruby – I don't believe it!'

'It was news to me too. I thought they were mates, more like brother and sister, the way they've always been. I had no idea it had developed into anything more.' I don't tell Andrea that it completely freaked me out, especially after the fallout from Ruby's crush on Darren. I couldn't help wondering if she was doing it on purpose, as some sort of sick revenge. Not that I said this to Alfie. I steal a look at Andrea. 'That's not the best bit.'

'There's more? Don't tell me Ruby's pregnant.'

'No! That would be a complete nightmare,' I say. 'The best bit is, Joanne. She thought it was wonderful that they had each other and said that if Alfie wanted to move in with Ruby, she didn't have a problem.' The sadness washes over me. I stop walking and look out across the valley and the vast landscape ahead. 'I think Joanne was punishing me. She wanted to take Alfie away from me and leave me with nothing.'

'Why?'

I feel a tear roll down my cheek and I shake my head. 'It doesn't matter now. Joanne's dead.'

Andrea comes to stand next to me and we both gaze out

at the vista. 'It's true about Ruby and Darren, isn't it? That's what you mean about Joanne punishing you.'

'Honestly, I don't know. We did have this big showdown with Joanne and Tris about it a couple of years ago, but Darren denied it all. We believed him – all three of us. Had no reason not to.'

'And now?'

'Well, I can't exactly ask him about it,' I say, a failed attempt at humour. 'I think maybe Joanne was never convinced and something has happened to stir it all up again. I don't know what, but whatever it was, she was probably going to confront me with it this weekend.'

'I didn't mean what I said about Darren being a paedo,' says Andrea. 'I was just cross, spooked, you know?'

'It's OK,' I say, with rather more grace than I feel. I'm so very tired, I'm finding it hard to delve too deeply into my bank of emotions. 'Ruby was eighteen at the time, so legally an adult. Although, ethically, it's another matter.'

'If it's any consolation, I don't believe Joanne would have taken Alfie on.'

'Why's that?'

'For the same reason you struggle to have a relationship with him. Don't take this the wrong way, but Alfie has a lot of issues he needs to sort out. He'd have been too much for Joanne; she couldn't have coped with the disruption to her nice organised life.'

I know it's irrational and unfair of me, but I can't help bristling at Andrea's opinion of my son. Yes, he is struggling, but I'm the one who's allowed to criticise him, no one else.

The irony isn't lost. I still feel massively defensive when it comes to Alfie, as any mother would. When someone else, no matter how close a friend, voices their negative thoughts, it doesn't sit well.

'He's good lad,' I say. 'He's not that bad.'

'This is me you're talking to,' says Andrea.

Whether Andrea intends it or not, I take umbrage. 'I suppose you think you've got the perfect family,' I snap, surprising myself at the level of my anger. 'You should look closer to home before you start criticising others.'

'What's that supposed to mean?' Andrea half turns to face me. Her foot is near the edge of the track. A steep hill falls away into the valley below us.

'Exactly what I say. Your son isn't perfect either.'

'You can't brandish things like that without anything to back it up. No one's kids are perfect, and mine isn't that bad. At least I can comment on Alfie with some authority. You've told me that he's not the easiest of kids to live with, not with the mental state he's in. And that mark on your back, I'll bet my last pound that was something to do with Alfie.'

'He might have some issues but at least he doesn't peddle drugs.' Somewhere in the depths of my mind, I'm conscious I'm lashing out because I'm hurt by Andrea's words. Someone once said the best form of defence is attack. I guess I'm fully embracing that philosophy.

'Drugs? What the hell are you on about?'

Despite acknowledging my reaction, I find myself snapping: 'Bradley. He buys weed and sells it to the kids in the sixth form. If he got caught, he'd be kicked out of school and reported to the police for drug-dealing. So, don't think your son is any better than mine.' The feeling of triumph and satisfaction at the shocked look on Andrea's face is short-lived. Almost immediately I regret my outburst. It is a childish and shameful way to carry on. But it's also too late. I can't retract the words.

Andrea is on the attack. 'I tell you what, Carys, you should be careful what you say. You can't go around accusing people of being drug dealers. Besides, a bit of weed is hardly crime of the century. If it were true, that is. You know what they say about people in glass houses.'

'Forget it. I shouldn't have said anything.' Realising that Andrea is now too close to the edge for my liking, I put my hand out to touch her arm. 'Come away from the edge.'

She snatches her arm away, the momentum throwing her backwards. When she puts her foot out to regain her balance, it makes contact with nothing but thin air.

Andrea screams. Her arms flail like a windmill as she tries to reach out to me. I lunge for her but my gloves can't get any purchase on her nylon padded jacket. The fabric slips through my fingers.

The look on Andrea's face is one of pure terror. She falls backwards and it is all I can do to stop myself falling after her. She screams again, this time longer and louder. More fearful.

I watch her plummet down the gulley, wincing as her head narrowly avoids hitting one of the many rocks along the way. Her feet fly up in the air and her arms and legs go in different directions as she tumbles backwards over the rocky hillside, gathering speed with each somersault. Then she is thrown to the side and disappears into some bushes.

'Andrea! Andrea!' I shout. 'Can you hear me? Are you OK?' It's a ridiculous question; how can she possibly be OK after a fall like that?

I peer into the gulley. I might be able to get down there, but I'm not sure I'll be able to scramble up again. Not without a rope and some chocks to wedge between the rocks for anchor points. The last thing I want is for both of us to be stuck down there. I call to Andrea again.

This time I hear a faint groan.

'Carys . . .'

The voice is weak but at least she is alive. 'Are you hurt?'

'I can't move. I think I've broken my ankle.'

'OK, erm . . .' My mind goes blank and it takes a moment before I can think straight. 'I'm going to head to the croft, get some rope and something to make a brace with for your leg.' I listen for a response. 'Andrea? Can you hear me?'

'Yes! Hurry up, my ankle is killing me.'

Before I leave, I look around for something to mark the spot where Andrea is. It might be difficult to remember the exact place when I return. I sprint over to the edge of the forest on the other side of the track and scan the area for a branch large enough to stick in the ground.

Eventually I find something suitable and push the stake into the rain-softened edge. To make certain I don't miss this marker when I come back, I pull out the foil blanket from my rucksack and use my penknife to rip off a length, which I fasten around the stick.

Happy that I'll be able to find the spot again, I shout reassurances down to Andrea before setting off at a run in the direction of the croft. I check my watch and estimate how long we had been walking and guess it will probably take me ten to fifteen minutes to get back. I'm used to cross-country running, but in hiking boots it's proving more taxing.

It's actually twelve minutes by the time I reach the croft. I'm about to hammer on the door when I realise it's ajar. I stop in my tracks, my hand stilled in mid-air. Zoe said she was going to lock the door. It was a condition of us leaving her here. I listen for any sound of life. I can hear angry voices coming from inside. One female and one male.

My heart hammers against my breastbone from the nervous energy coursing inside me. I push the door open and step on to the coir mat, the bristles folding under my weight. I can hear clearly now.

At first I think I must be imagining things. It's definitely Zoe's voice but the male voice sounds remarkably like Tris. As I listen more, I realise it is.

'Why didn't you stop them?' he's asking.

'I couldn't. Carys was adamant she was going. Andrea too. I thought if I at least stayed here—'

'Where did they say they were going?'

'I can't remember the name, but it's a town about fifteen miles away. Joanne pointed it out to Carys when we were up at Arrow's Head.'

'Gormston.' Tris lets out a sigh. 'What to do now?'

I can hear Zoe sniff. 'I'm sorry,' she says.

'Hey, sweetheart, it's OK. I'm sorry, I didn't mean to upset you. It's just the idea of those two going walkabout – it's dangerous.'

There's a pause in the conversation and I lean into the hallway further, not wanting to step on to the tile floor in case they hear me. I can see them through the crack in the doorframe. Tris has his arms around Zoe, comforting her. I watch as she looks up at him and then they kiss. A full-on kiss.

I manage to hold in my breath of surprise. So it's true. Zoe and Tris are having an affair. Joanne was right.

Lost in my thoughts, I nearly miss the pinging sound that comes from the living room. It sounds like a text message alert. I watch Tris and Zoe pull apart and then Tris take a mobile phone from his pocket. I'm confused. This is supposed to be a not-spot for mobile phones. I curse Joanne under my breath for lying to us. Tris swipes at the screen and reads the message. He pauses and then leans in to whisper something in Zoe's ear. Whatever he's told her, it's unnerved her. She looks over to the door, a worried expression on her face. I dip out of sight.

Then Tris is coming out into the hallway. I don't have time to dive outside. I have to think fast.

'Oh my God, Tris!' I say, injecting as much surprise as possible into my voice. I close the front door behind me. 'What are you doing here?'

'Carys! You're back. Thank goodness,' he says, coming towards me and giving me a hug. 'Zoe was telling me about your crazy idea about walking off to get help.'

He ushers me into the living room. I look at Zoe, who is

standing in front of the fireplace now, her hands clasped together and her eyes darting from me and then to Tris. Has she told him about Joanne? He's not exactly acting like a grief-stricken husband. Despite the fact he's obviously been having an affair, he must surely have had some feelings for Joanne.

'Carys, are you OK?' says Zoe, suddenly springing into life. She limps towards me, takes my arm and leads me to the sofa. 'Tris has only just got here.'

I look up at Tris. 'What are you doing here? I didn't know you were coming.'

'It seems I've caught everyone by surprise,' he says. 'Zoe wasn't expecting me either, but Joanne asked me to come. We arranged it all beforehand.'

Again, I look at Zoe. She's very nervous and goes to speak but changes her mind. I look at Tris. 'Has Zoe told you . . . ?' I leave the sentence unfinished. If he knows, then I don't need to say any more.

Tris dips his head and spreads his thumb and forefinger across his eyes. I watch him draw a deep breath and then let it out slowly. He continues to look down and gives a nod. 'Yes. Zoe just told me.'

'I'm so sorry,' I say. I stand and go to move towards him, but change my mind. This feels so awkward. I remember immediately after Darren had died, all I wanted was to be held and take comfort from caring human contact, but Tris appears to have got himself under control.

And then I remember why I'm here: Andrea is lying injured down a gorge. But before I can say anything, Zoe pre-empts me.

'What are you doing back? Where's Andrea?'

'There's been an accident. Andrea's fallen down a hillside and hurt herself. She thinks she's broken her ankle.'

'Oh, no! Not her too. Well, mine's not broken, but you know what I mean.' Zoe grimaces in the direction of her foot.

I dismiss the passing thought that Zoe doesn't seem too bothered about her injury; I'm more worried about Andrea right now. 'I need a rope so I can abseil down to her and try to get her out of there.'

'Whereabouts is she?' asks Zoe. 'You haven't been gone that long.'

'About fifteen minutes down the track. I've put a marker there so I'll know where to find her.' The panic and urgency that was momentarily on hold returns. 'There's a climbing rope. I saw it yesterday.' I am in mid-turn when I stop and look at Tris. 'Wait a minute. How did you get here? By car? You can drive us down there.'

It's at this point I realise I can't recall seeing a car outside when I ran up the track to the croft. I look out of the window and then at Tris. He's stopped crying now and fixes me with a gaze I can't read.

All my senses heighten at once. A primeval instinct tells me that I am surrounded by danger. I clench my fists as a sense of fight or flight takes hold. I don't understand my physical reactions; my brain isn't up to speed with my senses.

'The car's parked down the track,' says Tris. 'There was a landslide. I walked the last bit.'

'Oh, right.' I can't see how this can be true. If he'd walked up the track, then Andrea and I would have seen him. I edge a few steps in the direction of the door. 'Well . . . er . . . I'll get the rope and we can rescue Andrea.'

I've never felt a silence so stifling and oppressive. The air pressure in the room is suffocating.

'Good idea,' says Tris. 'You get the rope from outside.'

The blood pumps a little faster through my veins. He knows where the rope is. Or is it a random guess? I fight to appear calm and hope any anxiety Tris might detect in me will be passed off as distress over Andrea. 'I'm worried about Andrea,' I say, in a bid to reinforce this idea. I look at Zoe. 'Want to give me a hand?' I will Zoe to take the hint and come outside with me. There's something going on that I'm missing. The atmosphere in the room intensifies even more as I wait, for what seems like an age, for Zoe to answer.

'She can't,' says Tris, placing a hand on her shoulder. 'She's got a bad ankle, remember?'

Zoe's eyes widen and although I know she is trying to tell me something, I can't read her expression. She attempts to mouth a word at me. I can't be sure what she's trying to say. Run? Is she telling me to run?

Fear peaks within me and my skin feels clammy. Another glance at Zoe and this time there is no mistaking the silent words she mouths.

Get help.

'It's OK, I can manage,' I say. Without waiting for a response, I cross the hallway and head through the dining room into the kitchen, pushing the internal door closed behind me.

The walkie-talkie is on the worktop and I swipe it up

without breaking stride. Hurrying out of the unlocked door, I step out on to the patio and turn on the power. The handset crackles into life. I don't waste any time transmitting a message.

'Hello? I need to speak to the park ranger. Are you there?' I'm met with silence. Going over to where I'd thrown the rope, I pull it out with my free hand. All the time trying to get a response from the park ranger. 'Hello. Please? Anybody?'

The rope pools at my feet and I stoop to gather it up. As I stand, I happen to look down the garden and spy the wheel of a pushbike sticking out from behind the shed.

I know for certain the bike wasn't there before. An image of the tyre print in the mud flashes in front of me.

'Hello. Can anyone hear me?' I speak desperately into the handset for a third time.

And then I hear the unmistakable Scottish accent of the park ranger, except he is not on the other end of the handset, he is right behind me. A feeling of relief floods through me. It must be the ranger's bike. He's come to see if we're OK.

I turn and my hand falls limply to my side. Tris is standing there. A small smile of amusement playing on his lips. 'Aye, I can hear you,' he says. 'Over.'

Chapter 23

Tris is holding a walkie-talkie in the air with a smug look on his face.

'What's going on?' I ask, trying to keep the nerves from showing in my voice.

The smile drops from his mouth. 'Nothing. It was a joke,' he says, moving a step closer. I match this by taking a step away. He looks beyond me at the shed and back again. A shiver runs through me, not from the cold air but from the detached look in his eyes.

'You and Zoe – I don't care what's going on between you two,' I say. 'It's none of my business. I don't even care that you're here. All I want is to rescue Andrea.' I hoist the coil of rope on to my shoulder. 'You understand, don't you?'

He nods. 'I do. Of course I understand. Look, Joanne asked me to come up here. She gave me the walkie-talkie and said I was to pretend to be the park ranger if anyone made the call.'

'Why? Why would she ask you to do that?'

'She said it was a joke. She was going to play a trick on you all. I didn't know what she had planned. She told me I didn't need to know, my job was to come up here with my walkie-talkie at the ready and not to overreact to anything that was said. When you said there'd been a death . . . fuck, I thought it was all part of the game.'

Something about Tris's story isn't sitting right with me. It doesn't make sense. Then again, I don't know what Joanne had planned for us. Do I trust Tris, or do I go with my gut instinct? Countless thoughts jostle their way to the front of my mind, each demanding attention, but before I can settle on an answer, it's barged away by another.

Tris and Zoe are having an affair. That I'm sure about, but I don't know what the implications are. Did Joanne really ask Tris up here, or has he come because of Zoe? And why is Zoe telling me to get help? Something's wrong, it must be. Why else would Zoe be too scared to speak out loud?

Tris's eyes flick towards the rope on my shoulder and the noose which dangles near my knees.

'You're not going to do anything stupid with that rope, are you?' he asks.

'What?'

'I couldn't bear it if . . . well, you know . . . what happened to Darren . . . Joanne didn't tell you that story about mothers sacrificing themselves up in the woods, did she?'

My stomach lurches as I get what he's implying. Does he think I'm going to take my own life? The next thought knocks the air from my lungs. My natural reaction is to dismiss it, but I can't. Has Tris his own agenda in all this? Every fibre in my body is on high alert.

'I don't know what's going on here, Tris,' I say, surprising myself at how calm I sound when, inwardly, the panic is building. 'But I need to help Andrea. Whatever game you think Joanne was playing, it's over now. This is no game. This is serious.'

I take a few seconds to contemplate my next move. I need the rope to rescue Andrea but it's heavy and I won't be able to out-run Tris if I'm weighed down. He's pretty fit from all the 10K running he does, but I think I might stand a chance of beating him over cross-country terrain. He's used to the flat even surface of the road. If I can get a good head start, I might be able to do it.

In the next second, I can barely believe I'm thinking like this. It seems so surreal. Tris is scaring me. I think of Zoe in the croft. I'm uncertain where her loyalties lie. From what I saw earlier, I don't think she's in any danger from Tris, but with her ankle injury, there's no way I can take her with me. It's down to me and me alone to get help.

'Carys, you look terrified,' says Tris. He stretches out a hand to me. 'Don't be silly. You don't have to be frightened of me. I'm here to help you all.'

I take a step away. 'Why are you here? Was it to see Joanne, or to see Zoe?'

'I told you, Joanne asked me to come.'

'When did you see Joanne?'

'Carys, I don't know what all this is about—'

'When did you last see Joanne?' I insist.

'Wait a minute . . . are you asking what I think you are?' Tris gives a small laugh of disbelief. 'No. You can't be. You're not seriously asking me if I had anything to do with Joanne's accident, are you?'

I glance towards the shed. 'You're having an affair with Zoe,' I blurt out.

'That doesn't make me a murderer. Besides, Joanne fell. It was an accident.'

'You seem very sure about that.'

'I would never hurt Joanne. You're not thinking straight, Carys. It's OK, I understand, or at least I have some idea. I remember how difficult it was for you, finding Darren dead. So finding Joanne like that was bound to mess with your mind.'

'That's a cheap shot,' I snap. 'Anyone who finds their husband hanging is going to have a hard time dealing with it, but that doesn't mean I'm unstable now.'

'I didn't say unstable, I meant you would find this sort of thing particularly difficult. It's no wonder it's clouded your judgement. For Christ sake, I've lost my wife – whatever is going on between me and Zoe doesn't dilute that in the slightest.'

I almost believe him. Almost. 'I need to go,' I say, but still I hesitate, debating whether to sidestep Tris and run straight out of here. Will he let me? Can I take the risk?

But Tris isn't ready to end the conversation. As if anticipating my next move, he positions himself so he's blocking my path. 'From what I can tell, you had the motive,' he says. 'You know Joanne was pissed off with all of you. Andrea for the business deal. Zoe for having an affair with me, and you for what happened between Ruby and Darren.'

'Nothing happened.'

'That's academic now. What matters is that Joanne believed it.'

'I don't understand where all this has come from. We sorted it out between us. You and Joanne agreed it was nothing more than a teenage crush. A student smitten with her tutor. It happens.'

'Joanne said she had a surprise for you. She never told me what it was, but I got the impression she had recently found out something about you.'

'Like what?'

'I don't know. She didn't want to say.' He runs his hand through his hair. 'You know Ruby was devastated by what happened. Imagine how it must have felt for Joanne and me as parents, left wondering if their daughter had been seduced by her tutor, a man she thought she could trust? She was utterly heartbroken when he killed himself. And then, the final icing on the cake, your son and our daughter start to get closer and closer. Now she's got a thing for the son of the man who did this to her! Imagine how we felt when she told us. It's totally mind-fucking, Carys. Surely you can see that.'

Tris has a point. It's been hard for us all to get our heads around the fallout from one teenage girl's crush on an older man. I avoid eye contact with Tris, not wanting him to see the truth in my eyes.

'I don't know what to say.' I feel the weight of the past two years bear down heavy on my shoulders. Darren had promised me it was nothing more than a teenager with a crush and I had believed him then.

I had believed him then.

I glance up at Tris and meet his gaze, which momentarily paralyses me. He tilts his head to one side. 'What is it, Carys?'

I blink. I can't face my own thoughts. It's too much to bear. I need to get away. If Tris knows what I'm thinking . . .

The neuro pathways in my mind are numb as I try to push a command through to my feet. *Run! Run!* I can hear myself screaming in my head. *Get away! Now!*

Without warning, my body explodes into action, absorbing all the instructions at once.

I hadn't noticed Tris move closer. An error on my part, but there is still sufficient distance between us, which allows me to swing my body to the side and avoid contact. However, he catches hold of the rope on my shoulder and yanks at it. The force drags me off balance and I stumble, almost colliding with Tris. The rope drops to the ground and I must make a split-second decision. Pick up the rope and risk being caught, or try to out-run him.

I opt for the latter and sprint across the garden. The run to the croft has already warmed my calf muscles, so I hurtle up the incline towards the forest beyond. If I can get in amongst the trees, there's a chance I'll lose him.

The sound of his feet thundering on the ground behind me spurs me on. Every so often, he gives a grunt as we both leap, stumble and dodge the rabbit holes and dips in the ground. I don't know how close he is, but he's too close. I lean forward and with every ounce of energy and determination, I push myself harder. One last effort and I'm at the top of the hill, the grass and rock petering out as I charge into the forest.

I'm aware my bright-yellow jacket isn't helping to camouflage me, but taking it off will slow me down and then I'd have to carry it, as it would be foolish to discard it in this environment. I don't know how long I'm going to be out here in the wilderness.

'Carys! Don't be stupid,' Tris calls. 'Where are you going? Come back!'

My survival instinct kicks in as I sense I'm putting distance between myself and Tris. I veer off to the right in a bid to stay roughly parallel with the track. The trees are getting thicker and less daylight is breaking through the branches. I try to recall where Joanne had taken us on Friday when we had gone to the ancient clearing. I'm certain we had headed in a northerly direction, somewhere to my left.

I can no longer hear Tris's feet hitting the ground behind me, nor his panting or groans as he struggles with the terrain. For the first time, I look over my shoulder. I'm relieved when I can't see him.

I slow my pace to a jog, hoping to conserve my energy, and allow myself a more detailed look at my surroundings. There's a glimpse of movement behind me. It must be Tris. I duck down behind a large rock and peer cautiously over the top, tracking him as he runs steadily in and out of the trees. He can't have seen me. I've been lucky.

I watch as his pace slows and then he comes to a stop. He is about forty metres away from me. I hold my breath and crouch lower, keeping him in sight. He turns in a small circle, looking all around him. I duck completely out of view as he spins my way.

A few seconds later, I hear the crackle of the radio and Tris's voice breaks through the still air of the forest.

'Carys, I know you can hear me. Stop all this. It's gone too far. We need to talk.'

Shit! The radio I'm holding is still on. I fumble with the handset to turn the volume down. Has he heard his own voice from the walkie-talkie? Very slowly, I take another peek over the rock.

He's closer. Maybe thirty metres away. He must have heard.

I'm about to get up and make a run for it while I still have a reasonable head start, when I have an idea. I need to act fast. He's getting closer and closer.

'Caaaarrrys! I know where you are!' He's taunting me with a sing-song voice which reminds me of the child-catcher in *Chitty Chitty Bang Bang*.

I push the walkie-talkie into the pocket of my jacket and fasten the zip. From the ground, I select a small rock, the size of my fist. I have to dig my nails into the dirt to free it, but the ground is damp from all the rain and releases the stone without too much resistance. I try to make my breathing as quiet as possible as I wait for a pause in his calling.

'Come on, Carys, come out. It's no use hiding, sweetheart.'

And there it is. He's stopped. I can't hear his voice or any movement through the leaves and undergrowth. I take yet another sneaky look and good fortune is on my side. He has his back to me. As quick as I can, I throw the stone towards a clump of bigger rocks to his left.

As soon as the rock leaves my hand, I hide once more. I hear the rock hit the larger ones with a clonk and then bounce on to the forest floor with a noticeable thud.

'Oh, Carys!' His voice rings out. I hear his footfall as he

runs through the undergrowth towards the cluster of rocks.

Slowly, keeping as low as possible, I retreat backwards, further and further away from my hiding spot. My nerves break and I can no longer control my survival instinct to flee. I turn and run as fast as I can into the forest.

I hear Tris shout my name but he's further away now. This time there is no callous amusement, just pure anger at being duped.

I don't know where I'm running. I am certainly not on any path, but weaving and zigzagging my way through the trees. I'm running so fast, I can't stop myself as the ground dips violently and I half-fall down the side of a hill. My left shoulder whacks into the bough of a tree which makes me cry out in pain. Dirt and leaves scuff up as I tumble. I can't stop myself and can only pray I don't meet the same fate as Andrea or, worse, hit a tree head-on.

By some miracle, my path to the bottom is clear and I land in a stream, face down. I lift my head, spluttering, and spit water out. The stream isn't deep but the bed is stone and I can taste blood in my mouth. I think I've bitten my lip on the way down.

I stay where I am, stunned and winded. Somehow I pull myself on to my hands and knees, then take a moment to catch my breath. Above me I can hear Tris's voice calling my name. I don't think he can see me. Bushes halfway up the embankment act as a shield.

Slowly and as quietly as possible, I crawl to the edge of the stream. Keeping low, I practically belly-crawl out of the water, the walkie-talkie digging into my hip every now and then. I unzip my jacket and slip my arms from the sleeves. I have a quick look at the walkie-talkie. It feels dry, the water-proof outer layer of my jacket doing a good job at protecting it. I have no idea if it still works, but with Tris still too close for comfort I have no intention of putting it to the test. I push the handset into the pocket and zip it up again.

Trying to make as few and as quiet movements as possible, I turn the jacket inside out. The black fleece lining now on display will offer much more camouflage than the fluorescent yellow.

I'm not sure how long I have been lying here, squeezed up against the cold bank, but my toes are starting to go numb and my fingers are taking on a yellowy-white tinge. In fact, my whole body is damp and cold, my core temperature dropping fast after all that exertion. The last thing I need is to develop hypothermia. I must move.

I listen carefully but can't hear anything other than the wind rustling the leaves on the trees like tissue paper being scrunched up.

Making no sudden movements, I turn and peer up at the bank. I move from the sheltered position and take a cautious look around. There is nothing to make me believe Tris is still there.

I have no choice but to make a break for it now.

Chapter 24

The stream I'm following dips and dives its way through the forest with no sign of it meeting up with the larger river we paddled down yesterday. Was it only yesterday? It seems so much longer.

My sense of direction is telling me I am moving further into the forest and away from the track that leads from the croft. I picture the track in my mind, remembering how it sloped away to the east and then twisted and turned itself down into the valley and out on to a main road.

I use the term 'main road' lightly. Round here, that could be no more than a length of tarmac.

It has started to rain again and although the trees provide some shelter from the weather, they aren't enough to stop me from getting wet. I'm regretting taking off my hat and gloves at the croft and dropping them on the sofa. My ears and fingertips are numb with cold. At least my toes are faring slightly better, thanks to the two pairs of socks I put on before setting off this morning.

Tiredness is draining energy from my limbs and mind. I can feel my muscles burning in protest, a feeling I've often experienced when cross-country running. All I have to do is dig in as if I were competing. I can't stop now, I'm not confident my muscles will work again if I do. My priority now is to find shelter. Somewhere safe. Somewhere Tris can't find me.

The thought of Tris and the noose at the end of the climbing rope spurs me on, energising my body and mind. Like a never-ending whirlpool, my thoughts constantly return to Andrea. I hope her backpack made it down the hill with her. She'll have access to the high-energy snack bars we packed and the emergency foil blanket, plus drinking water. If she can get to all those things, she should be OK for at least twenty-four hours. Not for the first time this weekend, I find myself turning to religion as I offer a silent prayer that she will survive the night.

The energy rush is short-lived. After ten minutes, my body starts slowing down again. My walk turns to a slow plod as the terrain underfoot becomes heavier and boggier from the falling rain. I pull my rucksack round and take out my water bottle and one of the energy bars.

I need to think about how I will survive the night myself. Like Andrea, my backpack has a few emergency supplies, enough for one night. I don't in all honesty think I'm going to reach the town before dark. Daylight is already fading, and with my vision blurring from sheer exhaustion, I know I can't go on much longer.

I walk further into the forest and after a few minutes I notice that the trees are thinning out. Ahead, I can see daylight, albeit a dirty grey sort of hue.

I push a strand of hair from my face and blink as I look ahead. It's a building. A stone building.

My pace quickens as I hurry towards it.

'Please let someone be there,' I mutter out loud to myself. As I draw closer, I can see the building is about the size of a double garage, built from traditional stone like the croft. The ground is uneven as the land falls away at a shallow angle. I can see a small window in what I assume is the rear of the property.

I make my way around to the other side and find a larger window and a door. It must be a bothy; there are hundreds of them dotted around Scotland, former dwellings of labourers now used by hikers in need of refuge.

The bothy consists of one room with a fireplace on the end wall. Lengths of wood have been fashioned into crude benches, rather like the sort you get at school. On the other side of the room are two wooden beds; like the benches, they take rustic to a whole new level. There are two grey, rather dusty blankets hanging across a length of rope which stretches like a washing line from one side of the wall to the other.

Basic would be the most flattering way to describe the bothy, but I'm not in a position to be fussy. This will make an ideal place to spend the night, protected from the elements.

I inspect the fireplace and can see ashen remains of a fire in the grate. On the side is a box of matches. When I pick it up, there are only a couple of matches inside and the box feels damp. There is a small pile of twigs on the floor, which someone has kindly left to dry out for kindling. I make a mental note to do the same before I leave. All I need now are

251

some bigger pieces of wood to feed the fire once I've got it going.

Outside, I notice a small wood store. There isn't a huge amount of wood, just a few fallen branches that have been collected from the forest floor, but it will save me the job of trying to find dry firewood.

I gather the wood in my arms and go inside. I eye the blankets hanging up. I suppose they're better than nothing. I have a thermal-foil blanket in my rucksack and I can sleep on one of the blankets and drape the other over the foil. One underneath is worth two on top is what I tell the kids on the DoE weekends.

I set about making a fire and am rather pleased to discover a box of firelighters. Purist hikers would frown at the shortcut, but I have no qualms about using them. This isn't some outdoor adventure to fuel an inner-city need to get in touch with nature, this is real-life survival. I consider for a moment that the smoke may give away my hiding place to Tris but decide, at this point, he's probably returned to the croft. Besides, I'm cold, wet and tired. I need to keep warm to make it through the night.

I take off my jacket and remove the walkie-talkie from the pocket, standing it on the wooden bench. My fleece is a little damp around the cuffs and collar, so I take that off as well. Fortunately, my jumper and thermal long-sleeved T-shirt are both dry. Next, I take off my trousers and peel off the thermal leggings. They are both damp, as are my socks and shoes. The earth floor is cold on the soles of my feet; little bits of grit and dirt stick to my skin.

I move one of the benches in front of the fire and drape my clothes over it to dry and then rather dubiously, take one of the blankets down from the makeshift clothes line. Stale air wafts around the room as I move the blanket. Not relishing the thought of it on my bare skin, I take the emergency foil blanket from my rucksack and drape that over me first. I rummage in the side pocket of the rucksack and retrieve the small packet of white pills. I pop one into my hand, hesitate and then slide my fingernail across the foil of a second one. I swallow the guilt down with the tablets. These are exceptional circumstances and at least this way I'll be able to get some sleep and be better prepared for tomorrow.

The fire is alight but it's more of a smoulder than a raging burn and every now and then plumes of smoke billow down the chimney. I idly wonder when it was last swept. The upkeep of the bothies is down to volunteers and I guess those not so far off the beaten track are probably better maintained than this one. There seems to be a distinct lack of love here but, nevertheless, I'm grateful. Sleeping under the stars in the pouring rain is highly unappealing.

My stomach gives a little roll of angst as I think of Andrea. She's stuck on the side of that embankment, exposed to the elements. I can only pray she's managed to cover herself with the foil blanket. Perhaps the bushes above her on the embankment will offer some protection from the weather. I gulp down a hard ball of fear that tries to lodge itself in my throat.

'I'm so sorry, Andrea,' I whisper. 'Please be safe. Please make it through the night. Please don't think I've abandoned you.'

A scuffling noise outside makes me jump as fear shoots

through me. I leap to my feet and rush to the window, peering out into the leaching light.

I'm not sure how far I've come from the croft and can only hope that Tris hasn't been tracking me. As I moved through the forest, I constantly checked over my shoulder for any sign of him.

More for comfort than anything else, I pick up the penknife I laid out on the bench with my clothes. The long wooden handle is heavy in my palm and the steel blade nestles snugly in its slot. I open the four-inch blade, the polished metal reflecting the flickering flames of the fire. As long as I make sure it is always within easy reach, I will have something to defend myself with.

In all honesty, I'm not sure I have the nerve to use the knife on another human, but if my life depends on it, I hope my basic instinct to survive will take over.

I listen intently for any sound that would indicate someone moving around outside but all is quiet. Comforting myself with the thought that the noise I heard was probably a wood-land inhabitant, I put the knife down beside me, making a conscious decision to leave the blade open. My stomach is rumbling and I need some food inside me before my body starts to close down to conserve energy and warmth. I have three cereal bars in my rucksack and an apple. I decide to go for the fruit first.

From the corner of my eye, I notice the little red light on the walkie-talkie flickering. A thread of fear laces its way through me. It can only mean one thing: Tris. Does that mean he's within range? How far can these things transmit? I reach over, hesitating before touching the handset, the irrational notion that he will somehow know what I'm doing making me falter.

The red flashing light stops before I pick it up. Has he gone? Or was he there, waiting for me to reply?

Drawing the handset to me, I turn up the volume dial. There is silence.

And then Tris's voice comes so loud out of the speaker, I almost drop the handset. I adjust the volume control again to a more natural level.

'Hello, Carys, it's me, Tris. I hope you're OK. It's silly of you to be hiding out there in the forest. I know that I'm not going to be able to change your mind, but I have someone here who might.' There's a pause but I remain silent. 'Can you at least let me know you're listening. Can you hear me? Over.'

Part of me is screaming not to reply to him, but another part, a more insistent part of my brain screams louder.

I depress the button to speak. 'I can hear you.'

'Good stuff. Right, I'm passing you over now.'

There's a small silence and the next voice I hear takes my breath away.

'Hello, Mum. It's me, Alfie.'

Chapter 25

All tiredness, aches and pains are expelled as my whole body jolts into life. I jump to my feet, the blanket falling from my shoulders. My brain plays catch-up for a second as I process the fact that Alfie must be with Tris and I force myself to answer.

'What are you doing here?' I dispense with radio etiquette and the need to say 'over' each time.

'I . . . er . . . didn't fancy staying with Bradley any more.'

'Why?'

'We had an argument. I told him I was going to stay with a mate. I didn't say who and he didn't ask.'

'How did you know where to come?' Probably not the most pressing of questions, but I feel totally thrown by Alfie's presence.

'Ruby told me. It was all on Joanne's laptop.'

I take a moment to process this latest development. How or why Alfie's here is, on the scale of things, unimportant. All I can think of now is that he's with Tris, and my mind is filled with thoughts of his safety. 'But you're OK? I mean, really OK?' Will he pick up on what I'm asking? I can't think of any secret code I can apply.

'Yeah, sure, Mum. I'm fine,' he replies.

I listen hard for any inflection in his voice, any telltale hint that he might not be fine, but I can't hear any. He sounds pleasant and, if I'm honest, this is one of most civil conversations we've had in some time. Although, on second thoughts, I wonder if that in itself is the code? His usual grumpy grunting teenage self is conspicuous by its absence. Is he trying to tell me there is something wrong simply by pretending there isn't? Not for the first time this weekend, my thoughts are going around in circles. I simply cannot think straight.

'How did you get here?' I ask, focusing on more practical aspects.

Before Alfie can answer, Tris speaks. 'Carys, we can chat about those sorts of details in the morning. I assume you are coming back here. You wouldn't abandon Alfie, would you?'

Too fucking right I wouldn't. I stop myself from responding, for the first time grateful that the press-to-talk button gives me the second I need to compose myself. I don't want Alfie to know I'm frightened. If I suddenly fly off the handle at Tris, it might provoke him into doing something rash. What that something might be, I don't know.

'Yes, I'll be back tomorrow,' I say, aware there is no other option. 'But, Tris, I'm trusting you to look after Alfie for me. And, Zoe, if you can hear me, you will too, won't you? You'll look after him, like I'd look after one of yours?'

I hope Zoe is listening. I might not be able to predict what Tris will do, but Zoe is my friend, and like me she is a mother, so surely she won't let Tris do anything to harm Alfie.

'Don't be worrying now, Carys,' says Tris. 'We'll look after Alfie for you. Won't we, Zoe?'

'Yes, Carys. You have my word.' It's Zoe's voice, from somewhere in the background.

'There, you have Zoe's word,' says Tris.

'Do I have your word too?' I have to ask. My mother-meter is going off the scale.

'Of course you have my word too,' says Tris. 'Now, get some rest, you'll need your energy for tomorrow. Make sure you're here by eleven o'clock. No later.'

'Or what?'

There is silence from the handset. I'm not sure if Tris is still there. Then after a few seconds I hear his voice again. This time it is low and threatening.

'Listen, Carys, don't fucking mess with me. You get your arse back here in the morning.'

'Now you wait a minute. Listen to yourself, Tris. What in God's name do you think you're doing?'

'In case it's escaped your memory, my wife is dead. And I'm sure I don't need to remind you that your son is here. So don't mess about.' His breathing is heavy through the speaker and I hear a controlled, menacing tone to his voice. There's an iciness to it I haven't heard before and my skin prickles at the sound.

My mind is immediately filled with images of Joanne lying outside the porch of the croft. Is it possible that her death wasn't an accident? Is it a coincidence, Tris showing up? I have a sudden memory of Andrea telling me he was in financial difficulty. If he has been having an affair with

Zoe, would both these things be enough to make him kill her?

A wave of nausea hits me and I retch as my stomach convulses. Bile reaches my throat and I cough and splutter, forcing myself to swallow it down.

My mind is reeling from the knowledge that Alfie is in that house with Tris. I need to get him out of there. And then there's Andrea. I must think of a way to help her. God only knows how she's bearing up.

I consider setting off now, heading not for the croft but the village. I need to raise the alarm and get the police up to the croft as soon as possible.

'Carys? Are you listening to me?' Tris's voice breaks my thoughts.

'Yes. Yes, I am listening, but hear what I have to say first,' I reply. I can't reconcile the Tris I've known for over twenty years with the Tris I have conjured up in my mind. The Tris who wanted me to hang myself. There must be a more logical explanation for his behaviour. 'Joanne's death – what if someone was with her when it happened but they didn't mean for any harm to come to her?'

'What are you talking about?'

I swallow hard. 'What if you killed Joanne by accident?'

'Why the hell would I want to kill my wife?'

'Not on purpose but by accident,' I say. 'I know about your affair with Zoe and the money problems. If you had an argument with her and it got out of hand, maybe her death was an accident.' I'm aware that I'm throwing Tris a lifeline, but it's not for his benefit as much as mine and Alfie's. I don't want to believe that he is capable of something like that, but if he is, then convincing him that I believe it was an accident might be my only hope of getting Alfie out of there.

'You really are deranged. Joanne said you were on the verge of a breakdown. From what Zoe's told me, you're the one who had the argument with Joanne. You were the last one to see her alive. Anyway, we can sort this fucking mess out in the morning.'

'OK. I promise I'll be there. Let me speak to Alfie.'

'Hang on a minute . . . '

I assume Tris is returning to the room where he's left Alfie. The next voice I hear is my son's.

'Mum? You OK? You are coming back tomorrow, aren't you?'

'Yeah, sure I am.' I inject a cheer into my voice I don't feel.

'Where exactly are you?' says Alfie. 'Why aren't you here?'

'I was . . . erm . . . hiking in the woods and got caught by the bad weather,' I reply, thinking on my feet. I don't know what Tris has told him. I mentally cross my fingers for luck and hope Alfie won't ask about Andrea or Joanne. What can I say? I can't say I think Tris is responsible for Joanne's death. I don't want to burden him with this suspicion. I err on the side of ignorance being bliss. 'Look, love, I'd better go. I'm really tired. I'll see you tomorrow, yeah?'

'Yeah, sure.'

'Love you.' I wait for a response. I can't remember the last time Alfie told me he loved me. Was it the morning Darren committed suicide? Was it when he left for school that day, a happy, carefree young lad of fifteen? Was that the last time he paused halfway down the path, turned and waved, telling me he loved me too? He'd come home from school that day and his life had changed forever. As did our relationship. He hasn't told me he loves me since that day.

Tears leak from the corners of my eyes. He isn't going to tell me now either. My heart cracks a little more. I wish I could take away his pain and fix him. I would give anything to have my happy, loving son back, but each day I fear he moves further towards the horizon, getting closer to the absolute event, the point of no return, when he will be lost forever.

I don't stop the tears. I need to let them fall. After everything that has happened this weekend, coupled with Alfie being here, I have to let that emotion out. I sink to my knees and howl, rocking to and fro, letting the tears run down my face, hoping they will somehow wash away the pain.

Chapter 26

Tris took the walkie-talkie from Alfie. 'Well done.'

'What happens now?' Alfie sat down at the kitchen table, and twirled the spoon in his mug of hot chocolate.

'We wait for your mum to come,' said Tris.

'And what have you told everyone at home?' asked Zoe.

'Nothing. Just said I'd be staying at a mate's house.'

'And Colin didn't mind?' Zoe had switched to mum mode and it was irritating Tris.

'Leave the lad alone,' he snapped. 'He gets enough of this crap from his own mum, he doesn't need it from you too.'

'I can't help it,' replied Zoe. 'Sorry, Alfie. I know you're nearly eighteen. I keep forgetting you're one of the older ones in the year, whereas my Ben is one of the babies.' She looked over at Tris. 'August birthday.'

'Ah, right, gotcha.' He smiled at Zoe and motioned for her to go upstairs. 'Erm, right, Alfie. You OK there for a while? I'm going to give Zoe a hand sorting the beds out.'

'Oh, I can kip on the sofa,' said Alfie. 'To be honest, I don't want to sleep in someone else's bed, not without clean sheets anyway.'

'Listen to you!' Tris laughed. 'You'll be asking for Egyptian cotton sheets next.' He gave the lad's shoulder a squeeze. Maybe a little harder than necessary, but he wanted Alfie to know who was in charge. 'OK, you stay here. I still need to sort a few things out.'

They left Alfie in the kitchen listening to music on his iPod.

'What the hell are we going to do now?' hissed Zoe once they were in the bedroom.

He put his finger to his lips and closed the door. 'Keep it down,' he said. 'It's fine. Don't worry about anything. Alfie being here is working out well. He's the one thing that will make Carys come back. We've got to get her to trust us. What sort of friends would we be, if we weren't concerned for her?'

'I'm not following.' Zoe dropped down on to the bed and Tris sat beside her, putting his arm around her shoulders.

'Listen, I've got it all planned.'

'You're not going to do anything to hurt Alfie, are you?' Zoe looked genuinely concerned and it reminded Tris of all the reasons he loved her. She was so much more sensitive, kind and loving than Joanne ever was. Zoe had a vulnerability about her that he'd never seen in his own wife. Joanne had never needed him. Sure, she had wanted him, but never *needed* anything. She was always self-sufficient, independent and capable. All the things that made him feel inadequate. No, Zoe brought out the best in him. She allowed him to be the man, to wear the trousers. She wanted looking after and he wanted to be the one to do it. He kissed the side of her head and she moved her face up to him, their lips meeting.

Zoe pulled away first. 'I do love you,' she said. 'You know that, don't you?'

Tris side-stepped the pang of guilt. He held his hand to Zoe's face as if drawing on her inner strength. 'Yes, I know that. And I love you too. Very much.'

'What happened with Joanne, I know it's truly awful,' said Zoe, her eyes firmly fixed on his, 'but, in a way, it's a good thing.' He felt her jaw move against his hand as she swallowed hard. 'I mean, something good can come out of something bad, can't it?'

'Yeah, sure it can.' He kissed the top of her head again, breaking eye contact and, thereby, negating the possibility his doubt might be seen on his face.

'I hope Carys doesn't fuck everything up for us,' said Zoe, with uncharacteristic bitterness. 'She might tell the police that one of us killed Joanne. You can bet that's what she's thinking, why else would she have run away?'

'She won't. Look, Carys was the last person to see Joanne alive. She has the motive and the opportunity. She's on the back foot here.' Tris pinched the bridge of his nose and closed his eyes tight in a bid to quell his emotions over his wife's death.

'Are you OK?' asked Zoe. 'Come on, Tris. Keep it together.'

'Yeah. Sure. I'm OK.' He dragged his hand down his face and as he opened his eyes, his attention was caught by the objects on the dressing table: three mobile phones, lined up alongside each other on a blue cloth bag. 'What are they?' he asked, nodding in the direction of the dressing table.

'Er . . . mobile phones?' Zoe replied, hanging a questioning inflection on the last word.

Tris threw a scowl her way before speaking. 'Whose are they?'

'Mine, Carys's and Andrea's. We had to hand them over when we were first picked up. Joanne said she was keeping hold of them so we couldn't use the map app to pinpoint our location.'

'Where did you find them?'

'In her bedside drawer. I had a look earlier. I didn't tell the others though.'

'Why not?'

Zoe shrugged. 'I'm not sure. I was frightened after what happened to Joanne. I thought one of them might be up to something. I didn't know who to trust.'

Tris eyed Zoe speculatively. He couldn't follow her reasoning but decided to let it drop for now. 'Best put them back where you found them. We'll leave them there for the police to find. You can tell them how frustrated Carys was about not having her phone.'

'That's actually true,' said Zoe. 'She did tell Joanne she wanted her phone, but Joanne wouldn't hear of it.'

'Make sure you tell that to the police. They need to know how upset and frustrated Carys was about the no-phone policy. That she was clearly agitated and frustrated by Joanne's behaviour.'

'I wish I'd gone downstairs and broken the argument up, then none of this would have happened,' said Zoe, putting her arms around him. 'You could have left Joanne, but instead you're having to deal with her death. I'm so sorry for you.'

Tris took a moment to compose himself. He was finding

it hard to process the welter of conflicting emotions. At no point had he told Zoe he was going to leave Joanne. To do so would have been financial suicide. But now that she was dead, he stood to benefit from the insurance as well as the funds in her personal bank account. He clasped Zoe's hands, taking in her delicate features which had always seemed somehow at odds with her toned body and above-average height. 'Things don't always go to plan, Zoe. We have to adapt and make the best out of a bad situation. What was it you said, something good out of something bad . . . ?'

MONDAY

Chapter 27

Through sheer exhaustion, both physically and mentally, I find myself nodding off into a light and uneasy sleep which lasts for only a short while before I jolt awake. Immediately, the fear returns and I curl up in a ball on the wooden slatted bed and, once again, go over my plan for the morning.

When the craggy fingers of dawn find their way through the trees and slip through the window of the bothy, fear and anticipation battle within me at what I have to do.

Alfie is my priority. I need to get him away from Tris before I do anything else. Thoughts of Andrea's well-being are not far behind and I wonder what sort of night she's had. I hope she was able to protect herself from the overnight rain? Is she warm enough? I hope she's coping with the pain of her injury. 'I'll come for you as soon as I can, Andrea. I promise,' I say out loud. There's no one to hear my promise, but I offer it up to the little bothy all the same.

I unfold myself and, with the blanket still around me, move over to the fire which has long since died out. It was enough though to dry my clothes. I dress quickly and hope I'll start to feel warmer once I'm on the move.

It should be easy tracking along the water's edge, but I need to make sure I recognise the spot where I fell. Once up the side of the hill, I'll have to rely on luck and judgement to find my way.

It has been raining in the night and the going is slippery and wet. It takes me longer than I feel it should and I check my watch regularly to give me an indication of pace. Yesterday, while I had been hiding from Tris, I'd checked my watch and noted the time, which I also did when I arrived at the bothy. I estimate that, yesterday, I walked for approximately ninety minutes. If I pick up my pace and keep an eye on the time, that will give me a good indication of when I've reached the point where I fell.

I've only been tramping through the forest for about twenty minutes when the rain comes again. For goodness's sake, how much rain can one place get? I pull the zip up high on my jacket, which I'm still wearing inside out, and hope it will only be a small shower.

As it turns out, I don't need to worry about timing myself to where I fell. A little over an hour later, I spot the rock where I hid from Tris yesterday. All I have to do now is make it up to the top of the embankment.

Climbing is hard work. The rain-drenched ground offers little purchase and my feet keep slipping as I scramble to pull myself up over moss-covered rocks. It's only by luck that I missed these on my way down yesterday. Where the earth is bare, I kick toe-holes in with my boot to lever myself up. Finally, I drag myself over the top and on to the even ground.

I roll on to my back to catch my breath. The branches sway

in the wind, which has pushed the rain clouds away. The early-morning dawn has made way for sunlight; it punches its way through the gaps in the trees, warming the ground and releasing the aroma of damp earth and pine needles. In any other circumstances, it would be glorious to lie here, revelling in the peace and tranquillity. Funny to think that, before, I found comfort in the croft and fear from the forest. Now, it's the other way around.

Once I leave this forest, I will have all to play for.

Eventually, I find myself at the edge of the forest behind the croft. Crouching low and using the trunk of a tree as cover, I look down at the building. My gaze rests momentarily on the shed and I think of Joanne, wondering how it has all come to this.

I mustn't lose focus. Whatever the reasons, Joanne is now dead and my own life is in danger, as is my son's. The latter is the most pressing fear by far. Somehow I have to get Alfie out of there. We both need to get as far away from Tris as possible.

With my jacket still inside out, I pull the hood up over my head. Then I check that the walkie-talkie's volume is turned down; I don't want to blow my cover this time. I survey the ground between my hiding place and the croft. The biggest open space is from the edge of the forest to the shed where the bicycle still rests. I estimate it to be approximately fifty metres. Being on higher ground, I'll have the benefit of gravity; if I run in a direct line with the shed, keeping low, I'll minimise the chances of being spotted. I just have to hope that neither Tris nor Zoe choose that moment to look out of the upstairs window.

I take a deep breath, close my eyes for a second while I steel myself, and then with a quick glance around I burst out from the trees and into the open space beyond.

The ground is uneven, pitted with stones, rocks and rabbit holes that I can only see at the last minute but manage to leap over or swerve round. Wet strands of long grass whip the bottoms of my trousers as I hurtle towards the shed. I glance up at the house, but only briefly, the ground is too dangerous not to watch my tread. An unexpected rock causes my ankle to turn but I push on, gulping down the cry of pain which tries to break free. I don't have time to dwell on the possible injury. I stay on my feet and keep moving.

As I near the shed, I realise that my efforts to slow down are being hampered by the wet grass underfoot. Though I lean back and shorten my stride, it's not enough. I'm going to crash straight into the shed. I have two options. Either thump straight into the shed and risk the possibility of alerting Tris that I'm here, or dodge the shed but grab it as I go by, in a bid to stop myself.

I choose the latter and snatch at the corner of the shed. I feel a slice of wood dig into the ball of my hand, sending a searing pain that travels the length of my arm, but the shed does the trick and I manage to bring my uncontrolled run to a halt. I drop to the ground and sit with my spine pressed against the side of the shed, out of sight from the house, while I catch my breath and inspect my wounds.

'Shit,' I hiss, looking at my hand. A sliver of wood has sliced the palm below the base of my fingers and it stings. Blood oozes from the wound. There's also a large splinter embedded deep in my index finger. It's gone completely under the skin, leaving no end to pinch and pull out. It hurts like hell, but I've no option but to leave it for now. The cut concerns me more. I slip my backpack from my shoulders and rummage in the side pocket for the first-aid kit and set about cleaning the wound with a sterile wipe.

When I can see the cut more clearly, it is apparent that whatever first-aid I administer will be a temporary solution only. The shard of wood has dug a wedge-shape gash in the skin, the breadth of my middle fingers; it wags up and down like a cat flap. I'm going to need stitches, I'm sure. In the meantime, I will have to make do with a square of gauze and a narrow white microporous bandage. I rip the end down the middle and tie it around my wrist, using my teeth to pull it tight.

From my position at the edge of the shed, I have a clear view of the rear of the croft, about twenty metres away. I scan the downstairs windows but can't see anyone. Keeping low, I scurry across the garden and hunch down at the side of the porch.

I listen carefully for any sign that I have been spotted but it seems, so far, I've been successful. Slowly, I poke my head around the porch and, still crouching, move up to the door. Through the glass, I can see Alfie. He has his back to me as he stands at the worktop by the window overlooking the front of the property.

He appears to be making himself a bowl of cereal and a hot

drink. Filling the kettle and putting it on to boil. He's moving his head from side to side and his shoulders are bobbing too. He has his earphones in and is, no doubt, listening to some heavy rock thrash music that he doesn't have the courtesy to use headphones for when he plays it at home. He's wearing a hoodie and, for once, this isn't pulled up over his head. His jeans bag at the backside and bunch up at the top of his designer-label trainers. Ones he had wanted for his birthday, which I had bought him, even though I couldn't afford them. My only thanks had been a grunt and a 'ta'.

Alfie appears to be alone in the kitchen. This may be my only chance. I quickly slip out of the porch and, keeping as close to the wall as possible, I navigate the woodstore and reach the double doors of the living room. I hold my breath as very slowly I look through the window. Tris and Zoe are both in the room. I can see their heads over the top of the sofa. Then Tris gets up and I snatch my head away, praying he hasn't seen me.

A couple of seconds pass and I hear Tris talking. He's going to light the fire. I steal another look and this time he is kneeling in front of the hearth, raking the grate with a poker.

This is the opportunity I need. I hurry to the door and gently apply pressure on the handle, breathing a sigh of relief when there's no resistance: the door is unlocked. I slowly push against the wood and the door opens into the kitchen.

Adrenalin surges through me and my breathing quickens. Whether it's a subconscious thing or not, I don't know, but as I step over the threshold, Alfie turns to face me. His eyes grow wide and his whole face flushes with surprise. The cup he has just taken from the hook slips through his hands but he somehow manages to stick his foot out to break the fall. The cup still hits the floor, but only the handle breaks off.

I hold up my hand and pat thin air while putting my finger to my mouth with my other hand in a bid to silence him. He pulls out his earphones and stares at me.

'Everything all right?' comes Zoe's voice from the living room.

Alfie hesitates but I nod urgently and mouth for him to answer. 'Yeah. All good,' he calls.

I let out a breath. 'Get your coat,' I whisper. It's too cold outside to even think of venturing anywhere without at least a jacket. 'Hurry up.' Alfie seems rooted to the spot. 'Alfie!' I hiss as quietly as I can.

'It's in the hall,' says Alfie, giving another glance towards the dining room and hallway beyond.

I waggle my hand to urge him along. 'Get it.' Alfie looks down at the broken cup, but I tap his arm and almost push him out of the kitchen.

For once, Alfie does as he is told and fetches his coat from the hall and pushes the kitchen door closed behind him.

'We need to go,' I say. 'Put that on outside.'

As I turn to leave the way I'd come in, the kitchen door opens. 'I heard a clatter. Did you . . . ?' The question dries on Zoe's lips. Momentarily turned to stone, she doesn't move as she looks at me.

I clasp my hands together in prayer. 'Please, Zoe, please . . .' I don't need to say anything. We both know what I'm pleading for.

Then Tris calls, 'I could murder a coffee. Have we got any milk left?'

'I'll make it. You stay there,' says Zoe. 'Alfie's going out for a cigarette.'

I throw a look at Alfie, who shrugs. It's the first I know about him smoking. Zoe makes flapping motions with her hands and, nudging Alfie out of the way, picks up the kettle. She looks at me and for a second we stare at each other. I don't know what she's trying to convey.

'Come with us,' I urge.

Zoe shakes her head. 'I can't. You two go and get the hell out of here.'

'Not without you.'

'Please, Carys, go. I'm fine. I promise. I'm safe.'

I can't risk trying to change her mind. I can't stay any longer, not if I want to save myself and, more importantly, Alfie. I must put him above and beyond any friendship. I give Zoe one last look before turning and grabbing the sleeve of Alfie's jacket, which he has now put on, and yank him towards the door. Out of the corner of my eye, I spy a mobile phone. It's not one I recognise but, without giving it any further thought, I grab it and drop it discreetly into my pocket.

We run to the end of the garden and up the hill towards the trees.

'Where are we going?' Alfie pants.

'I'll tell you in a minute. Just keep running.'

Once we are two or three trees deep into the forest, I allow myself to stop and lean against a tree as I catch my breath. I look at the phone I snatched from the kitchen. It looks like a cheap basic model.

'Whose is this?' I ask.

'Dunno,' says Alfie.

I'm not entirely sure he's telling me the truth, but I don't question him further. Instead, I take a small waterproof pouch from my pocket and drop the phone into it, sealing it tight. The waterproof pouch is designed like a bum-bag to be worn around the waist, and I adjust the straps before fastening it in place. 'I'll keep it with me. It might come in handy,' I say.

'What are we going to do now?' asks Alfie.

'We can't go into the woods. We'll get lost. I've no idea how far or even where to go to get help,' I say, recalling my wasted efforts yesterday. 'We have two options: the road, only I think it won't take long before Tris catches up with us – he must have a car up here somewhere.'

'What's the other option?'

'The river.'

'The river?'

'Yep. There are two kayaks tied to the jetty at the water's edge in front of the croft. If we can get down there without being spotted, we can escape. Then we simply need to follow the river until we get to the nearest town. We can get help from there.'

'Mum, this is crazy. Why are we running away from Tris?'

'Because he's dangerous. You're going to have to trust me on this – I haven't got time to explain. Believe me, we need to get as far away from him as possible.'

'Mum—'

'Alfie, don't argue, not now. There's Andrea to think of too. She's fallen down a gorge and injured herself. She's been there all night. She needs urgent medical attention. Please, trust me.'

'Trust you?' Alfie's eyebrows rise above his fringe.

My patience snaps. 'Don't start. For once in your life, please do as I tell you. We're going to sneak down to the river and get in those bloody boats. Do you hear me?' I realise at some point I've grabbed his upper arms. I move my hands away.

'All right,' says Alfie in a way that says *keep your hair on*.

I'm relieved he's decided not to argue. We don't have time for that. Any minute now, Tris will surely realise Alfie has disappeared. I only hope Zoe's OK.

'Right, let's go down the track,' I say. 'And then we can double back. Hurry – we haven't got much time before Tris will be out looking for us.'

We jog through the forest, keeping parallel with the track until we reach the bend in the road and then drop down on to the track and make our way up the lane, thus keeping well out of sight of anyone looking out of the windows of the croft.

'We'll have to take our chances from here,' I say in a low voice. 'Keep close to this edge and on the count of three, we'll run down to the river. OK?'

'OK.'

'Ready?' I look at Alfie, who nods. 'One, two, three.' I sprint from the side of the track as fast as I can. Alfie's feet slap the ground behind me. We clamber up the embankment and then drop down the other side where the ground slopes towards the water.

The kayaks are exactly where we left them. I pull the rope to undo the slip knot on one of them.

'Take both of them,' says Alfie, pulling the rope free on the other kayak. 'We can set it adrift further up the river so Tris can't use it to follow us.'

'But it will slow us down,' I say. Suddenly Tris is at the top of the bank. He must have seen us through the croft window and chased after us. He begins to shout our names. I yell at Alfie. 'Get in the kayak! Quick!' We both push the boats out into the river. The temperature of the water sends shock waves up my legs. It is absolutely freezing but I don't have time to worry. As the water rises to my knees I glance behind me. Tris is now at the bottom of the bank and running towards the jetty.

I shout again. 'Come on, Alfie!' He has only just pushed the second kayak away. If he's not careful, Tris will catch him. 'Get in!' I yell as I throw myself into the first kayak and take up the paddle. The gash on my hand stings as I grip the wooden shaft of the paddle and I feel the wound under the bandage open.

I look over my shoulder. Tris is nearly at the water's edge. I urge Alfie with every fibre in my body to get in the boat and paddle.

The kayak rocks from side to side as Alfie hauls himself into the seat behind me. He hooks the rope of the other kayak on to ours and takes up the paddle.

'Go!' he shouts, plunging the paddle into the water. I follow suit, ignoring the pain in my hand as I drill down with my paddle. Alfie shouts the strokes and, despite dragging another boat behind us, we soon settle into a rhythm and move at speed through the water.

I hear Tris shout after us and I glance over my shoulder. He has run along the riverbank but now, realising he can't do anything to stop us, has ground to a halt. His hands rest on his hips as he watches us.

Chapter 28

We paddle hard, the current in our favour as the river snakes its way through the landscape, widening along the way. The banks on either side are becoming further apart and the wind whips across from one side to the other, battering us as it does so.

'How far are we going?' calls Alfie. 'My arms are killing me. Can't we stop?'

I rest the shaft of the paddle across my lap and turn to look at my son. 'I want to put as much distance between us and Tris as possible.' I look beyond Alfie at the other kayak we are still tugging. 'We can get rid of that now.'

'We'll ditch it in a minute. Let's stop for a rest now.'

'OK,' I concede. 'We'll stay in the kayak though, keep to the river in case Tris turns up in his car. I don't want to be at a disadvantage. We can let the current take us along for a while.' I move the paddle to place it lengthways down the kayak between our two seats. Alfie does the same with his. The sky ahead is grey and the temperature has dropped. 'I don't like the look of those clouds up there.'

'Doesn't look good from where I'm sitting either,' says Alfie.

I shift round on the seat of the kayak so I am now facing him. His voice sounds strange. Dark, like the sky. Cold, like the temperature. Hard, like the rocks that line the riverbank. His arms are resting on his knees. His long limbs scrunched up in the boat. His back is hunched and his head dipped, but under his thick lashes his eyes are fixed on me. He reminds me so much of Darren.

'You OK?' I ask. I lean forward to rest my hand on his arm in a comforting gesture. One that shows no challenge or confrontation. I've seen that look on his face before, rather too often of late. It comes and settles when he is brooding, when his mood is dipping and when I feel he is at his most volatile.

Alfie moves his arm a fraction, enough for me to know he doesn't want my sympathy. He is cross with me but I don't know why. We eye each other for a second or two but it is me who speaks first in an effort to dispel whatever ill feeling Alfie is experiencing. 'I haven't had a chance to ask, but how did you get here? And what exactly are you doing here? Why come all this way?'

'That's a lot of questions.'

'Like I said, I haven't had a chance to ask you.'

The kayak rocks gently in the current of the river as it carries us along. I have a sudden memory of rocking Alfie in a cradle when he was a baby, whispering soothing words to calm the angry little soul that he was. He's always been what I would term high maintenance, even before Darren died, but there was love there in those days. Something I'm aware I haven't seen in my son for a long time. I wish I could do something to help him. So many times I have questioned myself and my parenting of him as a youngster. Have I done something to turn him into this displaced, angry young man? All I've ever wanted is to love him, but he's never wanted that. Not from me, anyway. Darren was the one Alfie always sought approval from and, as was his due, he received it. They were a little club of their own at times, Darren and Alfie, but I never minded. I always thought of it as a father-and-son thing and it gave me immense pleasure, knowing they were so close.

Alfie sits up straighter and stretches out his legs. His fingers drum on his knee. 'I got the train to Aberdeen and then hitched a lift to here.'

Hitched a lift? I bite down on the urge to lecture him on the dangers of hitch-hiking. He is being particularly vague and there is an edge to his voice. He doesn't want me asking questions. However, I have him trapped in the boat, he can hardly storm off. I decide to push my luck. 'You hitch-hiked?'

'Sort of,' he says nonchalantly. 'I got a lift with Tris.'

'With Tris?' Surprise pitches my voice in a higher-than-normal range.

'For God's sake, Mum! Will you stop getting so freaked out by everything I say!' Alfie glares at me. 'It's your birthday, right? I knew from Ruby that Tris was coming up here, so I tagged along. I wanted to surprise you.'

I eye my son cautiously. He's not shown any interest in my birthday since Darren's death. Hasn't even wished me happy birthday, let alone given a card or gift. I can't help privately questioning his motivation today or the effort he's gone to.

'Well, you've certainly surprised me,' I say. 'What was Tris like when you were driving up? Did he seem agitated? Did he say anything about Joanne?'

'He seemed normal. Said he could do without the drive, but Joanne had insisted.'

'Was he cross with her?'

Alfie gives a dramatic tut to emphasise his annoyance. 'Can you stop with all the questions about Tris. Like I said, he seemed normal.'

'You do realise what's happened, don't you?' I ask. 'And that Tris is probably involved in some way.'

'What are you now, some sort of detective?'

I rub my temples with my fingertips. I want to get up and pace around, but obviously it's impossible in this little kayak. Even on open water, I feel blocked in. Deep breaths keep my rising hysteria regulated. I speak again, this time more controlled. 'I know you couldn't have realised what Tris had done, but you need to know . . . he's dangerous. We have to get to the police station and tell them. They'll want to talk to you about Tris. We can ring Seb and you can talk to him first. He could tell you what sort of thing to expect.'

'Firstly, I'm not a fucking child, so stop treating me like one. I'm quite capable of talking to the police. And secondly, do you seriously expect me to speak to that wanker?' says Alfie, his lip curling into a snarl. 'I don't think so.'

I look at my son, forcing myself not to admonish him for his language. My heart is heavy at the sheer amount of hate he harbours. I shouldn't have mentioned Seb. I had momentarily fantasised that Alfie would go to Seb for help and end up having a breakthrough bonding moment, where he'd finally accept Seb and realise he's a good guy. How perfect that would be? We could all have our happy ending.

It's nothing more than a fantasy though. Alfie is never going to accept Seb – and where does that leave me? I can't expect Seb to carry on the way we have been. He comes and stays with me on his days off, tiptoes around the house when Alfie's there, gallantly ignores Alfie ignoring him and has even, at my behest, kept quiet when Alfie's been rude to me. Although, the last time that happened, Seb did say he wasn't sure how much longer he could bite his tongue. He also said that he wouldn't be able to live under the same roof as Alfie.

I can't say I blame him. I wouldn't want to either. Equally, I don't want Seb witnessing the sort of disagreements I have with Alfie. I feel so ashamed. My only hope is that, assuming Alfie does go to university, things between us might improve. I cling to the thought that life could get better.

The kayak gives a lurch to one side and then the other. The weather has closed in without me noticing and the water has become choppier, the gusting wind propelling us down-river. The current has picked up too and we are moving faster now. Drops of rain begin to speckle my face. The river is a dark grey, a mirror image of the rain-filled clouds above us. And there is the sound of the river churning and turning as it tumbles over itself and bounces off rocks and boulders which jut out along the way.

Taking a good look around, I notice that the river has narrowed, thus increasing the pressure of the water now being forced through a smaller gap.

'I think we'd better start paddling,' I say, all thoughts of home life without Alfie relegated to the back of my mind. 'The river turns up ahead and there's no way of knowing what to expect, but we should be prepared. Cut that other kayak loose now, it will hold us up.' Alfie doesn't move. I pick up my paddle. 'Alfie, we need to paddle. Cut the kayak free.'

Still he doesn't move. 'You've not asked me what your birthday surprise is? Aren't you curious?'

'What?' I'm struggling to work out why, at a time like this, my birthday present is suddenly an issue.

'Well, aren't you?' He smiles at me but I see no warmth in his face.

'What's going on?' I can't hide the caution in my voice.

'I'm about to give you your birthday surprise.' The smile drops from his face and he fixes me with those blue eyes of his, so like Darren's. For the first time in two years, Alfie opens up to me and I catch my breath as I read his soul.

Chapter 29

'I know I haven't been the most attentive son when it comes to your birthday and I was trying to think of something you'd like,' he says, looking up to the sky in a mock-thoughtful way. 'I haven't got much money to buy you expensive presents, not like Dad used to.'

'It doesn't matter,' I say cautiously.

Alfie carries on with his speech. 'So, I thought I'd give you something money can't buy.' He smiles broadly at me. 'I thought I'd give you me. My heart, actually.'

'Your heart?'

'Yes, I thought I'd let you see into my heart and what I'm all about. Because, let's face it, Mum, we haven't exactly been close lately, have we?'

I shake my head. 'It's been difficult,' I say.

The boat rocks violently to the left and I grab the side to steady myself. The water is faster than ever now, thundering along and taking the kayak with it. My spine tingles with a sense of foreboding, a sensation not dissimilar to what I feel when I'm teetering on the edge of an argument with Alfie, only this time it's infinitely more intense. One wrong word now, or even the wrong tone to my voice, has the potential to send us spilling over the abyss and into the depths of an argument. Or worse.

I watch Alfie push the toe of his trainer under the stem of the paddle and flick it up to his outstretched hand. He holds the paddle with two hands and swings it round over the side of the kayak. A reflex reaction makes me duck out of the way, the paddle missing me by a few inches. 'Hey! Watch out!'

'I'm not the one who needs to watch out,' says Alfie. He dips the end of the paddle into the water for a moment before pulling it out and resting it on the side of the kayak.

I've long known that Alfie is unpredictable. He's volatile. He's nasty. And although I would never admit it to anyone else, he scares me. Today, if I was asked to rate my fear on a scale of one to ten, with ten being the highest, I would have to say I was at level nine right now. The high end of nine.

'I'm talking about you, Mum,' he says with a sneer. 'You need to watch out.' He begins drumming his fingers again, a sure sign his level of agitation is increasing.

If I can change the direction of the conversation, distract him, steer his mind elsewhere, I might be able to avoid a full-blown fight. Part of me thinks this is foolish. Diversion tactics have never worked before, not once he's locked in this blinkered mindset, but I must try. As a mother, I can't stop trying to help my son, no matter what happens or what he does or what I have seen lurking behind his eyes. Giving up on him is not an option. For a second, I revisit my fantasy of a life with Seb and harmony with Alfie. As I do, I'm struck by a moment of clarity: I will never be able to have both. It's got to be one or the other: Seb or Alfie.

I look down at the pool of water that has formed in the bottom of the kayak. The bigger waves are breaching the side of the boat. 'I think we could be in for a rough ride,' I say, nodding to the river. 'Shall we get ourselves through the next stretch? We can talk properly once we reach the village.'

'I don't want to talk later. I want to talk now,' says Alfie. 'You always do this. Try to stop me from talking. We always have to do it on your terms, when you're ready. Well, I'm ready now and seeing as you can't walk away from me this time, I guess that means you're a captive audience.'

'Alfie, please. Let's get to safety,' I plead. Acutely aware I am powerless, I pick up the paddle. My hand is shaking. As I lift the paddle to grasp it with both hands, Alfie lurches forward and grabs it. He twists it hard to the left, bending my wrist over to the point where, if I don't let go of the paddle, I will either tip over or break my wrist. I release my hold. Alfie snatches the paddle and throws it into the kayak behind us.

'You're going to listen whether you like it or not.' He fixes his eyes on me. I don't say anything for fear of antagonising him further. I know what will happen next if I do. I feel myself physically shrink into the seat. I realise that I am subconsciously rubbing the top of my arm. The bruise from his last attack has almost faded. It had been a particularly deep bruise. The memory of the pain makes me wince. It had hurt for days, my whole arm ached when I lifted it. Seb had questioned me about it, but I had passed it off as a knock from the newel post at the foot of the stairs. He'd looked unconvinced but hadn't pursued it, much to my relief. I think if he had, my resolve would have crumbled. There have been several times when I've been on the brink of confessing the toxicity of my relationship with Alfie, but I've always held back. Even in my most vulnerable moments, the desire to protect my son has been stronger. But everyone has their breaking point.

I take a deep breath and try a different approach. Conciliatory and unchallenging. It sometimes works. 'OK, Alfie.' I give a small smile as an indicator of my intent. 'That's fine. What do you want to talk about?'

'Thought you might have worked it out by now.' He lets out a long sigh. 'I'm going to have to spell it out, aren't I?' He raises his eyebrows and I brace for impact as he pauses to ramp up the tension like some reality talent show on Saturday-night TV. Then he launches his attack. 'I hate you. H A T E. Hate you. No, wait. Hate isn't strong enough. I *despise* you.'

I force myself to remain calm. This isn't the first time Alfie has said those words to me. They used to hurt a lot, but these days my invisible shield does a fine job of deflecting the spiteful comments. He doesn't hate me. He's angry, that's all. He hates what has happened, not me. I'm absolutely sure of that. It is not dissimilar to my own feelings about him at times. Not that I would ever admit that to anyone, but to myself, I can just about stomach the truth. Sometimes I don't like my son. I love him, but I don't like him.

Another silence sits between us as Alfie studies my reaction to his battle cry. I maintain my calm and unruffled exterior. 'I know you're angry with me and hurting because of what happened,' I begin, but am cut off before I can say anything else.

'Shut the fuck up!' He screams the words at me and for the second time I feel myself physically shy away from him. His face is only inches from my own. I can see the vein in the side of his temple pulsating and the ligaments in his neck look like they are about to burst from his skin. 'I do hate you, and yes I am angry, but it's all your fault and that adds to my hate. Do you get it? DO YOU?'

I nod. 'Yes. It's OK. I understand.' This isn't a new situation either. He needs an outlet for his anger and confusion, for his hurt and pain. I am his mother and, as my counsellor explained, I am the safe place for him to express himself.

The burst of anger subsides and Alfie sits down on his seat. The noise of the river and the wind blowing through the trees fades into the background as I watch my son. His leg is jiggling up and down, another sign of extreme agitation, and his fingers curl and then uncurl around the handle of the paddle. There's a shift in mood, and not for the better. His jaw is clenched and there is a hardness to his whole face which only serves to give a more dangerous undertone to his behaviour.

'You don't understand. You like to think you do, but you don't,' says Alfie. 'Sending me to those counselling sessions, as if that would make everything all right. I've heard you talking to Seb. Muttering to each other in the kitchen, thinking I can't hear you, but I can. Telling him that I need time to process what's happened, accept it and come to terms with it. All that bullshit shrink jargon.'

'I'm sorry. I thought talking to Doctor Huntingdon helped.'

Alfie looks up to the sky in exasperation. The raindrops bounce off his nose. He pushes his wet hair away from his forehead and then returns his gaze to me. 'It's all bullshit, Mum. I played along with it. In fact, it was quite amusing, seeing how far I could convince that stupid old bastard that I was coming to terms with it all.'

I notice the use of the past tense. '*Played* along with it?' I ask.

'Oh yeah, I forgot to mention. I sacked him.'

'Doctor Huntingdon? You don't see him any more?'

Alfie shrugs. 'It got boring.'

I take in this new information and try to find any link with Alfie's recent behaviour. Being brutally honest, I can't say there's been any obvious change, not that I've noticed anyway. He's been his usual pained self. 'It's supposed to help you.'

'Help me or help you? It didn't do anything for me, other than keep me amused. Sorry to disappoint you. I know you'd love me to be fixed.' His leg jiggles quicker. 'You'd be delighted if all my issues were resolved – that is the right expression, isn't it? Well, if they were, that would ease your guilt. And that would suit you fine.'

'The counselling wasn't for my direct benefit,' I say, although I'm aware that Alfie is pretty accurate. If Alfie hadn't been so badly affected by what happened, then I could have forgiven myself for my part in it. As it stands, I must take some responsibility for how my son is now.

'If you hadn't kicked Dad out, then he wouldn't have killed himself.'

'It's not as straightforward as that.'

'That's your stock answer.' Alfie shakes his head in disgust. 'Why did you kick Dad out?'

Alfie sounds like a schoolteacher trying to get answers from a bewildered student. And I'm the student, not knowing if I'm about to get a gold star or punishment. I can feel the trepidation rising through my airways, almost suffocating my voice. I cough to clear my throat before I speak. 'I didn't love your dad. Things had happened in our relationship that couldn't be put right.'

'Wrong! That's the wrong answer.' Alfie leans forward. 'You didn't believe Dad about Ruby.'

'That's not true. I did believe your father.' And I had. When Joanne and Tris had come round that evening, to confront us about Ruby's growing infatuation with Darren, I had never doubted for one moment my husband's side of the story. The other side was too preposterous to consider. I knew Darren wouldn't have got involved with an eighteen-year-old, let alone the daughter of our close friends. I look at Alfie. 'No one believed Ruby, not even her own parents.'

'Come off it, Mum. You know how angry and upset Joanne was. That's why you two fell out.'

'But that was because, like any mother, she automatically defended her own child. Once Tris had spoken to your dad properly, she realised it was all a silly crush Ruby had on your father.' Everything I'm saying is true and yet I am painfully aware that it is not the whole truth.

'Joanne never believed that. Why do you think she invited you up here for the weekend? She was going to tell you exactly how she felt about you.'

295

'I know that now, but Joanne's d—'

'Can we not keep going on about Joanne!' snaps Alfie. 'It's ruining my birthday present to you. Let's get back to you finding out about me. If that's OK with you?'

I give a small nod. 'Sure.'

'In order for you to find out more about me, I need to find out a few things from you.'

'OK. Like what?'

'Like why you didn't love me enough to let Dad stay. You might not have loved him, but I did. You didn't think of me then. All that mattered were your own selfish reasons for kicking him out. Never mind how much it would hurt me to see my dad in some seedy, dirty bedsit. To see him a broken man. All his self-esteem deleted, the hard-drive to his pride wiped clean. You didn't think how that would make me feel.'

'But staying together wouldn't have been any better. It would have been worse.'

'For who? For you – not for me. No, to have my dad there would not have been worse for me!' Alfie grabs at the paddle and bangs the end of the handle on the bottom of the kayak. 'You wanted him out of the way so you could get into bed with Seb. I bet you were carrying on with him long before you kicked Dad out.'

'That's not true!' I jump to my feet, forgetting where I am. The kayak tips violently to one side, sending both myself and Alfie off balance. For a moment, I think we are both going in, but the kayak tilts back to its central position, before returning to the rocking rhythm of the river. The extra width afforded to a tandem kayak is our saviour.

Alfie doesn't seem to notice. He gets to his feet. His hands clasped around the paddle. Rage colours his face a bright red. His eyes bulge as the suppressed tension erupts inside him. He lifts the paddle and draws it into the air behind him.

I hear myself gasp as, too late, I realise what he is planning to do. My hands fly to the air to protect myself as Alfie swings the paddle in a sweeping arc towards me and shouts, 'Happy birthday, Mum!'

It's amazing how the brain can process so many thoughts in a split second. Maybe because I've been expecting this moment, anticipating it, rehearsing this sort of situation for a long time now. Probably exploring it in my subconscious long before it ever reached the conscious part of my brain. This is the one and only opportunity I will have to make life better. This is my escape route.

Chapter 30

Tris had stood on the riverbank and watched the two kayaks and their occupants disappear under the stone bridge and out of sight. He gave a resolute sigh. There was no point trying to catch them. Even if he went and got his car, they'd be long gone by then.

He trudged up to the croft and was greeted at the door by Zoe.

'What happened? Where are they?'

'Gone. They took the kayaks.'

Whatever Zoe was about to say, she checked herself at the last moment and pressed her lips firmly together. Her features finally found an amicable setting before she spoke. 'Right, so, it's just me and you, then.'

'Looks that way. What about Andrea?'

'We need to get help. We'll take your car and head into the nearest town. There's no point us trying to find her, we can't do anything. We need to let the Search and Rescue team do their stuff.'

'We'd better go straight away or it will only raise questions why we didn't report this as soon as possible.'

Tris climbed on his pushbike and set off for the bothy he'd been staying in about two miles away. He'd left his car parked out of sight around the back.

Twenty minutes later he returned and began loading Zoe's belongings into the boot. He gave a last look at the croft before climbing into the car. He wouldn't admit it to Zoe, but he could feel a little ball of nerves rolling around in his stomach. They were about to give the performance of a lifetime at the police station. He wasn't naïve enough to think it would all be plain sailing, but as long as they held their nerve, they should be OK. He smiled at her. 'You all right?'

'Yeah, fine.'

Since she was clearly in no mood to talk, they sat in silence as the car made its way down the track and over the bridge. Tris's BMW wasn't the best of vehicles to be taking along the unmade road and he took it steady as it dipped and rolled through potholes, while small gravel stones pinged the wheel arches and the tyres crunched across the ground.

Eventually, they reached the end of the track and turned on to a small tarmac road which wound its way through the craggy hillside. Tris looked over at Zoe and was surprised to see she had a small mobile phone in her hand.

'Where did that come from?' he asked.

'It's a spare,' she said, without looking at him. Her thumb was clicking away on the keypad as she composed a text message.

'What do you mean, a spare? I thought we said we'd leave the phones at the croft?'

'Yeah, well, I forgot I had this one on me. It's an old one.

My just-in-case backup phone. It's not a smart phone, it can barely cope with messages and phone calls, let alone anything fancy like taking a decent picture.'

Tris took another glance at it. 'I see you've got a signal now.'

'Only one bar. I'm texting the kids to make sure they're OK.'

'You'd better not let the police know you've got that,' said Tris, feeling agitated that she'd not mentioned the spare phone before. 'In fact, probably best not to text the kids in case the police start checking phone records.'

'It's OK, it's a pay as you go. They won't be able to trace it.'

'Since when did you become an IT expert?' The agitation ramped up a level. 'For fuck's sake, Zoe. Put the bloody thing away. Switch it off!'

'I will. Soon as I've had a reply.' As if conjuring up the response, Zoe's phone made a ping-pong sound. 'And there it is,' she said.

'Now can you switch the fucking thing off,' snapped Tris. Not for one minute did he believe she was texting the kids. Keeping an eye on the road ahead while continuing to watch Zoe, he saw her switch the phone off and push it into the side pocket of her handbag. Somehow he was going to have to separate Zoe and her handbag so he could take a look at that phone.

'Before we go to the police station, can we stop somewhere so I can freshen up? I could do with going to the loo.'

Tris was about to tell her that it would probably look more authentic if they arrived in a dishevelled and hurried state, but changed his mind. A stop-off might give him a chance to look at the phone. 'Yeah, sure. There's a garage on the outskirts of Gormston. We can stop there.'

Fifteen minutes later, he pulled up outside the petrol station.

'I won't be long,' said Zoe. 'I'll grab a bottle of water while I'm in there. Do you want anything?' She reached down for her bag.

'Here, take my wallet,' he said, before she could pick up her bag. 'Use the cash in the side. I'll have a bottle of water too.'

Zoe took the wallet and trotted off into the garage. Tris wasted no time in diving his hand into her bag and whipping out the phone. It took ages to come to life, but eventually a little tune played out and the screen lit up.

'Bloody thing,' cursed Tris as he tried to work out how to get into the message box; this thing was a bloody relic. He was surprised to see an exchange of messages between Zoe's phone and another number. There was no name allocated to the other number. Tris glanced up at the petrol station to make sure she wasn't on her way out. He couldn't see her, so assumed she was still in the toilets.

He clicked open the message stream.

Message sent: All ok?
Message received: Yes.
Message sent: Completely?
Message received: 100%

Tris frowned and reread the exchange. He checked for other messages, but there weren't any and the contacts list was empty apart from this one number.

The car door opened, making Tris jump. Fuck! It was Zoe and he'd been caught red-handed.

'What are you doing?' she asked as she dropped into the seat. 'You've been in my handbag!' She snatched the phone from him.

There was no point in denying it or even pretending he was doing anything other than being nosy. 'I wanted to know who you'd messaged.'

'I told you. The boys.'

'Pretty glib conversation.'

'They're teenage boys. What do you expect?' She switched the phone off and replaced it in her bag. 'Now, let's get this over with.'

Chapter 31

Somewhere in the distance a dog is barking. It's muffled, as if the dog is a few gardens away where fences and a double-glazed window absorb the crispness of the sound. I strain to listen. I can hear shouting. Again, it's from afar, like Sunday-morning football noises from the park behind my house.

But I'm not at home. I'm not dozing on the soft duck-down cushions of my sofa, while gentle meditation wave music plays in the background. It takes a few seconds for my mind to reshuffle the deck of conscious and subconscious thoughts before finally dealing a full hand of stony ground, wet feet and rushing waters.

I open my eyes, now fully aware of my surroundings. I'm lying on my back on the riverbank. Water is lapping around my ankles and light rain tickles my face. I roll my head to the right and can see the river tumbling along. When I move my head to the left, I see Alfie. He's sprawled on his back, with one arm flung across his body and the other outstretched. His eyes are closed and his skin is pale, with blueness tingeing the edges of his lips.

We had gone into the water, been dragged downstream

through the rapids and somehow ended up being spat out the other side. I'm not quite sure how we've ended up here.

The dog has stopped barking and the shouting is reduced to one voice. A male voice. I follow the sound with my eyes and see several people line the other side of the river. A guy in a suit and waterproof jacket has his hands cupped around his mouth. I can hear his voice but I can't pick out the words. The man next to him is wearing a purple weatherproof jacket and a dog, also wearing a purple jacket, sits by his side. Search and Rescue?

There are two police officers in uniform standing next to the dog and several others are making their way down the embankment to join them.

Relief brings a trickle of tears and I rest my head on the ground as exhaustion overwhelms me. All I can think is that we have been found. We're going to be rescued. All sense of time was lost as I drifted in and out of consciousness, fatigued from hauling ourselves out of the river, fully clothed and drenched, coupled with what I suspect is a touch of hypo-thermia, adding to the tiredness.

From my first-responder training, I know that the point of rescue can be the most dangerous time. This is where the brain and body can give up fighting for survival, lured into a false sense of security that they are being rescued, passing over the responsibility to the rescuer. I fight to stay awake and alert. I can't let myself slip past that point now.

'Alfie,' I say. 'Alfie. The police are here. We're going to be OK.' I move to reach out to him, but pain shoots up my arm, preventing me. I look down and can see blood coating my hand like a moth-eaten glove. I don't think my arm is broken, I can wriggle my fingers, but it hurts like hell.

I either lapsed into unconsciousness again or fell asleep from sheer exhaustion, I'm not sure, but the next thing I'm aware of is the thundering sound of a helicopter above me and the downdraught from the rotor blades whipping up everything below, sending water spraying over me.

There's a thud and two black boots land on the ground a few metres away. A guy in an orange jumpsuit and a white safety helmet hurries over to me. He kneels beside me and places a reassuring hand on my shoulder and then leans down so I can hear him.

'Hi. My name's Rick and I'm here to help you.'

'My son, Alfie – he needs help,' I say. 'Help him first. Please.'

They haven't been able to tell me anything about Alfie yet. All I know is that he's under observation. I've emerged relatively unscathed: no broken bones, superficial cuts and bruises that the medical staff would expect to see from someone who has been tossed about in the water like we were. My injuries are minor. The most serious being my badly sprained wrist and a particularly nasty cut to my head which warranted shaving a small section of my hair and applying steristrips.

Alfie's injuries, however, are rather more serious.

'We're keeping him sedated for now,' says the doctor as we gather beside his bed in ICU. 'The brain's a marvellous thing; in situations like this it rests in order to repair itself. We'll give him a CT scan in the morning. By that time the swelling will hopefully have gone down.'

'What's your gut feeling?'

The doctor gives me a sympathetic look. 'I'm a doctor, I can't go on gut feelings. It wouldn't be fair of me to do that to you.'

I fiddle with the hem of the blanket which has been placed over my knees. The nurse insisted on bringing me down in a wheelchair, despite my assurances that I'm capable of walking. I feel such a fraud being pushed around.

'You should return to your own ward now, Mrs Montgomery,' says the doctor. 'You need to rest too.'

'One more thing,' I say, as I feel the nurse behind me lift the brakes from the wheelchair. 'How is Andrea Jarvis? Is she going to be OK? I did ask earlier but all they could tell me was that she had been rescued and brought here. Other than that, I don't know anything.'

'Your friend is going to be fine,' says the doctor reassuringly. 'A broken leg and hypothermia, nothing we can't sort out. She was very lucky to have a good emergency survival pack with her.'

'That's a relief. I'll go and see her tomorrow.'

'Please get some rest now,' says the doctor. 'Good night, Mrs Montgomery.'

I take one last look at Alfie before the nurse turns the wheelchair to face the door. He looks so peaceful lying there. I haven't seen such ease on his features in a long time. Not since Darren died anyway. I've yearned for the return of those days when life was simple, without complications. When Darren and I were a young married couple with a little boy, both of us deeply in love. Before life weighed too heavy on all of us. And now, it looks like I might be getting my wish, but not in the way I could ever have imagined.

I wipe away a tear that has found its way to my cheek.

'He'll be OK,' says the nurse reassuringly. 'You can come and see him in the morning.'

'Thank you.' I take one last look at my son before I'm wheeled through the door and out into the corridor. The nurse gives me a pat on the shoulder, a gesture to let me know that everything will be OK. I don't correct her. I allow her the indulgence.

TUESDAY

Chapter 32

I'm sitting in the chair, looking out across the hospital grounds, when the nurse comes in with the telephone in her hand.

'Detective Sergeant Adams wants to speak to you,' she says. 'Apparently, it's important.'

I take the phone from her and wait until she has left the room. 'Seb?'

'Hey, hiya,' he says. His voice is a balm to soothe the pain in my heart. 'I had to pretend I was phoning on official police business, otherwise they wouldn't put me through. Are you OK?'

'I can't tell you how happy I am to hear your voice,' I say, my own voice cracking with emotion. 'It's been such a terrible weekend. Did they tell you what happened?'

'Yep, I got a call from your mum. The police contacted her, but she's away on holiday and it's going to take her a while to get home. She phoned and asked me to come up. If I'd known, I would have been there sooner. I'm so sorry.'

'Don't be sorry. You weren't to know. Is my mum all right?'

'Yeah, she's worried, obviously, and frantic that she has to wait for the next available flight.'

'Did they tell you about Joanne?' I can feel my bottom lip begin to tremble.

'Well, not exactly. They wouldn't say much to me, but I've made a few discreet enquiries . . . I know what's happened.'

I note the hesitation. 'What have you heard?'

'That Joanne is dead. Her husband, Tris, is it . . . ?'

'Yeah. Tris.'

'Tris and Zoe turned up at Gormston police station and reported Joanne's death, along with Andrea being missing.'

'And me? What did they say about me?' Another hesitation, reminiscent of the days of satellite delays on long-distance calls, sets the alarm bells ringing. 'Seb, you must tell me. What did they say about me?'

'Look, Carys, don't be alarmed, it's all talk right now. The police will need to ask you some questions.'

'Seb, please. You're stalling. Tell me what you know.'

'OK . . . Tris and Zoe have been interviewed separately, which is standard procedure, but they're both saying the same thing.'

I bite back my frustration at Seb's inability to tell me straight and after yet another pause, he continues. 'They say you were the last one to see Joanne alive, and you argued with her. Tris is saying you two had an ongoing disagreement. They said you took off, taking Alfie with you. Is that true?'

My turn to hesitate. 'Sort of. Well, it is the truth, but it's not how it sounds.'

'You need to be more convincing than that when the local police show up there to interview you,' says Seb.

'What do you mean?'

'At the moment, it's not looking great for you.'

'But I didn't do anything!' The volume of my own voice surprises me. I check myself. 'I didn't kill Joanne. It was Tris. Or at least, I think it was. He's been having an affair with Zoe, for goodness' sake. He's got money problems. He'd be the one to benefit from her death.'

'Hey, hey, Carys, calm down. Listen, I'll try to get there before the police interview you, but if I can't, you must stay calm when you speak to them. Don't get yourself all agitated, it won't do you any favours.'

'I'm sorry, it's been such an awful weekend.' Before I can say anything else, the nurse returns. She makes an apologetic face and nods towards the phone. 'I've got to go now. The nurse needs her phone. Thank you for calling.'

'All right, remember what I said. Stay calm, tell the truth and everything will be all right. I promise. I love you, Carys.'

I can't answer. Even if the nurse wasn't there, I wouldn't be able to say anything. Emotion overwhelms me and I rest my forehead in my hand, willing Seb a speedy journey. I need him right now.

Despite leaving me in bits, I'm grateful for Seb's call. I'm heartened that he is at this moment on his way to me and, although I'm not looking forward to the local police turning up and questioning me, at least now I am prepared. I try to decide what sort of demeanour to adopt but after considering and dismissing several options, I come to the conclusion it is probably best to be myself. The police will no doubt see through any attempt to portray myself in a different light, and it will only serve to convince them I've got something to hide.

I don't have to wait long before I receive my official visit. I'm not sure whether this is a good omen or not.

'Hello, Mrs Montgomery?'

I turn in my chair to face a man I estimate to be in his mid-forties. 'Yes. Hello,' I say, taking in the dark hair, flecked with white at the sides, and friendly eyes which crinkle at the corners when he smiles.

'Hi, I'm Detective Chief Inspector Matt Chilton.' He holds out his police warrant card. I nod and he returns it to the inside pocket of his jacket. 'Can I call you Carys?'

'Yes, sure.'

'How are you feeling?' he asks.

'OK. Considering.' I adjust the blanket that covers my knees, more for something to do than for modesty's sake.

'May I?' Chilton indicates the plastic chair in the corner of the room. I nod and he picks it up with one hand, brings it over and places it opposite me. He sits down, gives me another smile and then begins: 'The nurse says you've had stitches.'

My fingertips automatically go to the dressing on the side of my head. I touch the self-adhesive square lightly. 'Three stitches and a drop of glue,' I say. 'Not to mention this rather fetching hairstyle.'

'You were very lucky, by all accounts,' says Chilton.

'Was I?' I drop my gaze to my hands, which nervously tease

the ribbon-edged blanket as I try to push away the still-frames in my mind of what happened on the river.

'Carys.' The detective's voice cuts through my thoughts. 'Yesterday afternoon, Tris Aldridge and Zoe Coleman walked into Gormston police station and reported the death of Joanne Aldridge. Mr Aldridge was very distressed, as you can imagine. They both were. They also reported Andrea Jarvis as missing, along with yourself and your son, Alfie Montgomery. I'm here to try to get to the bottom of what happened.'

'Yes. I realise that.' His patronising tone irks me. 'What did Tris and Zoe say?'

'That's not something I can discuss right now. What I want to do is to get your version of events.'

'Have you arrested Tris?'

'We are making enquiries. No one has been arrested, yet.' His voice is firm and his gaze steady. 'So, Carys, I need to ask you a few questions.'

'OK.'

'Can you run through the events of the weekend, just so I have them from your point of view.'

I take a deep breath. I remember Seb's words from earlier: stay calm and tell the police exactly what happened.

'I was invited to come away for the weekend by my friend, Joanne Aldridge. We arrived at the croft Friday lunchtime. Everyone was in good spirits. We had lunch and then went for a walk. In the evening we sat around chatting. Saturday morning, we went on a longer walk to Archer's Falls.'

'And how was the general mood of the party?'

'Fine. We were having a good time.' It's a rather audacious

lie, but I haven't got the energy to go into the undercurrents of the weekend. I'm not sure how much Chilton's been told and I decide to keep what I say to the bare minimum. 'Myself, Andrea and Zoe then returned to the croft by kayak.'

'Not Joanne?'

'No. She returned to the croft on foot, as far as I know.'

'Why was that?'

'She left us to abseil down to the riverbank. She said it was a bit of fun. A challenge, I suppose, to see if we could get back on our own.'

'This was an outdoor-adventure-type weekend, is that right?'

'I guess so. As I said, Joanne planned it all. It was a surprise for us.'

'OK. So, what happened when you returned to the croft?'

'We had tea. Joanne and I had a chat in the garden. I went indoors and later Zoe went out looking for Joanne. She found her . . . dead.'

'If we can go back a step: what did you and Joanne talk about when you were outside?'

'Our children.'

'Zoe Coleman says she heard the two of you arguing. What do you say to that?'

I can feel the heat rise up my neck and am sure my cheeks are on the verge of glowing red. 'It was nothing – a difference of opinion about my son, Alfie.' I take a second to swallow the lump of guilt that rises in my throat. 'I walked off in the end.'

I steal a look at the DCI as he takes a moment to contemplate my statement so far. He offers no comment but nods as if he has drawn some conclusion. 'When you and Andrea Jarvis left the croft to get help, Mrs Jarvis says you got into an argument with her. Is that right?'

'Er . . . yes. It wasn't a big argument though.' I'm thrown by the sudden change in direction.

'How would you describe it? Petty?'

'I suppose so.'

'And what did you and Mrs Jarvis argue about?'

'Is this necessary? How is that relevant?' The words burst out before I have time to check them. 'Sorry. I'm finding this all rather difficult.'

'Yes, I can imagine. But I do have to ask these questions, I'm afraid,' says Chilton. He genuinely sounds sorry. 'So, if you wouldn't mind answering . . .'

'Our children. We argued about our children.' I sound almost sulky as I say the words. I'm aware that this is not winning the DCI over to my side. 'I'm sorry, I'm just really tired,' I say, trying to recover lost ground.

'I'm sure you are. I have a few more questions and then I'll leave you in peace,' says Chilton. 'When Tris Aldridge turned up at the croft, what made you run away from him and Zoe Coleman?'

'When I returned to the croft to get help for Andrea, Tris was there, with Zoe. It was a very strange atmosphere. Nothing felt natural. I wanted to go back to help Andrea and I tried to get Zoe to come with me, but she couldn't. Tris didn't say anything, but he had his hand on her shoulder, stopping her from getting up. She mouthed the words *get help* and *run* at me.'

'And that's when you ran away?'

'I went in the garden to get some climbing rope and Tris followed me out,' I explain. 'I'd grabbed a walkie-talkie from the kitchen on my way out and tried to contact the park ranger – or at least, what I thought was the park ranger. Turned out it was Tris all along.'

'Mr Aldridge tells me that it was a joke. Something his wife had set up.'

I shrug. 'I don't know. It could have been, but by this time I was scared, I . . .' My voice trails away. I feel ashamed for leaving Zoe behind, even though I know she wouldn't have been able to run as fast as I could.

'So it was then you ran away?' prompts Chilton.

I compose myself and reply. 'Yes. Up to the forest. I knew I'd be able to out-run Tris.'

'I see.' I'm not sure what he sees, but he carries on before I can say anything else. 'Did you know Tris Aldridge had arranged with his wife to come up to the croft that day?'

I shake my head. 'She never said anything to me. I thought it was supposed to be only the four of us, but Joanne did like surprises.'

'Why do you think she asked Tris to come up?'

My shrug relays my inability to answer the question. Chilton cups his hands together and rests his elbows on his knees. 'Mr Aldridge says his wife was nervous about the weekend. Especially since you and she had fallen out recently.'

'Oh, for goodness' sake, he would say that, wouldn't he?' I catch myself again. 'Joanne and I were fine.'

'You hadn't fallen out?'

'No. Not recently. We had a disagreement a while ago, but that was all sorted out.'

'Would this have been the disagreement concerning her daughter and your late husband?'

My mouth drops open in true goldfish style. Tris must have told him; how else would Chilton know? 'That was all a misunderstanding. Their daughter had a crush on my husband, who was a tutor at the college where she was studying. Nothing happened between them. And the Aldridges and us, we were fine afterwards.'

'Let me get this straight. You had a history with Joanne Aldridge since this business with her daughter, you had an argument with Joanne this weekend, you were the last person to see her alive. You also had an argument with Andrea Jarvis, again, about children. You also had an argument with Tris Aldridge. There seems to be a common denominator here. Do you always argue with your friends?'

'No! You're making it sound worse than it is.'

We eye each other in an unspoken stand-off. I don't like the way this interview is going or the angle the DCI is approaching it from. 'I swear to you, I never did anything to harm Joanne. She was alive when I left her.'

'OK, let's move on to what happened on the river. You and your son decided to take the kayaks. Why was that?'

Again, I'm thrown by the change in direction. I can't help thinking this is a ploy to catch me out. I force myself to concentrate, despite the headache that is brewing. 'I was worried Tris might catch us if we took the road on foot, and we didn't have any other means of transport. No phones.

Nothing.' I dip my head and smooth my hands across the blanket draped over my knees, trying to dry my sweaty palms.

'You genuinely thought Tris Aldridge posed a threat to you?'

'Yes. Like I said, Zoe told me to run. I was scared of him. I was frightened about what he'd do to Alfie. He had already tried to . . . tried to get me. I think he was going to hang me and make it look like suicide.' The last few words are practically a whisper. After everything that has happened since then, I've hardly had time to process what Tris had wanted to do to me. Since then my main aim has been staying alive and rescuing Alfie.

I feel a sudden weight of reality settle on me. Tris Aldridge had wanted not only his wife dead, but me too, so he could pin her murder on me and pass off my suicide as an act of remorse. I swallow hard and blink away the tears.

'Take your time,' urges Chilton. 'When you're ready, tell me what happened once you and Alfie were in the kayak. Were you in one kayak or two?'

'We were in one, but we took the other one with us so that Tris couldn't use it. We were going to cast it adrift further down the river.'

The memory of the gushing waters, the noise of the current and the coolness of the wind returns. I close my eyes for a moment. I don't want to be transported back there. I need to keep a distance. I can describe it but I can't relive it. 'Sorry, this is so difficult . . . OK, it was all going fine until we rounded a bend in the river. There were rapids. The current was picking up speed, churning up as it hit the rocks and boulders. We couldn't get out of the current and were being swept along.' I pause and count to myself while I rein in my emotions. One . . . two . . . three . . . breathe. I can do this. I must.

'Were you in the front or the back of the kayak?' asks Chilton, his voice soft but firm. A voice that can't be ignored.

'I was in the front. Alfie in the back. He's stronger than me.' My stomach gives a roll and I think my breakfast is going to make a return journey. Once again, I call on the techniques I have learned to control the anxiety that is building up inside me. 'We had no choice but to sit tight and hope for the best. I don't know what happened next. I remember the noise. I could hear Alfie shouting but I didn't know what he was saying. Then suddenly there was a drop. It was like being on one of those log flumes at the amusement parks. We were airborne for a second, before dropping back into the water. We must have hit a rock because suddenly, I was thrown out of the boat and went under.'

'Did you have a life jacket on?'

'No. Those were stored in the croft. We didn't have time to get them.'

'Were you knocked unconscious at any stage?'

'I don't know. It's all a blur. I remember feeling I was being pulled down by the current and carried along underwater. I thought my lungs were going to burst. I was buffeted against rocks. I totally lost my bearings. And then, somehow, I was propelled to the surface. I looked round for Alfie but I couldn't see him. It was all I could do to stay afloat as I was swept along by the current . . .' I pause. My chest feels tight. I want to cry. I want to let out all the emotion, all the pain, both physical and mental. It is so hard to keep it under control. I fumble for another tissue, but the box slides on the Formica top. Chilton takes hold of the box and tugs at the contents. He hands me a tissue.

'Take your time. You're doing great.'

I wipe my face and nose several times before I feel able to continue. 'Then I saw Alfie, face down. The water was pushing him towards me. I managed to grab on to a rock to stop myself from being carried further along and as he went by I caught his sleeve. I nearly lost him, but somehow I managed to drag him out of the current.'

Again, more memories flood my mind. Snapshots. None of them joining together to make one complete narrative, but fragments jumbled up, all in the wrong order.

'How did you manage that with a bad wrist?' says Chilton.

His words jolt me from my thoughts. I look at him blankly. *How did I do that?* I shrug. 'I have no idea. I can't remember feeling any pain. I suppose the mothering instinct in me, the one that puts their child's life above everything else, must have taken over. All I remember is dragging him backwards through the water and on to the riverbank.'

'It was a shallow bank on that side. You were very lucky.'

Lucky? Lucky to be alive? I suppose I am, but that doesn't necessarily mean I am lucky in any other respect. I now have to live with what happened. That's not lucky.

'Have the doctors spoken to you about Alfie?'

I turn my gaze away and look at the treetops through the window. My heart is somewhere near the floor, the weight of the unhappiness within almost too great an encumbrance to bear. 'They have,' I manage to reply.

'He took a big blow to the head,' says Chilton. 'On one of those rocks in the rapids, no doubt. Did you see it happen?'

I move my gaze slowly across the window, turning my head until finally I am facing the DCI. 'There were rocks everywhere. He could have hit his head on any one of them. Everything happened so quickly . . .' My voice tails off as the tears make an unexpected comeback. The tissue in my hand is soft and wet, I close my fingers around it, so tightly that at first I don't register the pain. My nails are digging into the palm of my hand, but it's not until I feel the warm liquid of blood on my skin that I look down and see what I've done to myself.

I let out a cry of alarm, throwing the tissue away from me. It brushes across my knees and falls silently to the floor. A bright red crumpled ball of blood.

'Hey, hey, Carys. Are you OK?'

I flinch as something touches my arm. I look up and realise it's the detective. He is leaning over me, his hand resting gently on my arm. I look down at the tissue. This time I see no blood, only a white crumpled piece of tissue.

'I . . . I thought . . .' I look again at Chilton, then the tissue. I inspect my hand. No blood anywhere. 'Sorry, I'm not feeling good.'

'I know this is difficult, Carys, but I need to establish a chain of events.' He gives me a sympathetic smile. When he speaks, his voice is soft and full of compassion. 'If there's something that you remember, don't be scared to tell me. In my experience, people in extreme situations do extreme things.

Things they wouldn't ever contemplate under normal circumstances. It's frightening, I know, but if you can remember anything more, it would help me immensely.'

This time I look Detective Chief Inspector Matt Chilton straight in the eye. 'Sorry. I don't remember anything else.'

Chapter 33

DCI Chilton has been gone for about twenty minutes now. I watched from my hospital window as he left the building and crossed over to the car park. It's only a momentary respite. He's going to send someone over later today to take an official statement from me. I've been asked not to leave the area, in case he needs to ask me any more questions. I can read between the lines. I'm the chief suspect and he is biding his time while he gathers more evidence.

I've asked Seb to buy me a cheap pay-as-you-go mobile phone. My own one has been found at the croft and is currently being analysed. Chilton tells me it's standard procedure and the other phones are also being looked at. I've not been singled out, apparently.

From behind me, I hear the door to my room open. I turn, expecting it to be the mid-morning cup of tea, so am surprised when a big bouquet of flowers appears large enough to obscure the gift-bearer's face. My first thought is Seb and my spirits lift a little, but as I take in the jeans and the men's trainers, I realise I don't recognise either.

'Hello, Carys,' comes the voice. He lowers the bunch of flowers and smiles. 'Surprise.'

'Tris!' I want to leap from my chair but the drip in my arm prevents me from doing so.

He walks over and, without a moment's hesitation, drops a kiss on my cheek. If he notices me recoil from his contact, he makes no reference to it. 'Good to see you,' he says, with such ease I have to remind myself of the events of the past weekend. 'How are you feeling?' he continues, as he goes over to the sink and pops the plug in, before filling it with water and resting the flowers there.

'What are you doing here?' I say, finally finding my voice.

'I need to talk to you.' He takes the seat that Chilton occupied less than an hour ago.

'I don't want to talk to you. Go away. Now.'

Tris remains seated. 'I know you think I had something to do with Joanne's death, but I promise you, I didn't.'

'Why should I believe you?' I retort, glancing over to the door, wishing Seb would walk through it right now.

'Because you know me better than that.'

'Do I?'

'Of course you do.'

'Then why did you want to kill me?'

He gives an incredulous laugh. 'What the fuck? Kill you? Jesus, Carys, where did you get that idea?'

'You chased me. Through the fucking forest, Tris. You tried to hunt me down like some animal. Then you threatened me, saying if I didn't come back, something would happen to Alfie.'

'Have a word with yourself,' says Tris; the incredulous look remains. 'I was chasing you because I was worried about you. I could tell you had lost it, got all paranoid. Running off into the forest like that, I was worried something would happen to you. That's why I was chasing you.'

'No. No, that's not true,' I say, replaying the events in my mind. He had definitely chased me and it wasn't for my own well-being. Was it?

'Carys, think about it. When did I threaten you? What did I say?'

'You had the walkie-talkie, you pretended to be the park ranger and said you were going to help us.'

'Yeah, I did, but only because Joanne told me to.'

'Then why answer me that final time, when you came out into the garden?'

Tris pulls a pained expression. 'Sorry about that. Bad taste. I don't think I was thinking straight.' He runs a hand through his hair. 'You do know it was all Joanne's idea, me pretending to be the park ranger? But I swear to you, I didn't know what had happened the first time you called. I genuinely thought it was part of the game. Joanne told me to go along with whatever was said. I was doing as she asked. Or so I thought.'

'What?' I shake my head. Tris is throwing doubt on my thoughts. 'But you were going to harm Alfie.'

'When? I promise you, Carys, I would never harm that lad. God, he's been through enough already. You know how much I think of him. I was only letting you know he was there.'

'You're lying!'

'I am not! Think about it, Carys, when did I ever say I was going to harm Alfie?'

I dredge up the conversation we had over the walkie-talkie. I can't pinpoint the exact moment Tris threatened Alfie. Why is that? I plough deeper into my mind but come up with nothing. I cannot remember Tris making the threat, not in so many words. The little ball of doubt is growing in momentum, increasing in size as I try to locate the point of threat but fail. 'You said something, I can't remember. You're confusing me.'

'You can't remember because there's nothing to remember,' says Tris, with a calm sincerity that only serves to increase my anxiety. I am sure he can see the despair and uncertainty in my eyes. He raises his eyebrows in question. 'I didn't threaten you, did I?'

'You're messing with my head,' I say, frustration coating every word. I sit taller in my seat. 'Get out of here. You need to leave. If you don't, I'll call the nurse.'

'Don't get yourself stressed,' says Tris. 'It's not good for you.'

'I mean it,' I say, ignoring his supposed concern. I reach for the call buttons on the table next to me but Tris is quicker and moves the table out of my reach. 'What do you want?' I say, searching his face for any clues.

'I want to make sure you're OK. You suffered a nasty shock at the weekend, and a nasty bang to your head too, so I'm concerned about you.' There's a lack of sincerity to his words.

'Bullshit,' I snap.

'You need to stay calm. Don't get yourself worked up . . . again.'

'What do you mean, *again*?'

330

'Like you did when you saw me at the croft. I know what you've been through and . . . the destabilising effect it can have.' Tris presses his lips together and tips his head to one side in what is supposed to represent a sympathetic gesture. 'Seeing a friend dead like that can mess with your mind. Especially when you've a history of mental health problems.'

'I don't know what you're talking about.'

'Oh yes you do. When Darren hanged himself, you weren't too good then. I recall Joanne, God rest her soul' – he makes the sign of the cross – 'telling me how you were on anti-depressants afterwards.'

'That's none of your business,' I hiss, trying to hide the hurt I feel, knowing Joanne had betrayed my confidence. I hadn't told anyone else, not even Andrea, that I was on anti-depressants. Joanne only found out by accident. The tablets had fallen out of my bag one day and she had spotted them. She had quizzed me about them and I had felt compelled to tell her. At the time, it had been a relief, but now I wish I hadn't been so trusting. It was naïve of me.

I had been embarrassed about having to take them. It made me feel weak and ashamed; and then there were side effects, which left all my senses dulled, until lethargy and general tiredness became my new norm. Decision-making was hard work. All these factors had convinced me I was better off without the medication. Coming off had been difficult, but I had stumbled across a site on the internet where I could buy beta-blockers. It was anonymous. I didn't feel judged and there was no need for regular GP appointments where they asked too many questions. My online source had allowed me to battle on alone. The same way I have battled on alone with Alfie. And the same way I battle on with my life every day.

'Seeing Joanne dead was hard, but don't think for one moment it's broken me,' I tell Tris. 'I know what you're trying to do, but it won't work. It will be my word against yours.'

'Well, not quite,' he says. 'Haven't you forgotten someone? Zoe?'

I look warily at him. 'She's my friend. She'll stick up for me.'

'Oh, come off it, Carys. Don't play dumb. Zoe has already told the police how upset and irrational you were all weekend.'

'But I wasn't,' I counter. 'In fact, I was the one making all the decisions.'

'So you say.'

'Fuck off! Get the hell out of here. I don't have to put up with this crap from you.'

Tris stands and walks over to the window, his hands clasped behind his head. 'This whole thing sucks,' he says. 'If only Zoe had stayed in Hammerton and never bloody moved to Chichester, none of us would be in this mess.'

I watch him pick up the call buttons and press the blue circle with the silhouette of a nurse in the centre but my mind is reeling from what he has just said. 'Hammerton? Zoe lived in Hammerton?' I ask.

Tris looks up at me. 'Yeah, Hammerton. Why?'

I don't answer, I'm too busy joining up dots, making connections I hadn't been aware of before. Small, seemingly innocent and independent details start slotting into place. How did this happen? How did I miss this?

332

The door to the room whooshes open and a nurse swiftly enters. 'Everything all right?'

The ability to speak abandons me as my brain is overloaded with a maelstrom of thoughts and images of a place I believed I no longer had any connection with.

'Carys is getting upset,' Tris says, turning to face the nurse.

She looks over at me. 'Oh, you do look very pale, Carys. Let me check your blood pressure. When did you start feeling unwell?'

Tris puts the call buttons down on the chair. 'I was just going. Carys was with my wife when she died,' he explains, bowing his head. 'I think my being here has unsettled her. I merely wanted to make sure she was OK. It's very difficult for all of us.'

'I'm sure it is,' says the nurse; she rests a hand on Tris's arm. 'Don't worry, you head off. If you need a cup of tea before you go, the kitchen is down the corridor. I'll stay with Carys.'

'Thank you, that's very kind.'

'Get out of here!' I shout, suddenly finding my voice.

'Carys, please,' says the nurse, coming around to the other side of the chair, the blood-pressure sleeve and pump in her hand. 'Now, roll your sleeve up. That's it. Do you want some water?'

As the nurse fusses over me, Tris turns to leave the room. Pausing at the door, he gives me one final look. One that I can't read. I look away first.

I lean back in the chair and let the nurse carry out her observations as I once again go over everything in my mind.

First of all, there's the little nugget of information that Zoe used to live in Hammerton. Why has this never come up in conversation before? I try to remember if I've ever mentioned where Darren used to work. Quite possibly I have, so it seems very strange that Zoe hasn't said anything.

To be fair, I have bigger things on my mind. Like Tris and the impression of me he's trying to give to everyone. That I'm unstable and my problems with Joanne were too much for me to cope with. He's so sincere, I'm almost beginning to buy into it and start doubting myself.

Chapter 34

It takes some time for me to reassure the nurse that I'm fine. I let her perform her checks and drink the cup of tea that has been brought round.

'Have you had panic attacks before?' asks the nurse.

'I wasn't having a panic attack,' I reply. 'I just didn't want to speak to Tris Aldridge any more.'

The nurse doesn't appear to be listening. 'We can put you in touch with trained counsellors who can help you develop strategies to deal with panic attacks. I could ask the doctor to refer you to one of the mental health team. Perhaps some CBT—'

'Cognitive behavioural therapy,' I cut in, rather ungraciously. 'Yes. I know. Thank you, but that won't be necessary.'

'It was only a suggestion. It's up to you.'

I smile at the nurse, acknowledging to myself that she's only doing her job. 'Actually, I'd like to go up and see my son now. Do I need to keep this drip in?'

'I can take that out for you, but I don't want you wandering about the hospital on your own. You need to be in the wheelchair if you go anywhere. Perhaps when your boyfriend comes, he could take you to see your son.'

'But I need to see him as soon as possible. I want to know how he is.'

'I'll phone through for an update. You wait there.'

Before I can argue any further, the nurse has left the room. I thump the arm of the chair in frustration. I feel perfectly able to take myself up to ICU. In fact, I'm pretty sure I'll be allowed to go home today. I hate all this fussing.

A few minutes later, the nurse returns. Alfie has had his CT scan and is on the ward. 'He's regained consciousness, in so much as he's opened his eyes for a few short periods of time.'

'Oh, thank God,' I say. 'Has he said anything? Is he OK?'

'Nothing yet, but it's early days. It sounds promising though. As soon as someone is here, or one of us is free, you can go and see him.'

'What about my friend, Andrea? How is she today?'

'If I have any news, I'll let you know.'

I have to temper my frustration again. All I want is to know that the people I love and care about are OK. After the nurse has gone, my thoughts turn to Zoe. I wonder why I haven't seen her yet. I'm surprised she hasn't been to visit me or even called to see how I am.

The next two hours drag by, only broken up by the lunch-time interlude. The nurse doesn't reappear and I assume the staff have been too busy to take me up to see Alfie.

When Seb finally arrives, I'm so relieved to see him that I sob inconsolably in his arms for a good five minutes. He strokes my hair and kisses the top of my head, his strong arms wrapped around my body, making me feel safe. The pent-up emotions run riot until they eventually exhaust themselves.

'Oh, Seb, I'm so glad you're here,' I finally manage to say, my good arm firmly around his neck, the nurse having removed the drip earlier.

'I came as quickly as I could,' he says, hugging me tighter. He then pulls away and studies my face. His eyes take in the dressing on my head, the grazing to my face and bruising to my arms. 'How are you feeling?'

'Much better now you're here.' It's my turn to cast the cautionary eye. 'You look tired, you must be shattered from all that driving.'

'I'm OK,' he says, brushing away my concern. 'Any news on Alfie?'

'Apparently he's regained consciousness but he's not said anything. I haven't been able to see him yet.'

'I'll take you.' He looks over at the wheelchair. 'Is that your mode of transport?'

Seb wheels me along the corridors and up to ICU without even waiting to have a coffee or a rest. I'm touched by his selflessness.

'It's through there,' I say, pointing to the double doors ahead. 'We have to press the buzzer to be let in.'

Before we reach the doors, they open and I'm taken by surprise when the blonde-haired figure of Zoe walks out. I notice almost straight away, she's not limping. She stops in her tracks, her shocked look reflecting my own.

'Zoe? What . . . I didn't know you were here!'

'Hello, Carys,' she says and immediately I detect a wary

tone to her voice. Her gaze shifts to the ground, her whole body language broadcasting the awkwardness she is experiencing. She looks up and gives Seb a nod. 'Seb.'

Seb returns the greeting.

'What are you doing here?' I ask, unable to understand why she's coming out of ICU.

'I . . . erm . . . popped in to see Alfie.' Her eyes dart between me and Seb.

'I don't understand, how did you manage to persuade them to let you in? It's supposed to be family only.'

'Sorry, I kind of said I was related.'

I want to ask Zoe about Hammerton, but I quell the questions which are bubbling up. I need to check a few things first. I have to be sure of my facts. If I put a foot wrong here, the consequences could be disastrous. Instead, I force myself to focus on what is happening now. 'Why did you want to see him? Why haven't you been to see me?' I feel Seb's hand rest on my shoulder and give a gentle squeeze which I interpret as a pacifying gesture, telling me to cool it.

'I was worried about him. I heard what had happened. I don't know, I felt compelled to see him,' she offers as an explanation. 'I didn't think it would be a good idea to see you. Not with what's happened. I've had to give a statement.'

'Yes, we all have, but I don't follow.' As the words leave my lips, realisation dawns on me. 'Your statement, does it implicate me? Do you think I'm responsible for what happened to Joanne?'

'I really shouldn't talk to you about it,' says Zoe. She looks to Seb for support.

'It depends what you've said,' he replies.

'What have you said, Zoe?'

'Please, Carys,' says Zoe, her rigid body language and inability to make eye-contact growing more pronounced by the minute.

'You think I killed Joanne! For God's sake, why would you think that, let alone say it in a police statement? I thought you were my friend.'

'I am. I am your friend, but I also had to tell the truth,' says Zoe. 'I'm sorry. And I'm sorry about Alfie too. I hope he gets better soon.'

'Your ankle's healed, then,' I comment.

'It was only a sprain.' She steps to the side and almost hugs the wall to keep as far away from me as possible. 'I have to go. Bye, Carys. Seb.'

I twist round in my seat. Despite my calls for Zoe to come back, she doesn't break stride once as she disappears around the corner and out of sight. I look up at Seb. 'I didn't do it. Why is she saying that?' I can feel myself on the verge of tears but anger is welling up quicker. 'For fuck's sake, Seb, I can't believe this is happening.'

Seb moves the wheelchair to the side of the corridor and crouches in front of me, taking hold of my hand. 'Carys, it's OK. Keep calm. Listen to me. It doesn't matter what Zoe says, it's only her opinion. Without any evidence, you can't be charged. I totally believe you. I don't doubt you for one minute.'

'What if they say there's reasonable doubt?'

'The police haven't received the coroner's report yet. If it shows that she died from simply falling, by accident, then there won't even be a case to answer.'

'But how will they be able to prove that?'

'Different types of injuries will have different character-istics. Forensics will look at the scene – you know, blood patterns, things she could have hit her head on. The police can't charge you simply because you happened to be the last person to see her.'

'But you said I was under suspicion. Everyone thinks I have a motive.'

'Did you?'

I bite down on my lip. I haven't told Seb about Ruby and Darren and what happened between our two families. 'Look, I should have told you before, but Joanne's daughter had a crush on Darren once upon a time. He was her tutor at the college. Joanne and Tris confronted us about it and it was all sorted out – a misunderstanding on the Aldridges' part. The whole thing was long-forgotten. Or so I thought.' As I finish, I'm aware I have taken a conscious decision not to tell Seb the whole truth. How can I? It's best for both of us if he doesn't know.

'Right,' says Seb, drawing the word out and raising his eyebrows a fraction.

'Turns out, Joanne wasn't ready to let the matter go. She was planning to confront me about it this weekend. Honestly, Seb, it's crazy. She concocted this whole stupid game to get back at each of us. Me for standing by Darren over the whole Ruby thing, Andrea for conning her out of buying the gym and Zoe, get this, for having an affair with Tris.'

Seb's eyebrows shoot a little higher this time. 'Wow. Is that true?'

'There's a degree of truth to all three allegations.'

'So, you all have a potential motive.'

'Yes. So why am I being singled out as the prime suspect?'

'I take it you've explained all this to the police?'

I wince. 'No. I didn't want it all dragged up.'

'What! For Christ's sake, Carys, you should have told Chilton. It's bound to come out, and your failure to disclose it makes you look like you're trying to hide something.'

'I know. I wasn't thinking straight. I didn't want the whole Darren and Ruby thing dragged up. It doesn't look good on my part.'

'You must tell Chilton. It gives the others a motive, so the focus won't be entirely on you.'

'OK. I'll call him. He left his card in case I thought of anything else.'

'I'm not suggesting you lie, but maybe the knock to your head made you forgetful?'

Seb gives me a meaningful look and I silently translate the subtext. 'Yeah, that's what it was. A little bit of amnesia.'

Seb pats my leg. 'I'll make some enquiries and see if I can find anything out, off the record. I'm sure the police are being very thorough and considering all the possible motives,' says Seb. 'What about Tris? The spouse is always a prime suspect. If he was having an affair with Zoe, then that gives him a motive too.'

'I don't know. He came to visit me this morning. He was pleading his innocence.'

'For fuck's sake. He needs to stay away,' says Seb, rising from his squatting position. 'I can have a word with him if you like.'

341

'Oh, don't worry, I've made it clear to him that he's not welcome.' I let out a long breath of air. 'Let's go and see Alfie.'

A few minutes later we have been buzzed through into ICU. On the wall beside the nurses' station is a noticeboard. Staff pictures of the nurses and their names are displayed and I seek out Alfie's nurse, Dawn. She looks to be in her late thirties and has a motherly air to her, something which makes me wonder: have I been the best mother to Alfie I could have been? Or am I lacking some unidentifiable and elusive maternal instinct? Is that why Alfie is lying here in intensive care?

We use the alcohol gel to cleanse our hands before entering Alfie's room. Dawn is in there with him.

'Oh, look, Alfie, you have a visitor,' she says brightly as she smooths down his sheet. 'He's had a wash and I'm hoping I've done his hair OK.' She looks at Alfie. 'Don't hate me.'

Seb wheels me over to the side of the bed and helps me stand so I can make eye contact with my son. I'm aware of both Seb and Dawn melting away and leaving me alone with Alfie.

I hold his hand with my good one. 'Hello, Alfie. How are you?' The pause for a response is automatic and I remind myself what the doctor told me about Alfie's apparent lack of speech. I study his eyes. They look right at me, boring deep behind my pupils. His stare has the intensity to cause me to make a tiny and involuntary movement of my head away. He blinks but he carries on looking at me.

I break the gaze first and allow my eyes to travel to the bandage around his head. His injury appears superficial, giving no indication of the damage done on the inside. Nausea washes over me and I check the room to locate the en-suite bathroom in case I need to get there in a hurry.

Dawn re-enters the room carrying a stool-like chair with ratchet legs. 'I thought you might be more comfortable on this perching stool,' she says, beginning to adjust the legs. 'I don't want you fainting on me.'

'How he is doing?' I ask.

'You're doing OK, aren't you, Alfie?' says Dawn, guiding me to the stool. 'We're pretty sure you can hear us. You're just not ready to speak yet, are you, Alfie?' All the time she's making eye contact, using his name and smiling at him. Then she turns to me. 'Talk to him as you normally would.' She checks the screen on the cardiac monitor and looks at the printout. 'See here,' she points at the chart of the screen. 'This was five minutes ago, when you came in. His heart rate increased. That would indicate that he knows you're here. It's a good sign, it means he's responding to his surroundings.'

Dawn leaves us alone again and my eyes are drawn to Alfie's. 'I wish I knew what you're trying to tell me,' I say, and then wonder if that's true. I look at the cardiac monitor and the line graph Dawn pointed out with the heart rate shown in red numerals at the end of the line. The numbers are increasing, dropping now and again but the general trend is on the up. 'Please try to rest,' I say, trying frantically to think of something to say that isn't going to alarm him further. 'Nan is flying home from her holiday. She'll come and see you as soon as she can.'

Alfie moves his eyes away from mine and in what seems

a purposeful act, he closes them. If he could verbalise the action, he'd be telling me to leave, that I've been dismissed. He no longer wants to talk to me. This is the equivalent of walking out of the room and slamming the door behind him.

I sit with him for another ten or fifteen minutes, but he's lapsed into sleep. I can't help feeling hurt and rejected. Even in his hour of need, when he's at his most vulnerable, he still doesn't want me. He's never going to forgive me for what I've done.

Seb pokes his head around the door. 'You OK?' he asks in a whisper.

'Can we leave?' I shuffle into the wheelchair and Seb wheels me from the room.

'Give him time,' says Seb as we leave ICU.

'I've been giving him time for the past two years,' I say. 'I thought that was bad enough, but I think I've just extended it further.'

'Come on, let's go to the café and get a cup of tea.'

'No. Wait. I want to go and see Andrea,' I say, looking up at Seb.

'Do you think that's a good idea?'

'I don't know, but I need to see her. If Zoe's been to see Alfie, she's bound to have gone and seen Andrea. I want to know what Andrea thinks of it all.'

'OK, if you're sure.'

'Positive. Andrea's my best friend. I want to see how she is anyway.'

We make our way to the general ward Andrea is on and locate her bed in the far corner. She's in a sitting position on the bed with a blue blanket draped over her bottom half, covering her plastered right leg. Colin, her husband, is sitting beside her.

'Carys! I wasn't expecting you,' she says. 'Hello, Seb.'

'I wanted to see how you are. Hi, Colin,' I say as Seb wheels me closer to the side of the bed. I stand up and lean over to hug her. It's an awkward manoeuvre, one which lacks any grace. 'I'm so glad you're OK. I wanted to come back for you, but I couldn't. I had to get help.' I blurt out the unintended words.

'It's OK. They found me quickly,' she says.

This time there's no perching stool, so I sit down in the wheelchair.

'I need to make a call,' says Seb, taking his mobile from his pocket. 'I'll be back in a minute.'

Andrea and I exchange a look. 'Subtly done,' she says. 'Anyway, how are you?'

'Not so bad.'

'I heard about Alfie – Zoe told me. I'm so sorry, Carys. I hope to God he'll be OK.'

'Thanks.' I look down at my bandaged hand and think of Alfie's bandaged head. Not for the first time, I wonder how it all came to this.

'Have the police spoken to you?' she asks.

'Yes. This morning. A DCI Chilton.'

'Same one who spoke to me,' says Andrea. 'He asked me about the weekend. When was the last time I saw Joanne? Had I seen you and her talking outside?'

'What did you say?'

345

'The truth. I last saw Joanne when we got back from kayaking down the sodding river. That as far as I knew, she was in her room until Zoe found her outside.' Andrea pauses and takes a deep breath. 'Bloody hell, Carys. What the hell happened this weekend? Is it me, or is this some sort of bizarre alternative reality? I still can't believe she's dead. I'm half expecting Joanne to walk through the door any minute now and tell us it was one of her fucking jokes.'

'If only,' I say. 'What I don't understand is what Alfie was doing up there.'

Colin coughs and fidgets on his seat. 'Carys, about that. I'm sorry. The boys wanted to go to some party on Saturday night, over the other side of town. Said they'd get the bus there, meet their mates, stay the night and come home again Sunday.'

'A party? I didn't know anything about this,' I say, and then wonder why I'm so surprised. It's not like Alfie volunteers any information about what he's doing. 'Where was the party?'

'I don't know exactly.' Colin glances at Andrea. I'm not sure if this is for moral support or some sort of apology. 'They headed off into town Saturday morning. I went down the pub to watch some football. When I got home, about half-five, they'd already gone. Bradley texted to say they'd see me Sunday.'

'Weren't you concerned that you didn't know where they were going?' I ask.

Another pause. 'Not exactly. They're young men. I thought it would be good to give them some freedom.' There's a defensive tone in Colin's voice. 'I know what Andrea's like. Fussing over Bradley the whole time, wanting to know where he is, what he's doing, who he's with, all that carry-on. Young lads need to cut the apron strings, so I let them set their own agenda for a change. My mum had no idea where I was when I was their age.'

'It's at this point I feel I must apologise for my fuckwit of a husband,' says Andrea. She's clearly had this conversation with Colin before. He dips his head in remorse. 'Rest assured, Carys, I've explained in no uncertain terms to him why we have mobile phones and check up on our kids when they're out and about.'

I give a roll of my eyes to Andrea as a gesture of consolation. 'So, fast-forward to Sunday and Alfie is a no-show. What did you do?' I ask Colin.

'Nothing. He sent a text message to say he would be back Monday, that he was staying at another mate's house.'

'And you didn't check up on him? Ask the parents if it was all OK with them?' I ask.

Colin grimaces. 'I trusted him. Sorry.'

'Have you told the police this?' I ask.

'I take it he never said anything to you either?'

I shake my head. 'Alfie is like an Enigma machine, and sadly I don't have the code.'

An awkward silence fills the space around us, until Andrea speaks first, re-routing the conversation.

'The detective asked me about what happened on the track, when I fell.' I detect an air of caution in her voice.

'And?' I prompt, as my stomach muscles flex to take a blow.

'He wanted to make sure that my fall was an accident.' She says the words with care.

I sit up straighter in my chair. 'It was. You know that, don't you?'

She hesitates for a fraction. 'That's what I told him.'

'But it was. I tried to stop you from falling but I couldn't catch you.' I watch Andrea and Colin look at each other. 'Andrea, I'm telling you it was an accident.'

'Hey, don't start raising your voice,' says Colin, suddenly becoming all alpha male in what I suspect is an attempt to restore some respect in his wife's eyes. He rises from his seat. 'Andrea needs her rest.'

'Andrea?' I look at my friend.

'I'm tired, Carys. You look tired too. You've got a lot of shit to deal with right now. Get some rest.'

She closes her eyes and for the second time that afternoon, I'm dismissed with one simple action.

WEDNESDAY

Chapter 35

The following morning, I am discharged from hospital, much to my relief, although it has been on the condition that I am not left alone. Seb has been great and has been able to arrange an extra day off work so he can drive me home and stay until Mum arrives.

'Have you heard when they're moving Alfie?' asks Seb, as he helps me change into some clothes he bought from the local supermarket. I'm touched that he's got the right size and although we are only talking about a pair of loose trousers and a T-shirt, these are absolutely my style. He knows me well and this small act of kindness helps soothe my battered heart.

'They're waiting for confirmation there's a bed in the neurological ward in Southampton,' I reply, slipping my feet into a pair of soft canvas shoes, which are again the perfect size and style. 'They're better equipped there and it's less than an hour's drive from my place.'

'Did you want to see him before you go?'

'It's OK, I've already been. I went early.'

'How was he?'

'Awake for a while. Still hasn't spoken.' I fiddle unnecessarily with my shoe, as I can't bring myself to look at Seb.

'He'll be better at Southampton, they're specialists, right?' He sits beside me on the bed and puts a comforting arm around my shoulder. I deny myself the self-indulgent luxury of sinking into his arms. I must stay strong. I give a smile which is intended to be optimistic and thankful, but only manages resigned.

'I hope so,' I reply eventually.

As I stand to leave and Seb picks up my bag, there's a knock at the door and I'm taken aback to see DCI Chilton enter the room.

'Ah, great, you're still here,' he says, nodding an acknowledgement to Seb. 'I was hoping to catch you before you left.'

'Everything OK?' asks Seb, placing the bag down on the floor.

'Aye, there's been a couple of developments and I needed to check a few things.' Chilton looks at me. 'That OK with you, Carys?'

'Of course.' I sit down on the bed, and Seb sits next to me in what I take to be an act of solidarity. Chilton takes the lower ground on the bedside chair.

'Good to see you up and about,' he says. 'How are you feeling?'

'Not too bad,' I reply, wishing he would dispense with the niceties and get to the point.

'The nurses have brought me up to date with Alfie. I was hoping to be able to interview him but as I understand it, that may be some way off yet.'

'Interview him? Why do you need to do that?' Alarm bashes at my heart.

'I have to speak to everyone involved at some point,' says Chilton. 'Just so I have all bases covered.' He throws Seb a look and continues. 'I want to ask about the kayaks and the river.'

'Is this necessary?' asks Seb. 'It's distressing enough as it is.'

'I'm afraid it is,' says Chilton. 'You know how these things work.'

I can sense Seb is about to protest further, but I save him the trouble. 'It's OK. Please, Inspector, carry on.'

Chilton clears his throat before speaking. 'When you and Alfie went through those rapids, whose idea was it? What made you choose that route?'

'Erm, I'm not sure,' I say, trying to bide time to second-guess what Chilton's angle is. 'I think we got caught up in the current. It looked easier than it was. Everything happened so quickly, there wasn't time to think or to discuss it.'

'We've recovered the kayaks. They were further downriver. Amazingly, they survived the rapids,' says Chilton. He takes out his pocketbook and flicks through a couple of pages. 'Remind me again, which kayak you and Alfie were in.'

'The red one.'

'And you were in the front?'

'That's right.'

'Can you remember the colour of the paddles you used?'

'Erm . . . The red ones. I think.'

'Can you be sure about that?'

'As far as I can remember.'

'And prior to the rapids, was everything OK? Did you have any accidents or mishaps along the way?'

'No. I don't think so.'

'Are you sure about that?'

I glance at Seb for reassurance. Somehow, I feel I'm being led into a trap, one where I don't have the expertise to spot the hidden tripwire.

'Why's that?' intervenes Seb.

'We found some blood in the boat.' Chilton keeps his gaze fixed on me. 'Do you know how it got there, Carys?'

'Blood?' I repeat. I can feel the beginnings of a twitch in the corner of my eye. I think back to the kayak. 'Oh, yes, sorry. I did have an accident. I forgot. That must have been how I hurt my head. I caught it with the paddle when I was swapping from one side to the other.'

'Must have been quite a blow.'

'Yes. It did hurt.'

Seb squeezes my hand. 'I expect the panic and adrenalin that was rushing through you blocked out the pain,' he says. 'Amazing how the pain receptors can do that when your life is in danger.'

Chilton purses his lips and nods, although I suspect it's in response to some thought running through his mind rather than agreement with Seb. 'The thing is, the blood was on the yellow paddle. Not the red one you said you were using.'

I stumble over the question as I attempt to process what Chilton is saying and the possible implications, wondering if I've caught the tripwire already. 'Sorry, it's difficult to talk about. To remember everything clearly. I must have been using the yellow paddle. I can't remember now. I feel very confused.'

'Could we leave the questioning there?' asks Seb. 'It's very upsetting for Carys.'

'I do apologise but I have to ask all these questions to get a clear picture of what happened. I wouldn't be doing my job if I didn't.'

'I think Carys has had enough for one day, though,' says Seb. I've never seen him this adamant. 'She's still in shock.'

'One more question,' concedes Chilton, getting to his feet. 'Did you know that Alfie had been seeing Tris Aldridge for counselling?'

I hear myself gasp as my head jolts up to meet Chilton's gaze. 'What? Tris was counselling Alfie?'

'Yes. I take it you didn't know?'

'No. Not at all. Neither of them told me.' I am stunned by this revelation and yet, simultaneously, not surprised by Alfie's deception. 'How long has Tris been Alfie's counsellor? Surely that's a conflict of interest?'

'According to the medical records, Tris Aldridge took over several months ago. I spoke to the secretary there and apparently Tris told her specifically not to advise you, in accordance with Alfie's instructions.'

'I had no idea,' I say. 'No idea at all.'

'Alfie's previous counsellor, Doctor Graeme Huntingdon, felt increasingly uncomfortable about this and said he wrote to you saying as much. Did you receive a letter from him? He had his concerns and felt you should know.'

'What concerns? Did he say?' asks Seb.

'Only that he felt there was a conflict of interest and that Tris Aldridge and Alfie seemed too close. He'd had an argument with Aldridge about it and as a result was spurred into writing to you. Says, he wishes he'd written sooner,' explains Chilton. 'Did you receive a letter?'

I shake my head. I'm certain I would have remembered a letter like that. 'I don't think so. Oh, wait! I did get a letter, the day before I left.'

'Was it from Doctor Huntingdon?' presses Chilton.

'I don't know. I didn't open it. I put it to one side and got distracted with the invitation from Joanne and all the details about the weekend.' I put my hand to my mouth to quell the tremble of my lip.

Chilton pulls out a folded sheet of A4 paper from his inside pocket. 'I have a copy of it here. Huntingdon's secretary emailed it over.'

I take the paper from him and unfold it.

Dear Mrs Montgomery

As you know, your son, Alfie, has been under my care for some time now, regularly meeting for counselling sessions. However, three months ago Alfie took the decision that he did not wish to meet with me any longer and asked that he could see Dr Tristan Aldridge instead.

As I understand it, Dr Aldridge is a close family friend and while this is not wholly unethical, I feel it is my duty to raise this matter with you. It is, of course, Alfie's prerogative to see whoever he wishes, but I feel obliged to make you aware of this recent change.

Yours sincerely
Dr Graeme Huntingdon, BSc(Hons) PhD

Seb takes the letter from my hand and reads it. 'Is this significant to the investigation?' he asks. 'You think there's some connection?'

'It's a line of enquiry we're pursuing,' replies Chilton.

Chapter 36

The journey home was long and arduous. My wrist ached and my back was sore from where I'd hit several rocks in the rapids. The bumps in the road were jarring my spine against the seat, rubbing the grazes. I wish now I'd let the nurse dress some of them but I had been in such a hurry to get out of that place that I hadn't let her.

Originally, I had wanted to travel with Alfie, but he was being flown down to Southampton and there was limited space for passengers. In the end, I'd watched as they took him out to the air ambulance and hoped he would remain sedated for the journey.

Seb settles me in the living room and brings me in a cup of tea, while I listen to the message Mum has left on the answerphone.

'She's on her way,' I say, taking the cup from Seb. 'She's going to come straight from the airport. She should be here by about six o'clock.' Seb makes an effort to check his watch discreetly. I know he's got to leave soon to get back to work. 'It's OK, you don't have to babysit me, I'll be fine.'

'I could call in and try to arrange to start work later,' he says.

I can tell from the poorly disguised concern on his face that it's not something he wants to do. Not because he doesn't want to be with me, but because he's under pressure from work to be there.

'Honestly, Seb, I'll be fine. It will only be a couple of hours at the most. It will give me time to have a little nap before Mum gets here. She'll be fussing round me when she arrives, I need time to prepare for the onslaught.' It's a feeble attempt at making light of it. Mum does fuss and I'm not sure how much of it I'll be able to cope with.

Seb sits beside me and we watch the TV, although I'm sure neither of us is taking any of it in. It's nice to sit quietly and feel safe with Seb by my side. Alfie is constantly on my mind and I wonder what must be going on inside his head. Although he's not speaking, he's conscious and I wonder if he can process his thoughts. Can he remember what happened on the river? How does that make him feel now? The hospital phoned to say he'd arrived safely and they were making him comfortable. I'm going to visit tomorrow with Mum.

I doze and my half-dreams are filled with images of Alfie as a young child. When I awake, I can feel a physical pain in my chest as I recall those magical years. I have an urge to sift through all the baby photos and the pictures of him growing up. I need time to grieve for Alfie. I have lost the son I was given in life and been left with one I neither know nor understand. I still love him, but I feel broken when I think about what has happened. I need time alone with my thoughts and feelings, some of which I feel ashamed to even acknowledge. I won't be able to do that with Mum here. She won't understand. Sure, she'll be fussing and clucking over me, she'll be able to offer sympathetic words and comforting hugs when words are not enough, but she won't truly understand. How could she? She's never been through what I have gone through. I'm her only child and I have always loved and respected her. Mum won't understand the level of emotional pain I'm feeling or the scarring it will undoubtedly leave behind.

I want to look at the photographs of Alfie before Darren's death, when Alfie was a baby, a toddler, a little lad and a teenager. I want to drink in those photos, absorb and harbour all those happy times, all that love I had for him and he had for me. I need to feel that again, to remind myself that I did once have a loving son. It will help me counter the emotions I am dealing with now and those yet to come. Or at least I hope it will. I'm not quite sure how I'm going to get over this.

Far too soon, Seb is gently rousing me. 'I'm sorry, Carys, but I've got to go,' he says, kissing the top of my head.

I snuggle into him, my cheek resting against his firm chest and I breathe in the fresh zingy scent of his body wash. I wish he could stay but I don't want to put any pressure on him. He's done so much for me already. 'I'll miss you,' I say.

'Shit, I'm going to miss you too. And worry about you. Are you sure you'll be OK?'

'Yes, please don't worry.' I look at my watch. 'Mum will be here soon.'

'I could hang on,' says Seb, again.

He is so thoughtful and yet so not needed right now. I don't have the heart to tell him. 'Please, Seb, I do appreciate it, but I will be one hundred per cent fine. Besides, I could do with an hour or two to prepare myself mentally for Mum. After all, she's having to deal with what's happened to Alfie too.' An irritated tone clips the last few words which I immediately regret when I see a small flicker of hurt dash across Seb's face. 'Thank you, anyway,' I tack on the end to soften the blow.

'I'm sorry. I'll get off, but if you need me, call. I can come right back.' He kisses me and hugs me gently one last time. 'Make sure you lock the door behind me. I'll ring you when I get there.'

'Be careful,' I say, following him out to the front door.

Seb picks up his overnight bag and stops on the front step. 'I love you, Carys.'

I watch him pull out of the drive and disappear down the road. I close the door and flick the Yale lock, remembering to put the chain across. I'll run myself a bath and dig out the photographs while I'm upstairs.

In the bathroom, I pour my favourite bath cream under the running tap. The sweet smell of coconut fills the steamy air. My bath is notoriously slow at filling and I potter around in my bedroom sorting out clean nightclothes. Ideally, I'd like to wash my hair but am unsure how I'll manage with only one good hand. Perhaps I'll have to wait for Mum to help with that tomorrow.

The sound of my mobile, the new one Seb bought me, rings out from downstairs in the living room. I nip downstairs and pick up the handset. It's Mum.

'I'm so sorry, darling. The flight was delayed and now the traffic is horrendous. I'm not going to be with you until at least nine this evening. Is that OK?'

'Of course, don't worry,' I say. 'Are you driving now?'

'I'm on the hands-free,' she replies. I hear an impatient blast of the horn. 'Bloody idiot! Not you, Carys, the moron in the BMW, just cut across me to get into a different lane.'

'Look, Mum, you go. Concentrate on your driving and I'll see you when you get here. Take your time.'

I put the phone down on the arm of the sofa and notice something out of the corner of my eye, tucked around the side. It's the bag the hospital sent home containing all the belongings I had on me when I was airlifted from the riverbank.

I take it into the kitchen, emptying the contents on to the stripped-pine surface of the table. My clothes had been given to Seb yesterday and are now languishing in the washing machine, waiting for Mum to attend to when she gets here. Mum had been insistent that I was to do nothing and, to be honest, I don't have the energy to argue. I know letting Mum help in a practical way will give her far more satisfaction and a sense of being useful.

Amongst my clothing, I spot the little waterproof bag I had hung around my neck when Alfie and I took the kayaks. My mouth dries as I run my fingers over the plastic. I can feel the outline of the mobile phone. Alfie's phone. Only one person knows I have this and they will be equally keen to make sure it stays out of the hands of the police.

I drop the phone into the pouch and pop it into my pocket. I'll hide it at the back of my wardrobe in the box where another time-bomb silently ticks. One that I don't fully understand but the sense of anticipation that it's about to go off any day now is getting stronger and stronger with each thought.

'Hammerton,' I say out loud. Once again, I take the stairs to my room, stopping at the bathroom to switch off the bath. The built-in wardrobes face me. Darren had them specially designed to maximise the space either side of the fireplace. I slide the right-hand door open. This part of the wardrobe, nearest to the chimney breast, has a set of drawers. The top drawer is only half the depth of the other three and at first glance, once the clothes are in, socks in this case, you wouldn't notice the false back. I take out the drawer completely to reveal a secret hidey-hole, precisely the right size for a hotel-room-style safe. I tap in the number and the little red LED turns to green.

I haven't opened this safe for nearly two years. The ghosts of my past have been secreted in a dark corner of my room, not a dissimilar place to where they have been buried in my mind. I close my eyes, take a deep breath and open the safe.

Inside is a brown A4 envelope marked 'Private' with my name on it, written by my own hand.

Sitting at my dressing table, I empty the contents on to the glass surface. A newspaper clipping. A photocopy of a student profile from college. A feather and a small message card, the type you leave on a bouquet of flowers for someone's birthday. Or funeral.

I think of Darren's funeral and the crowds of students who had come to say their last goodbyes. I had found it particularly moving, seeing those young people who Darren had a real affinity with, seeing his affection for them so clearly reciprocated. I had felt compelled to comfort their young broken hearts, despite my own heartache. It was a touching moment and I am sure they gained as much from the gesture as I had.

When I turned away, however, I had seen one lone student. She hadn't noticed me looking at her. It was the abject sorrow that filled her eyes and the pain so clearly etched on her face that caught my attention first, that and several plaited strands of hair, wrapped in multicoloured thread, finished off with a feather attached to the end. I had approached her, to try to offer some form of comfort, but as soon as I said hello and asked her if she was one of Darren's students, she had gone such a deathly white, I thought she might faint. She had backed away from me, taking two or three steps before turning and running out of the cemetery. It was later, after going through Darren's paperwork, that I found a printout of her student profile. Leah Hewitt. I'd been able to find her on Facebook but her privacy settings didn't allow me to find anything else out.

I had asked about her at the college, but was told she had left and even if they had a forwarding address, the admin staff couldn't possibly pass it on to me. The next time I went to look at her Facebook account, it had been deactivated.

There was something about Leah Hewitt that told me she wasn't your average student. She appeared to keep herself apart from the others, for a start, but that on its own wasn't what had made me want to find her. There was something I saw in her eyes, a deeper level of emotion that disturbed me. Something which I knew I would have to deal with at some point. Maybe not then or in the immediate future following the funeral, but I knew she would ultimately come back into my life. I had never managed to find her and became so caught up in the aftermath of Darren's suicide that, although I didn't forget about her, I put her to one side and concentrated on my own child who very much needed me.

I pick up the feather. I had found it down the side of the passenger seat in Darren's car a few weeks after his funeral. I had been hoovering the car when I noticed the multicoloured feather poking out from under the seat, between the seatbelt holder and centre console. When someone finds a feather, it's supposed to be a sign that a loved one who has passed away has come to visit. In an unusually sentimental gesture, I had kept the feather and taken it indoors. It wasn't until sometime later that the significance dawned on me.

I turn my attention to the student profile printout. At the beginning of the academic year, when the students return to college, staff are given temporary registers with a printout of each student's details and a photograph. Once the first three weeks are complete and the students have enrolled, the temporary registers are replaced with permanent electronic ones. I remember thinking there must have been a reason why he had kept hers, but my brain had been fogged with grief.

I look at the black-and-white photocopy of Leah Hewitt's face, studying each feature both separately and as a whole, looking for the slightest resemblance. Is it the eyes? The nose? The mouth? I can't tell. The knot in my stomach tightens the longer I look at the young woman's face underneath the words *Hammerton College of Further Education*.

Now the grief-laden fog is lifting, I can see the reasons he kept her profile emerging from the bleak and distorted corners of my mind, forming into the monster I've been hiding from these past two years.

Chapter 37

My head is a morass of thoughts, swirling around, like a Viennese waltz, making me dizzy as I try to untangle them. And there's that tugging heavy sensation of my heart as if it's about to drop into the pit of my stomach, it's teetering on the edge of realisation. I'm not quite there yet, but when the music stops and my head stops spinning, when my thoughts line up nicely in an orderly fashion, then I know my heart will plummet.

The earlier urge to look through Alfie's old photographs has deserted me. I can only deal with one painful realisation at a time. Robotically, I take myself downstairs to the living room and hunt through some CDs, hoping the music will help clear my thoughts. If I keep all the doors open, I will still be able to hear it when I'm in the bath. It might even help to drown out my thoughts of Alfie and Darren, dark thoughts which are never far from the surface.

The soft tones of James Blunt drift up the stairs. I wish for a brief moment that I had taken the hospital's offer of something to help me sleep. My beta-blockers got soaked in the river and with no more at home, I seek out the alternative and pour myself a glass of wine.

I must have put more bath cream in than I realised. A big foaming mass of white bubbles swirls on the surface of the water. I turn on the cold and swish it around with the hot.

As I perch on the edge of the bath, my good hand trailing a figure of eight through the water, I have a creeping sensation I am not alone. I spin round and almost topple backwards into the bath, letting out a small yelp of surprise.

I can see the top of Zoe's head as she stands at the foot of the stairs. I walk to the landing and look down at her, wondering how the hell she got into my house.

'You left the kitchen window open,' she says, as if she can read my mind.

We stare at each other in a mutual silence and in those few seconds, all the pieces of not only last weekend but the two years leading up to it now begin to fall into place. I grab the top of the banisters for support as my legs go weak.

And then, Zoe is taking the stairs two at a time. I let out another scream, this time one with more conviction. I rush across the landing and into my bedroom, slamming the door closed. I look frantically for something to push up against the door, if only to buy myself a few extra seconds. The bedside table is my only option, but one-handed, I won't be able to move it quick enough.

'Carys! Carys, don't be silly.' Zoe's voice is getting closer. She's at the top of the stairs. I can hear the loose floorboard on the landing groan under her step.

'Go away. Leave me alone,' I shout. 'I'm on the phone to the police right now.'

'Tut, tut, don't tell lies. I have your mobile and the house phone is downstairs.' She's outside the bedroom door. 'So, are you going to come out so we can talk, or do I have to come in there?'

I consider standing my ground and going for an all-out physical fight with Zoe, but with only one arm and Zoe's height advantage, the odds aren't in my favour. She's clearly recovered from her bad ankle, although I doubt now she was ever hurt. I suspect it was all a ploy to unsettle me more and a reason for her to stay at the croft. I edge myself around the bed towards the window. Would I make the drop? There's a small porch that runs across the front door and the living-room bay window. It would break my fall. I grapple with the key in the window lock, cursing myself for insisting they were installed when we had first moved in. The locks were supposed to be a protection from the dangers outside, not to prevent me escaping the dangers lurking in my home.

'Looks like I'm going to have to come in,' calls Zoe. The handle moves and the door inches open.

I've managed to get the lock undone. I grab hold of the cord for the blinds and yank at it, pulling it to one side to lock the blinds in one place but before I can do anything else, Zoe is around the bed and pulling me away from the window.

'Get off me!' I yell, trying to pull myself free from her grip. My bandaged hand is a hindrance. My bare feet make no impact on Zoe's shins. She grabs my arm and twists it agonis-ingly behind me, grabbing a fistful of my hair with her other hand and tugging my head backwards, before marching me out of the room.

'Zoe, what the hell are you doing?' I cry out, holding on

to my hair with my one free hand. If she tugs any harder, I'm sure she's going to pull it out at the roots.

'Told you. I want to talk to you. Let's go downstairs, shall we?'

'I haven't exactly got any choice,' I say. 'Please can you let go of my arm, you're hurting me.'

'That is the general idea,' says Zoe. She stops short of the top of the stairs and for one awful moment I think she's going to launch me to the bottom. 'Nice and easy, one step at a time.'

Zoe steers me towards the dining room but only to grab a chair. She releases my arm and with one hand still firmly clutching my hair, she uses her free hand to drag the chair out into the hall. She pushes me into the seat and from her trouser pocket produces several red cable ties.

As Zoe lets go of my hair to attach my wrist to the arm of the chair, I take what I think will be my only opportunity to escape. I lift my knees up and push her hard in the stomach with both feet. Zoe groans and moves to the side, but she doesn't let go of my arm, squeezing tightly around my damaged wrist. A red-hot poker of pain shoots through me and I'm immobilised immediately.

'That wasn't very sporting of you,' says Zoe as she deftly straps my wrists to the carver arms.

I shout and scream, kick my feet and bang my heels down on the wooden floorboards in the hope that one of the neighbours will hear me. Being in a detached house, I know this is unlikely, but I can't sit here and give in to whatever Zoe has planned for me. I am under no illusion that a cosy chat is on the cards.

'For fuck's sake, Carys, give it a rest!' shouts Zoe. She grabs at a bag I hadn't noticed before and pulls out a roll of gaffer tape. She rips off a strip with her teeth and places it firmly over my mouth.

Zoe sits on the floor and catches her breath, resting against the wall opposite me, her knees raised and her arms languishing on top of them. 'I'm knackered now,' she says. 'You shouldn't have bothered putting up a fight. You'll need to conserve your energy for later.'

I can't answer and I struggle to free my arms, but the cable-ties are too tight and my left wrist and shoulder too painful to have much effect. I decide to take Zoe's advice and save my strength.

After a moment or two, Zoe heaves herself to her feet and dusts down her trousers. 'That's better, nice and quiet.' Then, humming an unidentifiable tune to herself, Zoe fishes around in the bag and brings out a rope. She turns and smiles. 'Remember this?'

My eyes bulge and a new wave of fear washes over me. The rope is the climbing rope from the croft, the one with the noose on the end.

I watch in horror as Zoe ascends the stairs. Stopping halfway, she ties one end securely around the banister between two spindles, with the noose trailing down, swinging in front of me at eye level. I'm mesmerised by the sight. Images of Darren flood my mind. I can't deal with this. Tears swamp my eyes and I feel them cascade down my face. I struggle against the ties holding my wrists in place and then try to stand by pushing my arms back and moving the chair out from under me. The pain in my wrist and shoulder is excruciating. Hunching forwards, I head for the front door but only make it as far as the foot of the stairs before Zoe blocks my path.

'Don't be silly, Carys,' she says. 'If you're too impatient to stay put, we'd better get this show on the road, sooner rather than later.' She resumes her humming as she effortlessly pushes me into the chair. Unfortunately, the chair is now on the rug at the end of the hall and all Zoe has to do is to drag the rug to move me back to where I started from.

I'm screaming through the gaffer tape but it is too tight and muffles any sound. Zoe pulls the noose over my head; the knot pushes against the base of my neck. Then she heads up the stairs and I feel the slack leaving the rope as it bites into my skin. I stretch as high as I can, but still Zoe pulls on the rope until my windpipe is being squeezed. I struggle to inhale enough breath through my nose.

She returns to my side and reaches into her bag. Her hand emerges holding a Stanley knife. I try to move away from the blade as it glints in the sunlight streaming through the door. A rainbow of colours reflects around the room like a disco ball, but this is no party. Zoe slices the cable ties and my hands ping free from the chair. Immediately I grapple at the rope around my neck, trying to relieve some of the pressure. I manage to stand and the tension decreases, but not for long. Zoe takes hold of the loose end of the rope and pulls on it, sending me to my tiptoes as I try to stop myself being choked.

'Stand on the chair,' she orders.

I do as I'm told. I have no option. Momentarily the pressure

372

around my neck is once again released, but no sooner am I standing on the chair than Zoe starts pulling on the rope again, making it shorter. I lose contact with the chair as Zoe ties the rope off around one of the spindles in a series of knots.

My feet flail in mid-air as I try to find something to take my weight. I make contact with the arm of the carver, my tiptoes just touching it.

Zoe stands admiring me for a moment. She folds her arms and smiles. 'You look rather like a ballerina there,' she says.

I pull the tape from my mouth, which burns my skin as it is forced away. 'For God's sake, Zoe, stop this. Please don't do this.' I'm crying and gasping for air all at the same time. 'Stop now before it goes too far.'

'Where's the phone?' she asks, fixing me with her dead soulless eyes. 'Alfie's phone. The one you took from the croft. Where is it?'

As Zoe mentions the phone, another piece of the puzzle slots into place. 'It was you who texted Alfie. Not Tris,' I say.

'Oh dear, have you only just realised that?' says Zoe. 'Of course it was me.'

'The police said Tris was Alfie's counsellor. I thought he had got to Alfie somehow, but it wasn't him at all. It was you. How?'

'Honestly, Carys, you're as bad as Tris and the rest of them. You know I should get an Oscar for my performance. You all thought I was a dizzy blonde who always thought the best of everyone, didn't you?'

'You played us,' I say.

'Totally. The funniest bit was up at the croft when you came back and found Tris there. You know, when I did the big goggly eyes and told you to run!' She recreates the face she made at the croft and mouths the words *run* and *get help*, before laughing to herself. 'It was hilarious. You totally believed me.'

'You and Tris were in on it together?'

'Oh, please, I wouldn't take that loser with me.' She inspects her fingernail and then looks up at me. 'The trouble with Tris is that he's all cock and no brain when it comes to women. Pay him a few compliments, bolster his macho image – yeah, I played up to that and I played him.' There's a look of satisfaction on Zoe's face. 'I let him believe he was helping to shift the suspicion from me to you. I told him that the affair would come out and if there was any suspicion that I was involved with Joanne's death, then he would be in the frame too. If we made it look like you'd gone nuts and killed Joanne, we'd both be in the clear.'

'You used him?'

'He was a means to an end, the same as Joanne was.'

'What do you mean?' I genuinely want to understand Zoe's thought process, not least because keeping her talking is buying me time. I have no idea how I'm going to get out of this, but my survival instinct is in the driving seat.

'I'm sure you've worked it out by now,' says Zoe, picking up the student profile picture she'd taken from my room. 'Leah Hewitt was my daughter. I had her when I was very young – her dad buggered off as soon as he knew I was pregnant and I was left to bring her up on my own.'

'Was? Leah Hewitt was your daughter?'

A flash of pain briefly crosses her face. She looks at the photograph of her daughter before she speaks, ignoring my question. 'Your husband took advantage of Leah. She was a vulnerable student, searching for a father figure.'

She folds the student profile in half and places it in her bag. 'When Hammerton College told me Darren had left, I went to a lot of trouble to track him down. To find out where he lived. I watched him for quite a few weeks. I watched you too. And Alfie.' Zoe stands in front of me with her arms folded. 'I wanted to know what sort of pervert your husband was. I was going to confront him. Make him own up to what he'd done. Force him into admitting what sort of scum-bag he was.'

I wonder how many times Zoe had watched me and my family go about our daily routines. It's unsettling to think that she had been stalking us and we were totally oblivious. Or at least, I was. 'Did you confront him?'

'No. I didn't get the chance. The coward hanged himself.'

'Didn't that make you feel better, like there had been some sort of justice?'

'Like I said, he was a coward but I might have been tempted to leave it there if it wasn't for Leah.' Zoe gulps and again I see the flash of pain cross her face. 'My Leah, my beautiful daughter, she couldn't cope with his death. She was heart-broken. She was still under some silly illusion that he'd eventually leave you for her.' Zoe holds her hands over her face and takes a deep breath before lowering them. 'She hanged herself two days later. It was like some bad Romeo and Juliet story. She was so besotted with him, she couldn't live without him.'

I let out a gasp. 'Oh, Zoe. I'm so sorry.'

Zoe slams her fist against the bookcase. 'I don't want your apologies!' she shouts. 'What good are they? They're meaningless. They won't bring my daughter back.'

'But neither will all this.'

'Someone has to pay.' Her voice is cold and heartless. She paces up and down the hall several times, before coming to a halt in front of me. 'I decided you owed me. You must have known what was going on or at least had an inkling. I can't forgive you for standing by and doing nothing.'

'Zoe, I promise you, I had no idea.'

'Shut up. I'm not interested in your lies.' Zoe gives the chair a nudge with her foot, causing it to judder and the rope to bite into my skin. 'After Leah passed, every night I went to bed and cried myself to sleep, wishing I could have done something to help her. Been more insistent at the college. Confronted Darren. Then one day I woke up and saw an article in the newspaper about this man whose daughter had been attacked. He'd gone out and beaten the man up who'd done it. Beat him to within an inch of his life. The judge took pity on him. Said it was a crime of passion. I remember thinking what a good father he was to defend his daughter like that, to show his daughter how much she meant to him. He was quoted as saying if he'd done nothing, he would have been letting her down. I knew then, I may not be able to bring Leah back, but I wouldn't let her down either.'

'And that's when you decided to come after me?'

'You're catching on,' says Zoe. 'I had to be careful though. Take my time. I befriended Joanne at the gym. I'd seen you with her several times. I'd seen her at the school with you. It was easy to make friends with Joanne and to make extra sure I was allowed into your special friendship circle. I even fucking moved here.'

'All that time and I never suspected a thing.'

'When I found out that Joanne's daughter had been in Darren's class, I thanked the gods for such luck. It was being handed to me on a plate.'

'I don't understand.'

Zoe lets out a sigh of impatience. 'I haven't got much time, but I'll tell you anyway.' She smiles, preening herself about how clever she's been. 'Joanne confided in me once about Ruby and her crush on Darren. She told me how you had stood by him. She told me everything. I saw in Joanne the same feeling of helplessness that I had experienced. It doesn't go away. It festers inside. That and the fact that you stood by your husband, despite his habitual penchant for female students.'

'That's a lie.'

'Come, come, Carys. We all know it's not. Darren Montgomery had done it before. That's why he had to leave Hammerton. I've no doubt my daughter wasn't his first conquest, although Ruby appears to be his last.'

'Shut up!'

'Sorry if you don't like what you hear.' Zoe smiles and cocks her head in a faux sympathetic way. 'Right, where was I? Oh, yes. In my eyes, you were as guilty as your husband.

So I fed Joanne's obsession, encouraging her to out you, show you up for what you are. All the while, I was biding my time, waiting for the moment to strike. When she told me about her plans for the weekend, I knew it would be the perfect opportunity to let you feel the pain and misery I have felt.'

'You bitch,' I mutter.

Zoe grabs the arms of the chair and gives it a shake, throwing me off balance as I try to regain my tiptoe footing. 'I'm not the bitch. You are! You stood by that sleazy husband of yours.'

'Why didn't you go to the police?'

'They wouldn't believe me. My own daughter didn't want to give evidence against Darren. You know, she loved him.' I see the anger leave her body as her shoulders drop and her grip eases on the chair. 'Even after he killed himself, she still loved him.'

'I know,' I say softly. 'I've only just realised that I saw her at the funeral. I mistook her sadness for that of a young student shocked about her tutor's death. I was wrong, she was a young woman grieving for someone she loved. I am so sorry, Zoe. I didn't know.'

'You should have done,' she snaps at me, her mood changing like a sail tacking against the wind.

'Zoe, please. Let me down. We can talk about this properly.' I am pleading with her. Surely, she isn't planning to carry out this lynching. She only wants to scare me.

Zoe's next mood swing veers from conciliatory to attack. She grips the chair and looks at me menacingly. 'The phone, Carys. Where's the mobile that Alfie had at the croft?'

'My pocket.' The words croak out as my legs wobble and the rope bites tighter into my skin, constricting my airways.

Zoe pats the pockets of my fleece and locating the mobile, takes it out. 'Thank you,' she says, dropping it into her bag. 'You know, you fooled me for a while up there in Scotland. At the riverbank, replying to my text messages.'

'I thought you were Tris,' I say, watching her features to try to gauge her mood.

'Alfie was supposed to text me so I knew it would be OK to raise the alarm. I wanted to wait at the croft, but Tris was insistent that we go and report you missing. In the end, I had to send the text message. So, very good, Carys. Go to the top of the class, you fooled me there.'

My calf muscles are aching from being in this precarious position, all the time having to make tiny adjustments to maintain my balance. I wish Mum had got here on time; perhaps then things wouldn't have got to this point. On the other hand, maybe Zoe would have tried to harm Mum in some way. I decide if I see Mum coming up the path, I'm going to scream with every ounce of energy I have left to warn her. Maybe she'll be able to call the police before it's too late. In the meantime, I need to keep Zoe talking. 'How did you get Alfie involved in all this?'

'Oh, that was the easy bit. I knew from Joanne that Alfie was having counselling with Tris . . .' She lets the sentence hang alongside me in the air.

'You knew?' Dismay fills me and I feel the familiar thread of jealousy that once again, Joanne knew more about my son than I did.

'Soon as I knew that, it wasn't hard to . . . how shall I put it? To *distract* Tris and then, while he was showering, to nose around in his briefcase. You should have seen me, I was like an MI5 agent, firing up his laptop and copying the files on to a memory stick!' Zoe's face is full of glee as she recounts her actions. 'That way, I could read all about Alfie at my leisure. After that it was simply a case of gaining his trust and taking my time to plant the idea that he could get his revenge and even the score.'

'And you did all this without Tris knowing?'

'Absolutely. I thought the weekend would be a good place to counter Joanne's surprise with my own. As it happened, things turned out much better than I could ever have antici-pated. Your private tête-à-tête with Joanne gave me the perfect opportunity to confront her. Shame it ended the way it did. I didn't mean to hurt her. One minute she was calling me a whore for sleeping with her husband and the next thing I knew, I had whacked her with a log. I didn't even realise I'd picked it up, I must have got carried away in the heat of the moment.'

'You killed Joanne.'

'It was an accident, but I couldn't take the risk of being charged with murder or manslaughter. As it happened, you managed to put yourself in the frame. No one is even looking at me. It's perfect.'

'You're sick, you know that, don't you? You fooled us all.'

'Like I said, I deserve an Oscar. It was so easy, all I needed was to lure you, Joanne and Andrea into a false sense of security, so none of you would think I was any kind of threat.

But, you know what, it's a shame. I think you and I could have been great friends. I see a lot of me in you.'

'Don't flatter yourself,' I say, my anger getting the better of me.

'We both have blood on our hands,' she says, her top lip curling. 'I killed Joanne after you had spoken to her. I admit that. You need to admit you killed Darren.'

'Shut up! You know nothing!'

'I know everything. I read the notes Tris made, the transcripts from his sessions with your son. Alfie heard you and Darren arguing in the kitchen the morning of his death.'

'Stop it,' I whimper. 'Please.' But Zoe's enjoying herself too much to stop.

'Darren told you he felt like killing himself, that his life was over without you. And you told him that he would be doing everyone a favour if he went ahead and did it.'

'I didn't mean it,' I say, as the tears fall freely down my face.

'You said that the sooner he did it, the better.'

'I was angry. I thought he was attention-seeking. He'd threatened me with that so many times before.' My nose is running and I momentarily let go of the rope around my neck with one hand, to cuff the snot away.

'Alfie heard every single word. Now do you understand why he hates you so much? He blames you – and he has every reason to.'

I cry silently, unable to dispute what Zoe has said. Every word is true. I never knew Alfie had heard me say what I did that morning. I hadn't meant it, but Darren had punished me in the one way he knew how to hurt me. He wanted me to suffer for the rest of my life. So far, he's succeeded. Suddenly, dying doesn't seem like a bad option. All I would need to do would be to tip the chair over with my toes. I could do that easily.

Zoe is talking again and the sound of her voice brings me back to reality. I don't want to die. 'Please stop this, Zoe,' I beg.

'It is far too late to stop now. Even if I wanted to, I can't,' she says. 'I've been waiting for this day for a long time. Why would I want to stop now, just when I'm about to make my dream finally come true?'

'Zoe, we can talk about it. I promise you, I didn't know anything about what happened at Hammerton. I swear on Alfie's life I didn't.'

'If you didn't know anything, why are you mentioning it?' says Zoe, sitting cross-legged on the hall floor looking up at me. 'Why have you got these souvenirs?' She waves the picture of Leah in her hand.

'I only made the connection earlier and I'm not even sure I understand it all yet.'

'Let's play a game. In honour of Joanne – we all know how she loved games.' Zoe rests her hands together under her chin. 'You tell me what you think you know and you'll get rewarded or punished depending on what you get right.'

'Zoe, this is ridiculous. Please, let's talk.'

Zoe checks her watch. 'I haven't got much time, so let's not debate this any further. Come on, tell me the first fact. Tick-tock.'

I take a few gulps of air and try to keep as still as possible.

With every jolt the rope bites into my neck. 'OK, have it your way. Darren used to teach English at Hammerton College where Leah Hewitt was a student.'

'Keep going. I need more than that for a reward.'

'They became very good friends.' I pause, waiting for Zoe's reaction. She purses her lips and makes a hurry-up gesture with her hand. 'They were very close.'

'For fuck's sake, Carys, stop beating about the bush.' Zoe jumps to her feet and pushes the chair out from under me. My feet frantically paddle thin air. My bodyweight is dragging me down and I can feel my airways being squeezed. Then, as suddenly as the chair was taken away, Zoe restores it to its original position under my feet and I wheeze thankfully as I'm able to hold myself up again. 'That's the punishment for getting it wrong. You need to say it out loud, so I can hear you, otherwise this is going to be a very short game.'

I don't doubt for one moment she means it. I force the words from my mouth. 'Darren and Leah had a relationship.' I see the spark of anger flare in Zoe's eyes and quickly add, 'They had an affair. Darren and Leah Hewitt were lovers.' Self-preservation has no qualms about voicing my darkest thoughts, but I inwardly flinch all the same.

'That's better.' Zoe is walking backwards and forwards in front of me. 'Carry on.'

'I'm not sure what happened, why it stopped, but Darren left Hammerton College. He said he had been passed over for promotion and the management had changed. He wanted a new job nearer home.'

'Interesting,' says Zoe. 'The college never elaborated on

Darren's departure, only that it had been by mutual agreement.' She stops right in front of me. 'You must have known you were married to a perv. Don't tell me you never suspected.'

'I didn't!' I protest with a raspy voice. 'I honestly didn't. He never ever gave me any reason to suspect. He abused his position of trust, I know, but Leah was twenty. She wasn't a child.'

'She was MY child!' Zoe's voice leaps several decibels. 'Leah Hewitt was my child. Your husband took advantage of her. He promised her all the wonders of the world.' Her voice is calmer now.

I find it hard to believe. Or have I always been in denial? Even to myself. I knew he was a charmer, loved women, said he loved everything about them, but I had always thought it was a respectful admiration. 'I'm sorry, I didn't have a clue. You have to believe me.'

'I don't think you're in a position to dictate the rules,' says Zoe. 'Anyway, back to our game. What do you think happened next?'

'I . . . I don't know.'

Zoe gives an exaggerated look up to the ceiling in exasperation. 'It's no fun if you don't even guess.'

I can't take any more of this bullshit from Zoe. She's toying with me and has no intention of letting me live. Not now she's confessed all. I have one last chance to save myself. If I can get her close enough to aim a kick to her face, hard enough to knock her out, then I reckon I can swing my leg out and reach the bookcase. If I can twist myself round and keep my balance I ought to be able to maintain enough slack in the rope to get it off my head.

All I need is to get her close to me, and the only way she's going to do that is if she wants to take the chair out from under me. It's a gamble, but I realise no one else is coming to my rescue.

'You know what, Zoe, you can go fuck yourself with your stupid game. I'm not playing any more and I don't give a shit what you do about it.'

'Well, my dear friend, you're the one who looks fucked to me. And I don't mean in the carnal sense either.'

Chapter 38

'How's it going up there?' asks Zoe, leaning against the hall table and looking up at me. She's been standing there watching me for several minutes. 'I hope all this hanging around isn't getting too boring for you?' She laughs at her own sadistic joke.

'You know I sent a copy of those text messages to my own phone,' I say. I'm grasping at straws now. My feet are tottering on the top of the chair. I look at Zoe, willing her to believe me. 'I sent them to Seb as well.'

Zoe cocks her head to one side and flicks Alfie's mobile phone from one hand to the other. 'Did you now? And I'm supposed to believe that? I can easily check the phone and see what messages have gone out.'

Shit. I hadn't thought of that. My plan to entice Zoe over to me so I can attempt to free myself isn't working. If only Mum wasn't stuck in that bloody traffic jam or I'd taken Seb up on his offer to stay. A tear escapes from my eye and rolls down my face.

'Oh dear, Carys. Don't cry,' says Zoe. 'You know you could always kick that chair away and it would all be over in a few seconds. You wouldn't have to hang around for much longer.' Again, she laughs. 'Go on, Carys. Do it.'

She pushes herself away from the table and for a moment I think she's going to either kick the chair away or come close enough for my foot to make contact with her face. I need to kick her hard. On the side of the head. I read somewhere the temple is a weak point. If I can stun her, maybe I can whip this noose off. A few seconds, that's all I need.

Zoe's attention is drawn to something outside. She stands in the doorway to the living room and peers around the corner of the door. Is it Mum? Do I try to free myself now or call out to Mum? If there's no one there and I start shouting, Zoe is bound to put the tape over my mouth again. My moment of indecision costs me. Zoe rushes over to me, but the space between us is still too great a span for my reach.

'Keep your mouth shut, otherwise, I promise, I'll pull this chair right out from under you.' She gives the chair a kick, causing it to wobble. 'Make a sound and that's your lot. By the time whoever it is gets in here, you'll be doing the perfect impersonation of Darren.'

I let out a whimper. 'Please, Zoe. Stop this now.'

'Shut the fuck up.'

My left leg begins to shake involuntarily and I struggle to keep my balance. My hands are clasped around the rope above the noose, taking some of the weight from my feet, but my arms are hurting from being above my head and the lack of blood flow is causing my muscles to burn, making it increasingly difficult to maintain this position. My spine is being stretched to full capacity and my shoulder blades are searing with pain.

There's a rapping of knuckles on the door, followed immediately by three insistent rings of the doorbell, the last held down for several seconds. Through the distorted glass of the door, I can see the indistinct figures of two people.

'Carys! Are you there? It's the police.'

An enormous shock wave of relief floods through me. The police are here. They can rescue me. I look down at Zoe. She gives a warning look. I must make the decision now. I don't have time to dwell on it. I might never get this opportunity again. The police may turn and leave and then what? Zoe will be rattled, but she'll carry out her plan to make my death look like suicide. I'm not bloody well going to give her the satisfaction.

I close my eyes, tighten my grip on the rope and brace myself before shouting as loud as I possibly can.

'HELP! HELP ME!'

'You stupid fucking bitch!' hisses Zoe, and she pushes the chair away.

She's not quick enough, I have already committed myself to pushing off as much as I can with my tiptoes and swinging my leg over to the bookcase. The weight of my body is immense and as my feet frantically try to make contact with the bookcase, I realise I won't be able to hold myself for more than a second or two.

Somewhere in the midst of it all, I am fleetingly aware that Zoe has run towards the kitchen. I'm on my own. No one can save me other than myself.

My toe catches the edge of the bookcase. The rope is digging deeper into my neck and I can feel the power in my arms beginning to fail.

The police officer is banging on the door again. Shouting my name. I try to reply but my airways are being crushed and only a rasping noise comes out. I've managed to get a foot on the bookcase, but it's not enough. I need to try to get my other foot on there and swing my body round. Have I misjudged the length of the rope or, more importantly, my own stamina and body strength? My vision begins to blur, my peripheral vision disappearing as I head down a silent black hole, my arms dropping to my side and my feet slipping from the bookcase.

And then I am weightless. I'm floating.

'Cut her down, for God's sake!'

The voice penetrates my thoughts. Suddenly, I'm aware of arms around my body. Holding me up. The pressure is instantly relieved from my throat. I open my eyes but my vision is bleary. And then I am being lifted down. My feet touch the ground, but I have no feeling and cannot hold myself up.

'Set her down on the floor.' I think it's the same voice who was shouting through the door to me. 'And get that fucking rope off her neck.'

'Someone radio for an ambulance.' A female this time.

As the rope is removed from my neck, I feel a rush of air to my lungs. It makes me cough violently as I wheeze for breath and for a moment I wonder if I'm going to choke despite being rescued. The coughing subsides and I take deep breaths, filling my lungs and brain with much-needed oxygen. I put my hand to my neck, which is sore to the touch, and when I withdraw my fingers, the tips feel sticky.

'Try not to touch your neck,' says the female officer kneeling beside me. 'The skin has been broken a little. The paramedics will clean it up when they get here.'

The sound of raised voices and scuffling is coming from the kitchen. I turn my head towards the door. I blink. I must be seeing things. I blink again. No, it's not my imagination. Zoe is lying face down on the floor and Seb is sitting on top of her, holding her hands while another officer handcuffs her.

'Zoe Coleman, I am arresting you on suspicion of the attempted murder of Carys Montgomery. You do not have to say anything, but it may harm your defence if you do not mention when questioned something which you later rely on in court. Anything you say may be given in evidence.' Seb's voice comes out loud and clear.

I almost cry in relief as I hear Seb arrest Zoe. I cough and roll over on to my side so I can sit up.

The police officer eyes me carefully. 'You OK?' she asks. 'I'm fine. Just need to sit up.'

And then Seb is by my side. He holds me tightly. 'Thank God we got here in time.' He inspects my neck and his unchecked wince tells me it must look quite nasty.

'I'm fine. Honestly.'

Seb helps me to my feet and sits me on the chair. The noose sprawls on the floor next to me. Seb kicks it away with his foot.

He puts a protective arm around me and one of the uniformed officers leads Zoe out of the house and into a police squad car whose arrival was announced by sirens and two-tone blue lights bouncing through the open front door.

'What made you come back?' I ask. 'How did the police know to come here?'

'It was down to luck,' says Seb. 'When I left you earlier, as I came to the junction at the end of your road this bloody hatchback turned in, taking the corner so wide that I had to swerve to avoid hitting them. I didn't get a chance to see who it was before they sped off down the road. Anyway, I didn't think any more of it at the time, but when I stopped for coffee I thought I'd give the local nick a call and see what the latest was,' explains Seb. 'Turns out they had put out an APB on a blue Fiesta registered to Zoe Coleman. Apparently, there's been a major development in Joanne's case and Zoe was to be held for questioning until DCI Chilton got here. He's on his way now.'

'I still don't understand, what made you turn around?'

'I was rattled. I knew from bumping into Zoe at the hospital with you yesterday that she was shifting the suspicion to you. And what with the Fiesta that nearly took me out, it sent all sorts of alarm bells ringing.'

'So, you told the police about the near miss in the car?'

'Yeah. I tried to call you, but your phone was switched off.'

'Zoe must have done that.'

'I rang the house phone too, but that just rang and rang.'

'I didn't hear anything.'

Seb picks up the house phone and inspects the receiver. 'It's on silent, that's why.'

'Zoe,' I mutter.

'I'm sorry to interrupt.' We both look up and a paramedic

is coming through the door. 'We need to get you to hospital for a check-up.'

'I don't need to go. I'm all right,' I say.

'You most certainly do need to go,' says Seb. 'Look, I've got to go down to the station and hand Zoe over. There's some paperwork to take care of, but I'll come and see you as soon as I can. I'm guessing one of the local officers will be along to take an initial statement from you.'

'I'm becoming an old hand at this statement-giving lark. Unfortunately.' I let out a sigh.

Seb walks me out to the waiting ambulance. 'I'll get hold of your mum too.'

As I climb into the ambulance, I can't help but wonder what I've done to deserve such a loyal and caring man as Seb. If he knew the truth about me, I'm not sure he'd want to hang around. As the doors close and the engine starts, I shut my eyes and play out the possible reactions to Seb finding out the truth. None of them are in my favour.

Chapter 39

By the time Seb finally gets to the hospital, I've given my preliminary statement to the police, been seen by A&E and told I'm allowed to go home.

'Sorry it took longer than I expected,' says Seb. He sits down in the chair next to me. 'Those developments I mentioned earlier, I'm not sure of the detail, but Chilton is on his way down from Scotland and is going to charge Zoe with Joanne's murder. Or, so I've heard.'

'If I hadn't heard it from her myself, I'm still not sure I'd believe she was responsible,' I say.

'It won't entirely rest on your statement, but it will certainly add weight.'

'Do you know what the other evidence is?'

'I don't know the details, but they've got some forensic evidence linking her to the murder weapon.'

I sense Seb's hesitation and guess he's probably holding back on the detail, trying to protect me. 'Tell me. I'll find out sooner or later.'

'She used a lump of wood to hit Joanne on the head,' he

says carefully. 'They found traces of blood matching Joanne's DNA on the wood and a fibre which matched a jumper of Zoe's.'

'That was a stroke of luck.'

Seb nods. 'It happens like that sometimes. It also helps that Tris has decided to save his own arse and cooperate with the police.'

'To be fair, I don't think Zoe planned it. And I don't think Tris had any idea what she was up to.'

There's a silence that follows and I sense that Seb wants to say something else, but is working out how to do so. Eventually, he speaks. 'The police found a mobile phone in Zoe's holdall that she had at your house. You don't know anything about it, do you?'

'A mobile phone? No. Why would I?' I nearly choke on my lie.

'She had two phones on her. Unregistered. There's a text message conversation between the two.'

'Oh?' I keep my voice level.

'The tech guys are going to run a cell-site analysis on them. See if they can work out where they've been used, that sort of thing.'

I want to tell Seb the truth but something is stopping me. If I tell him, then I'll have to confess to Alfie being involved. Then they'll start asking questions and I don't know if I can keep my nerve. Chilton has already questioned me about the blood on the paddle. I'm sure he has suspicions about my version of events as to what happened in the kayak with Alfie.

'You know they'll be able to track back and find out when and where the phone has been used.' Seb speaks gently, all the time holding my hand and stroking my palm with his thumb.

I look at Seb. I don't want another relationship based on lies, but if I do as he's asking the whole world will know how my own son hated me so much, how I was blind to the truth about Darren and Leah Hewitt, how I dismissed claims about Ruby and Darren, and how I taunted my husband and encouraged him to take his own life, even if it wasn't my intention.

I close my eyes and rest my head against the wall. I'm tired. So very tired. Maybe I should just let the truth come out. Or at least some of it.

'The phone was Alfie's. I took it from the croft. I sent those replies. Zoe thought she was texting Alfie.' Seb nods. He doesn't look surprised. 'You'd worked it out,' I say.

'I did wonder. Don't be frightened, Carys. I know how much this hurts you, but it's not Alfie that will be on trial, it will be Zoe. Alfie had nothing to do with Joanne's murder or what happened here today.'

I feel a sense of relief that I have told Seb almost everything. I let him lead me out to the car. 'I don't want to go home,' I say as I fasten the seatbelt. 'Not tonight. I don't think I can face it.'

'No problem. We'll find a hotel room. I'll give your mum a call and let her know what's going on. She wanted to see you tonight, but I managed to put her off until tomorrow.'

'Thanks. I'll give her a call. Tomorrow, can you take me to see Alfie?'

'Sure.'

The doctors tell me Alfie's condition has stabilised with no sign of improvement. They use the term 'unresponsive wakefulness syndrome', which is a new name for being in a vegetative state. He has lost awareness of himself and his external surroundings.

'I'm sorry, we can't tell you any more than that right now,' says the doctor.

I thank her and she leaves me and Seb alone in the medical room with Alfie.

'I'm so sorry,' says Seb.

'I need a few minutes alone with Alfie,' I say.

'Sure. I'll wait for you in the coffee room.' He kisses my cheek before leaving.

I move closer to Alfie. He is breathing on his own but is wired up to monitors and other medical equipment.

'I'm sorry, Alfie,' I whisper, taking his hand and holding it in mine. 'I'm sorry I wasn't able to bring you up to know right from wrong, that I wasn't able to steer you along the path to happiness. But most of all I'm sorry I left you in this state.' I wipe the tears from my cheeks. 'I never knew you had heard me that morning when I argued with your dad. I never meant what I said. It was in the heat of the moment. I never for one moment believed he would carry out his threat. He'd threatened me before and I thought I'd call his bluff. I got that so very wrong. If I could turn back time, I'd give anything to change what I said that morning. I truly would.'

For a second, I think I see Alfie's eyes flutter. I freeze, studying his face intently, looking for any movement of his lashes, a twitch from his face, even a small movement of a finger. Anything to let me know that he's heard me. That he can forgive me. Have my words been able to penetrate the barrier in his mind that is preventing communication?

'I hope you can forgive me, Alfie. We have both done things we wouldn't have normally done. I forgive you. I forgive you for trying to kill me in the kayak. I know you were suffering, have been suffering for so long, and you haven't been able to think straight. I never wanted it to end this way. Never.' I lean over and kiss Alfie's forehead. 'I wish things had been different, my darling. I'm so sorry.'

I find Seb sitting in the coffee room as he said he would. He's been an absolute rock to me and I don't know how I would have managed without him. He slips his phone into his pocket. 'That was your mum,' he says, standing up and placing a guiding hand on my shoulder. 'She's going to meet us at the hotel.'

'Thanks, I appreciate that.' When I spoke with Mum earlier today, I let her talk me into going to stay with her for a few days. The police have finished gathering evidence from my house but I still don't want to go back there. I'm not sure when, if ever, I'll feel able to. It's the house where my husband killed himself and the house where my so-called friend tried to kill me. The house represents sadness, anger and danger.

'I'll miss you,' says Seb.

I offer Seb a smile. 'I'll miss you too but it's only for a couple of weeks. Once you've got some leave, I'll come up and stay with you.' Seb doesn't challenge me about this and how I'll be able to leave Alfie; perhaps he thinks I'll change my mind before then.

Seb reaches over and holds my hand, lifting it to his mouth and kissing it gently. 'I love you, Carys.'

'I know.' I want to say I love him too but my feelings are weighed down by a blanket of sadness. It is hard to find the love when it is smothered by so much pain. I hope Seb understands.

He trades a resigned smile for an upbeat one. 'Oh, I had a call from Andrea,' he says. It seems Seb is now my unofficial PR officer.

'What did she want?'

'To say that she was thinking of you and when you're back, ring her and you can take her out for a coffee. She said she was sure Colin would be driving her fucking nuts by then, especially all the time her leg is in plaster and she's stuck in the sodding wheelchair. Her words, not mine.'

I give a small laugh. 'Sounds like Andrea is on form,' I say. 'What you see is what you get, that's for sure.'

'I also have news on Tris. He's being charged with perverting the course of justice. They were going to try for accessory to murder but there's not enough evidence.'

'Despite everything, I'm pleased. Ruby and her brother, Oliver, are going to need their dad even more right now.'

'Poor kids. All that to deal with.'

When we arrive at the hotel, Mum is waiting in the foyer with two suitcases. One full of her clothes that she's brought home from her holiday and the other with my clothes she picked up from the house earlier.

She had gone to see Alfie last night as I hadn't been able to face it. I can see from her eyes she must have cried a lot in the night. The makeup can't hide the puffiness of her eyelids or the dark circles underneath.

'Hello, darling,' she says, giving me a hug.

'Hi, Mum.'

'All set? The parking valet is bringing my car round. Oh, look, how's that for timing?'

Mum's silver Mercedes draws up outside the hotel steps and the porter takes the suitcases down to the car.

As Mum supervises the loading of our bags, I turn to Seb and hold him tight. 'Thank you,' I say, 'and I'm sorry you've had to deal with all my shit. I wish things hadn't turned out like this.'

'Carys, you can't change what happened. You're not responsible.'

'I wish I'd taken what Ruby said about Darren more seriously,' I say. 'I should have asked Darren more about why he was leaving Hammerton, but I took it all at face value. If I'd known or even suspected about Leah Hewitt, then maybe when all that came up about Ruby, I would have believed her and none of this would have happened.'

Seb holds my face in his hands and looks into my eyes. 'You're not to blame. You mustn't torture yourself. Zoe is to blame. No one else. Zoe took the conscious decision to get her revenge. It was premeditated. When she found out Darren was dead and couldn't be brought to justice, she came after you. Listen to me, you have done nothing wrong. Nothing whatsoever.'

I feel a traitor to Seb's absolute belief and confidence in my innocence. I should have told him the whole truth earlier but I'm too far down the lie to do that now.

Images of Alfie and I struggling in the kayak play out before me. I will never forget the moment when I saw into my son's soul and saw the tortured monster he'd become. As he swung the paddle down towards me, I knew at that point our lives were on another path. I realised that Ruby was never the ticking time-bomb, she was never the black hole in my night sky – Alfie was. He was the supernova of black holes. He sucked in all love and life around himself and squeezed it so tightly that nothing could possibly survive.

The force of the blow had knocked me out of the kayak. As I had struggled to get in, grasping at the sides, the kayak had tipped violently, sending Alfie flying into the river as well. The current was fast and had caught Alfie, dragging him under and spitting him up a few metres downstream. I had launched myself after him, swimming with the water, gaining ground on him, until finally I had managed to grab hold of his jacket. We were tossed and turned in the river, but eventually we made it through the rapids and out the other side into calmer waters, where exhausted, we had dragged ourselves on to the riverbank.

I don't know how long I had lain there, coughing and spluttering as I got my breath back. It was not long after that

I'd got the text message which I wrongly assumed was from Tris.

It's academic now.

'You'd better go. Your mum's calling you.' Seb's voice brings me from my trance.

I give him one final hug and kiss goodbye.

Sitting in the passenger seat next to Mum, I take a long and lasting look at Seb. He's a good man. He doesn't deserve to be saddled with someone like me. If I can do one good thing with the rest of my life then it will be to let Seb go.

I can't stop the tears that fall as we drive away from the hotel. I don't know how I'm going to manage without him. If I was selfish, I wouldn't be letting this happen, but Seb deserves so much more than a liar like me.

It wasn't supposed to end like this. You weren't supposed to walk away with just a few cuts and bruises and a sprained wrist. You were supposed to pay dearly for what you have done, for the pain and suffering you have inflicted upon me. You were supposed to drown in that river but you couldn't even do that for me, could you?

But, then again, maybe it's turned out for the best after all. I mean, I may spend the rest of my wretched life confined to this building, this room even, but to be honest, I don't give a shit. Not any more. Maybe my revenge is knowing you will spend eternity in abject misery and suffocated by guilt.

Even if you can't bring yourself to visit me, because you cannot bear the pain seeing me brings you, I am satisfied that you are suffering every day of your life knowing you did this to me. You put me here.

I didn't see the rock in your hand, I was too busy enjoying the look of disbelief and horror on your face as I very slowly began squeezing your neck with my bare hands when we had finally dragged ourselves out of the water. I should have been more vigilant. I should have known you wouldn't go that easily.

I underestimated you. I didn't think you had it in you to harm your own flesh and blood. It was a wrong call on my part.

And now here I am, trapped in this useless body of mine, with no means of communication. No one will ever know the truth but they don't have to. Your ever-lasting remorse and anguish is my sweet revenge.

Acknowledgements

Without the eternal patience and support of all my family at home, I'm not sure I would have ever finished writing this book. Thank you, gang!

As always, both my agent and Commissioning Editor have been super supportive and I'm more than grateful for this.

Huge gratitude also to my two editors, Emily and Anne, who have worked so hard with me on this book. Their feedback has been invaluable, challenging and rewarding.

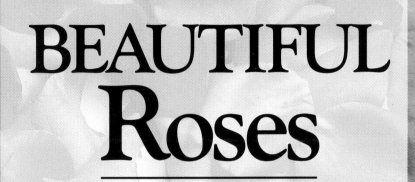

BEAUTIFUL
Roses

WRITER
BOB DOLEZAL

PHOTOGRAPHER
KIRK AMYX

ILLUSTRATOR
DICK COLE

NK
LAWN & GARDEN

Acquisition, Development and Production Services by BMR, of Corte Madera, CA

Acquisition: JACK JENNINGS, BOB DOLEZAL

Series Concept: BOB DOLEZAL

Developmental Editing: BOB DOLEZAL

Photographic Director: ALAN COPELAND

Cover Photo: ALAN COPELAND

Interior Art: DICK COLE

Copy Editing: NAOMI LUCKS, JANET REED

Proofreader: TOM HASSETT

Typography and Page Layout: BARBARA GELFAND

Index: SYLVIA COATES

Horticulturist and Site Scout: PEGGY HENRY

Color Separations: PREPRESS ASSEMBLY INCORPORATED

Printing and Binding: PENDELL PRINTING INC.

Production Management: THOMAS E. DORSANEO, JANE RYAN

Film: FUJI VELVIA

First Edition

ISBN: 1-880281-01-5

Library of Congress Catalog Card Number: 91-67353

91   92   93   94   95   10   9   8   7   6   5   4   3   2   1

Special thanks to Robert Van Deist, Eric Nelson, Keith Zary and Nancy Butler of Jackson-Perkins Rose for their dedicated assistance in selection and photography of the rose varieties in this book. Also, thanks to John Dallas, John's Rose Garden, Napa, CA, and Sequoia Miniatures, Visalia, CA, for their help in providing plants and locations.

Additional photo credits: Bear Creek Gardens, pages 24–41, for the following: Grand Masterpiece, Oklahoma, Crimson Glory, Glory Days, Barbara Bush, Pristine, Fountain Square, Redgold, Peace, Blue Nile, Intrigue, Climbing High Noon, Lavender Jewel. Nor' East Nurseries, pages 38–43 for the following: Party Girl, Minnie Pearl, Cupcake, Jennifer, Nighthawk, Centerpiece, Winsome, Pacesetter, Julie Ann, Center Gold, June Laver. Ray Spooner/Oregon Miniature Roses, pages 38–39, for Maurine Neuberger. Kristine Milaeger Reisdorf/Milaeger Garden, pages 48–49, for Alba Meidiland.

Notice: The information contained in this book is true and complete to the best of our knowledge. All recommendations are made without any guarantees on the part of the authors, NK Lawn and Garden Co., or BMR. Because the means, materials and procedures followed by homeowners are beyond our control, the author and publisher disclaim all liability in connection with the use of this information.

BEAUTIFUL ROSES

ROSE FAMILY TREE

Roses are ancient plants whose relatives are found all around the world. Every modern rose stems from these *species*—that is, native—roses. Today thousands of beautiful rose varieties, or *cultivars*, thrill gardeners with their beauty, fragrance and many forms and colors.

Grandifloras

Floribundas

Hybrid teas

"La France" hybrid tea (1867)

Miniatures

China species (1752)

8

Polyanthas

Climbers and ramblers

Old Garden roses

Miniature Climbers

Wild Species

9

CREATING NEW ROSES

Each year growers offer many new roses for sale. They are created from the hundreds of existing varieties—called *cultivars*—of modern roses, from *species* or wild roses or by accidents of nature, called "sports." See pgs. 60–61 for step-by-step information you can follow to create a new rose variety.

Growers experiment with thousands of rose variations each year, but only a few are selected for commercial development. The first step is *hybridization*. In this process a flower of one cultivar is used to fertilize the flower of another cultivar.

Each rose flower has both male and female parts. Care is taken to prevent self- or cross-*pollination* by removing the petals and pistils from the target flower, waiting until it matures, then brushing its stamens with pollen from the anthers of the fertilizing flower. The flower is then bagged and labeled to prevent stray pollen from causing unexpected results.

If the cross is successful, the bud swells with ripening seeds, turning red, orange, pink or golden yellow. The seeds are harvested and prepared, then planted to grow into small rose plants.

Next, the roses flower and promising cultivars are chosen. All the rest are discarded. They are rated for color, form, disease resistance, fragrance and other desirable characteristics. Then they are "budded"—small cuttings are used to create new plants—before being grafted onto hardy rootstock.

Field trial propagation—growing in commercial quantities—is next. Only a few roses survive. A successful variety is patented, rewarding its breeder for all his or her efforts and granting the breeder exclusive property rights for its sale.

ROSE FORMS AND STYLES

Modern roses come in all sizes and shapes. Their growth and blooming habits divide them into five major groups, each with five growing forms or styles. Choose roses that fit your garden's size and design, from loose and natural ramblers to formal tree or standard roses.

Miniature Roses
Standards, bushes or climbers 6–18 in. tall and ideal for indoors.

TREE OR STANDARD FORM

BUSH FORM

CLIMBERS
Either large-flowered climbers (10–20 ft.) or small-flowered ramblers (6–12 ft.).

Grandfloras
Hybrid Tea and Floribunda parents. 3–6 ft. with single or clustered flowers.

Polyanthas
Grow 24 in. or less, ideal for hedges and hills. Flower spring to fall.

FIVE ROSE GARDENS

Roses add grace and beauty to any garden setting. Plant them as formal rose gardens, as a colorful cascade, to decorate a border or in containers or on arches. Roses are easy to plant and forgiving to grow. Choose your garden's look: formal or casual.

Raised Bed Garden. Good where space is small, soil is poor or large yields per sq. ft. is desired.

Terrace Garden. Garden walls hold flat benches of soil and slow water runoff.

Small-Space Garden. Tiny areas produce planned portions of selected fresh vegetables.

Container Garden. For city dwellers with green thumbs or country kitchens.

Flat rows. Traditional row vegetables for those blessed with flat sites and ample space.

CHOOSING A SITE

OPEN Competing trees rob roses of sun, water or nutrients.

SUNNY Full sunlight at least 5 hours per day.

SHELTERED Structures and shrubs block damaging winds.

GOOD ROSE GARDEN SITES

Roses are hardy and forgiving, but carefully choosing the site for your rose garden will pay back many times over. Good location will prevent pest and disease problems, reduce the need for watering and avoid damage from winter's cold. Always consider these key points:

Sunlight Roses need full sunlight for at least 5 hours each day. If these needs are not met, roses become leggy and develop fungal diseases. Roses do best in sunny sites that get 5–7 hours of sun per day. In the arid Southwest and hot South, choose a site that gets full sun from morning until early afternoon, but turns shady in mid-afternoon. Such sites help prevent sunburn and wilting.

Wind Avoid sites with strong winds, or take protective care by planting or building windbreaks. Winds rob moisture from plants by evaporation, killing leaves and blossoms. Winter winds are especially harmful—they freeze-dry rose canes.

Competition A good rule of thumb is to plant roses twice as far away from trees or large shrubs as the rose's fully grown height. Large plants rob roses of nutrients and water.

Soil Nearly any soil can be made suitable for rose growing (see pgs. 18–19). Be sure that it is well-drained, with lots of decomposed plant matter. Roses prefer soil that is neither too alkaline nor overly acidic. Check yours with a soil test.

The best sites will be well protected, yet sunny. Create terraces on steep hillsides, and dig lots of well-rotted leaf mold into the new rose bed for ample nutrients and good drainage (see pgs. 20–21).

IDEAL ROSE SOIL

Silt is larger than clay and smaller than sand, 1/100–1/10,000 in. It retains water well, but lacks air space between particles.

Clay particles are dustlike, less than 1/10,000 in. in diameter. Wet clay is sticky and hard to work. Dry clay is hard, locking out air and water.

Sand has the largest soil particles, 1/25–1/100 in. It contains lots of airspace but holds water and nutrients poorly.

Loam contains nearly equal parts of clay, silt and sand. It is the finest, most easily worked soil. It holds water, air and nutrients easily.

SOIL AND DRAINAGE

The best rose soils drain water at a moderate rate, neither too fast nor too slow. They are neutral to slightly acidic (pH 6.0–6.5).

Clay soils, made up of millions of tiny clay particles, all roughly the same size, drain poorly. When soaked, they become sticky; when dry, they harden until they are nearly cementlike. Rose roots drown in such soils, because the water they hold displaces the air between the clay particles. They also build up deadly salts and water-soluble nutrients over time.

Sandy soils are the opposite of clays. Because sand grains are large, the spaces between the sand allow water to run through quickly. Such soils lose their nutrients and cause plant roots to dry out even with frequent waterings.

Ideal rose soil, made from either sandy or clay soils, is loam. Add about one-third decomposed plant matter by volume to fix drainage and alkaline-acidity problems.

To measure your soil's drainage, dig a hole 1 ft. wide and deep at least 5 days after the last rain or irrigation. Fill it with water, then time how long it takes the water to soak in completely. Soils that drain in less than 5 minutes are too sandy, while those that take more than 15 minutes are too high in clay.

A RAISED-BED ROSE PLANTER

Raised planter beds for your roses are easy to build and provide a simple answer to hopeless soils. You can completely ignore the native soil and fill the planters with rich loam. Besides giving a neat, attractive look to your rose garden, they drain well and make care easier. Follow these simple instructions:

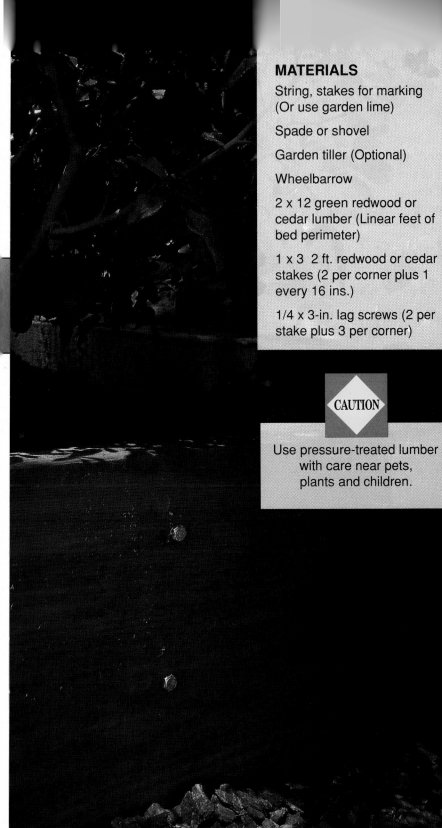

MATERIALS

String, stakes for marking (Or use garden lime)

Spade or shovel

Garden tiller (Optional)

Wheelbarrow

2 x 12 green redwood or cedar lumber (Linear feet of bed perimeter)

1 x 3 2 ft. redwood or cedar stakes (2 per corner plus 1 every 16 ins.)

1/4 x 3-in. lag screws (2 per stake plus 3 per corner)

CAUTION

Use pressure-treated lumber with care near pets, plants and children.

Raised-Bed Planter

First Choose and mark site. Remove any weeds or turf.

Then Till soil. Dig shallow trench along border.

Next Fasten edge boards to stakes with lag screws. Bottom is 2 in. under soil surface.

Last Fill bed with soil and added fertilizer. Mix thoroughly.

MODERN RED ROSES

Chrysler Imperial

Hybrid Tea, Lammerts, 1953

Large, shapely flowers, intense rich fragrance. Vigorous. Good for warm climates. AARS 1953, Gold medal, Portland, AARS John Cook Medal.

American Spirit 6083

Hybrid Tea, Warriner, 1988

Upright vigorous growth, bright red with 5-in. blooms. Rose of Year 1988.

Red Masterpiece 3508

Hybrid Tea, Warriner, 1974

Classic dark red, well-formed buds, opens to rich red 5-in. blooms. Very fragrant. Rose of Year 1974.

Olympiad 5519

Hybrid Tea, MacGredy, 1984

Brilliant clear red blooms on extra-long stems. Grey-green foliage. AARS 1984.

Crimson Glory

Hybrid Tea, Kordes, 1935

Famous the world over for rich damask fragrance and dark color. Very vigorous. Gold medal, RNRS England.

Mister Lincoln

Hybrid Tea, Swim & Weeks, 1965

Large, pointed buds, rich velvet red petals, powerful damask rose fragrance. Vigorous, upright growth. AARS 1965.

Europeana

Floribunda, de Ruiter, 1968

A superb, deep red floribunda with many flowers, deep green foliage and vigor. AARS 1968, Gold medal, The Hague.

Ingrid Bergman 6264

Hybrid Tea, Olesen, 1988

Vigorous with dark green foliage, disease resistant. Cold tolerant. Outstanding. Gold medals in The Hague, Madrid and Belfast.

ProudLand

Hybrid Tea, Warriner, 1969

Vigorous and upright, urn-shaped deep red buds open to velvet red flowers. Very fragrant. Rose of Year 1969.

Showbiz 4844

Floribunda, Tantau, 1985

Bright red flowers borne in plant-covering clusters. Compact, good as border or mass planting. ARS 1985.

Grand Masterpiece 4767

Hybrid Tea, Warriner, 1984

Long-stemmed clear red. Excellent for cutting, perfect high-centered form. Rose of Year 1984.

Oklahoma

Hybrid Tea, Swim & Weeks, 1964

Darkest of reds. Rich old-rose fragrance. Large plant and foliage. Gold medal, Japan.

25

MODERN PINK ROSES

Fragrant Memory 3423

Hybrid Tea, Warriner, 1974

Medium pink, large, extremely fragrant flowers on long stems ideal for cutting. Disease resistant.

Sheer Elegance PPAF

Hybrid Tea, Twoomey, 1991

Large, well-formed pink blend flowers on vigorous, disease-resistant bush. Outstanding. AARS 1991.

Tournament of Roses 6725

Grandiflora, Warriner, 1989

Deep coral pink buds, large coral pink flowers. Very disease resistant, cold tolerant. AARS 1989.

Unforgettable PPAF

Hybrid Tea, Warriner, 1992

Large, pink flowers with excellent form. Vigorous. Dark green leaves. Sweet, light fragrance. Rose of Year 1992.

Touch of Class 5165

Hybrid Tea, Kriloff, 1986

Coral buds open to warm pink, shaded blossoms dark on edges and cream in center. Vigorous with ideal form. AARS 1986.

Mon Cheri 5156

Hybrid Tea, Christensen, 1986

Coral pink buds open with scarlet at petal tips and coral centers. Deep green, disease-resistant foliage on vigorous, rounded plant. AARS 1982.

Queen Elizabeth

Grandiflora, Lammerts, 1955

Famous the world over. Large, long-stemmed clusters with clear pink blooms. Disease resistant, glossy green foliage. AARS 1955.

Glory Days PPAF

Hybrid Tea, Warriner, 1991

Huge, coral pink to pink blooms on long cutting stems. Tall and vigorous with deep green, shiny leaves. Fragrant and disease resistant.

Sexy Rexy PPAF

Floribunda, MacGredy, 1988

Tremendous production of medium, pink-ruffled blooms. Dark green, semi-glossy foliage is disease resistant. Compact growth.

First Prize

Hybrid Tea, Boerner, 1970

Huge, pink rose with exhibition form from bud to petal drop. Extra vigorous and large-leafed. AARS 1970.

Color Magic 3998

Hybrid Tea, Warriner, 1978

Salmon pink blooms change to scarlet pink with age. Fruity fragrance. Dark green leaves, vigorous growth. AARS 1978.

Pleasure PPAF

Floribunda, Warriner, 1990

Warm coral pink buds open to delightful, ruffled flowers. Compact growth, disease resistant. AARS 1990.

Barbara Bush PPAF

Hybrid Tea, Warriner, 1991

Large, excellent, soft coral and cream flowers. Vigorous, dark green foliage. Good for cutting.

First Kiss

Floribunda, Warriner, 1990

Unusual, light pink flower with top form. Many blooms on very disease-resistant, vigorous plant.

Seashell 3685

Hybrid Tea, Kordes, 1976

Beautiful salmon and shell pink, iridescent flowers. Profuse blooms, vigorous plant. AARS 1976.

MODERN WHITE ROSES

Sheer Bliss 6282

Hybrid Tea, Warriner, 1987

Classic form, creamy white with pink-touched center. Spicy scent, vigorous bush. Disease resistant. AARS 1987.

Pacali

Hybrid Tea, Lens, 1969

Long-lasting, soft, creamy white flowers. Vigorous, disease resistant, dark green leathery leaves. Gold medal in The Hague.

Class Act 6515

Floribunda, Warriner, 1989

Bright white with constant blooms and dense growth. AARS 1989.

French Lace 4848

Floribunda, Warriner, 1982

Cream white to pale apricot. Flower clusters on long cutting stems. Disease-resistant, dark green leaves. AARS 1982.

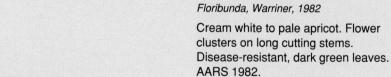

Garden Party

Hybrid Tea, Swim, 1960

Large, ivory white flowers touched with pink. Vigorous growth, bushy, with medium green leaves. AARS 1960, Gold medal in Bagatelle.

White Lightnin 4670

Grandiflora, Swim & Christensen, 1981

Crystal white blooms, heavy citrus fragrance. Healthy, dark green, glossy foliage. Good for cutting. AARS 1981.

Pristine 3997

Hybrid Tea, Warriner, 1978

World-recognized for form, white with pink blush on petal edges. Tough, disease-resistant foliage. Vigorous. AARS 1978.

Fountain Square

Hybrid Tea, Huminek, 1992

Pure white sport of Pristine with same outstanding form. Vigorous, disease resistant.

Honor 4167

Hybrid Tea, Warriner, 1980

Enormous, pure white flowers on long cutting stems. Dark green, disease-resistant foliage. Vigorous growth. AARS 1980.

Iceberg

Floribunda, Kordes, 1958

One of world's top 10 roses. Best for landscape use. Crisp white, profuse flowers. Hardy, disease resistant. Gold medals in England and Germany.

White Delight PPAF

Hybrid Tea, Warriner, 1990

Exquisite, full-petaled white blooms with pink center blush. Fragrant with many cutting stems. Rose of Year 1990.

MODERN YELLOW ROSES

Brandy 5168

Hybrid Tea, Swim & Christensen, 1982

Big, apricot blooms on long cutting
stems. Large, dark green leaves.
Tender and requires protection.
AARS 1982.

Amber Queen 5582

Floribunda, Harkness, 1988

Wonderful apricot gold with sweet
scent. Constant blooms. Disease
resistant. AARS 1988.

Shining Hour

Grandiflora, Warriner, 1991

Bright yellow flowers, disease
resistant foliage. Rounded plant good
for landscapes. AARS 1991.

Graceland

Hybrid Tea, Warriner, 1989

Big, rich yellow blooms with excellent
form. Large with vigorous, disease-
resistant foliage. Rose of Year 1989,
Gold medal in The Hague, Bronze in
Rome.

Sunbright 4438

Hybrid Tea, Warriner, 1984

Big, chrome-yellow flowers from
bright yellow buds. Upright, dark
green foliage. Disease resistant.
Rose of Year 1984.

Gold Medal 5177

Grandiflora, Christensen, 1983

Buds start deep yellow brushed with orange, open to shapely, deep golden yellow. Fruity fragrance. Vigorous, deep green, disease-resistant foliage.

Redgold

Floribunda, Dickson, 1971

Novel gold-yellow flowers edged in scarlet. Vigorous and healthy. Excellent for cutting. AARS 1971.

New Day 3228

Hybrid Tea, Kordes, 1977.

Vigorous growth of medium green foliage. Healthy. Sunshine-yellow, fragrant flowers from pointed buds. Rose of Year 1977.

Peace

Hybrid Tea, Meilland, 1946

Perhaps world's most popular rose. Huge, lemon-yellow flowers edged with pink on glossy green foliage. Easy to grow. AARS 1946. Gold medals in England, The Hague, Portland.

Sun Flare 5001

Floribunda, Warriner, 1983

Low-mounded, glossy growth covered everywhere with clusters of bright yellow flowers. Good landscape rose. AARS 1983.

Oregold 3415

Hybrid Tea, Tantau, 1975

Large, pointed buds open to bright yellow flowers. Upright growth with glossy green leaves. Good cutting flower. AARS 1975.

MODERN
MULTICOLOR ROSES

Mikado 6470

Hybrid Tea, Suzuki, 1988

Velvety, scarlet red flowers with
yellow base and lighter reverse.
Upright growth, vigorous. Shiny dark
green leaves. AARS 1988.

Chicago Peace

Hybrid Tea, Johnson, 1962

Sport of parent Peace. Rich pink
flower with canary yellow to copper
yellow at base of petal. Apple green
leaves, vigorous growth.

Double Delight 3847

Hybrid Tea, Swim, 1977

Very popular. Creamy buds open to
cream brushed with cherry red. Color
deepens with age. Spicy fragrance.
Disease resistant. AARS 1977, Gold
medals in Baden Baden and Rome.

Love 4437

Grandiflora, Warriner, 1980

Bright red flowers with clear white
reverse. Vigorous and productive.
Dark green foliage. Disease
resistant. AARS 1980.

Voodoo 6121

Hybrid Tea, Christensen, 1986

Bewitching yellow, peach and deep orange. Vigorous. Glossy, dark green foliage is disease resistant. AARS 1986.

New Year 5428

Grandiflora, McGredy, 1987

Eye-catching, clear yellow and orange blend. Foliage is deep, glossy green. Disease resistant. AARS 1987.

Perfect Moment PPAF

Hybrid Tea, Kordes, 1991

Deep yellow with broad, red edge. Compact growth, disease resistant. Dark green leaves. Good for cutting. AARS 1991.

Dynasty 6443

Hybrid Tea, Warriner, 1991

Big bright orange flowers are bold yellow on petal underside. Vigorous, with long stems. Rose of Year 1991.

MODERN VIOLET AND LAVENDER ROSES

Blue Girl

Hybrid Tea, Kordes, 1964

Beautiful, clear lavender with light, fruity fragrance. Very vigorous, upright growth. Dark green foliage. Disease resistant. Gold medal in Rome.

Blue Nile

Hybrid Tea, Chabert, 1981

Large, deep lavender, fragrant flowers with good form. Olive green foliage, long cutting stems. Gold medal at Bagatelle.

Paradise 4552

Hybrid Tea, Weeks, 1979

Clean lavender with ruby red edges. Fragrant and easy to grow. Disease-resistant, dark green foliage. AARS 1979.

Intrigue 5002

Floribunda, Warriner, 1984

Deep purple buds yield plum-colored, fragrant flowers on long stems. Bushy, well-rounded plant with dark green foliage. AARS 1984.

Angel Face

Floribunda, Swim & Weeks, 1969

Urn-shaped buds open to ruffled, lavender flowers with heavy scent. Low, bushy growth. Healthy. AARS 1969.

Sterling Silver

Hybrid Tea, Fisher, 1957

Famous greenhouse cut flower and garden rose. Novel silver, fragrant flowers on long cutting stems with dark green leaves.

Heirloom 3234

Hybrid Tea, Warriner, 1972

Surprising deep magenta buds open to pure lilac color. Very fragrant. Deep green, leathery leaves on healthy plant.

CLIMBING ROSES

Climbing Don Juan

Climber, Maladrone, 1958

Deep, velvety red, 5-in. flowers. Vigorous, very fragrant. Blooms on new and old wood.

Climbing Pinata

Climber, Suzuki, 1978

Bright yellow and orange red blooms. Canes grow 6–8 ft. high.

Climbing America 3682

Climber, Warriner, 1976

Well-formed, large, coral pink blooms. Flowers have rich, spicy scent, form on new and old wood. Long canes. AARS 1976.

Climbing Royal Gold

Climber, Morey, 1957

Deep yellow "Hybrid Tea" blooms with stems long enough to cut. Fragrant. Blooms on new and old wood.

Tempo 3652

Climber, Warriner, 1975

Bright red flower clusters cover from spring to fall. Bright, dark green foliage. Blooms on new and old wood.

Climbing Blue Girl

Climber, Kordes, 1964

Sport of parent Blue Girl. Large, fragrant lavender flowers. Vigorous. Blooms on new and old wood.

Climbing Joseph's Coat

Climber, Swim & Armstrong, 1964

Very popular multicolor climber in shades of pink, red, orange and yellow. Blooms on new and old wood.

Climbing High Noon

Climber, Lammerts, 1948

Lemon yellow, large, fragrant flowers set off by shiny green foliage. Disease resistant. Blooms on new and old wood. AARS 1948.

Climbing White Dawn

Climber, Longley, 1949

Constant blooms of clear white, ruffled flowers on a vigorous, disease-resistant plant. Blooms on new and old wood.

Climbing Golden Showers

Climber, Lammerts, 1956

Masses of fragrant, pure yellow, ruffled flowers. Good climber. Blooms on new and old wood. AARS 1956.

Climbing Blaze

Climber, Kallay, 1932

Most popular climber. Masses of bright red blooms in large clusters form on new and old wood.

MINIATURE ROSES
RED AND PINK

Party Girl 4598

Miniature, Saville, 1981

Flowers are soft apricot flushed with pink, borne one to a stem. ARS Award of Excellence.

Jean Kenneally 5637

Miniature, Bennett, 1986

Apricot pink and constantly in bloom. Tall, vigorous. ARS Award of Excellence.

Jennifer 5857

Miniature, Bernadella, 1985

Light pink, white on reverse. Strong fragrance. Tall. ARS Award of Excellence.

Cupcake 5484

Miniature, Spies, 1983

Easy to grow with pretty soft pink buds and flowers. Compact, rounded growth. ARS Award of Excellence.

Minnie Pearl 5097

Miniature, Saville, 1982

Soft pink, high-centered flowers grace upright, vigorous and rounded plants.

Nighthawk 6951

Miniature, Hardgrove, 1989

Crimson red blooms are long-lasting and high centered. Upright, dark green growth. ARS Award of Excellence.

Little Sizzler PPAF

Miniature, Warriner, 1988

Glossy dark green foliage sets off bright red buds and flowers. Disease resistant.

Galaxy 4580

Miniature, Moore, 1980

Clusters of bright red, ruffled flowers on very compact plant. Glossy green foliage.

Starina

Miniature, Meilland, 1966

Red-orange flowers with very pointed buds. Easy to grow. Highest-rated ARS miniature.

Centerpiece 5692

Miniature, Saville, 1985

Medium to dark red, velvety blooms. Good cutting roses. ARS Award of Excellence.

Maurine Neuberger PPAF

Miniature, Spooner, 1990

Bright crimson red flowers on long cutting stems. Tall and vigorous plant.

Black Jade 5925

Miniature, Bernadella, 1985

Near-black pointed buds open to very dark red flowers. Vigorous, disease resistant. ARS Award of Excellence.

MINIATURE ROSES
LAVENDER, MULTICOLOR AND WHITE

Winsome 5691

Miniature, Saville, 1985

Deep lavender purple pointed buds open to well-formed flowers. Disease resistant. ARS Award of Excellence.

Little Artist 6907

Miniature, MacGredy, 1984

Unusual, fragrant flowers have red petals with white "eyes" and reverse.

Rainbow's End 5482

Miniature, Saville, 1986

Bright yellow to orange-red buds and blooms. Bushy, compact growth. ARS Award of Excellence.

Debut 6791

Miniature, Meilland, 1989

Ivory yellow with broad red edges. Disease resistant, compact growth. AARS 1989.

Lavender Jewel 4480

Miniature, Moore, 1979

Excellent lavender color with great form. Upright plants with vigorous growth.

Blizzard PPAF

Miniature, Warriner, 1992

Pure white miniature with low, spreading growth and constant blooms. Good border or accent.

Sweet Chariot 5975

Miniature, Moore, 1985

Cascading sprays of fragrant blooms start deep purple, turn lavender. Disease resistant and good for hanging containers.

Magic Carousel 3601

Miniature, Moore, 1972

White with fine red edge. Flowers heavily. ARS Award of Excellence.

Pacesetter 4513

Miniature, Schwartz, 1981

Fragrant, pure white blooms on dark green foliage. ARS Award of Excellence.

SPECIES ROSES AND SPECIES HYBRIDS

Hansa

Rugosa hybrid, Schaum & Van Tol, 1905

Mauve roses with deep scent on vigorous, 4-ft. shrubs. Hardy, disease resistant.

Pink Grootendorst

Sport *Rugosa* hybrid, Grootendorst, 1923

Clusters of small, pink double blooms with frilly petals. Winter hardy.

Rosa roxburghii

"Chestnut rose," species hybrid

Large, bright pink blossoms open from chestnut-like calyx.

F. J. Grootendorst

Rugosa hybrid, Grootendorst, 1918

Double, fragrant red blooms adorn a 5-ft. shrub. Very hardy.

Celsiana

Damask, pre-1750

Intense, fragrant, large pink flowers. Probably best of the Damask roses.

Rosa rugosa

Species rose, 1845

Parent of many species of adaptable, disease-free hybrids with textured leaves. Sets large, colorful hips.

Rosa pavlii

Species hybrid

White, single flowers on deep green foliage.

Rosa rubrifolia

Species rose, pre-1830

Pink, 2-in. flowers bloom in June on gray-maroon foliage. Survives cold to minus 50°F.

Rosa complicata

Species hybrid

Deep pink with large yellow center on smooth, dark green foliage.

Rosa soulieana

Species rose

Small, 5-petaled white flowers on a dense, 3-ft.-high bush.

Rosa eglanteria

Species rose, 1551

Sweetbriar is the rose of Shakespeare. Pink, clustered flowers on tall plants.

45

OLD GARDEN AND HERITAGE ROSES

Rose de Rescht

Damask

Cross of *R. gallica* female and unknown male (probably R. phoenicia) parents.

Madame Hardy

Damask, 1832

Popular with very double, fragrant white flowers opening flat around their green center.

Baroness Rothschild

Bourbon, 1868

Originated on the Indian Ocean island of L'Isle Bourbon, or Reunion Island, in the early 1800s.

Gloire des Mousseux

Moss, 1852

Fragrant pink blooms appear in June. Very cold tolerant.

Maiden's Blush

Hybrid Alba, 1704

Clusters of fragrant, light-pink flowers open to white. Cold tolerant.

Golden Moss

Moss

Moss roses—sports of Centifolia roses—have green, mosslike growth on their sepals. Gold flowers open to pale yellow.

Honorine de Brabant

Bourbon

Fragrant with dark pink flecks on blush pink petals. Very cold hardy.

Marie Louise

Damask, 1813

Fragrant with mauve pink, 3-in. blooms in June. Very cold hardy.

Jeanne D'Arc

Alba, 1818

Cold tolerant with very fragrant blooms of tight, ruffled white petals.

Kathleen

Hybrid Musk, 1922

A blush pink repeat bloomer with fragrant, ruffled flowers.

Catherine Mermet

Tea, 1869

Elegant with light pink petals.

Great Western

Hybrid Bourbon, 1840

Deep mauve, whorled petals.

Prince Camille de Rohan

Hybrid Perpetual, 1861

Fragrant, dark red flowers.

Madame Alfred Carriere

Noisette, 1879

Large white flowers with a hint of pink in their center.

Shrub Roses

Roller Coaster PPAF

Shrub, McGredy

Startling red and white, striped flowers on tall, arching canes. Disease resistant.

Confetti 5399

Hedge Rose, Christensen, 1984

Bright yellow and red flowers in large clusters. Healthy, fast growing.

Bonica 5105

Shrub, Meilland, 1987

Fast-blooming, spreading growth with excellent disease resistance. Pink flowers and good repeat bloom. AARS 1987.

Simplicity 4089

Hedge Rose, Warriner, 1975

Most popular rose in the world. Upright, early and constant-blooming pink hedge. Disease resistant.

Pink Meidiland 5956

Hedge Rose, Meilland, 1985

Upright shrub with simple pink flowers. Blooms all summer.

White Simplicity 6666

Hedge Rose, Warriner, 1989

Snowy white blooms cover dark green foliage. Disease resistant with fast, upright growth.

Alba Meidiland 6891

Shrub, Meilland, 1989

Large, arching plant blooms heavily throughout summer. Disease resistant.

Sea Foam

Shrub, Shwartz, 1964

Creamy white, 3-in. blooms cover this trailing shrub. Disease resistant. Gold Medal Rome, ARS David Fuerstenburg Prize 1968.

Bloomin' Easy 7157

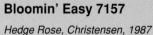

Hedge Rose, Christensen, 1987

Bright, ruby-red blooms. Hardy, disease resistant and fast growing.

Scarlet Meidiland 6087

Shrub, Meilland, 1987

Mounding groundcover with deep red blooms in early summer.

Red Meidiland 7116

Shrub, Meilland, 1989

Low, vigorous groundcover. Flowers are bright with a white eye.

Special Situation Roses

COLD CLIMATE ROSES

Pick these hardy roses if you live in a very cold climate. They thrive where more delicate roses can't live.

F. J. Grootendorst

Hansa

Pink Meidiland 5956

Rosa Rugosa

HOT AND DRY

Best choices for the desert southwest, where heat and low humidity are a problem.

Pristine 3997

Olympiad 5519

Iceberg

Pride n' Joy PPAF

Touch of Class 5165

Gold Medal 5177

HOT AND HUMID

Roses thatresist fungus, mildew and other diseases do best in climates with cool winters and hot, moist summers.

Class Act 6515

Sheer Elegance PPAF

Sun Flare 5001

Tournament of Roses 6725

Ingrid Bergman 6264

FRAGRANT FLOWERS

These roses delight with heady perfume as well as beautiful flowers.

Chrysler Imperial

Fragrant Memory 3423

Intrigue 5002

Angel Face

Sheer Bliss 6282

ROSE LANDSCAPES

You can find ideas for using the roses you have chosen for your garden in many places—magazines, books or other gardens. Four common landscape uses for roses are shown here. Keep the mature size of the roses in proportion to the size of your garden, and match colors carefully.

Pick roses with low-growing, mounding growth habits

Control growth with careful seasonal and annual pruning

OLD GARDEN ROSES

PILLAR

HYBRID TEAS

FLORIBUNDA GROUPING

MINIATURE

CRUSHED

SCALE 1" = 4'

OLD GARDEN
ROSES

FLORAS

ROSES

HYBRID

TEAS

NG AREA

STANDARD
TREE
ROSES

FLORIBUNDA
GROUPING

MINIATURE

BORDER

ROSE

ROCK

PATHWAY

ROSE GARDEN PLAN

40' by 24'

Cover high supports with climbers,
low walls with Grandifloras

MAGIC RUB
FaberCastell
1954

UNDERSTANDING ROSE PLANTS

Most modern rose plants have been grown and budded into the forms you buy at your nursery or garden store. A sturdy rootstock—usually from a wild, or species, rose plant—forms the base. This helps the rose resist disease and be more vigorous. The blooms that form appear on the cultivar, which is budded onto the rootstock. In tree roses another budding forms the trunk.

Flower bud

Flower

Petals

Anthers

Pistils

Rose Hip

New season growth

Stamens

Last season canes

Bud union

Rootstock sucker

Rootstock

Mulch

Roots

Some insect pests that attack roses include aphids, beetles, scale, mites, budworms, thrips, caterpillars and leafhoppers.

Common diseases found on roses are blackspot, mildew and rust. Crown gall is a serious, uncommon disease.

Roses grow when buds on old canes begin to swell into new shoots, forming foliage and flower buds.

Damage includes broken canes and foliage, wilting and fertilizer burn.

CHOOSING ROSES

Roses may be purchased as bare-root plants or in containers. Bare-root plants are available in springtime and offer a wide selection of varieties. Container-grown plants are usually older than bare-roots but are also more costly. Either provide good results in home gardens.

Healthy bare-root roses have green, thick canes with at least 3 healthy, undamaged roots. Pick Grade 1, the highest rating.

Examine canes for pests, disease and damage. Healthy canes will be plump and green. Avoid withered or dried-out plants.

Holding bare-roots through winter weather is easy—heel them in a protected spot in a V-shaped trench of moist sawdust and dirt.

Strong, thick canes

Variety, type and grade

Disease- and pest-free foliage

Large container

CHOOSING ROSES

Select either bare-root or container rose plants. Container plants usually can be found in full leaf, sometimes with flowers blooming. Bare-root plants require better knowledge of the varieties desired and the rose grading system.

Bare-root roses are dormant and ready to plant when purchased. You may hold them in a damp and cool place for up to five days, or heel them into a V-shaped trench filled with moist sawdust and covered with dirt for longer periods. Don't allow them to freeze.

The bare-roots are graded as 1, 1-1/2 and 2, with 1s as best. While there are grade variations depending on the type of rose, grade 1 Hybrid Teas and Grandifloras usually have 3-4 heavy canes 18 in. long and at least 1/8 in. around; 1-1/2s have two or more canes 14 in. long; and 2s have 2 canes just 12 in. long (avoid these, they may be weak or very young). Similar grading standards exist for Floribundas, Polyanthas and climbers.

Examine plants for root development; damage and disease; number and quality of canes; general condition—avoid dried plants; and absence of crown gall—a cork-like growth near the bud union where the rose has been grafted to its rootstock.

Container-grown plants are more mature and you can easily judge their health and vigor. Examine the foliage for pests or signs of disease, including aphids, rust, blackspot or physical damage. Always shop in the spring. You'll find more varieties—even annual bloomers can be seen in flower—and the roses will have a chance to become well-established before they face the stress of summer heat. Always buy in large containers—5-gal. roses are best. Avoid sparse, weak or sickly plants.

PLANTING ROSES

After you have choosen your rose varieties, prepared the rose bed and the weather is right, planting begins. Most planting involves bare-root plants, container plants or transplanting into a container. Each is easy if you follow these simple steps.

After planting add chipped-bark mulch to limit weeds, reduce amount of water needed and moderate soil temperatures. Fertilize (see pgs. 64–65). Water regularly for the first month.

TIME AND DEPTH TO PLANT

Coldest Winter Temperature	Planting Time	Bud Union to Soil Surface
Below –10°F	Early Spring Only	–3 in.
–10°F to 10°F	Late Autumn/ Early Spring	0 in.
Above 10°F	When Ground Workable	+2 in.

Bare-Root Roses

First Soak rose for 4–6 hrs. Dig hole 6 in. wider and deeper than roots. Trim broken roots.

Then Mix 2 oz. 0–10–0 fertilizer with soil, mound to support plant (see table). Firm.

Next Fill 2/3 full with soil, then water. Adjust plant height and let it soak in.

Last Fill until 8 in. mound covers top of hole, including bud union. Gradually wash

Container Roses

First Dig hole that clears container by 6 in. on all sides. Mix 2 oz. 0–10–0 fertilizer into removed soil.

Then Turn plant upside down. Tap free; don't pull by stem.

Next Score rootball to cut circling roots. Firm 6–8 in. of soil in bottom of hole.

Last Level plant (see table) and backfill. Water and adjust, add soil until full.

Transplanting Roses

First Select largest container possible with bottom drain hole.

Then Mix compost, peat, leaf mold and liquid fertilizer into rich potting soil.

Next Partially block drain with broken pottery or wire screen to prevent blockage.

Last Pot following basic steps for bare-root or container plants. Leave soil 1–2 in. below top of container.

REPRODUCING ROSES

Roses grown from seed may look like their parents or turn out much different. Copy the rose growers and try your hand at hybridizing. If you are particularly fond of one of your roses, grow another just like it with cuttings, or bud an offspring onto sturdy rootstock.

Hybridizing Roses

First Select a half-open rosebud. Remove petals.

Then Remove stamens. Cover with bag to prevent self-fertilization.

Third Brush dried pollen from other parent on stigmas when ripe and sticky.

Fourth Recover with bag. Hip swells and matures.

Next Store seeds in dry jar at 40°F for 4–6 wks. Plant 1/2 in. deep.

Last Carefully transplant germinated seeds.

Softwood Cuttings

First Cut 6 in. piece of growth stem with two leaves.

Next Dip in root hormone compound, set halfway into moist potting soil. Bag.

Last New growth begins in 5–6 weeks. Transplant after 8–10 weeks to sheltered shade.

60

Hardwood Cuttings

First In fall, cut 6 in. lengths of mature canes. Dip in rooting hormone.

Next Cover cutting with peat or sand. Hold at 40°F until spring. Keep moist.

Last When frost danger ends, transplant rooted cutting.

Budding Roses

First Cut *scion* of dormant bud and surrounding bark from parent with budding knife.

Then Make shallow T-shaped cut in rootstock and completely insert scion.

Third Bind tightly with grafting tape or budding rubber.

Fourth Bud develops in 3–4 weeks.

Last In fall, after plant goes dormant, remove rootstock foliage above bud.

CAUTION

Budding is difficult. Keep trying until you succeed.

61

Basic Rose Care

Roses are hardy, vigorous plants that need attention throughout the year to produce beautiful flowers and healthy foliage. This care includes regular deep watering, fertilizing, annual and seasonal pruning, pest and disease control and winter care.

WATERING

After planting in rich, well-drained soil in a sunny site, your roses will need regular, deep watering. To absorb water easily, the soil should be lightly cultivated 1–2 in. deep beneath the mulch. Rake back the mulch and cultivate at least twice each season. Don't cultivate deeper than 3 in.; rose roots spread around the plant and could be damaged.

A good layer of mulch is important to the roses in several ways. It moderates the temperature of the ground on hot days; it helps prevent rain from splashing mold spores up onto the rose bushes or washing away the soil; and it slows evaporation to save water. The mulch layer should be 3–4 in. thick and replaced each year in spring.

Roses need regular watering, but take care not to overwater or water too lightly. Always water the base of the plants, using a bubbler head. Don't water the foliage unless it can dry thoroughly by nightfall to prevent mildew or other diseases.

Water whenever the soil is no longer damp to the touch 2 in. or more beneath the soil surface. A good test is to plunge a trowel into the soil to examine it.

Roses need 4–8 gal. of water per week, usually applied all at once. If the soil is compacted, water until runoff begins, allow it to soak in, then repeat until the full amount has been applied. Or build watering basins 24 in. in diameter and 2 in. deep around each plant.

Only roses in very hot and dry climates need as much as 8 gal. weekly, beginning in late spring as days turn hot. Water 4 gal. per plant every 3–4 days through summer, cutting back again as days cool in fall.

Install automatic drip watering to save water. It's easy to do, inexpensive and time-saving.

FERTILIZING ROSES

Proper fertilizing is necessary for showy roses with healthy leaves and flowers. If roses become stunted, or have brown leaf tips or edges, and you're sure that watering isn't the problem, your soil may lack phosphorus or potassium—a soil test is in order. Otherwise, regular applications of slow-release fertilizers rich in nitrogen—such as bonemeal—will be all that's needed.

CHOOSING AND APPLYING FERTILIZERS

Most fertilizers carry N-P-K numbers on their label to tell how much nitrogen, phosphorus or potassium they contain. A 5-0-0 fertilizer, for example, has 5 percent nitrogen by weight, 0 percent phosphorus, and 0 percent potassium. A 100 lb. bag holds 5 lbs. of nitrogen.

Choose a fertilizer that is *balanced* (equal parts of all nutrients) or *complete* (contains all three nutrients), or one higher in nitrogen (for foliage development), phosphorus (for vigorous growth) or potassium (for strong roots). Fertilize when planting and every 3–4 weeks, all season long.

Organic, "natural" fertilizers are made from things like fish, bone, manure and minerals. They usually are long-lasting. Some may be bulky, have odor, or be difficult to use or control, but give good results when used as the label instructs.

Synthetic fertilizers are manmade, usually from petroleum or its by-products. They often give quick results, but are concentrated and may burn plants. They must be applied frequently, according to the label recommendation for use.

Fertilizers come in three forms: applied dry, mix dry-into-liquid and liquid. A special category of liquids are *foliar* fertilizers, applied and absorbed by plant leaves and foliage instead of to their roots and the soil.

Fertilizers labeled as "rose food" may have no special ingredients or benefit. There are also fertilizers that contain systemic insecticides that kill rose pests.

Plants can't tell manmade from natural fertilizers, nor does it matter what form they take. Use the fertilizer that fits your purpose and plan.

PRUNING ROSES

INTRODUCTION

To retain their beauty and health, roses need two separate kinds of pruning: major annual pruning and seasonal pruning while growing and flowering. Pruning removes dead and diseased growth, encourages healthy new growth and blooms, and restores shape, size and beauty. Pruning must be done with care, for roses use their canes and roots to store nutrients needed to emerge from dormancy in the spring.

ANNUAL PRUNING

The timing of the annual pruning depends on when the rose blooms. Prune modern and recumbent—low-growing—roses near the end of dormancy, just when buds begin to swell on the bare canes. Prune old garden roses, some ramblers and climbers, shrub roses and species roses that bear their flowers on second-season wood just after they finish blooming. Cold-climate roses should be lightly pruned, just eliminating dead wood. In warmer climates choose moderate to heavy pruning to stimulate new growth and larger flowers.

SEASONAL PRUNING

Seasonal pruning is needed to remove spent blossoms before they swell into seed pods, called *hips*. If hips remain on the canes, flowering stops. Seasonal pruning also removes diseased or broken growth, trains or halts growth, eliminates suckers and makes flowers larger and more showy.

   Always use the right equipment, and be sure it is sharp. You'll need hand pruners, long-handled lopping shears, and occasionally a fine-toothed pruning saw for large canes. Make all pruning cuts at 45° angles except those at the bud union or main stem, and cut 1/4 in. above a dormant bud eye.

CAUTION

In cold winter areas, limit pruning to minimum necessary.

Annual Pruning

First Cut away any dead wood. For annual bloomers, wait until flowers have faded.

Then Remove any weak or spindly canes, and ones that grow inward. Leave 6–8 strong canes.

Next Remove any suckers growing from below the bud union. Top canes at 14–24 in. tall.

Seasonal Pruning

First Prune as flowers fade, cutting 45° angle just above 5-leaflet foliage.

Next Pinch off unwanted secondary buds to grow larger flowers on terminal buds.

Last Gather and remove all pruning debris to prevent disease and insect pests.

CLIMBER AND RAMBLER ROSE CARE

Bend long, springy canes over and tie securely to supports to promote growth of lateral shoots that bear buds and flowers.

Remove old canes that have lost vigor and don't bloom profusely, usually 3–4 years old. New growth will fill in and bloom the following spring.

CLIMBING ROSES

Without pruning and training, climbers, pillars and ramblers will grow only stems and foliage and become too tall. The end result is an unsightly bramble with few flowers.

The reason they prefer to grow upward is because almost all their energy goes to the last bud on each cane. To train them and avoid this tendency to be too tall, bend the long canes over in a gentle arch, tying them to a support fence, arbor, post or wall. The buds along their length will develop laterals that form flowers in spring.

Annual care of climbers is limited for the first few years. Until they are fully established, limit pruning. Remove dead canes and branches, spent flowers and any weak or flimsy growth. Train new canes into position by tying them to their supports as they grow. Stretchy plastic tape is good for this since it grows with the plant yet is strong enough to support its weight.

During this period observe your rose's flowering habit. If it blooms only once, in the spring, begin to give it an annual pruning after the bloom is finished. If it blooms repeatedly, treat it like a climbing Hybrid Tea (see pgs. 66–67) and prune it in the spring before it resumes active growth. Gradually remove older canes that have begun to produce less flowers and train new canes into place.

Seasonal care should aim at encouraging the plant's good habits and discouraging its bad ones. Prune away dead or diseased canes. Removing old blooms is not necessary.

Pillar roses should be pruned like Hybrid Teas (see pgs. 66–67) and trained along their supports. Prune ramblers after flowering, when new growth reveals their intention. Keep all canes with new, long shoots and new ones growing from ground level—remove older spent canes.

Extreme Winters

First In severe winter areas, protect roses by carefully freeing root ball of soil on 1/2 of rose.

Next Carefully tip plant to mulched ground and stake down. Roots left in ground provide nutrients and water.

Last Cover plant with burlap, then hay mulch and, finally, cover with soil. Remove coverings and tip up in spring.

WINTER PROTECTION

With regard to roses, climates can be divided into three classes: those that are *mild* (winter temperatures never dip below 10°F), *intermediate* (coldest temperatures between 10°F and −10°F), and *severe* (temperatures lower than −10°F).

In mild winter climates, no special protection is necessary. Simply mulch the soil of the rose bed to moderate temperature fluctuations and cut back on fertilizer and water. Let rose hips form in autumn to slow the plants' growth before onset of the winter dormant season. In very mild climates, strip all leaves with pruning shears in late autumn to force the plant into dormancy. The annual pruning may be performed at the same time in such areas.

In intermediate winter climates, leave spent flowers on your roses after September. They will mature, hardening the plant before temperatures turn colder. With the first freezing nights, mound soil over the bud union and the base of the canes. No further protection should be necessary. Wait until spring to remove the soil and perform the annual pruning. The uncut canes store needed energy and nutrients to keep the dormant plant alive.

In severe winter areas, extra measures are needed to help roses survive. Best results will come from planting cold-resistant varieties (see pgs. 50–51). Mulching the ground with 3–4 in. of insulating mulch is essential. Then wrap the entire plant in burlap or other breathable fabric, mulch with hay and cover with soil. In the coldest climates, where temperatures may drop below −30°F, follow the step-by-step instructions shown to protect roses from severe freezing damage. Annual pruning in severe climates should only remove dead wood killed by the cold, and canes should be left as long as possible.

CONTAINER ROSE CARE

You can grow beautiful, fragrant roses indoors in containers. Choose a sunny location. Most homes are ideal for miniatures, but some allow larger varieties. For best results choose the largest container allowed by your decorating plans.

Fertilize with dry or liquid houseplant fertilizers every month, water thoroughly, drain.

Repot each year. Use fresh sterilized native soil and planter mix in equal parts.

Stop fertilizing in early autumn and move outdoors. Return inside as soon as nighttime temperatures reach 20°F.

DISEASE AND PEST CONTROL

AVOIDING PESTS AND DISEASES

Prevent fungal diseases and insect pests by choosing resistant varieties, planting them properly and giving them the very best care—regular watering, fertilizing and pruning. Always remove clippings and dead plant material as soon as possible. They are ideal hiding places for pests.

Inspect your roses regularly, looking closely for problem signs: yellow or brown leaves, insect pests, blackspot or other diseases. The best time to inspect them is when you prune spent flowers away. Be sure to look under leaves for pests.

Most rose diseases can be controlled easily with a fungicide. Choose one specific to the disease condition that your plant is suffering. When mixing, applying or disposing of fungicides, read the label carefully, following all warnings and instructions completely.

Early infestations of sucking and piercing insect pests can be controlled by washing the rose with a soapy-water solution of 1 tbsp. dishwashing detergent mixed in 1 gal. of water. Repeat the treatment every three days until the insects are gone.

Advanced insect attacks may require use of systemic or topical insecticides. Systemics are sprinkled or sprayed on the ground surface, watered in and absorbed through the plant's roots. They kill insects that suck plant juices or eat their stems or leaves. Topical insecticides are dusts, liquid sprays or powders that coat the plant and kill insects by contact. Choose from natural or synthetic insecticides and always follow the label instructions carefully and completely.

HEALTHY LEAVES
Not yellowed, spotted, burnt or withered.

CLEAN MULCH
No clippings or fallen petals to hide pests or disease spores.

CAUTION

Always use chemical controls carefully and follow all label directions exactly.

Disease Control

First Measure and mix fungicide powder or liquid as directed on label.

Then Spray rose, including leaf undersides and ground under plant.

Last Dispose of empty fungicide container only as directed and wash equipment thoroughly.

Systemic Insecticides

First Apply systemic granules to ground, following all label directions.

Then Rake granules into soil or mulch with rake or hand tool.

Last Water rose thoroughly so insecticide will dissolve and be absorbed.

ROSE TOOLS
AND EQUIPMENT

Spade

Pruning
Shears

Rake

Pruning
Saw

Cultivating Tool

Watering Can

Grafting Tape

Budding Knife

Twist Ties

Lopping
Shears

Spray
Applicator
Bottle

Bubbler
Hose
Head

Hose

Hose-end
Sprayer

Hand
Trowel

Barrow

INDEX